Life After Death

(book 4)

KR Bankston

All rights reserved. No part of this series of books may be used or reproduced by any means, graphic, electronic or mechanical, including, photocopying, recording, taping or by an information storage retrieval system without the written permission of the author or publisher except in the event of quotes embodied in articles and reviews.

The work is a work of fiction. All of the characters, names, incidents, organizations, and dialogue in this novel are either the products of the author's imagination or are used fictitiously.

Copyright © 2012 Kirabaco Publishing/ KR Bankston. All rights reserved.

The views expressed in this work are solely those of the author and do not necessarily reflect the views of the publisher, and the publisher hereby disclaims any responsibility for them.

Liberation is not a gift bestowed upon us from our oppressor. It is taken and owned by the decision that NO ONE can keep them from it.

For too long we've watched silently as we've been violated by our government at every turn. The rights and needs of the poor, minorities, and women have been ignored and trampled upon. It's time to stand up and say no. You have the power to make a difference and it is as simple as casting a ballot in your local, state, and federal elections.

If you haven't registered to vote, you may do so in the following ways:

- Contact your Secretary of State and request a voter registration form by mail
- Register at your Public Library
- Register at the DMV when you renew your license
- Register when you renew your TANF/Food Stamp benefits

Registering to vote doesn't automatically sentence you to jury duty. If you get a jury summons, don't avoid it! We need rational voices to keep our men and women from behind bars!

Convicted felons are not barred from registering! States such as Rhode Island, South Carolina and Utah automatically restore your voting rights upon completion of your sentence. Check your state laws for complete information on restoring your voting rights if you've been convicted of a felony.

To Report Voter Issues: call the Civil Rights Division toll-free at (800) 253-3931, or contact them by mail at:
Chief, Voting Section
Civil Rights Division
Room 7254 – NWB
Department of Justice
950 Pennsylvania Ave., N.W.
Washington, DC 20530

Your right to vote was secured through blood, sweat, and tears. Exercise it to the fullest without relenting. Social change and justice for people of color is not optional: it is mandatory. Make them know this by registering your voting voice today!

Acknowledgements & Thanks

Thanks be to the *Divine Creator* for the gift and talent, as well as the ability to finish another novel. To *Big Daddy*, the best husband ever; and *Ms. Finesse*, the best daughter ever. To the multitude of readers, fans, friends, who encourage me on a daily basis. My test readers who put up with my craziness and still tell me the truth. To each and every person who has ever given my work a chance, I hope I've done you proud yet another time.

How can I forget you when you're always on my mind?
How can I not want you when your all I want inside?
How can I let you go when I can't see us apart?
How can I not love you when you control my heart?

Unknown

The Gianni Legacy

Detective Dwayne Marchant continued to study the case file. He looked at the documents again and again, searching for anything that would give him a clue concerning the identity of the person or persons who killed both Thomas Bradford and Christopher Lynch. Officially the case remained cold for two years, but for Marchant it still wasn't over. He hated the thought that somewhere out there, someone got away with murder. *That's not the only reason you want to know,* his subconscious piped up. The thought brought a deep guttural sigh from him. Marchant glanced up toward the small bulletin board in front of the desk where he sat. The photographs of Kayla stared back at him; her beauty and radiance in stark contrast to the bland beige of the walls, absent of picture or decoration. The only things in the office that brought a semblance of humanity were the hand-carved oak desk and matching leather chair. Marchant knew he was in too deep where the woman was concerned, but no matter how hard he tried, he couldn't shake the feelings. *She may not be as innocent as everyone thinks she is,* his mind was back. Marchant was more than toying with the idea of the woman being a femme fatale; getting her boyfriend to do the dirty work but being the mastermind behind the murders. He sipped the scotch in his glass still staring at the smiling images.

"Are you fooling all of us," he mumbled never looking away.

Marchant closed his eyes then, imagining her scent as he recollected standing near her bedside at the hospital, the softness of her skin as he kissed her forehead and gently stroked her cheek. *Let this go and move on,* he heard the warning in his mind's eye. The thought that she may have fooled him too brought the anger to the forefront. Something was very foul in the world of Mrs. Mikayla Bradford. He was asking plenty of questions, but so far not getting anything near the right answers. Marchant began looking through the files again this time taking note of the small blurb written in the margin of one of the dog-eared pages concerning Kayla's bank accounts.

"Hmph," he remarked, seeing that the funds were all transferred immediately before her husband's death to an institution in Bermuda.

Almost like she knew she would be leaving and wanted everything in order, he brooded, the suspicions gaining momentum. The woman left without a trace, completely disappeared, not even forwarding her mail. *Is that where she went,* Marchant questioned. It made sense his mind continued to tell him. If he were a criminal having masterminded a crime, he wouldn't want to be anywhere inside the continental United States either. More and more Marchant was seeing a Black Widow pattern emerging, and Kayla was smack dab in the center of it. Armed with the sliver of information, Marchant pulled up Google and began to search for banks near Pembroke

Parrish, the name scribbled in the blurb. He found three and decided he would start there. Marchant knew to be careful. He held absolutely no jurisdiction outside of North Carolina, let alone, the United States. Still he felt justified, telling himself he was only seeking justice for the two slain men and their remaining family. *Yeah right, liar,* his conscience scoffed; his pride and ego were also heavily involved at this point. Pushing it away Marchant promptly emailed the three banks, sounding as professional as possible and pushing the limits of truth when he informed them he was investigating a murder case with possible ties to their banks. He also made a note to visit the bank where the transfer took place and have an off the record chat with the clerks. Maybe he would get lucky and find out which one of them actually handled the transaction, perhaps gaining even more knowledge to unravel this case.

Crossing his fingers, Marchant hoped he would get a hit from both the emails and the bank clerks. *Then what,* his mind again piped up. He wasn't thinking that far ahead; he would worry about that later. Right now Marchant simply wanted a hit. He wanted to find Kayla Bradford and ask her a few more questions about her late husband and her ex-boyfriend. That was yet another strange twist to the case in his mind. The woman dated Christopher Lynch years ago, a fact he learned both men were apprised of. Marchant made a quick note to do a thorough background check on Kayla Bradford. He looked at the photos again, studying the woman's eyes. They seemed innocent, almost unaware, but Marchant knew it could be an act. He met plenty of criminals over the years. Some of them were phenomenal actors and actresses, making you believe their innocence, when in fact they were as guilty as the day was long.

"Is that what you are Kayla," Marchant murmured aloud. "A great actress," he questioned, still sipping the liquor and looking at her photos.

Sighing intensely he realized that until he heard back from the banks there was nothing else he could do except wait. Glancing at the clock, he rose and headed into his kitchen. Stepping into the small cabinet lined space, Marchant's aloneness again hit him full force. He missed the days when his cozy home was filled with the sound of laughter and joviality. Sonia was the light in his otherwise dismally dark world. A beautiful woman with an effervescent laugh, she always made coming home a joy. Sonia was also on the force. She worked vice and was a veteran officer with fifteen years in. They met at work, forging an instant friendship. For Marchant it quickly grew into something far deeper and he found himself proposing marriage some eight months later.

The microwave's loud ding broke his thought as Marchant hustled the frozen dinner from the contraptions innards and set about removing the stuck on plastic coating. Moving his treasure of roast beef, mashed potatoes and green beans to the small two seat nook table, he began to eat. His mind, however, was already across the ocean to the parish in Bermuda. Marchant prayed once more that he was finally on the right track. He wanted, no needed, closure to this case. *You want to find her and bring her back,* his mind accused as Marchant's appetite left him. He couldn't lie anymore. He did. He wanted to find Kayla, talk to her, and make her admit her part in this entire fiasco. Marchant was convinced she knew far more than she ever admitted to him. He hated how he was attracted to her, allowing that attraction to dull his otherwise sharp discernment to the point he only mildly interrogated her that day when she came to the precinct.

"Won't make that mistake again, you can count on that," Marchant murmured angrily.

Dwayne Marchant didn't like being made a fool of and he wanted to clear his name, take back his reputation, and prove to the world that the sweet, innocently smiling woman in all these photos, was truly a black hearted, greed inspired, murderess who seduced men to her beck and call as she continued to grow rich and prosper from their deaths. *What about the boyfriend,* his mind again questioned as he frowned deeply. "Whatever is necessary," he murmured irritably, not above any amount of violence to achieve his goal.

Rising, Marchant threw the half-eaten meal into the trash, and grabbing the scotch bottle, decided on a liquid dinner for the evening.

KR Bankston – The Gianni Legacy

Life After 1 Death

Marchant was up bright and early, having slept little the night before, his mind still racing thinking about Kayla and the suspicions he held. He needed to find out all he could about her background. That would provide a few answers to the nagging questions. Who was the boyfriend? Where did he come from? How long were they having an affair? Marchant made up his mind the two must have been seeing each other long before the trouble with her husband. *Entirely too quick to have just met,* he continued to reason, turning his shower on full throttle. Going back into his office he picked up the phone and called the station.

"Gaynelle Hudson speaking," the voice shot into the phone as he smiled slightly.

Gaynelle was one of his friends from the street beat, when they walked the worst neighborhoods in the city together. She was on a desk now, finding it much more to her liking, as did her husband and four children.

"Hey Gaynelle, its Dwayne," he answered as she cheerfully returned his greeting.

"I need a favor," he began as she groaned somewhat waiting for him to finish the request.

"I need you to dig up some information for me on Mikayla Bradford."

Gaynelle paused before speaking again.

"Reverend Thomas Bradford's widow," she questioned.

"Yes, the very same," Marchant told.

"Dwayne, Capt. has said to leave it alone," she warned quietly.

Marchant knew it as well, having been pointedly told by the Captain himself that the case was for all intents closed, and he was not to investigate it any longer.

"I know Gaynelle, but it's just not sitting right in my gut," he returned, pleading. "I need to find out what the hell happened in that house and how that woman is involved," Marchant obstinately replied.

Life After Death

Gaynelle exhaled deeply again, thinking, he knew from his experience with her.

"I'll see what I can find without raising the radar," she told him quietly.

"Thanks Gaynelle, call my cell if you find out anything," Marchant responded.

Promising to do just that, she disconnected and Marchant finally stepped into his shower. *You're going to get yourself suspended, or worse,* his common sense tried to again intervene. Pushing the warnings away Marchant showered, exited the bathroom and began to dress. He stepped to his computer and checked his email again. To his delight he received a response from two of the three banks emailed. They were both basic form letters telling him there were no account holders with the names supplied and gave names and contact numbers should he need any further assistance.

"Dammit," he mumbled aloud sighing deeply.

He prayed the last bank was a hit or he was effectively at the end of the road. *Unless Gaynelle gets a lead,* Marchant thought, grabbing his shield and weapon, putting them on and exiting the house, climbing into the government issued unmarked police cruiser and backing out of his driveway.

•••

"Sir," the agent spoke, addressing the man standing beside the large plate glass window looking out of it.

"Yes, what is it," he questioned, turning and taking the man in.

"There's been activity on TCG," he informed, as the man's blue eyes narrowed and he nodded slightly.

The agent left his office as the man sighed deeply and walked over to his desk picking up his phone.

"This is Keller, I need to know who is accessing TCG and why," he said simply as the other party answered and they disconnected.

Michael Keller felt the headache starting to throb right at the base of his neck. He prayed the file was disturbed in error, any other reasons being all disastrous in his mind.

"It's been years," he murmured as the phone rang and he answered seeing the party's identity on his caller I.D.

"What do you have," Keller questioned.

"Precinct in Chapel Hill, North Carolina," the voice informed as Keller frowned deeply.

"Get me sight and sound," he said now.

"Silent," he added as the party again assured him they understood and disconnected.

What the hell is the Chapel Hill police department up too, he mused walking to the small black file cabinet next to his huge mahogany desk. Producing the small silver key, Keller pushed it into the slot and turned it, unlocking the drawer and removing the files contained.

Spreading them on his desk, Keller opened the first one and looked at the photograph.

"Dezi Gianni," he spoke calmly, the 'classified' stamps covering each document concerning the man.

He looked past those, finding the file for Mikayla DeWitt Black Bradford. North Carolina was the last location they had for her. They knew she now resided with Gianni in Bermuda. *So why the hell is this file being disturbed,* Keller wondered. File TCG stood for The Clique Gianni. It was what they coded it back during his tenure with the FBI. Keller since moved to on to bigger and brighter endeavors here with the CIA. This was still one case however that, given the right circumstances, could topple several important and influential members of their government, past and present.

"Someone's searching," he mumbled and sighed again.

Whoever was trying to find Mikayla was treading a dangerous and deadly path; they needed to be derailed, rerouted, immediately. Keller would wait for the eyes and ears on their way to Chapel Hill to give him the specifics, then he would make the necessary moves. *These people have no idea what kind of evil personified they're stirring,* he thought once more as his assistant entered the room reminding him of the luncheon date with Senator Crowler.

"Thank you," Keller returned, smiling slightly as she returned the smile and left him alone.

Keller placed his blackberry in his pocket, the secondary droid in his suit breast pocket and left the office. For now, all he could do was wait.

●●●

Life After Death

Marchant saw the small email icon on his phone and clicked on it, pleased to see the final response from the banks contacted. Opening it, he smiled slightly seeing the response. Pembroke Capital Investments Bank did indeed have an account holder by the name of Mikayla Bradford. She remained a loyal customer for the past three years. The letter told Marchant they could not release any more information without an order from the courts. He didn't care about that. He got a hit, which put him closer to finding her. Marchant quickly googled the airport, looking for a flight into Pembroke Parrish. *What are you gonna tell the Captain,* his mind again questioned. Marchant sighed softly. He needed to slow down. He knew where she was, and Kayla was clueless he was looking for her so she wouldn't run. He needed to collect more evidence, put the pieces together before he went traipsing off to Bermuda. *I need enough to get the locals to cooperate, arrest her, and help me extradite her back to North Carolina,* Marchant thought and slowed his breathing. He checked his text messages hoping Gaynelle might have contacted him. There was nothing.

Glancing up Marchant saw the man he was looking for. Crossing the street he headed into the small antique shop to speak with him.

"Judge Alston," Marchant greeted as Maurice turned his attention from the small pocket watch he held and smiled slightly.

"Hello," he greeted recalling the detective from their previous meeting during Thomas's arrest.

"How are you Detective Marchant," Maurice returned alerting Marchant he did indeed recall who he was.

"I'm fine your Honor," he returned trying to stay on Maurice's good side.

"Your Honor, I'm still trying to find out who killed Reverend Bradford and Pastor Lynch," he told him as Maurice frowned slightly.

"Yes, tragic," he remarked quietly.

Maurice was unsettled for months after the two men were killed, fearful he may have been next on the revenge list, sure that was the reasoning for their deaths.

"I need your help," Marchant began anew.

"I wanted to ask what you knew about Mrs. Bradford," he questioned carefully.

It was no secret the Alston's thought very highly of Kayla and Donovan Black.

"She's a wonderful woman," Maurice answered immediately, slightly offended by the question.

"I don't doubt that your Honor," Marchant again replied diplomatically. "I was simply curious seeing how she was dating almost immediately after leaving her husband," he threw out.

Maurice sighed deeply.

"Detective, Kayla's marriage to Thomas was strained for some time," he told the man evenly. "If you recall, Thomas entered an affair as well, with major consequences," Maurice finished, his tone indicating the conversation was over.

Marchant graciously didn't push. He knew the judge would be no help. He was too close to the woman. *Maybe his wife,* he thought fleetingly before dismissing it as well. The woman was almost obsessed with the daughter, Mariah, so she wouldn't say anything detrimental toward Kayla either. *Someone in this town knows something,* Marchant thought, his cell vibrating and breaking his thought. He looked at the display and clicked on the message icon. He quickly dialed Gaynelle as she requested.

"What you got," Marchant questioned trying to stay his excitement.

"Well just basic stuff," Gaynelle replied. "She used to live on the West Coast, that's where she met the first husband, Donovan, the FBI agent," Gaynelle told him as he grunted.

That much he knew.

"Moved to Virginia Beach for a little while, then she came here with Donovan," she finished as Marchant thanked her and disconnected.

Start at the beginning, his mind told him. He needed to find out about her life on the Coast. What she used to do, who her friends were, who she used to date. *The case where she met Donovan would be a good start,* Marchant continued to think as he walked back to his car and opened it getting inside, starting it and heading back toward the precinct. He would put in his eight hours and then he would go home and get started on unwrapping the mystery surrounding Mikayla Bradford.

●●●

"He's heading toward the precinct," the man said calmly as he and his partner followed the navy blue cruiser.

Life After Death

"Stay with him," Keller instructed. "I want to know what he knows, see who he sees, hear what he hears."

The agents again acknowledged their assignment continuing their surveillance, their target completely unaware of their presence. Keller continued to cogitate, toying with several ideas, but maintaining his composure. He would wait until all the facts were in and then he would decide.

"Dwayne, Dwayne, Dwayne," he exclaimed quietly once again tapping the classified folder and praying Marchant wouldn't force his hand.

The phone rang as if on cue and Keller answered, prepared for the onslaught he knew was about to unfold.

"Good evening, Senator," Keller greeted the man.

"What the hell is going on," Senator Layton Crowler questioned.

They shared lunch earlier but Keller didn't bother to enlighten the man of the latest developments; a mistake on his part.

"Right now sir, there's no reason to be alarmed," he tried to soothe.

"Are you serious," Crowler replied growing more agitated. "I thought we contained this problem twenty years ago," he growled.

Keller assured him the problem was still contained. "Gianni is not in the country, nor has any plans that we've been made aware of, to come back to the United States," he told the Senator hearing the man sigh panting.

"Then why is someone dredging up the past," he questioned slightly calmer now.

"A low level detective," Keller returned. "I'm having everything thoroughly checked out," he added as Crowler again grunted.

"You know as well as I, Keller, we cannot allow this detective to get too close to Gianni," he told Keller who assured him again he realized the gravity of the situation.

"Relax Senator," he told the man. "I'm going to make sure that Detective Dwayne Marchant doesn't cause any unwarranted chaos for us."

"I'm holding you to that Keller," Crowler told him. "And remember if anything goes down, you'll be left out to dry all alone."

"I understand sir," Keller returned calmly as the Senator bid him goodnight and disconnected.

Breathing intensely Keller headed for the small bar in his office and made himself a drink. Sitting behind the huge mahogany beast he garnered as a desk, he began reading the Intel that was already coming into his office on Dwayne Marchant. *What's your angle,* he questioned seeing the man's files and his exemplary service record. *Why are you so damned determined to dig into this case, of all cases, why this one,* Keller continued to ponder as his cell rang again and he answered, listening carefully as one of his operatives began filling in some blanks for him.

Life After Death

Life After 2 Death

Kayla, Mariah, and Jackie, were enjoying their day shopping at the local boutiques, deciding they wanted to head over to one of the seaside café's and have lunch.

"I love that blouse mommy," Mariah told Kayla of the multicolor strapless blouse she just purchased.

"Yes, the colors are really vibrant," Kayla remarked picking up the menu as their server approached the table.

"Hello ladies," the young man greeted smiling brightly.

The three ladies returned his smile and greeting, asking for water and fruit juice. Turning he left their table to retrieve the drinks as they all began to peruse the menu.

"Good afternoon ladies," the deep baritone voice spoke.

Kayla looked up from her menu and smiled, returning his greeting.

"Hello Stephan, how are you today," she greeted amiably.

Jackie did the same, with Mariah reluctantly following suit.

"I'm fine Mrs. Gianni," he replied looking into Kayla's eyes now.

Even though she and Dezi weren't legally married, she used his name and no one on the island questioned it.

"How are you today Mariah," he questioned now, turning his attention to her.

"I'm fine Stephan, thank you," she returned guarded but politely.

He smiled again.

"Have a great afternoon ladies," he spoke before finally walking away.

"So what was that about," Jackie questioned, not missing the tension between the two.

"Is there something you should tell us," Kayla questioned now.

The server returned with their libations, setting them on the table before them and asking for their order.

"I'll have the snapper, with sweet potato pudding and bananas," Kayla told him handing the menu back.

"I'll take the Mahi Mahi, fried, with Johnny cakes," Jackie ordered.

Mariah opted for the mussels, steamed and potatoes on the side.

"Thank you so much, your food will be right out," the server told them, smiling again as he left them alone and the scrutiny once again fell on Mariah.

"Out with it," Jackie accosted.

Mariah sighed deeply glancing across the street finding the man still staring intently at her. She quickly averted her eyes and picked up her water, sipping it for a moment gathering her thoughts. Kayla gave Jackie a look and her best friend shrugged slightly, both of them waiting on the young woman to speak.

"I think he likes me," Mariah said softly as the women both smiled.

"Honey that's very natural, you're a beautiful woman," Kayla told her patting her hand softly.

"Girl yes, the man isn't blind or dead," she teased as Mariah chuckled.

"Has he done anything or said anything out of the way," Jackie questioned.

"No, not really," Mariah told them. "It's just the way he looks at me, and talks to me."

"Well he knows you're married, so let the man have his little crush," Jackie again spoke as Kayla chuckled and Mariah joined in, feeling silly about the entire episode.

The server returned moments later with their food, setting it before them, asking if they needed anything else before leaving them alone to enjoy.

"Is Livvy coming this weekend," Kayla asked in between bites.

"Sure, that's fine," Mariah sighed softly.

Truthfully she felt as if her daughter wasn't her own most times. Dezi and Kayla spoiled her scandalously and Livvy actually preferred to spend time at their home as opposed to her own.

"You and Dezi have got to stop spoiling her though mommy," Mariah tried.

"Honey, we don't spoil her," Kayla protested.

Life After Death

"Mommy, seriously," Mariah retorted, giving her mother a look.

Jackie burst into laughter and agreed with Mariah.

"You and Dezi give that girl anything she thinks she wants," she told Kayla.

"Well as grandparents, we can do that," she promptly told them.

"She's impossible when she comes home though mommy," Mariah told her mother of her almost four year old daughter.

"OK, OK, I surrender," Kayla told them laughingly. "We won't spoil her this weekend," she told them as Mariah rolled her eyes and shook her head, and Jackie gave her a long side eye.

"Yeah right," she quipped as they all burst into laughter again.

Mariah already knew Dezi wasn't hearing anything along the lines of no when it came to Livvy. The child spoke fluent Italian already, leaving both her parents totally clueless at times when she sat and talked to them.

"So where too after lunch," Kayla questioned.

"Abby's," Mariah replied of the exclusive boutique.

"Yes, I love Abby's and I saw a dress just perfect for the Parade of Islands celebration," Jackie said aloud as the two women agreed and continued eating their meals.

•••

"Hey Stephan," Jacob greeted his friend.

They were both on the police force, and both shared ideals and ideas of grandeur and power far beyond their current statuses. Jacob Minions and Stephan Eveson made excellent partners. They kept each other's secrets and there was no mud too dirty for them to wade through or throw out to accomplish their goals.

"What are you doing, watching traffic," he questioned only half joking.

"Watching her," Stephan said calmly, his eyes still trained across the street.

"Aah, I see," Jacob returned seeing the three women.

"You haven't gotten over her yet," he questioned, having a bad feeling about the attraction.

Jacob knew very well who Mariah's husband was. Mr. A Gianni was as deadly as Mr. D Gianni.

"I want her, and I damned well plan to have her," Stephan growled angrily.

He didn't give a damn who her husband was. Truthfully he loathed the Gianni's; his deep seeded jealousy at their wealth and social standing. Stephan grew up dirt poor, struggling for every scrap or morsel he obtained. He thought by finishing school and joining the police force, he would earn respect as well as a decent salary. He barely got the former, and the latter, while not leaving him destitute, did little to remedy his lust of real wealth and power. Seeing Mariah when she and Aidan first attended the policeman's social with Dezi and Kayla, he was instantly smitten. Beautiful women were something else Stephan spent his life trying to acquire, only to be rebuffed, sometimes painfully so, by them as being inferior. Mariah was very different. She was continually pleasant, never arrogant or condescending of her position. She was, in his estimation, his perfect companion. There was still the issue of her being very married however. Soon though, everything would change, even her marital status. Stephan was planning a rise in power, knowing the current chief Kareek Anketil was loyal to Dezi, allowing the man to basically do whatever he wanted on the island without consequence. He was making allies though. Powerful and strong allies who wanted to see an end to the Gianni regime as much as he did. Allies who would help him become even more wealthy and powerful than the men, bringing a satisfied smirk to his face.

"Stephan, don't start a war because of your lust," Jacob admonished giving him a look.

Stephan regarded his friend, eyes narrowed, face twisted in fury.

"What I feel for Mariah is well past lust," he growled. "I can fuck any woman on this island I want, anytime I want," he fired as Jacob cringed, sorry he opened the can of worms.

Calming slightly, Stephan returned his attention to the women now rising to leave the café.

"I want to build a life with her, marry her, have children of our own," he spoke softly now, almost to himself.

"There's still the matter of her husband, and his father," Jacob told him jolting Stephan harshly back into reality.

"Hmph," he replied simply, turning and beginning to walk down the street.

Jacob caught up quickly matching his much taller friends stride as they walked.

Life After Death

"I am going to see Vanessa tonight," he told Jacob who nodded.

Vanessa Trufont was the daughter of one of the most powerful politician's on the island, Arroyo Trufont. He and Dezi were friendly, but not excessively close, at least not yet. Stephan wanted to make sure that never happened. He needed Arroyo on his side. With that kind of power and backing, removing Kareek would be child's play. Arriving shortly after they started walking, they headed inside the small police precinct.

"Chief is looking for you," one of the officers quickly informed Stephan and Jacob.

Sighing deeply and reminding himself of his plans, Stephan turned and headed in Kareek's office.

"Hello Chief, you wanted to see us," he spoke, taking the man in.

Kareek was medium height, 5'10 or so, thick but neither muscular or fat, just solid. He was dark as midnight with small feral eyes always seeming to dart to and fro as if searching for something.

"Yes, sit down," he told the men regarding them for a moment before sitting back in his chair.

"I will be out of the office for a few days," he informed as Stephan fought the urge to smile, and Jacob listened intently.

"You will be in charge while I'm away Stephan," he told the man as the smile continued to fight for freedom.

Kareek gave him the tasks list, as well as contact information should anything arise their jurisdiction couldn't handle.

"I'll be back in three days," he told them, noting the he left on Thursday, two days from now. *He won't be back until Sunday*, Stephan contemplated, knowing he would need to move swiftly. If he could get everything in place, when Kareek returned he would already be the former chief and Stephan would be the new chief.

"Any questions," Kareek queried.

Shaking his head no, Stephan and Jacob rose leaving the chiefs office and heading straight to the locker room. After assuring themselves it was empty they both smiled brightly and clapped each other on the back.

"This is going to be easier than I thought," Jacob replied as Stephan chuckled.

"You're exactly right," he returned.

"Come lets shower and get out of here," Stephan spoke now. "I want to go celebrate a bit before I see Vanessa and put the rest of the plan into action," he told him chuckling still as they both headed for the showers, remarking yet again on their stroke of good luck.

•••

"Come in Dezi, have a seat," Arroyo greeted smiling.

The two men were finally getting the opportunity to talk privately and compare notes. Dezi needed to make alliances with the politician for the next leg of his business venture. He was about to procure a fleet of ships and enter the shipping market.

"I've heard very good things about you and your enterprises," Arroyo told him, sipping the cognac they were both enjoying.

Dezi smiled slightly returning the compliment, taking in the lavishly furnished office. The handcrafted Italian woods shone beautifully in the natural lighted office. He and Arroyo sat in the handsomely crafted high back leather chairs, deep mahogany red in color.

"Arroyo, my plans are to make this island a utopia for those who have worked hard to deserve it," Dezi told him calmly, regarding him as he spoke.

Arroyo nodded thoughtfully.

"And you have a new venture in mind," he questioned.

"Yes, as matter of fact," Dezi told him, going on to elaborate.

"It sounds like a very novel, ideal, and lucrative endeavor," Arroyo returned after hearing the idea.

"I do believe it will benefit us all," Dezi returned, his meaning obvious.

"I don't want you to rush into anything," he began anew. "Why don't you come with me this weekend," Dezi invited. "My son, Aidan, my partner Big D, and I, are going deep sea fishing," he told the man as Arroyo smiled broadly.

He liked Dezi Gianni now that he got the opportunity to meet him one on one. The man was cunning, calculating, and deadly; ideal traits to keep him and his family safe and his fortunes hefty.

Life After Death

"That sounds like a wonderful idea," Arroyo returned.

"Excellent," Dezi returned going on to tell him they would be leaving Thursday morning around 6:00AM.

"You have a yacht," Arroyo questioned.

"I actually have several yachts," Dezi smiled somewhat.

"We're taking one I just acquired," Dezi again spoke.

The more he heard the more impressed Arroyo Trufont was with Dezi Gianni. True, he wielded his own share of money and power, obviously it was paupers change compared to what this man wielded.

"I've never been deep sea fishing," Arroyo conceded.

"There's nothing to it," Dezi chuckled.

"We actually don't have to do anything except drink and sit there," Dezi told him still laughing lightly.

"We have people who bait the poles, cast them for us, who take the fish off the hook we catch," he explained as Arroyo laughed now.

"Ohhh, I see," he replied still smiling.

"We'll relax this weekend, tell you more about the venture, and you can see for yourself the benefits of aligning yourself with us," Dezi told him rising now and preparing to leave the politicians office.

"I do believe I'm going to enjoy this weekend immensely," Arroyo replied as the two shook hands and Dezi left the office, promising to send a car to pick him up on Thursday morning.

Still smiling, Arroyo walked back to his desk and sat down, his feet atop it, as he thought of the new alliance he was about to make and the money that would quickly follow.

Life After 3 Death

Marchant was on the trail again. He called in a few favors and received some background information on Kayla.

"West Coast," he mumbled leafing through the papers.

That was where he would need to start. Marchant knew he was fighting an uphill battle. The woman was removed from the place for more than twenty years, still he had to start someplace and he believed he would find the beginning of her blood trail there. *She's no amateur,* Marchant coldly thought looking over the various photos of Kayla from the file he was sent. She always beautiful it seemed. *That's how she trapped these men before she killed them,* Marchant continued to think as he jotted various points of interest onto the paper.

"Adrian Roberts," he murmured seeing the name in a file dealing with an organized crime ring of some sort.

"Was she mixed up in this," he again spoke aloud.

Marchant was getting antsy. He found way too many questions and not nearly enough answers. His cell rang and disturbed his research as he answered amiably seeing Gaynelle's name on the caller I.D.

"Hey, what's up," Marchant greeted.

"Captain wants to see you, right now," she returned, voice strained and thick with tension.

Shit, Marchant thought, praying none of the banks he contacted had called his superior.

"What about Gaynelle," Marchant tried.

"Get here quick Dwayne," she returned instead of answer and disconnected.

The knot in Marchant's stomach tightened as he closed the folder putting it inside his desk and locking it. Grabbing his jacket, he headed out of the door, car keys in hand and got into the cruiser, backing out of the driveway and heading toward the precinct. He tried Gaynelle again, the call going directly to voicemail. *Your ass is gonna get suspended,* his mind told him as Marchant sighed deeply. This case was important to him. He needed to find

Life After Death

out the truth; to know once and for all if Kayla was truly guilty or innocent. If she was innocent, then no harm, no foul. If she was guilty he vowed to bring her back to North Carolina and put her on trial. *She will pay for taking those men's lives,* Marchant thought angrily, pulling into the first available parking space upon his arrival at the precinct.

●●●

Maurice was thinking about his conversation with Detective Marchant, frowning slightly. *Why is he still dredging up that case, let it rest,* he thought uneasily. Thomas and Chris's death shook him more than he wanted to admit. Maurice was no fool. Someone viciously murdered the two men and his gut told him it was because of Kayla and the things Thomas did to her.

"Wrong place and time," Maurice murmured thinking of Chris.

After all the publicity died down, the whispering about Kayla's leaving stopped, things went pretty much back to normal. Normal was what Maurice wanted and normal was what Captain Wilmont promised after he made the call to her office. Whatever one man demolition route Marchant was on, Maurice wanted it stopped. *My family needs to be safe,* he thought concerning his wife, Sandra, and their grandson, Reese. Maurice smiled thinking of the precocious little boy, eternally grateful he was here. He still missed David without measure, but through his grandson, they were able to still have some small piece of him in their midst.

"Judge Alston," Maurice answered as he picked up the receiver.

"Hello your honor," the voice said on the other end.

"This is Agent Cassandra Deale," she told him her voice soft and feminine, yet commanding and assertive.

"Good morning Agent Deale," Maurice returned, completely perplexed. "How can I help you?"

"I need to see you concerning a case that has been recently brought to our attention," Cassandra explained.

"Discretion is at an utmost premium your honor," Cassandra spoke once again.

"Yes, yes, of course," Maurice returned, his mind whirling.

"Can we get together for brunch," the agent inquired.

"Certainly, what time and where," Maurice asked, which she calmly supplied.

"I will meet you there," she added before disconnecting.

Now what, he wondered that uneasy feeling returning. Maurice buzzed his clerk alerting her he would be out of the office for a little while.

"I won't be available via cell phone, so please take messages," he instructed as the clerk acknowledged his direction.

He picked up his briefcase and keys heading to the parking deck and retrieving the Benz. Maurice reflected on his life as he drove thinking of his new position and all the prestige that came with it. Vowing that he would allow nothing to get in the way of, or derail it, Maurice pushed away all the warnings and premonitions, making up his mind to cooperate fully with the Agent and whatever requests were being made. His resolve was further shored after arriving at the restaurant and coming inside, being greeted by Agent Cassandra Deale; one of the most beautiful women he laid eyes on in a long time.

●●●

Marchant arrived at Captain Wilmont's office with a deep seeded sense of trepidation. Caroline Wilmont was no joke. She was the first female, African American, captain in the department, making sure everyone knew she got their on her merits, not her looks or connections. After tapping lightly on the frosted glass portion of the door bearing her name, Marchant entered, hearing her admonishment to come in. He took the captain in, admiring her soft feminine features. She was a beautiful woman without doubt; dark almost midnight, soft pouty full lips, expressive brown eyes and two small, but adorable dimples adorned the cheeks. She wore her hair natural, small twists, dyed a soft shade of brown, almost auburn.

"You wanted to see me Captain Wilmont," Marchant carefully questioned, taking the seat she beckoned him to while she finished the paperwork she was working on.

Her silence spoke volumes as Marchant's sense of dread deepened even further. Finishing up five minutes later, Caroline laid her pen down and sat back in her chair regarding the detective in front of her.

Dwayne Marchant was a good detective in her book, one of the best on her force. Still, he had a penchant for angering the wrong people and today was no exception. Judge Alston was adamant in his assertion that the detective

Life After Death

was doing more harm than good by continuing to question the murders of three years ago. Caroline patiently explained that as an open homicide case, it was well within Marchant's scope of duties to try and follow up on the case and eventually solve it. *"That's all well and good, but he's endangering people, especially my family and I will not stand for that,"* Maurice told her angrily. Caroline sighed deeply then, promising to talk to the detective.

"How are you this afternoon Marchant," she questioned as he glanced at the clock and noticed it was indeed after 12:00PM.

"I'm fine Captain," he replied as she grunted slightly and sighed again.

"You've been asking questions again about the Bradford, Lynch murders," Caroline asked as Marchant steeled himself.

"It's still an unsolved case," he returned in his defense.

She nodded slightly, taking a thoughtful pause.

"Dwayne," she began her tone calm but firm. "I want you to stop investigating this case," Caroline spoke. "I've told you that before, and normally I would look the other way when you disobeyed my orders since it may end up with you solving the case," she went on as Marchant endured. "Sometimes though, things are bigger than the both of us, and as much as we might like, we have to know when to surrender," she patiently explained.

"It's our sworn duty to try and find the perpetrators of these crimes," Marchant again threw out. "I'm simply trying to give some families closure."

Caroline again grunted, fully understanding his intentions, unaware of his ulterior motives.

"Listen Dwayne, if you insist on investigating this case, stay way under the radar," she began basically conceding defeat.

The detective was right. It was their job to solve crimes, not brush them under the rug.

"You're getting way too much attention," she added as Marchant nodded, understanding.

"I'm sorry Captain, I promise, no more rippled waves," he told her sincerely as Caroline eyed him carefully for a while before speaking.

"Please do that Dwayne," she told him. "You're a great detective and I would hate to lose you over egos and power trips," Caroline ended, giving him a knowing look.

Marchant nodded contritely; glad she was only chewing him out, not suspending or firing him for disobeying a direct order.

"You have my word," he told her standing now as Caroline nodded and allowed him to leave her office, praying he wouldn't force her hand.

•••

Maurice was still enjoying Agent Deale's beauty when she began to speak again. He wasn't really listening as he watched her supple lips move and heard the melodic hypnotic resonance of her voice. The woman was statuesque, standing he was sure somewhere around five feet, ten inches. Voluptuous curves adorned her hips, thighs and firm butt. Agent Deale was toned in every area his eyes roamed. Her breasts were firm melon mounds on her chest; the beautiful soft brown eyes were enchanting. Maurice felt ten years younger sitting here with her, enjoying the view of her long shapely legs now that she crossed them, continuing to speak. He knew he shouldn't have been thinking of the woman that way, but things at home weren't good since David's death. Sandra seemed to only exist for Reese. He was her entire world, leaving Maurice very much in the cold. He tried talking to her; getting her to see a therapist, but nothing seemed to break the spell and after a while Maurice simply gave up.

"So as you can see your honor, we really do need your help," Cassandra spoke waking Maurice from the lust filled thoughts and returning him to the table where they sat preparing to enjoy lunch.

Maurice cleared his throat slightly, praying his voice didn't betray his earlier thoughts when he spoke.

"Are you sure that your information is accurate," he questioned as Cassandra smiled slightly.

"I understand your hesitation your honor," she replied.

"Maurice," he replied amiably. "Please call me Maurice."

Cassandra smiled demurely and complied, using his name now.

"Maurice, this is a matter of national security honestly," she told him looking into his eyes.

Cassandra Deale was good at her job, hence why she was sent. The man sitting across from her showed all the classic signs. He was arrogant but powerful in his own right; women were his Achilles heel and from the lust in his eyes as he took her in, things were very cold in his bedroom at home.

Life After Death

Cassandra could also tell affairs were nothing new to the judge, and his conscience concerning them took hiatus long ago. Sliding the file across the table, she looked up at him, capturing him with her eyes once more.

"The things in this file are confidential, but I feel you need to know them," she told him as Maurice nodded absently, already picturing her naked.

Forcing his eyes away from hers Maurice opened the file and began perusing the information contained.

"Wow," he said simply after reading it, closing it and pushing it back to Agent Deale.

"How can I help," he questioned, several questions already answered for him after being enlightened by the file.

"We need to know that when we're ready to move your hon--, I'm sorry, I mean Maurice, that we have a judge who understands the seriousness of the situation and will be able to sign the necessary documents," she told him, casting the bait.

Maurice felt the semi erection become full blown when the beautiful agent unconsciously licked her lips.

"Yes, of course," he returned emphatically. "I will help in any way that I can," he added as Cassandra smiled.

"Thank you Maurice," she told him, lightly stroking his hand now.

"I knew you were the right choice," she added, removing her hand and sipping her water now.

"Please understand Maurice, it is of utmost importance that our meetings be kept strictly confidential," Cassandra told him as Maurice nodded vigorously. "Not even your wife can know," she iterated.

"I promise you, our meetings will be held in the strictest of confidences," Maurice assured.

"Good, here's my cell number," Cassandra told him, sliding the small card across the table. "We'll communicate that way, and meet when necessary," she added as Maurice cleared his throat and took a deep breath.

"Agent Deale, I know this may seem forward, but do you think we could maybe have dinner and talk more," he questioned, feigning a heavy court calendar today and his having to leave.

Cassandra smiled graciously knowing he was lying, having already done a thorough check of the judge and all his cases.

"Certainly, that would be fine," she replied, not calling him on the deception.

Maurice thanked her, rising and assuring her he would call her later as he left the restaurant. Cassandra watched him leave, pulling out her cell and making a call.

"He bit," she said simply.

"Good, make the next move," Keller replied as Cassandra acknowledged his direction and disconnected.

Life After 4 Death

Stephan watched her as she shopped in the fresh market. He loved the times she was out alone; it meant he would get the opportunity to talk to her. Stephan was careful however. He knew both the Gianni's were very obsessive and paranoid where the women were concerned, not past having someone watching them as they went about their daily tasks. Slowly Stephan made his way to Mariah standing in front of a large display of ripening melons; the fragrant aroma's cascading through the warm morning air. Stephan snagged a fresh ripe apple, biting into it as he continued to walk and observe her. *Patience, this weekend will change everything,* he thought and smiled slightly, discarding the apple and swallowing the fruit in his mouth.

"Hello Mariah," he spoke now as she turned and regarded him, her expression slightly concerned.

"Hi," she returned calmly, returning her attention to the melons in her hand.

"The yellow ones are sweeter," Stephan told her, still standing in front of her.

"Thank you," Mariah returned putting his suggestion in the small handcart she held.

"May I," Stephan asked, taking it from her and walking with her now as she continued to shop.

He could sense her discomfort, but he was enjoying every moment of his time with her.

"Hello Stephan," Vanessa spoke, making sure both he and Mariah saw her.

Stephan saw the jealousy in her face as she regarded him holding the other woman's cart.

"I'll take this," Mariah told him, taking the handcart as Stephan grudgingly surrendered it.

"Hi Vanessa," Mariah spoke now, smiling slightly.

Vanessa quickly put on a fake smile and returned the woman's greeting. Mariah saw her opportunity and took it, leaving the two alone as she quickly headed for the vegetable section.

"What's that all about," Vanessa questioned angrily.

Stephan took a deep breath not wanting to lose his temper. The woman in front of him was still an integral part of his plans and he couldn't afford to offend or alienate her just yet. He would explain things to Mariah later, once they were together. She would understand; she was that kind of woman, Stephan reasoned internally.

"Why are you so jealous Vanessa," Stephan threw out. "Mariah is a married woman," he added giving the woman a look.

"I saw how you were looking at her," Vanessa fired, not appeased.

Stephan sighed heavily, shaking his head slowly.

"That was clearly your jealousy and imagination at work," he told her, gently stroking her face now. "Vanessa, you can't be jealous of every woman I talk to," Stephan chided gently.

She continued to regard him quietly, angry with herself for not being able to stay mad at him. Stephan was sexy and he knew it.

"Alright, I believe you," Vanessa finally acquiesced.

"Thank you," Stephan replied kissing her cheek gently.

"Oh, I was coming to see you to tell you that daddy won't be home this weekend, soooo," she trailed off giving him a look.

Stephan controlled the urge to frown, quickly trying to calm himself. He didn't want to hear what she just said. Stephan needed Arroyo Trufont in place. He needed to talk to him, get his plans in motion.

"Where is he going," Stephan questioned innocently.

Vanessa shrugged slightly.

"On a fishing trip," she replied nonchalantly.

"Oh I see," Stephan replied smiling at her, knowing her plans, but not really caring.

His mind was on overdrive right now thinking of how he would approach and see the politician before he left. He had to move Kareek out of the way quickly. *First him, then both the damned Gianni's and I can finally have Mariah and*

Life After Death

everything else I've ever wanted on this island, Stephan was thinking as Vanessa continued to talk.

"He's leaving Thursday morning, so you can come over after work Thursday evening," she told him seductively batting her eyelashes at him.

"That sounds like a plan," Stephan managed another smile.

"I'll see you then," he replied as she smiled again.

"I have to leave, but call me later," Vanessa informed as Stephan's mind leapt for joy.

"I will," he replied still smiling as she sauntered out of the market directly into the waiting car sitting at the curb and the driver whisked her away.

•••

Kayla had a bad feeling about Dezi's trip, but didn't voice it. She dismissed the thoughts as being foolish and didn't want to dampen his enthusiasm. He was excited about both the trip and Arroyo Trufont coming along. Still she couldn't shake the small voice that kept telling her not to let him go.

"Hey baby," Dezi greeted coming into the bedroom.

"Something wrong," he questioned reading her expression and knowing his woman very well.

"No, I'm fine," Kayla returned, brushing her hair now.

Dezi exhaled softly and walked over to her, pulling her into his arms and looking into her eyes.

"Kayla, you do realize you're a terrible liar right," he teased as she chuckled and playfully rolled her eyes.

"What's wrong baby," Dezi questioned once more.

"I'm just being silly Dezi, nothing is wrong, I promise," Kayla again tried as he continued to watch her a few moments more before kissing her.

"OK, I'll let you have this one," he teased as she smiled.

"What are you, Mariah, and Jackie, getting into this weekend," he questioned, kissing her neck gently.

"All day spa, shopping, not sure what else," she returned, biting her lip as Dezi began kissing the center of her chest.

Returning to her lips, he easily unzipped her dress removing it as he kissed his way down her body, lifting her and laying her onto the king size bed, his lips meeting her sex, his tongue breaching her threshold, as Kayla moaned deeply and arched her back to enjoy all he was offering. All dark thoughts, warning, or trepidation was instantly dissolved as Dezi brought her to a dizzying and drenching climax. Kayla cried his name, gasping as the second wave of the orgasm hit and she remembered why she loved this man so much.

"Dezi, yess," Kayla breathed, feeling his tongue slowly make its way up her body, stopping at her breasts and giving each individual arousal.

Kayla was moaning steadily, on fire and wanting to make love. Dezi's lips found hers as they began to kiss passionately and he entered her, thrusting deeply enjoying the feel of her.

"Baby, mmm, so good," Kayla moaned as Dezi spread her widely, riding her clit high and hard as she came yet another time, screaming his name aloud.

Dezi smiled slightly knowing she was enjoying his efforts, placing one leg on his shoulder and dropping his hips lower, going deeper inside her.

"Yes, oh god, yes," Kayla continued to cry out, her body showing its appreciation.

Dezi felt his own end nearing, the warm tightness of her space turning him on in a major way. Kayla began gripping him with her sex, his breathing more and more erratic the closer he got. She came one last time, her sex contracting and lubricating his hardness, finally pushing him over the edge as Dezi's manhood expanded and his finish escaped, going deeply inside Kayla as he collapsed atop her, breathing hard, but fully satisfied. She was stroking his back, kissing his neck as they held each other now. The thoughts were back and the feeling of dread was even worse. *Stop it, the man is only going fishing,* Kayla told herself. Dezi removed himself from her lying beside her now and pulled her into his arms.

"Everything is going to be fine baby," he told her looking into her eyes again, reading her thoughts.

"I promise," Dezi added kissing her softly.

Kayla smiled, reassured by his strong arms and those piercing gray eyes, finally believing him and dismissing her own fears once and for all.

●●●

Life After Death

Mariah couldn't describe how happy she was when Vanessa interrupted Stephan following her. She thought about the advice her mother and Jackie gave, but there was something about the man that scared Mariah deeply. There was a darkness; an evil aura that seemed to cling to him.

"Hello Mrs. Aidan," the woman behind the register greeted.

Mariah smiled and returned her greeting. She wondered if anyone even knew her name. They all called her by Aidan's name or his initial. Mariah didn't really mind. It actually served as deterrent and kept a lot of the more unsavory element from harassing her. *Too bad it doesn't seem to work on Stephan,* her mind threw out as Mariah immediately chastised herself for the thought. Stephan was an attractive man. She would concede that much. He was tall, slightly shorter than Aidan, nice build, not thick or thin, but pleasantly in between. She supposed the radiant smile he possessed could be called his best feature, but again, she couldn't help feeling there was something very cold and detached behind the gesture.

"Did you find everything," the familiar voice spoke as Mariah turned to find Stephan once again in her personal space.

"Yes, thank you," she replied politely, gathering her bags and preparing to leave the market.

"Please, allow me," Stephan spoke, taking the bags from her and walking with her to the car parked outside.

Mariah unlocked the trunk, asking him to put the bags there. Stephan complied taking a quick mental inventory of the contents, before closing it and regarding her once again.

"Thank you so much for your help, Stephan," Mariah spoke smiling slightly.

"You're very welcome Mariah," he replied still looking into her eyes.

"Are you and Vanessa dating," she questioned since he seemed determined not to leave immediately.

She saw his face shadow, reminding her of the earlier thoughts, before he quickly recovered himself and answered.

"We're friends, we occasionally date," he replied vaguely as Mariah nodded slightly.

"She seems like a very nice woman," she tossed back as Stephan grunted but didn't comment.

"Yes, she's nice enough," he replied, still holding her eyes hostage.

"Do you miss the United States," he questioned out of the blue.

Mariah frowned slightly. It was an odd question.

"Sometimes, but not often," she answered.

"I'm happy here, I have a great family, friends," she added as Stephan smiled and nodded slightly.

"I've never been, but I would like to go one day soon," he told her.

"Any particular destination you have in mind," Mariah questioned.

"California or New York perhaps," Stephan replied.

"Definitely lively places," Mariah returned chuckling slightly.

Stephan loved seeing her true smile. The dimples were beautiful, sexy, and alluring. He wanted so much to kiss her, to hold her, make love to her. *Patience,* his mind told his libido as he slowed his thoughts and continued talking to her.

"Where did you live," he questioned.

"I grew up in North Carolina."

"I've never really heard of it," Stephan answered honestly.

"No, I'm pretty sure you wouldn't have," Mariah returned still smiling.

"How are the children," Stephan asked now.

He didn't mind that she had the two. They were still young enough to adapt and would accept him as their father.

"They're fine, enjoying time with their father," she replied, fishing in her purse now, looking for her keys.

It took all of Stephan's will not to frown when she mentioned her husband. He honestly hated acknowledging the man's existence.

"That's nice, gives you some alone time," he returned amiably as Mariah found her keys.

"True," she replied stepping to the driver's door. "Thank you again Stephan, but I need to get home," she told him.

"Have a great afternoon, Mariah," he graciously told her, standing and watching as she drove down the road and out of his line of sight.

Life After Death

"Time to go see Arroyo Trufont," he murmured heading for his own car.

●●●

"Hello father," Vanessa greeted Arroyo coming into his office without knocking.

"Oh, I'm sorry," she spoke once she saw the man inside, vaguely recognizing him.

"That's why you are supposed to knock," Arroyo spoke, giving his daughter a chastising look.

"Aidan Gianni, this is my daughter Vanessa," he continued, introducing the two.

He's as attractive as his father, she thought behind the cordial smile gracing her face. "Hello Vanessa," Aidan greeted amiably, returning his attention immediately back to her father.

"What did you need dear," Arroyo questioned noting his daughters prolonged attention to his guest.

"Huh, oh, I was coming to see if you needed anything before I leave for the evening," Vanessa returned, mind still on the strikingly handsome man sitting in the high-back Victorian chair, casually sipping the drink he held.

"No," Arroyo returned. "I'm fine, you can go ahead and leave, I'll be home shortly," he finished, dismissing her from their presence.

"It was a pleasure to meet you Aidan," Vanessa spoke sweetly, eyes locking with his once more.

"Pleasure meeting you as well, Vanessa," Aidan replied, smiling yet another time as she forced her feet to move and turned leaving the office and them to their business.

Vanessa bit the corner of her bottom lip, her breathing heavy as her heart pounded. Aidan effectively seduced her in that simple look, the gray eyes alluring and mysterious.

"How in the world did Mariah manage to land him," she murmured jealously.

You're with Stephan, and Aidan is married, her mind quickly reminded. Vanessa sighed softly but didn't completely dismiss the idea of being with Aidan. Maybe he wasn't happy with little miss perfect. Maybe he wanted to sample some of the islands flavor, Vanessa thought and chuckled walking toward her own office. Entering she was surprised to see Stephan waiting for her. The smile faltered ever so slightly before she turned it on full speed and said hello.

"What a wonderful surprise," Vanessa told him as Stephan rose and walked toward her.

"Hello beautiful," he greeted, kissing her lips feather soft.

"I'm actually here to see your father, but I see he's busy," Stephan told her doing an excellent job of hiding his loathing of the man he knew to be in Arroyo Trufont's office.

"So I came to wait inside your office, hoping you would show up," Stephan lied, kissing her neck at the end of his sentence.

"Mmm, he might be a while Stephan," Vanessa breathed as his lips began to go lower, the tops of her breasts being greeted.

"Stephan, we can't, not here," Vanessa tried as his hands palmed her butt, his lips brushing the nail hard nipples as she bit her lip once more to stay the moan wanting to escape.

"No one will know Vanessa," Stephan returned, pressing his erection against her.

His lips found hers once more as they kissed and he slowly guided the zipper on her dress downward. Vanessa didn't protest further, wanting and needing the release dangling before her when he removed her bra and put her nipple in his mouth.

"Aaah, Stephan," she murmured, opening her legs wider to allow his searching fingers inside her fortress.

Stephan caressed the hardened clit, walking her backward until the desk stopped her progression. He nimbly lifted her, sitting her on the desk continuing to kiss her while he stroked her clit, fingers coated with her arousal.

"I want you so much right now," Vanessa moaned, unzipping his pants, pulling them to his knees and freeing his erection from the underwear she managed to get mid-thigh.

Stephan returned the favor, sliding her thong off, stepping between her legs, the head of his manhood rubbing her clit soliciting more soft moans and groans.

"You're so beautiful Vanessa," Stephan spoke, really needing to enter her.

Life After Death

He was beyond horny after his conversation and time spent with Mariah earlier.

"Stephan, mmmh," she moaned, thrusting her sex forward.

Taking her lead he slid deeply inside her, both of them murmuring as their bodies shuddered lightly from the contact. Stephan began a wicked ascent to release thrusting hard and deep inside Vanessa as she held on tightly and enjoyed the ride. "Right there, ahh yes, Stephan," she groaned aloud, lying back onto the desk, her legs now on his shoulders as he pounded her mercilessly.

Eyes closed and rolled back in his head all Stephan could see was Mariah. He licked his lips, picking up speed and velocity inside Vanessa, seeing Mariah's beautiful body naked, her sex dripping slowly as his tongue captured each and every ounce of her sweet and syrupy nectar.

"Oh god Stephan, I'm about to cum," Vanessa again moaned, her cries falling on deaf ears.

The only sounds he heard were Mariah's kitten like purring's as she came hard and her creaminess covered his manhood, the erotic scent wafting to his flared nostrils bringing him to the peak of release. Stephan's cry was low and baritone filled as he thrust one final time into Vanessa and his semen burst from him, body tense, trembling in delectable ecstasy, biting his own lip to stay the name Mariah on the tip of his tongue from escaping his lips.

"Mmm, that was so good, you're a beast Stephan," Vanessa told him tiredly, still heaving slightly trying to steady her breathing.

"You bring that out in me," he lied smoothly, fixing his pants and zipping them.

"I'll see your father later," he told her bringing a smile to her face.

"Alright," Vanessa returned. "Do you want me to tell him you stopped by," she questioned the tiny smirk on her face.

Stephan chuckled shaking his head no as he kissed her lips and left her in the office alone with her thoughts and plans.

Life After 5 Death

Bumping up in here tonight for a change, JaDon thought making his way inside the crowded club and toward the bar. Tonight was Friday, the end of one very long and arduous week.

"Hey, what's up," the bartender greeted.

"What can I get for you," she questioned as JaDon looked her over.

Not bad, a little too butch for my tastes though, he decided of the raven haired, fair complexioned woman still waiting for him to speak.

"Hennessy, ice," he spoke as the woman nodded and quickly grabbed a glass, throwing in the frozen cubes before adding the caramel liquor and handing it to him.

"$12 bucks," she spoke, JaDon handing her the twenty and telling her to keep the change.

Walking away he began looking for a table. Hopefully tonight wouldn't be a total waste and he would find some hot and willing pussy, or dick for that matter, to take home. He chuckled at his thought, but JaDon prided himself on being honest. He didn't have time for love just yet and he enjoyed a great night of intimacy with either sex. The latter however he kept very close to the vest. The FBI wasn't quite that sexually liberated yet. There were still plenty of people who would frown on his choices, people who could and would make his tenure even harder than it was currently. Right now his entire focus was on making his career. JaDon Ivory was a freshman FBI agent, lowest of the low, and the senior agents never let him forget it. Since graduating law school and his father pulling some strings to get him into the agency, he worked his ass off to prove his worth.

"Just need that one case," he mumbled into the Hennessy spotting familiar faces and bringing a smile to his lips.

"Look who's slumming tonight," the woman teased as JaDon drew close enough to be noticed.

"Wow, why does it have to be like that," he bantered back as she invited him to sit down.

"JaDon, this is Harry, Lina, and your already know Gar," the woman introduced.

Life After Death

JaDon said hello to the group, everyone greeting him warmly. Everyone except Edgar 'Gar' Simons, and he already knew the reason for that.

"You work for the FBI too, JaDon," Lina, the petite Asian beauty asked smiling at him as she sipped the margarita.

"Yep, he's bottom rung like us," April returned laughing again.

April Sutton was the reason Gar couldn't stand him. The man carried a serious case of heat for her, but she wouldn't so far give him the time of day.

"Whatever April," JaDon answered laughing, beckoning the server over wanting another drink.

"You wouldn't have that problem April if you worked for a real agency," Gar threw out condescendingly, giving JaDon a look.

Harry and Lina rolled their eyes, causing JaDon to chuckle aloud.

"And you do what for the CIA, Gar," JaDon threw back giving him a look.

"You're a records clerk, so please shut the hell up," he added as the rest of the group howled with laughter at the scathing jibe.

Gar however was not amused as his expression darkened and he drained the beer in front of him, ordering two more.

"Stop it you two, damn," April spoke up, hating the tension between them and not wanting it to ruin the evening.

His ass has about one more time, JaDon thought behind the small smile as he caught a glance of Gar from the corner of his eye. Feeling perfectly devious, he leaned close to April and spoke in her ear.

"What are the chances of you coming home with me tonight," JaDon whispered nastily, blowing softly on her ear.

He was actually attracted to the woman, at least sexually, simply keeping her at arm's length because they worked together. April was no slouch in the looks department; porcelain smooth skin covering every inch of her taunt body, breasts a bit small but perfectly proportioned to the hips and curvy butt, graduating down the dancer toned legs. Her lavender eyes were set deeply inside her face giving her a uniquely mysterious aura, the pouty ruby red lips begging to be kissed.

"Hmm, depends on how drunk you can get me," April teased back, her eyes giving him the yes her mouth tried to conceal.

"I can do that," JaDon quipped ordering her a triple shot of tequila, bringing another round of laughter to the table.

"What case are you working on at the Bureau, JaDon," Gar questioned, still visibly pissed at the closeness between the man and April.

"We don't discuss our cases," JaDon quipped, not wanting to admit he wasn't working on anything.

So far he was doing nothing more than Gar; typing and filing reports on a daily basis from the senior agents.

"Mhmm," Gar returned giving him a knowing look. "Not like the Bureau gets any of the real cases anyway," he added, the alcohol beginning to loosen his tongue.

"What's that mean," JaDon questioned, paying more attention.

"Means the Agency is the one who gets the good stuff, the classified stuff that can ruin nations," he slurred.

"Oh shut up Gar, damn," Harry threw out, growing tired of the routine.

"Let's dance," he told Lina.

JaDon casually looked Harry over again. *Hmmm, might be worth a conversation or two,* he thought instantly picking up vibes the man wouldn't be adverse to being approached. Lina giggled and complied leaving the three of them at the table alone.

"I'm going to the restroom," April spoke a bit annoyed now herself.

JaDon didn't move. His instincts told him even though Gar was drunk and rambling, there was something going on underneath the nonsense that he needed to hear. April rejoined them just as Gar began again.

"Yeah, we stay cleaning up the stuff the Bureau fucks up," he threw out once again, arrogantly.

"Yeah, like what asshole," JaDon baited, shaking off the liquor and putting his listening skills to work.

"Like a case so fucked up by the Bureau the Agency had to triple classify that shit," he threw back getting belligerent and angry.

April frowned slightly, hoping Gar was just running his mouth, but getting a bad feeling.

Life After Death

"Let it go you guys, seriously," she tried to interject. "Let's have some fun," she added, throwing JaDon a pleading glance.

Normally he would have backed off, but his curiosity was peaked. JaDon needed something that would catapult his career hurriedly up the ladder and Gar had his radar wide open.

"What case? You always talking shit, name it," JaDon baited a final time.

"I'm going out on the dance floor," April spoke testily, sick of the testosterone at the table, rose and left them.

"Like a muthafucka so dangerous he can kill across continents," Gar told him, swallowing the last of his beer and rising.

"But don't worry bitch boy, the Agency took care of it, don't hafta worry about big bad Devastator no more," he finished haughtily staggering onto the dance floor trying to dance with April, who quickly dismissed him and returned her attention to Lina and Harold.

JaDon quickly typed the name into his phone deciding to follow up Monday morning when he got back to the office. Rising he headed to the dance floor, pulling April close and sweetly apologizing, his mind having not forgotten his manhood still wanted release tonight.

●●●

"Why the fuck was a records clerk in my office," Keller raged, furious that the file was disturbed or seen by anyone under the restricted classification.

"He files records sir," the agent returned, praying his boss didn't bust him down to the same rank for the error.

"I want all his information," Keller returned furious.

There was enough issue trying to keep things under wraps without some freshman records clerk wanting to play international spy and leak it to any unscrupulous parties.

"Yes sir, right away," the agent returned as Keller dismissed him from his presence.

"Edgar Simons, you better be cleaner than a Buddhist Monk," he growled, preparing himself a drink.

The private line in his office rang and Keller answered still irritated.

"Things are quiet for now," the voice spoke, calming Keller slightly.

"Let's hope for Detective Marchant's sake, he obeys his captain and backs off," he spoke hearing a subtle sigh.

"I hope so too, but just in case," Cassandra replied sipping a dry martini of her own.

"We still have everything and everyone in place to keep an eye on our resourceful little friend," she threw back taking another sip.

"Hmph," Keller returned, still thinking. "How are things going with the Judge," he queried hearing the woman laugh.

"Things are fine," Cassandra returned. "He'll do anything we ask if the time comes," she assured her boss.

"You slept with him yet," Keller questioned calmly.

"No and I don't plan too," she returned.

"You may have too," Keller returned, with conviction.

"I won't have too," Cassandra confidently replied.

She was more than sure she possessed enough feminine charm and finesse to get the good Judge to do whatever she needed him to do. *All he wants is the promise of sex,* she thought before Keller's voice shook her from the ponderings.

"Well if it comes to it, then you better spread for him and pretend you like it," he told her garnering a huge frown unseen by him.

"Our lives, literally, are on the line with this bullshit," Keller told her growing angry again. "Dezi Gianni is a fucking nightmare that will put us all in eternal sleep if we don't nip it in the bud right now," he added, Cassandra quickly agreeing with him.

"I know what's at stake here, trust I will do my part, whatever that may be," she fired, angry herself now that he just put her out there like a common prostitute on the street.

"I know you will," Keller returned. "Because you like freedom, because you love money, and because if you don't I'll kill you personally," he fired disconnecting before she could speak.

Rising Keller walked over to the huge plate glass window once again looking down on the nation's capital. The slip up tonight could not happen again. Hopefully they would be able to corral and contain Edgar before he caused any real damage, or the man was going to very soon meet with a life ending accident. Keller wasn't going to prison. He wasn't going to be labeled a traitor and disgraced, and he certainly wasn't going to be broke looking over his shoulder for the rest of his life. Walking over to the painting hanging near his desk, he removed the small photograph and opened the safe behind it. Reaching inside he extracted the clear case with the nondescript DVD inside, turning it over in his hands as his mind raced. *Survival of the fittest,* Keller thought before dropping the case and the DVD into his briefcase and securing the latches. Making a couple more calls and once again being assured by his chief assistant that Edgar Simons would be found tonight, Keller headed toward the elevator and his car. He reached the darkened deck and quickly got into the government issued Ford and started it, turning up the radio and driving out of the deck, quickly merging into traffic. Keller's mind was on his issues, his instincts on mini hiatus, explaining why he didn't notice the car that followed closely his every lane change.

"He just left," the man following Keller in the silver Cadillac spoke.

"Follow him, I want to know where he goes and what he's up too," Layton spoke calmly.

"Yes sir," the man replied disconnecting and concentrating fully once again on the target in front of him.

•••

"I swear you and Gar act like two kids sometimes," April told him as they arrived at her place.

JaDon liked it better going to the woman's house. It made his escapes that much easier once the sex was done.

"Aww April, just friendly competition baby," he murmured, pulling her to him and beginning to undress her.

"Slow down," she teased, snaking out of his arms and casually strolling into the kitchen.

JaDon caught the frown before it came. He was horny and his mind was still on overload with the slip Gar had made earlier this evening. He wanted to get laid, get his nut, and get to work; all in that order.

"Come on," April again spoke, breaking his thought as he saw the bottle of Hershey's syrup and marshmallows in her hand. The smile on his face grew wider as she managed to lose a piece of clothing with each step toward her bedroom.

"This is more like it," JaDon teased, stepping up behind her, taking a breast in each hand.

"Mm, nice," she moaned softly, allowing him to palm the small melons, pinching the nipples.

"You're still dressed," she pouted, pulling away and seductively crawling into the queen bed.

JaDon wasted little time stripping from his own constraints and climbing in with her, as she quickly took the lead, flipping him onto his back, chocolate syrup in hand, squeezing it all over his body.

"And the marshmallows," he questioned as she began slowly licking his chest.

"Those are for you, for me," she told him giving him a knowing look.

JaDon smiled but didn't speak. He honestly held no intention of eating her out. As much as he would enjoy screwing her, April gave it up just a bit too easily for him. There was basically no work at all involved for him to get it. It made his mind wander how many other men were in this bed covered in the same chocolate syrup. That contemplation didn't last long however, once her mouth struck gold and she began slowly and methodically licking the syrup from his stiff member. JaDon closed his eyes enjoying every lash from her tongue, the sucking of his head when she popped him into her mouth wanting to get every remnant of chocolate that remained.

"You're delicious," she told him as his hand found her clit, massaging it as she grew wet to the touch.

JaDon allowed her to kiss him, stroking her harder, sliding three fingers inside her as she began to ride them up and down, up and down, moaning loudly, her pleasure obvious. *Enough of this, I need to bust one*, he thought behind the closed lids, needing to move so he could get the condom in his pocket. Slowly, JaDon began to decrease his rhythm even as April continued to ride his fingers desperate for release.

"Hold on baby, I'ma take you there, just a sec," he spoke in her ear, withdrawing his fingers completely hearing a loud disappointed hiss.

Hastily rising, JaDon scored the condom, put it on and climbed back into bed, pulling April back onto his lap, her wetness still ample to allow his engorged offering smooth entrance inside.

Life After Death

"Mmm JaDon, yes, fuck me, right there," April began to scream, her hips bucking wildly as he held on for the ride, her tight hole slamming down on his erection again and again, his cum slowly ascending the shaft.

This trick is wild as fuck, he thought not unhappily as she threw it to him once again and he fell over the edge, the cum rushing out in a huge gush just as April came screaming out his name and string of expletives that would make any sailor blush.

"Damn, that was great," she told him still breathing hard as she climbed off his waning erection.

"Yes, it really was," JaDon replied truthfully.

With that urge satiated, he could fully concentrate on the other business at hand. April drifted off almost immediately with him lying beside her fully awake for the next thirty minutes before stealthily rising, dressing, and leaving her apartment.

Life After 6 Death

Marchant took in the city once again shoring his resolve that he was doing the right thing before hanging a left and walking down the busily hurried street and heading for the precinct he managed to dig up in his research. *West coast is highly overrated,* he thought taking in the sensory overload of all the flashing neon signs, creative, and gaudily dressed characters walking by him, oblivious to his existence outside of their own selfish pursuits. Marchant was praying that his trip to the city wouldn't be in vain. He wasn't able to find a lot pertaining to Kayla's history. Just a small bit here and there he heard in passing and from talking to various people who knew her, Donovan Black, or Thomas Bradford. Marchant was perspiring heavily, the midday heat and smog almost unbearable. He was used to hot weather as North Carolina definitely had its heat stroke days, but the heat was different here. It was stagnant, no breeze, no mist, just hot and muggy. He checked his directions and took another left on Howell street, which according to the sheet of paper in his hands, meant the precinct was only another two blocks.

Marchant noticed that no one said hello in the entire six block walk. He passed at least a dozen people and not one of them made eye contact or said hello. *Unfriendly bunch,* he again mused, finally seeing the precinct and breathing a small sigh of relief. Coming inside he took in the station. It was busily buzzing as criminals were whisked to and from, some quietly with complete cooperation, others belligerent and noisy, resisting even the smallest of commands. Marchant noted the same drab government accessories from the wanted posters, to the crime stoppers photos, to the sandstone and gray metallic chairs that lined the waiting area. Glancing around Marchant finally made contact with the desk sergeant's area. The man was large and imposing, graying hair and wrinkles plentiful from years of frustration, stress and worry, Marchant was sure. Taking a deep breath, he made his way to the station, waiting patiently for the man to get off the phone.

"Yes ma'am, you need to come in and file a report, bring a photograph," he told her without enthusiasm. "Yes, anytime ma'am, yes, you have a good day too," he added, disconnecting before rolling his eyes and turning his attention to Marchant.

"Missing dog," he spoke in explanation as Marchant smiled slightly.

Life After Death

"Hi, my name is Detective Dwayne Marchant, from North Carolina," Marchant spoke as the Sergeant continued to give him the plain expression. "I spoke with a Detective Canfield," he added as the man finally nodded.

"Oh Marty, yeah okay, hang on a second," the man, who's badge identified him as Stutgard, replied and picked up the phone.

"Yeah, you got a visitor, a detective from North Carolina," he spoke with a slight sneer.

Marchant didn't react choosing to ignore the rudeness and conduct his business. He was reasonably optimistic that this trip would give him more to work with than the near nothing that was his companion at the moment. Two minutes after Stutgard disconnected another man walked into the room, the first two buttons on the oxford undone, tie hanging slightly askew.

"How are you Detective Marchant," he greeted smiling. "I'm Marty Canfield," he returned as Marchant took him in.

Marty was a heavy set man, shorter than his own six foot frame, midsection giving away his love of food and beer.

"Come on with me," Marty told him amiably. "We can talk in my office."

Marchant followed the detective, seeing more of the inner working of the department, unimpressed by anything they passed. It seemed that for the most part, all precincts were the same; granite tiled floors, over waxed and under cleaned. The paint here was a dismal gray, uneven and chipping. Thankfully there were no photos to further aggravate the presentation, the flaking paint of the holding cell they passed handling that task all on its own.

"Have a seat," the detective told Marchant, taking a seat behind his small desk, pushing a couple of rogue papers and folders from their path.

"I gotta say I was really surprised to hear from you about a case this old," Marty spoke, looking directly at Marchant.

The other detective knew he was being sized up. He returned the man's gaze taking in the small, questioning eyes in the broad face, nose slightly upturned at the end, lips thin and seemingly used to being drawn tightly. His skin was blotchy, several capillaries in his face engorged giving his otherwise bland and pasty appearance a rosy, almost cherubic, glow.

"Well honestly," Marchant began carefully. "The case I'm looking into is far more recent, yours simply has ties to one of the persons of interest, so I'm covering all my bases," he told the man who nodded thoughtfully.

"Well there's not a lot to give you detective," Marty began again. "The woman you questioned, Mikayla Bradford, aka Mikayla DeWitt, doesn't have a record to speak of," he told Marchant who nodded knowing that much.

"The only reason her name pinged at all is the guy she was dating at the time," Marty told Marchant who began to grow slightly excited.

He was finally about to get some information he could possibly use to light fire to his case and bring Kayla back to the United States and put her in a jail cell. *Is that what you really want to do to her,* his mind tried as Marchant angrily pushed the thoughts away yet another time.

"What about him," he questioned instead, allowing Marty to continue.

The detective sat back in his chair and sighed deeply.

"He was bad news of the worst kind," he told Marchant evenly, giving him a look. "He was head of one of the most vicious cartels the city had back then."

"So you arrested him, broke up the cartel," Marchant questioned, knowing they didn't.

He read all the background information and knew that Donovan Black and the FBI were the ones to put the cartel out of business. It all seemed to get fuzzy there however. Even the man's name was a mystery. Marchant gathered archived old newspapers only to find the information conspicuously missing.

"No," Marty spoke and he could hear the irritation in his voice. "He unfortunately had enough money to employ some of our less dedicated," he admitted with malice.

Marchant nodded sympathetically, needing the man to continue talking.

"The FBI came in, began to systematically break down the defenses," he told Marchant, his tone taking on an air of nonchalance.

"Oh okay, I see," Marchant replied.

"I heard through the grapevine, they took him out with a sniper," Marty spoke and Marchant continued to remain quiet.

Life After Death

"Anyway," Marty shifted gears. "What did you need to know," he questioned, pushing the ball back into Marchant's court.

"Hmm, his name would be great for starters," he replied. "I'm trying to investigate everyone this woman knew to see what kind of ties we can find," Marchant gave up.

He knew he had to give a little to get what he needed.

"His name is, hmm," Marty told him skimming the notes again.

"Well that's strange," he spoke almost to himself.

"Something wrong," Marchant questioned seeing the look on his face.

"It just refers to him as Subject X," Marty spoke the frowned deeply creased in his brow.

"Hang on detective, maybe one of the old heads will know," the man spoke rising and walking from the room.

What the hell, Marchant wondered. *What kind of heavy hitter was this guy that his name has been removed even from the police records,* he continued to think praying Marty got a hit with one of the other detectives. The shroud of mystery surrounding this case was growing deeper, peaking Marchant's interest even more.

●●●

"Your honor, I'm so glad you could make time in your schedule to see me," Cassandra spoke amiably, sipping the water in her glass and smiling at him across the table.

"Cassandra, I told you before, call me Maurice," he replied, chastising her lightly.

Feigning forgetfulness, she chuckled briefly.

"I'm sorry, Maurice," she corrected.

"It's never an imposition to see you," he told her, flirting openly now.

Cassandra smiled again, allowing the moment to pass before she began anew.

"Things are unfortunately a little worse than before," she told him baiting the trap.

Maurice frowned, leaning forward, eyes directly on hers.

"How so," he questioned.

Cassandra loosed a weighty sigh for dramatic effect before answering his query.

"I'm afraid our fears are being confirmed, there is widespread, high level corruption in your police force," she told him earnestly, watching the words sink in.

"Absolutely reprehensible," Maurice replied, his irritation obvious.

"What would you like to do about it at this point," he queried as she lazily drew circles on the condensation outside the slowly warming glass of water.

"At the moment, we want to simply gather more Intel, see just how high up this goes," Cassandra told him as Maurice nodded.

"I just need to know you're still on our side, Your Hon--, I mean, Maurice," she corrected, playing on his attraction.

"Of course Cassandra, whatever you need," he immediately replied as she smiled again.

"Good, that's great to hear," Cassandra returned. "You don't know what a weight off my shoulders that is," she went on, drawing him in deeper. "There have been so many judges we've trusted only to find out they were part of the problem later on," she spoke, shaking her head sadly.

"No worries," Maurice returned, reaching out and placing his hand atop hers.

Cassandra forced the blush as Maurice smiled, removing it a few moments later.

"Have you had a chance to see any of our lovely city since you've arrived, Cassandra," Maurice questioned as their entrees arrived.

Spreading the white linen napkin across her lap, Cassandra returned her eyes to his finally.

"No, haven't made time really," she told him. "This case is very sensitive since it's still in the beginning stages," she added, having a feeling where the conversation was headed.

"Hmm, well I understand that," Maurice returning slicing his chicken breast. "But everyone needs a chance to relax," he spoke, glancing up at her.

Life After Death

"Why don't you let me show you around a bit after dinner," he requested, placing the small portion of chicken in his mouth, watching and waiting for her answer.

Cassandra finished her mouthful, gingerly dabbing her lips with the napkin, her mind turning over his request. She didn't forget the admonishment given by Keller or the threat of death by his hand if she failed.

"That might be nice," she returned with a small smile. "I don't want to inconvenience you or keep you out too late," Cassandra added.

"I don't want Mrs. Alston angry with me," she threw in reminding him she knew of his marital status.

"No worries," Maurice returned with a quick wave of the hand.

He wasn't concerned about Sandra, she was busy fussing over Reece, and as soon as she put him to bed she would procure her nightly glass of wine and sedatives, retiring to their bedroom for another night of comatose sleep. *Hmm, with names so similar can't get in trouble calling out the wrong one,* he mused almost laughing aloud, secure in his desire to bed the stunning agent sitting across from him.

"Well, if you're sure it's okay," Cassandra returned, shoring her own resolve that she not fail.

Her life depended on it yes, but her heart was the real reason she stayed the line and obeyed his every order, no matter how personally distasteful. *He doesn't love you like that,* her mind told her of Michael Keller. *He could,* she threw back as they finished dinner and Maurice smiled at her asking the waitress for the check. Smiling back, Cassandra prayed she could put him off just a little while longer.

●●●

Marchant was getting antsy. He flew across the country on a hunch and he prayed it wasn't merely a matter of time and money wasted. Fifteen long minutes passed since Marty left him in the small office alone. *Maybe it's a sign that you need to let this thing rest,* his mind began to speak. *The woman is gone, out of the country, the men are dead and buried, no one is asking questions about this case except you,* it steadily fed his conscious mind. *Live your life and let this obsession with Kayla Bradford go,* the common sense tried one last ditch effort as Marty glided back into the office ending the persuasive session.

"Any luck," Marchant questioned.

The man smiled brightly, giving Marchant renewed hope.

"Found one of the old heads from back in the day when this guy would have been big news," he told Marchant, who finally saw the papers in his hand. "These are his personal notes, I made you a copy," he told him handing him the three sheets of paper. "It's not much because they didn't keep him on the case long, especially once the Feds swooped in," Marty told Marchant as he glanced over the papers.

He was about to burst sitting here holding them, but didn't want to be rude and read them while the man was still talking.

"Thank you so much, Detective Canfield," Marchant told him rising from his chair.

"No biggie," Marty returned, rising as well. "I just hope they help you out somehow," he told him.

"I'm not sure, but there is an unsolved double homicide that leaves me with a bad taste in my mouth," Marchant honestly replied as Marty sympathetically nodded.

"I totally understand," he told the man arriving back at the lobby. "We've got far too many ourselves," he added, reaching out to shake Marchant's hand.

"Good luck Detective," Marty spoke in parting as Marchant smiled and walked from the precinct, paperwork in hand.

"Marty," came the shrill voice of Stutgard.

"Yeah," Marty returned, turning to look at the Sergeant.

"Captain wants to see you," he told him as Marty nodded.

"NOW," he bellowed and the sinking feeling immediately came to the pit of Marty's stomach as he turned and headed to the elevator and upstairs to his Captain's office.

Marty's mind rode with the elevator, wondering about the detective who just left, the case he questioned, the woman involved and how they all tied together. Marty was equally curious why the man's name was removed from all the official reports. *This guy must have been Al Capone reincarnate or some shit*, Marty pondered as the elevator ground to a halt and the doors opened. Stepping out he walked toward the lone glass door, gold lettering displayed that held the name, Scott Artest, their Captain.

•••

Life After Death

The walk seemed like nothing to Marchant as he glided purposefully back to the hotel and to his room. His excitement was at an all-time high as he grabbed himself a bottle of water from the small mini fridge and plopped down on the queen bed the room held. Unfolding the paperwork he'd taken from his pocket, Marchant began reading the cops notes, taking in every detail. This report had something to do with a murder, suicide, it seemed. *Who is Eric Greene, LaTaea Everett,* Marchant quizzed, jotting the names in his own notebook. He continued to read, there were more notes about a group called The Clique, another note Marchant jotted. *What does any of this have to do with Kayla,* he wondered finally coming to the last page of the notes. *'Eric Greene aka Dirty, is the right hand man. Order more surveillance, see if organization cracks, talk to confidential informants tonight,'* the notes read as Marchant's mind continued to try and make the connection. *'LaTaea Everett, girlfriend, best friend, Mikayla DeWitt, boyfriend, Dezi Gianni, head of The Clique,'* the notes ended with another small blurb about increasing surveillance.

"Hmph, just like I figured," Marchant murmured aloud. "She was dating this guy, he's dangerous, teaches her about the life, she plays the innocent role, gets him to teach her about the art of murder without a trace," he continued to put together from the sparse notations on the pages of paper.

"Not this time Kayla," he promised, finishing the water. "This time you're going to pay for your crimes and your looks won't help you at all in a court of law," he fired angrily, rising and tossing the papers onto the bed, heading into the bathroom wanting to take a shower and wash away not only the sweaty perspiration of the day, but the grimy filth he felt knowing how deeply infatuated with the woman he was at one time. *You still are liar,* his mind decided to chime in as Marchant looked at his reflection in the mirror.

Sucking his teeth, Marchant instead stepped into the shower, his head under the spray drowning out his mind and the surroundings. He never heard his door slowly open, nor saw the lone figure enter the room, gun in hand. The visitor saw the papers on the bed, walking to them and picking them up with a gloved hand. The soft click of the camera shutters didn't penetrate the watery fortress where Marchant was still entombed while the visitor finished his business. He took photographs of everything in the room, the entire contents of Marchant's luggage and briefcase. He stealthily took the back of the cell phone off, attaching the almost invisible transmitter to it and returning it to its original condition and placement. Slipping out the same way he entered, the visitor was nonexistent as Marchant emerged from the bathroom, refreshed and ready to get back to North Carolina, and back to business.

Life After 7 Death

"I will return in three days," Kareek was speaking as Stephan pretended to listen. He was pissed his plans would be delayed and his new regime not put in place. He still was yet to arrange a meeting with Arroyo Trufont, and unfortunately it was beginning to look as if the man would be lost to him, connecting with the Gianni's and thus becoming yet another enemy and obstacle Stephan would need to overcome. *Damn them both,* he thought venomously of the two legendary men he both envied and hated.

"Everything should run smoothly, you should have no issues," Kareek concluded, waiting for acknowledgement from his lead deputy.

"Yes, I'll be fine and I have all your orders," Stephan returned calmly, seething inside.

Kareek gave him a short smile before gathering his briefcase, key, sunglasses and hat, departing the office.

"Smug bastards," Stephan again mumbled, walking from the Chief's office.

Sighing deeply he settled at his own small wooden desk, promptly placing his feet atop it. If Arroyo connected with the Gianni's it would be all but impossible to unseat them. *There has to be some way to keep that from happening,* he continued to muse before another thought took precedence in his subconscious. *Mariah will be alone for the next three days,* his mind told him as the smile burst into his face. Her husband would be on the boat with Arroyo, Kareek, and their other partner, Big D. The women would all be here alone, and free of hindrance.

Stephan was still smiling when Jacob walked inside the small precinct and regarded him.

"And what has you in such a good mood today," he teased, coming over and sitting down next to Stephan at his own small wooden desk.

"Kareek is gone for three days," he told his friend as Jacob chuckled now as well.

"Good, three days to relax without him shouting orders at us," he spoke wistfully.

Stephan laughed aloud agreeing with his estimation.

Life After Death

"Also three days free of the Gianni's," he added as Jacob grunted now.

"Ahh and three days Mariah is free hmm," he again teased as Stephan smiled even wider.

"Yes," he replied calmly as Jacob shook his head and reclined in his chair, his own feet propped upon his desk now as well.

The phone rang on Stephan's desk and he answered sounding official.

"It's only me lover," Vanessa returned as the smile vanished and the frown replaced it on his face.

"Hello Vanessa," he greeted, able to sound friendly.

"Father left almost an hour ago," she pouted as Stephan rolled his eyes, controlling the heavy sigh that wanted to escape.

"I'm at work, Vanessa," he tried diplomatically.

Stephan was actually glad to be at work, not wanting to see her at the moment.

"I know silly, but you get off in two hours," she purred. "I'll be expecting you thirty minutes after you get off," she told him, knowing how long the drive from the station to her villa was.

Stephan frowned again, but didn't voice his displeasure when he spoke.

"Alright, I'll see you then," he told her, no real excitement or emotion in his tone.

Vanessa, oblivious to his nonchalance, excitedly spoke again.

"I'll be waiting honey, and I have a surprise for you," she added, disconnecting without him speaking.

"Looks like Mariah will have to wait," Jacob teased having overheard the conversation. Stephan threw him an evil look, eliciting another burst of laughter from the man. "Relax, go and see Vanessa, do whatever it is you enjoy doing to her, then stop by the Gianni compound when you leave," Jacob spoke, shrugging at the end of the statement.

Stephan admitted inwardly it made sense. He was law enforcement; they patrolled on a nightly basis. Mariah wouldn't think anything of it. He will have worked off all his stress sexing Vanessa, so he could be patient and forge their budding romance, giving it the gentle nudge it needed to get her moving in the right direction. *She's faithful to her husband,* his mind spoke of the woman, causing Stephan to frown again. *She's afraid of him, she doesn't really love him,* he told himself, needing to convince his mind in order to justify his heart.

"I'm going out for a while, do a little patrolling," Stephan told Jacob who was on the verge of nodding off while he relaxed.

"Hmm, yes that's fine, I'll be here," he sleepily returned.

Stephan shook his head and turned away walking out of the station, the midday heat engulfing him instantly. Stephan felt the sweat beads popping from every orifice as he made the short walk to the patrol car.

Quickly jumping inside, he started it turning the air conditioning up full blast, all vents directly on him. No particular destination in mind, Stephan simply drove the various streets of the downtown area. Noticing the bank, he remembered needing to make a deposit and sign some documents. Pulling into the first parking space, Stephan shut off the cruiser, dreading having to open the door and again be assailed by the scorching heat and humidity. Shoring his resolve however, he did just that some three minutes later grimacing and rushing toward the cool comforts of Pembroke Capital Investments Bank.

"Hello Stephan," Cass greeted him.

She was a daily fixture in the bank, acquainted with Stephan for years.

"Hi Cass," he returned smiling at the woman, taking her in once again.

She was pleasant to look at, nothing really outstanding in her appearance, but she was extremely sweet and kind, which definitely added to her appeal.

"Hot enough for you," she questioned, finding the documents he needed to sign.

"As always," Stephan returned as Cass chuckled shortly, still shuffling papers.

"Cass, did you answer this inquiry," the man questioned walking over to where she and Stephan sat.

He recognized and disliked him instantly. Kamau Ladrus was an ass by just about everyone's standards in the parish. He was rude and arrogant, known to treat his employees very badly. Stephan suspected it was his repressed sexual aggression that accounted for the nastiness.

"Yes, I answered it a couple of weeks ago," she returned as Stephan continued to sit and observe.

Life After Death

"You have worked here long enough to know better," Kamau told her meanly. "We do not divulge information about our account holders, it is an invasion of their privacy," he fired.

Cass took a deep breath, to stay her anger Stephan was sure, before answering the man assailing her.

"Mr. Ladrus, the party identified themselves as a law enforcement officer," she told him patiently.

"It's an email Cass, how do you know he was an officer," Kamau returned. "Anyone could have written this," he added growing more agitated.

"Mr. Gianni is one of our largest clients, and his wife as well," he fired and Stephan stopped daydreaming, giving them his complete attention.

"Have you been in contact with this person since you answered," he questioned.

"No sir," Cass meekly returned.

"Is there a problem Kamau," Stephan interjected tired of the man badgering the woman and his personal curiosity aroused.

The bank manager seemed flustered momentarily by the question before regaining his wits.

"No, well, probably not," he returned.

"May I," Stephan questioned, hand held out for the papers Kamau held.

The man regarded him a few moments more, he assumed deciding if he would comply, before handing over the documents. Stephan read the email from one Detective Dwayne Marchant, inquiring about Mikayla Bradford. Fascinated by the implications, Stephan's mind began to race.

"I don't see anything harmful here in the response, Kamau," he told the man chastising him. "Cass only said yes you have an account holder with this name," he added as Kamau looked away anxiously.

"No harm done," he returned. "I will follow up on this and make sure this Marchant person is legitimate and not up to anything funny," he added as the manager now threw him a thankful look.

"Thank you Stephan," he told him quickly. "I don't want any problems," he added and Stephan knew he was thinking about the elder Gianni.

"Thank you for helping me Cass, I'll drop these off later," he told her sweetly of the documents she finally found that required his signature.

Cass gave him a grateful smile.

"That will be fine, Stephan."

"I'll contact you Kamau if there is anything askew about the email, otherwise, don't give it another thought," Stephan told him as Kamau nodded and scurried away.

"Horrible human being," Cass murmured as Stephan quickly agreed with her, turning and leaving the bank, document in hand.

No sooner than he got into the car and started it, again engaging the air conditioning, Stephan read the email over. There was a return email address, but also a phone number. He went back and forth in his mind for a while which method was most effective. *They can trace the call if you make it from the station,* he thought not wanting to alert anyone that anything was amiss immediately. Deciding he would email the detective and break the ice, Stephan began driving toward the precinct. *What could this man be after and how was Kayla involved,* he continued to muse, intrigued. *Might be just the tool I need to dethrone the self-proclaimed king,* Stephan thought jovially of Dezi. Even though his main fight wasn't with the father, destroying him would definitely have the domino effect and rid of him the son as well.

"Let's hope this pays off," he remarked, arriving at the station once again and heading inside, straight for the computer, and pulling up his email.

Life After Death

Life After 8 Death

Inhaling deeply Arroyo smiled brightly. He always loved the water and today was perfect for the fishing and sailing they were doing. The winds were mild but cooling, the surf rolled harmlessly along the bottom of the expansive yacht they were passengers aboard. Dezi Gianni was proven to be the consummate host so far. Arroyo was exceptionally pleased with the man's taste not only in the boat, but the food, the drinks, even the crew. All the men chosen were experienced at their task, not a moment of worry or duress since they set sail almost eight hours ago.

"Are you alright sir, can I get you anything else," the ships mate questioned as he stood before Arroyo who was relaxing on deck in the oversized chair.

"Hmm, another bottle of water would be good," he replied as the man nodded shortly, scurrying away to get it.

This is a lifestyle I could quickly become accustomed too, he thought as two men came into view.

"Catch anything," Big D queried, smiling at Arroyo.

All of them set poles up, but did little more than walk by them from time to time, men in place to handle the actual task of monitoring them.

"Not even a nibble so far," he returned amiably.

Arroyo met Big D once they embarked. He was very impressed with both the man's knowledge and expertise as they all talked earlier.

"So Arroyo, do you think you would be interested in the uniting of forces," Aidan questioned, taking a seat on his left, as Big D sat to his right.

"I'm definitely all for that," he returned without hesitation. "I just need a bit more information and then there are the financial divides to discuss," he added just as Dezi walked up.

"Where's Kareek," Arroyo questioned, not seeing his Chief of Police.

"He wanted to learn more about the boat and such," Dezi returned calmly. "He's at the helm with the captain," he added as another server appeared with liquor glasses.

"Let's go down into the hull, much cooler there," Dezi spoke, removing his glass from the tray and sipping the liquor. "We can discuss everything and come to agreement," he added as Arroyo, Big D, and Aidan all rose and followed him.

Arroyo was again mesmerized by Dezi's tastes and money. The private yachts interior was amazing. There were chocolate blinds covering the windows to block the heated noon sun, a crème and chocolate sectional adorned the main room, with a mid-sized wicker coffee table, also chocolate in color. The cabinetry was a faux oak color, built in bookcases, as well as entertainment center.

"Cigar," Dezi inquired, producing the box.

Arroyo took one as did Big D. Aidan did not, continuing to sip his drink as they all made themselves comfortable on the sectional and began to talk yet another time.

"So you export illegal substance," Arroyo questioned Dezi as they all sat.

"Not exclusively no," he returned.

"It's actually only a very small part of what we do," Aidan enlightened.

Arroyo frowned slightly in confusion, bringing a small smile from all three men.

"We ship things that people would rather keep from customs and the light of day most times," Big D now calmly explained.

"Procured goods that might be frowned on by the powers that be," he added as the light came on for Arroyo.

"Of course we export the legal wares that are listed on our manifests and delivered to suppliers," Dezi commented, taking another drag from his cigar.

"I see," Arroyo returned.

He knew the black market was big business and evidently the three men in this room mastered its ins and outs with precision.

"So what do you need from me, Dezi," Arroyo now questioned.

"Doors opened, connections," he told him, explaining further.

Arroyo understood. He was surrounded by political elite. People who could, for the right price, make life a lot easier for all of them with laws, rules, regulations etc.

Life After Death

"We would know things ahead of time, like when the guard was patrolling for instance," Big D spoke, giving Arroyo a look.

The man nodded, seeing their point, definitely wanting to be a part of the enterprise.

"How would my portion be split," he questioned, not wanting to be crass, but curious nonetheless about his financial gain.

Aidan and Dezi both smiled slightly. Big D emptied his glass, rising to grab another drink, refilling Dezi's glass at his request.

"You would get a twenty percent cut of the profits made for that month," Aidan replied as Dezi thanked Big D for his drink and sipped it.

Arroyo wasn't stupid. Twenty percent of the purported half million dollars they made each month wasn't small change at all. He would be a millionaire in no time flat, enabling him to provide even better for his daughter, Vanessa. His wife had been dead for the past few years and while he wasn't struggling, Arroyo certainly wanted more.

"That's a very generous split," he returned eloquently.

Dezi smiled as did Aidan and Big D.

"Simply good business," Dezi replied rising. "I think I'll get a small nap while we fish," he spoke as the men all burst into laughter.

"Sounds like a good idea," Big D replied, rising and heading to his quarters, as did Arroyo.

Aidan stretched out on the sectional once they all left closing his eyes and drifting off quickly. Arroyo's mind again commended him for a decision well made when he walked into the spacious cabin once again. The bed built into the wooden platform, stained and varnished to a high shine. The was another mini sectional encompassed in the room, windows with snow white treatments in place and two port hole windows on the other end. There was no expense spared it seemed when Dezi acquired the yacht. *Soon I'll have one to rival his,* he thought pleasantly as he stretched out, closing his eyes, sweet dreams of riches and the softly tousling waves sending him quickly into a deep sleep.

●●●

"You don't have to be bashful honey," Vanessa purred, walking into the sitting room where Stephan was making them a drink.

She was wearing a see thru negligee, gold in color, matching thong panty.

"No one is here except you and me," she added taking the red wine from his hand and walking away, her butt switching from side to side.

Stephan felt his erection growing despite his minds distaste for the current situation. He would have much rather been with Mariah, laughing, talking, simply enjoying her beauty. He exercised his authority earlier, swinging by the mansion under the guise of checking on her and the children.

"Hello Stephan," Mariah spoke, smiling pleasantly. "What brings you by," she questioned as he returned the smile.

"I was out patrolling and thought I would check on you and your mother since both Mr. Gianni's were out on the ocean," he told her alerting the woman he knew her husband's whereabouts.

"Oh, that was nice," she returned. "We're fine though, everyone is fed and getting settled in for the evening," she added chuckling a bit.

Stephan loved her laugh, her smile, the dimples. He loved the sweet smell of her perfume wafting through his senses at the moment. Nothing could have made the space in time more perfect except a kiss between them.

"All right, well you have a great night, and if you need anything please don't hesitate to call," Stephan told her, giving her a look.

"Thank you, I'll keep it in mind," Mariah returned, the smile in place, but her eyes cautious.

"Are you going to stand there all night," Vanessa teased breaking his thought as he looked her over again.

"Come on," she told him as Stephan licked his lips.

He couldn't have the one he wanted, but Vanessa would suffice as a means to satiate the hunger he held for Mariah. Coming into her bedroom he began undressing, his eyes never leaving her partially nude form. She removed the thong and was propped on the bed, legs agape, giving him an uninhibited view of her femininity, the lips glistening with her desire as she watched his clothing leave his body.

"Mmm, why don't you come lie down," she crooned, eyes glued to his hard member.

Stephan climbed into the huge king bed, quickly pinning her down, his fingers on her clit gliding back and forth her lubrication plenteous as she moaned softly and he kissed her neck. Vanessa snaked her hands down his body, grabbing hold his firm manhood, stroking it turning him on more and more.

"I want to taste it," she murmured in his ear bringing a smile to his face.

Vanessa helped him turn his body so his glory was in her face. She flicked her tongue over the head, a deep hiss leaving Stephan's mouth as she chuckled a bit, sucking just the head, her tongue again flicking across it in rapid succession. Stephan tensed, the pleasure undeniable. Deciding he would give her a taste of her own medicine, he parted her gleaming, moisture laden, lower lips, licking her throbbing clit, hearing her catch her breath.

Continuing to play tit for tat, they pleasured each other's erogenous zones with Vanessa reaching orgasm twice, Stephan's manhood encased deeply in her throat cavity, the cum rushing forward and sliding harmlessly down her throat. Able to gather himself and remove his semi hard member from his mouth, Stephan began sucking her nipples, his member rubbing back and forth on her clit, growing harder as she grew wetter.

"Mm, yess, Stephan, mmm," Vanessa moaned with each contact of flesh, her clit throbbing and thumping.

Stephan, again steel hardened, put her legs on his shoulders and rammed himself inside her viciously thrusting deep and fast. He wanted to punish her, wanted her to know he was in charge, he was the man of the relationship and she would comply.

"Lover, slow down, oh god," Vanessa told him, scared and exhilarated at the same time.

Stephan never took her this violently before and she was ashamed to admit she was loving it. Her cave gushed with pleasure each time he went inside and hit her hard.

"Yes Stephan, yes, give me more," Vanessa screamed cuming hard, her juices flowing freely, the gushing become louder and more melodic, the musty scent of their joining arousing her even further.

"You're my bitch Vanessa," Stephan growled, smashing her again and again.

"Yes, Stephan, I'm your bitch, fuck me," she screamed back as they came hard, his cum spurting inside her sopping cave, the two satisfied and satiated beyond words as they clung to each other, calming finally and drifting off to sleep.

Life After 9 Death

JaDon was finally able to follow up on the information the liquor plied from Gar almost a week ago. Things were extremely busy and hectic at the Bureau, usurping his private time, but today he was on a mission. Recalling the things Gar spoke, the case was old. Not wanting to call any unwanted or unwarranted attention to himself or his quest, JaDon headed downstairs to sub-basement level one. That's where the old paper files were housed. There would be nothing to raise suspicions of his activity since he was for all intents and purposes a file clerk at the moment. The elevator ride was pleasant and he found himself relaxed and unhurried as the doors opened and the musty smell of ancient paper descended his senses. Stepping out, JaDon stood for a moment deciding which direction he should choose. These files were slated to be added electronically to the system, a tedious process that so far was near the very bottom of everyone's list of priorities. *Good thing for me,* he thought finally walking to his left and down a long corridor of huge cabinets, each filled to capacity with file folders.

"Hmm, Devastator would be under D," he murmured looking up at each cabinet as he passed it.

Right now he was on the rows filled with R. Turning back the way he came, JaDon made his way to this right this time, deducing that the beginning of the alphabet would be on that end. It took him another fifteen minutes of walking the various rows to find the beginning of the D file names.

"Day, Darvet, Deitch," he was speaking aloud still walking.

The rows were long and seemingly endless, JaDon began to think finally arriving at the De's.

"Deale, Deem, Deutch," he spoke growing impatient before finally finding the folder he sought.

"Damn, took long enough," JaDon again groused, pulling the file marked Devastator from the long drawer.

Examining it he saw confidential stamped all over it. Undeterred JaDon flipped it open hoping to find something of interest. The file contained various notes and scribbles, a few official documents, but nothing that would have warranted the kind of attention that Gar bragged worthy of

Life After Death

CIA attention. *What the hell,* JaDon thought crossly. He was pissed for allowing Gar to make him look like an idiot chasing a smoke screen.

He was just about to close the file when a small notation caught his eye. 'Gianni, D,' it stated and JaDon knew it was a cross reference. Excited once more, JaDon returned the original file to its proper place and began his trek to find the G's. His cell went off surprising him since he thought a signal wasn't found this deep underground. It was a text. 'Spoelman is looking for you,' it read. JaDon frowned, irritated because he would have to leave now. Vernon Spoelman was his boss; a no nonsense man who made him feel every bit the peon they all saw him as.

"Shit," he murmured before texting April back and thanking her for the heads up.

JaDon quickly headed for the main elevator. He would come back later. At least he had a lead now, a new direction. *I hope this really does pan out to be something I can catapult my career with,* he thought the elevator ascending to the fifth floor where he was sure his boss was waiting with an angry scowl on his face. JaDon heard the soft ding of the elevator and took a deep breath, steeling himself. As he predicted, the doors opened and Vernon fixed him with a venomous glare. JaDon strode purposefully across the floor careful not to show the irritation he felt and jovially addressed his boss, listening quietly as the man chewed him out before finally enlightening him to the task he needed performed. *I cannot wait to be from under this bullshit,* JaDon thought as he began his project, his mind on the sub-basement and getting back down there as quickly as possible.

●●●

Gar knew he was still being watched and scrutinized. He kicked himself mentally again and again for the mistake and prayed he wouldn't face any blacklist or additional fallout from the filing incident. *Shit, they pay me to file, so dammit,* he groused but knew he was wrong. Gar knew very well anything marked restricted he wasn't supposed to touch. Not only did he break protocol and file it, he actually read parts of it. *Thank goodness they don't know about that,* he mused silently. His career would have been over before it began if they did. Still, their reaction led him to believe that he was onto something. The case was over twenty years old, why still be that concerned with the security of it. Gar's mind also went to the drunken night at the club, April and JaDon. *I sure as hell hope no one remembers anything I said,* he worriedly began to fret. He talked to April only briefly a couple of days ago, but everything seemed fine. He didn't talk to JaDon at all if he could help it, having an extremely healthy dislike for the man. *That sonofabitch would definitely be trouble if he remembers,* Gar thought as sighed deeply reaching his small cubicle and sitting down behind the desk.

His mind went back to the Gianni file and the things he read. The man was seemingly a one man wrecking crew, the street name Devastator, fitting him perfectly. *Why is keeping this guy under wraps so important,* he wondered, doodling on the small lined yellow pad on his desk. Gar recalled the cold, unemotional face of Deputy Director Keller as the other agent questioned him about the file. *That guy's shit list is not one I plan to end up on,* Gar resolved. He picked up the phone and dialed April's number before disconnecting, recalling all the conversations were recorded from any of the desk phones. Rising Gar quickly went outside to the smoker's area, though he didn't smoke, and pulled out his cell calling her again on her own cell number.

"Hi Gar," April greeted whispering, alerting him she was inside the building.

"Hey, I know you're busy, but can you give me a call back later when you take a break," he returned. "It's important," he added quickly.

"Sure, call you back in about thirty, okay," April returned and disconnected without his response.

"Please let this end right here," Gar murmured before returning inside, anticipating April's return call.

●●●

JaDon was back in the sub-basement again, this time on the G isle, methodically tracking down the name he'd scored from the Devastator file.

"Gaze, Gazebo, Gia, Giancandro, Gianni," he spoke smiling as he scored the thickly padded file folder, pulling it out and using his hip to push the open drawer closed.

"Let's see what's in here that has it triple classified," he grumbled moving under one of the florescent lights.

JaDon finally noticed the red tap securing the file causing him to quickly glance over his shoulder feeling the specter of being watched. *Chill, there are no cameras on this level,* he reminded himself as his fingers ran along the edges of the tape. JaDon didn't want a sneak peek, he wanted the time to completely absorb and dissect the contents of the folder.

"Not going to happen here," he spoke aloud an idea forming in the recesses of his mind.

Life After Death

JaDon wanted the folder on his own turf, at home, in his home office. *How do I get these out of here,* he pondered. They left through checkpoints at the end of the evening, laying their bags, cases, purses, etc. on the belt to go through the x-ray machine.

It wouldn't have been an issue if he had the clearance to carry files home, but he didn't. The security officers were well apprised of the clearance level of employees. If he tried to take the file out without permission all sorts of alarms would sound and that was something JaDon planned to avoid, period. *So how then,* his mind threw back as he continued to stand with the yet sealed file still in hand.

"Shredder," he murmured.

Each night they shredded files that were converted electronically. The Bureau was trying to move away from all forms of paper records. JaDon knew where the bin was, and what time the pickups were made. *I could put it in there, specially marked, then retrieve it right before I leave,* he thought, the checkpoint coming to mind again.

"OK JaDon, think dude, you can do this," he bolstered himself.

JaDon wanted this file. His gut told him the things in it would make his career and propel him past the likes of even his annoying boss Special Agent Vernon Spoelman. "That would be sweet as hell," he murmured again before another idea came on how to actually get the file out of the front door.

"Yeah, that could work, real talk," JaDon continued to converse with himself as he tucked the file under his arm and headed back toward the elevator.

Pushing the number two button, JaDon continued to think over his plan. He didn't see any issue and all that was required, was being normal when he walked through the checkpoint. *Don't draw attention to yourself,* his mind told him as he stepped onto the second floor and spotted the large blue bin marked shred. JaDon casually walked toward it, opening the lid and peering inside. Files littered the bin, thrown inside in every conceivable position. There was no order at all to the chaos. *OK, so how do you put it in here so you can find it later,* his mind was whirling as he continued to look inside the bin for any ledge or pocket he could place the file that would prevent it from being mixed into the rising sea of disorder.

"Shit, shit, shit," JaDon murmured still not finding an answer to his issue.

Glancing quickly at the exterior of the bin, he noticed a small opening near the rear, perhaps to have held product information or safety notification. He tried sliding the folder inside. Thankfully the opening was deep enough, even if extremely snug. The thick girth of the folder used every spare inch the area offered. JaDon looked it over after placing the folder inside, pleased that neither the manila paper or the red tape was readily visible to anyone walking by.

"Cool," he mumbled before heading back to the elevator and finishing his day.

•••

"Hey Gar, sorry about earlier," April told him returning his call almost forty minutes later.

"No problem, hang on a sec okay," Gar told her glancing furtively around to ensure no one was paying any attention.

Still unsettled he again rose and headed outside to the smoking area. One of the few perks of his first floor office was the quick exit afforded into the outside haven.

"I was calling about that night at the club," he told her.

"What about it," April questioned without malice.

"Well, I just wanted to make sure I didn't say or do anything really stupid," Gar fished praying he wouldn't have to spill the truth of his quest.

April sighed before speaking.

"Nothing more than you and JaDon having a stupid macho contest as usual," she told him slightly irritated.

"I apologize again for that April," he told her contritely. "I don't know why I keep letting that guy get under my skin," he added as she sighed again.

"Me either Gar," she returned. "You two really need to let that go and move on," April continued. "We all have great jobs with great agencies and we should act like the lucky dogs we are to have them."

Gar agreed in theory with her words. He just expected to be far more in the CIA than the file boy.

"I hear you April and I promise to be better," Gar told her, convinced he hadn't said anything out of the ordinary.

Life After Death

At least not to her, his mind chimed in, reminding him that he and JaDon were alone at the table for a few moments while April went to the ladies room. *Damn, do I have to call that jerk too,* he continued to ponder as April chatted pleasantly about the meeting up for a drink later in the week.

"Sounds good," Gar replied, paying attention again. "Set it up and let me know the when and where," he told her. "You can even invite JaDon," Gar added deciding he could kill two birds with one stone.

He would carefully pick the man to see if anything was recalled, and prove to April he was a good guy. His attraction to her was still strong and he wanted her to see him the way she saw JaDon.

"Cool, I promise I'll call in a couple days," April returned preparing to disconnect.

"Thanks Gar for being a good sport, have a good night," she added as they said goodbye and disconnected.

"Almost safe," Gar mumbled and returned inside, only thirty more minutes until quitting time.

•••

Be cool, be yourself, JaDon continued the pep talk as he strolled toward the two checkpoints, x-ray machine whirring quietly. April was two people ahead of him, placing her bag on the table, keys in the plastic tray, as the officer flirted with her and she entertained him. *This has to work,* JaDon's mind was still working. The man in front of him placed his case on the belt, keys in the tray, stoic and quiet as he walked through the metal detector and stood on the other side waiting for his belongings to be returned.

"Have a good evening sir," the guard spoke stiffly.

The man nodded shortly, picking up his case and keys, turning to walk out of the building. JaDon guessed he must have been one of the directors from his demeanor and the guard's reaction to him. It was his turn and he was fighting tooth and nail not to show the anxiety and fear he felt at the present.

"Satchel on the belt sir," the guard spoke giving JaDon a look.

"Oh, sorry," he apologized with a smile, quickly pretending he to be preoccupied with his phone.

The guard gave him a small smile before turning his eyes onto the screen as the satchel passed through. JaDon walked through the metal detector unscathed and now stood where one of the directors was moments earlier, praying his army green satchel would emerge from the flapping plastic curtains of the x-ray machine without hindrance.

"Thank you sir, have a great night," the guard returned with another small smile.

JaDon returned it, picking up the satchel and forcing himself to walk, not run, from the building and to the parking deck. Getting inside the Honda, he started it and turned onto the street out of the deck and headed home, finally allowing himself to breathe and relax. *Who would have thought,* he congratulated himself. JaDon retrieved the file some twenty minutes before he left, placing it between a thick newspaper and three magazines. Obviously the only thing the security guard saw was what JaDon planned for them to see. *Can't wait to get this thing home and unlock this mystery,* he thought hearing his stomach growl as he smiled. Pulling into the drive thru of the fast food joint he was passing, JaDon made a quick order and drove to the window, paying for it and driving away, both appetites at full throttle.

Life After 10 Death

"Captain Wilmont wants to see you," the officer told Marchant as he made his way into the station.

Damn, now what, he thought wearily making his way down to the office he was summoned too. Marchant noticed the new cracks in the plaster as he walked, shaking his head at the state of disrepair the station found itself in. The walk was short or maybe he was simply anxious, but either way, he found himself standing in front of Caroline's door, knocking lightly.

"Come in," the woman called out.

Marchant took another deep breath and came inside; taking a seat in the wooden chair she beckoned him toward.

"You wanted to see me, Cap," Marchant questioned.

He was racking his mind for any infraction he committed that could have landed him here. He honestly was neglectful on the Bradford-Lynch murder case since returning from the precinct on the West coast.

"Yes Dwayne," she began sipping her coffee gingerly, frowning at the obviously disagreeable taste of it.

"I have a new assignment I need you on," Caroline told him giving him a look to gauge his reaction.

"OK, what is it," Marchant questioned without malice.

"It's providing backup on an undercover surveillance case," Caroline told him. "It shouldn't be more than thirty, maybe forty-five, days," she added as he frowned slightly.

Marchant was pretty sure the assignment would send him back to his least favorite shift, night or swing. He hated the hours, fighting long and hard to get on, and stay on, days.

"What kind of surveillance," he questioned carefully, gaining a sigh from the Captain, further bolstering his dread and suspicions.

"Stolen goods tied in with drugs," Caroline answered. "It's going to require long hours Dwayne, I won't lie to you," she continued as Marchant sat stoically. "You'll be working 3PM until 6 or 7 AM," she laid out, the frown increasing in intensity on Marchant's face.

"Jeez Cap, seriously?"

"I know it's not your favorite shift, Dwayne," Caroline began diplomatically. "But I need your seasoned expertise on this one, and Hillingson says he trusts you to have his back," she tried, hoping to soften the news a bit.

She was aware of Marchant's distaste for working split shifts, but she was pretty much depleted. This was a huge operation and they invested months already.

"I mean yeah I can definitely handle it, Cap, that's not an issue," Marchant returned defeated and disgusted, but doing a plausible job of hiding both.

"When do I start," he questioned praying that she said next week or so.

He needed to do just a bit more investigating into his case.

"Tonight," Caroline returned once again plummeting Marchant's hopes. "So go on back home, climb into bed and report to Vice at 2:30PM," Caroline instructed, glancing at her watch and seeing the 6:45AM time.

Rising Marchant addressed her once more. "I appreciate the confidence Cap, both from you and Derk," he told her, referencing Hillingson. "I'll definitely do my best so we can bust these thugs and take some dope off the street, stop some of the theft going on," he added as Caroline smiled slightly.

"Thanks Dwayne," she told him sincerely. "And I promise as soon as everything is handled and the dust settled, you'll be right back on days," she added as he smiled and thanked her, leaving the office and heading back down the same dismal gray hallway.

Great, just great, Marchant was thinking as he walked straight out of the double glass doors at the front of the station, getting into the unmarked cruiser and starting it up, heading for his home. There wasn't a lot he could do with the case right now truthfully, he pondered thinking about Kayla and what he perceived her role to be. He needed time to research some of the things he got from Detective Canfield.

"Shit, guess it will have to wait a little while longer," Marchant mumbled, not at all pleased that once again Kayla seemed to be getting a reprieve.

Life After Death

He pulled into his driveway and got out going inside, oblivious to the dark blue Chevrolet parked across the street, the two men inside observing his every move.

●●●

Stephan was edgy and irritable. Kareek was of course back from his fishing trip as were the Gianni's and Arroyo. The chief continued barking orders from the time he arrived, complaining about the cleanliness of the station, the lack of reports filed, and other minor tribulations he was finding as he walked through the small office area and checked on varying items of interest. *I cannot wait to push his ass out of the front door,* Stephan continued to angrily muse. He was also irritated that he received no response from the email he sent to the detective in the states. Sitting down and booting up the antiquated computer, Stephan waited drumming his fingers impatiently on the desk before him. *I wonder if Mariah will be at the market today,* his mind wandered as the screen sputtered to life before him. Stephan smiled thinking of her. He also thought of Vanessa and the torrid sex they enjoyed all weekend. She was good in bed he readily admitted, but Stephan felt nothing for her past pure physical lust. His heart belonged fully to Mariah and he was growing impatient having to continually share her with the husband who certainly didn't deserve anyone as unique and special as she was.

Finally online, Stephan went directly to his Yahoo account and logged in. His mailbox appeared with several unread messages. He scrolled through them finally seeing the one that caught his interest. It was a failed send notification.

"What the hell," he mumbled clicking on it after seeing the address and knowing it belonged to the detective.

Stephan frowned deeply thinking the mailbox was closed, when he noticed the small transposition of two letters which caused the error.

"Dammit," he murmured, drafting a new email and carefully typing in the address.

Satisfied some ten minutes later with the content, and triple checking the email address, he hit send.

"Stephan," Kareek called out distracting him.

"Coming," he called back, the acidic frown plastered on his face.

He was careful however to look perfectly normal some three minutes later when he materialized in front of the Chief.

"Yes sir, you called," Stephan questioned.

"Yes, sit down," Kareek instructed still studying the papers in front of him.

Stephan did as he was told, watching the man as they both continued to sit in silence.

Looking up from his papers after completing his perusal, Kareek addressed him. "I'm sending you to the training symposium this year," he told Stephan.

Definitely displeased with the words spoken, the internal struggle was fierce to keep the frown from his brow, the anger from his voice, as he spoke.

"Thank you Chief, that is an honor," Stephan lied.

Any other time he might have been excited, as it gave him the chance to network and make new allies he was sure would come in handy for his long range plans. Right now however, it served as a complete hindrance. He would be gone for at least three or four weeks. He wouldn't see Mariah, couldn't get to Arroyo and feel him out, and wouldn't be able to meet with the detective once he answered his email. The timing was most assuredly not of his liking, but he was impotent to do anything about it except be frustrated.

"Good, I'm glad you're excited," Kareek returned smiling. "You will leave in two days, I'll assign Jacob and Joell some of your more mundane duties," he added, as Stephan again nodded.

Stephan didn't care much for Joell. The man was a total Kareek ass kiss in his book and he always felt like the man was spying on him specifically to take information back to the Chief.

"You will enjoy it, trust me," Kareek iterated, rising from his desk, handing the papers to Stephan. "Read them over and familiarize yourself with everything," he told the deputy. "Please finish any open reports you have on your desk today, and make a list of things Jacob, Joell, or I need to attend to while you're away," Kareek told him. "Then you can leave for the day and take tomorrow off to prepare for travel," he finished amiably.

"Thank you Chief, I will," Stephan returned leaving the man's presence and heading back to his desk.

Life After Death

He was furious. *I need to go to the market and at least see her again before I have to leave*, he thought as he scribbled on the paperwork in front of him. He had a couple of reports to finish, a few to file, then he would compile a quick list. That would put him right about the mid-morning hour and he would be able to head over to the fresh market and begin his stakeout waiting for Mariah to arrive. *I need to see Vanessa too*, he thought and chuckled silently. Stephan decided he wanted to get laid once more before he left for the symposium. *I'm pretty sure I can find some willing women while I'm there as well*, he again thought giddily. Female cops weren't all that plenteous or even willing for that part, but there were always the servers, the hotel workers, the locals looking for some fun. Pulling out his cell, he texted Vanessa asking if he could see her today. 'Of course baby, what time,' came the quick reply. Stephan told her he would be off after three, allowing time for him to see Mariah and hopefully talk to her today. 'I'll be waiting,' she again typed as he sneered and deleted her responses.

"Stupid," Stephan mumbled yet another time as Jacob walked into the room.

"Lucky dog," he teased his friend.

Stephan shrugged and gave him a lazy smile, keeping his true feelings a closely guarded secret.

Life After 11 Death

JaDon's mood was euphorically cautious as he continued to read the forbidden stolen file in front of him. He scribbled notes furiously on the notepad to his right as his eyes read, his brain absorbed, the words set to page.

"This man was a damned nightmare," he mumbled of Dezi Devastator Gianni.

He spent the better part of the week getting acquainted in his off time with the file and all its occupants. He was very intrigued with the mention of the woman, Mikayla DeWitt, as well as the involvement of the agent on the case at the time, Donovan Black. The file went on to tell of their marriage later and even Agent Black's early demise trying to apprehend a fugitive.

"So he fell for her during the investigation," JaDon again spoke, looking at the photograph of Kayla some twenty plus years earlier.

"She's hot, no doubt about that," he murmured, putting it down and going back to the file.

Surprisingly there were notations as late as five years ago. The woman, Mikayla, was again intertwined, as her daughter Mariah, and evidently Gianni's son, Aidan Preston, were dating.

"Freaky ass coincidence for real," JaDon yet another time addressed to the empty room.

Doing a quick search through the rest of the folder, he noticed that everyone associated with the earlier case was dead with the exception of Demetrius Wilson, aka Big D., and one Adrian Roberts. No one saw Demetrius for years, leading JaDon to believe he was either incarcerated again or dead.

"Quick crosscheck will tell me which one," he went on, thinking about Big D but still looking at Adrian's information.

There were no hits on Big D, but Adrian Robert's last known address was notated as London, England.

"I would definitely like to talk to him," JaDon murmured before his mind questioned what exactly he was hoping to find with this ancient case.

Life After Death

"Can't be that ancient if Gar was filing it," he spoke getting up and heading for his kitchen, stomach leading the way.

Someone must have been reading it recently and I doubt it was just for the historical value, he continued to muse as he looked into the refrigerator rumbling through the various takeout containers. Opting for the Chinese he bought two days ago, JaDon popped the small square container into the microwave and hit three minutes. His mind whirled while the microwave rotated and his food reached the desired temperature. Why in the world would the CIA be looking into this case again? By all accounts it was settled years ago with the death of Dezi Gianni and the ultimate demise of his organization.

"Some next level shit going here and I'm going to find out what," JaDon vowed just as the small chime on the microwave sounded and the tray inside stopped rotating.

He took it out carefully, opening the lid allowing the steam to escape as he grabbed a fork from the dish rack and headed back to his home office. Sitting down, JaDon began scooping the noodles into his mouth, his eyes back in the file. There must be something he was missing. On the surface there was absolutely no reason to reopen this file, none at all. For JaDon that meant there were some far more sinister rationale and purpose in the seemingly harmless gesture.

I need to get some more info from Gar's worrisome ass, he thought still enjoying his dinner.

"If I can find out WHO requested the file, that would definitely set me on the right path," he mumbled, burping loudly as he finished the food and tossed the empty carton into the small metal wastebasket at his feet.

JaDon wasn't sure how he would accomplish that task however, given Gar's hatred of him. He also didn't want to make the man suspicious and thus create an unwanted obstacle to his breaking the case wide open and gaining the notoriety and fame he sought. *Maybe go see this Adrian Roberts guy,* his mind began to swirl.

"And say what," he murmured aloud trying to think of a plausible cover.

Maybe he could convince the man he was training and this was part of some assignment, JaDon thought, not totally dismissing the idea. The case was old, closed from every indication. There would be nothing to really raise the man's suspicions that he wanted anything other than to fulfill a portion of his assignment.

"Might just work," JaDon spoke the small smile playing on his face.

KR Bankston – The Gianni Legacy

Going back to the file he found the portion concerning Adrian, typing in the address listed in the Google search bar and hitting enter. The address was viable, but there was nothing he could immediately find to indicate if the man was still there.

"One way to find out, hell," JaDon groused clicking another tab and checking his bank account.

Pricing the flights he saw the he would be cutting it extremely close. *It'll be worth it if you can hit some pay dirt, find out any little thing of why they would have this file open again,* his mind urged as JaDon nervously bit his fingernail. Common sense was telling him not to go as it calculated his bills versus his savings. His sense of curiosity and yearning for recognition told him it was a necessary investment. Twenty minutes later, curiosity won and JaDon booked his flight for London.

•••

"This is bullshit," Gar complained of his added job duties. He knew it was punishment for the file fiasco almost two weeks ago. They placed him deep in the crypts of the CIA cleaning old files, dusting, removing documents that were long past shredding date and putting them into bins to be disposed of. He sighed slightly, thankful he was only given extra duties and not reprimanded or even dismissed. The error of touching a triple classified file like the Gianni file was normally the kiss of death for a budding career in this building. *Guess Keller was feeling slightly generous,* he thought once more of the Deputy Director. The man was coolly aloof during the verbal reprimand, but Gar wasn't stupid. Michael Keller had deadly written on him. *Wonder how many secret cases that guy has been a part of that will never see the light of day,* Gar pondered, coughing slightly as he dropped the last of the file folders into the huge bin, dust rising from the ancient papers, assaulting his sinuses bringing on a round of sneezing and watery itchy eyes.

Trudging his way back to the elevator, Gar pushed the heavy cart still cursing his fate and tapped the up button upon his arrival, waiting for the car to descend and deliver him from the dank hell of the file vault. *Maybe you should see what's so touchy about this Gianni guy,* his mind wandered while standing at the elevator bank. To say his superiors were angry was an understatement. They grilled him for almost two hours. What did you see? Who did you tell? Did you make copies? Are you working for a foreign government? An outlandishly crazy thing as far as Gar was concerned, but they were serious; viciously so. The ding of the elevator broke any further contemplation as the doors opened and Gar once again put his back into it and pushed the cart inside, making just enough room to squeeze himself in

Life After Death

and touch the button for L3, the sublevel just below the main offices. This is where he needed to drop off his bin and finally rid himself of its burden for the evening. The ride was smooth and quick, the elevator delivering him moments later to his destination. Gar pushed the cart out, finding strength in his impatience, and quickly placed it near the other three identical bins he filled over the course of the week. Checking his watch he saw it was already after 8PM.

Deciding to take the stairs the two flights up to his office, Gar disappeared into the stairwell and began walking. *Maybe you should read it, hell you're already in trouble for it,* his mind started up again about the Gianni file.

"No thanks," Gar spoke aloud already knowing if anyone even thought he was trying to access the file again he would be drummed out of the CIA and probably brought up on charges.

Still need to find out if JaDon remembers you running your mouth, the fear reminded. Gar prayed the man was just as tipsy as he and not thought anymore about it. Knowing JaDon's hound like tendencies, Gar definitely prayed that amnesia was the order of the evening. He exited the stairwell, a bit winded, but glad to be off and headed home. It took all of three minutes for him to stop at his small cubicle, retrieve his keys and backpack before heading to the main lobby and security, which he had to pass through each night, in order to leave the building.

His cell vibrated as soon as he picked up his book bag from the conveyor belt, adjusting it on his one shoulder. It was run through the x-ray machine each night to ensure nothing was being taken from the building that shouldn't leave. Satisfied, the security guard bid Gar a good night and returned his attention to the monitors before him. Gar glanced at the message and smiled. April accepted his invitation to have a drink. He was happy for the opportunity to spend time with her, but he was also plotting. He would get her a few drinks then casually question her again about their last outing, see if she recalled anything or if JaDon said anything to her since then. He arrived at the older model Corolla and climbed inside, throwing the book bag into the passenger seat and starting the car. Gar popped in the Maroon 5 CD and turned it up as he left the parking deck and turned onto Central, heading for the wire district, where he and April set for their evening of drinks, inside the small bistro they found on an earlier excursion. *It would definitely make my night to get laid too,* he chuckled glancing at his reflection in the rearview. He was a decent looking guy, Gar surmised; sandy brown hair, blue eyes, strong chin. His nose was slightly protruding, but it didn't stand out like a ski slope or anything, Gar again thought as his turn came into view. For whatever reason April was always very aloof when he tried to take the romantic route. *Maybe the liquor will help tonight, that and JaDon not being there,* his mind spat causing a slight frown. Gar disregarded the thoughts seeing her Acura and parking beside it.

"Game on," he murmured popping the breath mint and exiting the car, locking it and engaging the alarm before heading inside and finding her waiting already enjoying a house margarita.

Life After 12 Death

Maurice kissed her lightly, smiling at her as the lashes fluttered slightly and her eyes opened. They finally crossed the threshold last night and made love.

"Hi," she whispered quietly as he continued to smile and say nothing.

Cassandra stretched before turning the covers back and rising from the king bed, heading into the bathroom. Maurice lay back on the pillows after she closed the door thinking how much he enjoyed being with her. Glancing at his phone he frowned slightly. It was after 3AM. He honestly didn't want to leave, but he needed to keep up appearances. Sandra wouldn't raise a fuss. Maurice frowned thinking about her. Their marriage was over for all intents and purposes. They slept separately, she didn't interact with him unless it was something that concerned Reese, so he knew there would be no mention of his late nights or his indiscretions. He heard the water in the bathroom and reeled his mind in. Even knowing what was happening between him and the CIA Agent was temporal, Maurice allowed himself to feel for her. Cassandra Deale was a beautiful woman, warm and funny, passionate and desirable. She opened the door walking back into the room nude as Maurice again took in her exquisite frame finding himself becoming aroused all over again.

Cassandra fluidly slid back under the covers, turning on her side to face him.

"Don't you have to leave," she questioned when Maurice pulled her close and she felt the erection.

"Yes," he murmured nuzzling her neck. "But I want you so much right now," he admitted as she smiled out of his sight.

Cassandra closed her eyes allowing Maurice to arouse her, as her mind spun and she thought of Michael. Her body immediately sprang to life, images of the man she loved dancing in her minds eyes. She felt his lips as the warm tongue ran over her hardened nipples, Michael's fingers as they massaged ever so slightly her throbbing clit.

"Yesss," Cassandra breathed, orgasm very close.

The spell wasn't broken even when Maurice's lips connected with hers and his tongue slid into her mouth. Cassandra was making love to Michael Keller, irrespective of who the man was in her bed. The orgasm came without further warning, her back arched, moaning loudly as Maurice's fingers slid inside her saturated opening milking more of her creamy offering from her.

"Mmm, don't stop," Cassandra murmured urgently, feeling yet another wave of the delightful release.

Maurice kissed her again, the transition from fingers to hardened member, seamless as he thrust deeply inside her gently pulsating walls.

Cassandra gasped loudly. Michael was riding her hard and fast, his engorgement sliding against her clit rapaciously, her lubrication drenching them both with another delectable orgasmic release.

"Fuck me, yes, just like that," Cassandra was writhing as she hoarsely cried out her pleasure.

Maurice held her tightly going deeper, fully turned on by her outburst and the feel of her nails pressing trenches into his back.

"Mmm, yes, harder, fuck me harder," Cassandra again cried out, her sex contracting as the orgasm showed favor and graced her once again.

Maurice was almost over the edge. She was tight, wet, hips bucking wildly as he drilled her reminiscent of his college years. He couldn't recalling feeling as alive, vibrant, stimulated, as he did right at this moment with this beautiful woman beneath him, grinding her phenomenal sex against his pubic bone and telling him how good he was making her feel.

"I'm almost there baby," Maurice murmured, feeling Cassandra's hands slide down his back, gripping his butt pulling him deeper into her.

Her muscles continued to contract, squeezing his member tightly and urging his finish forward.

"Oh goooodddddd, that's it, yeeesssss," Cassandra screamed as Maurice pounded her, exploding on the third thrust, his semen rushing forward, body trembling in ecstasy hearing her satisfied purring as they both lay in each other's arms trying to gather themselves.

●●●

Keller sighed intensely as the phone rang and he answered.

Life After Death

"Hello," the voice spoke amiably.

"Hello," Keller returned.

"How are you this evening," he questioned amiably trying to gather his thoughts.

"I'm fine Vernon, but I'm sure you didn't call me at this ghoulish hour to ask me that, so what's going on," Keller questioned calmly.

Taking another deep breath, Vernon finally spoke.

"The Gianni file is missing," he said simply, imagining the look on the man's face right now.

"What do you mean missing," Keller questioned.

"It's gone, taken from the vault," Vernon again spoke.

Keller's mind was racing. Vernon Spoelman was his final link to the FBI and its inner workings. He was thankfully high enough on the food chain that he could move about freely to gather information Keller may have requested when he needed it. He alerted the man of the Gianni breach in the CIA when it occurred a few weeks back and told him to keep his eyes open.

"Has it left the building," Keller returned, gathering his thoughts.

"I'm almost certain, yes," Vernon answered, further infuriating Keller.

"Dammit," he groused hearing his friend sigh.

"I'm running tapes now of the security camera, quietly of course," Vernon told Keller.

"Great move," he spoke. "Let me know as soon as you find anything Vernon, and I do mean anything."

"You know I will," Vernon spoke. "I don't want this shit to get started again just like you," he went on. "We all have far too much invested and too much to lose if this psycho is successfully revived," Vernon ended, speaking aloud all the things Keller was feeling.

They made Gianni promises and so far he kept his end of the bargain. Keller knew that all hell would break loose if they didn't keep theirs. He made mental notes to contact Cassandra and see what she found out. He also wanted the surveillance stepped up on Dwayne Marchant. With the FBI file now missing and them having no idea who took it or where it might be, this small glitch turned into a major catastrophe and it was up to him to make sure damage control was in place. *Damned right because Layton will leave your ass out to dry without thought,* his mind told him.

"Give me a couple of days," Vernon again spoke aloud bringing Keller from his musings.

"OK, but make sure you call me," Keller again iterated before disconnecting.

He immediately rose and headed for his bar. He needed a drink.

"This has got to end quickly and quietly," Keller murmured throwing back the vodka, without chaser.

He never forgot about the wreckage caused by Gianni during his task force days with the FBI. *"What do you see for your career Agent Keller," Layton Crowler asked calmly as they met inside his private villa in San Juan. "I want to succeed sir, perhaps become Director one day," Keller answered calmly, his head spinning. When he received the invitation via his mentor, Lucas Wenters, he was blown away with the things the man confided. Lucas opened his eyes, showed him his inexperience. Keller quickly learned that working within the confines of the bureau would leave him burned out, disillusioned, and left behind. Men like Layton Crowler were the future Lucas instructed before they boarded the plane. "Listen Michael, let's cut the bullshit, and get to the real business at hand," Layton returned.*

"And the rest as they say, is history," Keller spoke aloud recalling his deal with the devil.

They whisked Gianni out of the country, triple classified his file. Keller gave his resignation to the Bureau and quickly assumed his new role with the CIA.

"Now this bullshit is back," he muttered, mind tumbling.

Keller knew Crowler held a vested interest in keeping Gianni out of the states and dead in the minds of those who mattered; but what he didn't know was the true reason why.

"Maybe it's about time I should," he murmured finishing the third shot of vodka and heading back to his bed.

Tomorrow he would add another quest to the growing pile he found himself surrounded by.

•••

Life After Death

Cassandra cursed herself for being so weak, hating the tears that rolled down her cheeks. She despised the vulnerability that Michael Keller exposed in her otherwise perfectly crafted armor. Why did she love him? He never showed her more than a fleeting interest at best. *That's not true, liar,* her mind told her recalling the extremely brief fling they shared. He was exquisite in bed and he pleasured her to no end on the occasions he allowed himself to relax and be with her. Cassandra learned quickly that Keller's first and only love was his work. Everything else was merely a minor diversion. Still she allowed him to use her, to pull her deeply into his dark web, and now she was trapped. If Keller went down, so did she. Her career was over, her life was over, and her freedom along with it. Forcing the tears to stop, Cassandra pulled herself together. She was going to have to call him in a few hours to report her progress. *Will he be jealous,* she wondered knowing that she would tell him about sleeping with Maurice.

Sighing Cassandra again felt defeat, knowing that even if he were, Michael Keller would never tip his hand and let her know it.

"This has got to end quickly," she murmured aloud thinking of Maurice.

She opened the door. Now it would need to be seen completely through. *You're only here for a little while,* her mind told her. *He's not a bad lover, and he's a nice man,* it continued to try and soothe. Cassandra conceded that much, but he still wasn't Michael.

"Do your job," she spoke aloud, hearing Keller's voice in her head.

Turning on the shower, Cassandra adjusted the water temperature, deciding she would call him after she dressed and ate breakfast. Her cell vibrated, disturbing her preparations. Picking it up she clicked on the message icon. 'Last night was perfect, I am looking forward to more like it,' the text read. Cassandra exhaled again, simply selecting a smiling emoticon and hitting send.

"Do your job," she repeated yet again, the defeat thick in her voice as she stepped into the scalding hot shower and prayed it burned away the shame and muck she felt as her mind replayed the sex she engaged with a married man last night.

● ● ●

"You got in late," Sandra remarked, giving Maurice a look.

They were enjoying breakfast in the massive dining room. She insisted upon it once Reece was old enough to sit in a normal chair, instead of his high chair.

"Mhmm," Maurice returned without explanation.

"Are you in love with her," Sandra questioned, sipping her juice, face neutral.

Maurice put down his coffee cup and regarded her a few moments longer.

"Why would you care," he replied coolly.

Sandra swallowed, took another deep breath, before addressing his response.

"Maurice, we have to keep this family together," she told him. "For Reese's sake," she added quickly as her husband sucked his teeth.

"Yes, I forgot, it's all about appearances," Maurice snidely remarked seeing the tears come to her eyes.

He didn't care. Maurice was sick of Sandra's coldness. She was continually pushing him away, yet wanted him to pretend everything was just fine with the world.

"Maurice, you don't have to be so cruel," Sandra replied sniffling slightly.

"I realize I don't excite you anymore," she continued. "I just don't want you to leave and Reese's world to be turned upside down," Sandra told him. "Your grandson adores you," she added as Maurice again regarded her.

"Sandra, for months and I do mean months, I begged you to sleep with me," Maurice told her voice tight with anger.

"I think you're beautiful, sexy," he went on eyes boring into her. "And month after month it was the same thing, no I don't feel like it, no Reese might hear us, no, no, no," Maurice mimicked. "How damned long did you expect me to do without," he fired growing angrier.

Sandra glanced furtively around not wanting Reese to walk in on their argument.

"To answer your question, no, I'm not in love with her, but we make damned powerful love when I'm with her," he finished, throwing the linen napkin on the half-eaten plate and rising, striding from the table.

Sandra took a deep breath, dabbing at the errant tear that rolled down her cheek. She couldn't let Reese see her crying. Her mind replayed her husband's words while her conscience condemned her for how she treated him.

"Hi Gramma," Reese's little voice piped up, shaking the darkness as Sandra looked into his beautiful brown eyes.

"Hello darling," she greeted the little boy picking him up and hugging him tightly.

Reese giggled allowing her to squeeze him a moment longer before squirming to get down. She smiled with delight watching the toddler as he climbed into the dining room chair his booster seat in place, reaching immediately for the muffin she placed on his plate. Sandra added the eggs and bacon strip, enjoying his chatter as Reese ate and told his grandmother about his morning cartoons.

"Hey champ," Maurice greeted coming back into the dining room to tell him goodbye.

"Hi Grampa," Reese grinned as Maurice kissed the top of his head, ignoring Sandra's presence.

"Be a good boy today and I'll take you for ice cream tonight when I get home," he promised.

"I will Grampa," he quickly assured as Maurice chuckled again.

"I'll see you later," he grudgingly told Sandra, careful to keep his face neutral and Reese oblivious to his still lingering anger with the woman.

Sandra bid him a good day, watching his back as he left the pain and fear returning. *So what are you going to do about it,* her mind kicked in. *You going to just roll over and play dead, let her have him, or are you going to fight for him?*

●●●

"What have you got," Keller barked into the phone.

His patience was short and his mind on overload. Pleasantries were not high on his list of priorities at the moment.

"Marchant has been reassigned temporarily," Cassandra returned trying to keep the hurt from her voice.

He didn't even greet her with a simple hello, how are you.

"What else," Keller again gruffly questioned.

"There's been no further movement or contact between him and Detective Canfield," she continued referring to the man he met with on the West Coast, praying the conversation would end soon.

What the hell is wrong with me, why am I so damned emotional, Cassandra pondered her mind half listening as Keller began to speak again. *No, that can't be,* she thought as a horrid realization came to her mind.

"Are you listening to me," Keller raged.

He was furious with her silence.

"I'm sorry, something came across the computer," Cassandra quickly lied.

"It better be damned good for you to not pay attention with all that's at stake," he fired yet another time.

"What did you get from the judge," he asked now, referring to Maurice.

"I'm picking up the files from Thomas and Kayla Bradford's divorce, and Thomas Bradford's case with the dead escort in about twenty minutes," Cassandra returned, mind still swirling.

"I'm sure that came with a cost," Keller threw back wanting an answer.

Cassandra exhaled acutely but didn't speak.

"Was he at least a good lay," Keller questioned again.

"He was fine," she returned confirming his suspicions and answering his query.

"Hmph, well that's the way it goes sometimes," he returned successfully mastering the show; no hint of his true jealousy or anger, plainly a statement of fact.

"What else do you need me to get," Cassandra questioned wanting to change the subject.

"For now nothing," Keller told her. "Simply keep his honor entertained and cooperative, we may be needing him in short order," he finished and Cassandra picked up the underlying tension in his voice.

"Has something happened," she asked.

"Yes, but that's not for you to be concerned with at the moment," Keller quickly returned. "I'll let you know if I need you on that end."

Cassandra again swallowed hard the earlier thoughts returning to her mind.

Life After Death

"You're really okay with me sleeping with him," she ventured, holding her breath for his response.

"We're professionals Cassandra," Keller told her squarely. "We do any and everything that we have to do to accomplish our goals and keep everyone safe," he added, not answering her question directly.

"That's not --," she got out before he interrupted.

"It's extraneous," Keller told her, unwittingly hurting Cassandra's core yet another time.

"Do your job, get the information, let's put this time-bomb to bed and move on," Keller added as a final thought, still struggling inwardly, before disconnecting.

Cassandra burst into tears, furious with herself once again as she headed into the bathroom and grabbed her cosmetic bag. Opening it she found what she was looking for. Five minutes later she was sobbing, quasi-hysterical, as the wand lying on the counter showed two plus signs and Cassandra confirmed the one-night stand with Senator Layton Crowler produced more than securing her future with the CIA.

Life After 13 Death

London, England. JaDon took in his surroundings exiting the taxi at his requested stop, throwing the small carry bag across his shoulders. He packed very light. The trip itself was costing him a small fortune; he didn't want to add baggage fees to the mix. He had enough to stay one night so he was determined to make his visit with Adrian count. *What if he's not home, has moved, you've wasted time and all your money,* his mind barraged as JaDon heard the click clack of his shoes on the stone street. He passed a telephone booth, red, oblong, with multiple windows, chuckling to himself how a 007 movie immediately came to mind as he did.

"Can't find one of these in the states," he murmured still walking, passing a bike rack outside of a small roadside café, filled to capacity with the two wheelers, some of them casually leaning against the metal rail, unlocked and unguarded.

Continuing his walking JaDon passed a long row of shops, peering into each window as he passed it. Glancing around he saw the large four story building that took up almost the entire block, just as the double decker bus passed him, again giving JaDon a feeling of Hollywood nostalgia. Checking the name on the building, South Kensington, he took a deep breath and walked inside the lobby immediately in front of him.

JaDon took a moment to acclimate himself, pulling his phone from his pocket and checking the address he stored inside. Satisfied he was in the right place, JaDon walked over to the elevator, once he managed to locate it, and pushed the up button. His wait was short as the door almost instantly opened and he stepped inside pushing six, the top floor, and waiting to be delivered to his destination. Stepping out once the elevator stopped and allowed him exit, JaDon cleared his throat slightly and looked up and down the short hallway. He saw number 12403 in front of him, deciding to go left, which turned out to be the wrong way some three doors down. Turning around JaDon went back the way he came, passing 12403 again and continuing forward. He found the apartment he sought moments later, 12414, and shored his nerve before knocking. JaDon went over his cover story for a second time in his head making sure he remembered it perfectly. He checked his pocket for the FBI credentials, finding them intact. Deciding he was ready, before his apprehension talked him out of it again,

Life After Death

JaDon made a fist and knocked on the intricately carved, white enameled, door in front of him praying he struck pay dirt.

● ● ●

Adrian took in the handsome man standing on his doorstep, giving him a questioning look.

"Hello," JaDon greeted, growing a bit nervous under the man's intense stare.

"Who is it luv," another male voice spoke as JaDon heard footsteps and knew the man was coming toward them.

"I'm not sure yet," Adrian replied.

JaDon cleared his throat and opened his mouth another time.

"My name is JaDon Ivory," he told Adrian. "I'm with the FBI, Mr. Roberts," he added seeing the distrust instantly mirrored on the man's face.

"No, there's nothing wrong sir," JaDon hurriedly explained, seeing Adrian relax slightly.

"Well, since I don't enjoy having my neighbors all in my personal affairs, come in," Adrian told him moving aside finally and allowing him entrance.

"Who is he," the man questioned having arrived, standing protectively at Adrian's side. JaDon looked him over noticing the youth and deciding that Adrian liked them younger. In this case, considerably younger, he continued to muse knowing the lover was closer to his own age.

"Mr. Ivory, this is Nesby," Adrian introduced without further explanation.

"Would you like something to drink," he questioned being hospitable.

"Some water would be fine," JaDon replied as Adrian smiled slightly.

"Nesby, get Mr. Ivory some water, and bring me coffee," he told the young man who grudgingly complied leaving them alone in the beautiful sitting room.

This guy is loaded and attractive, JaDon thought behind the calm exterior. The room was exquisite. White and exquisite, he continued to muse taking in the bay windows leading to adjoining balcony doors. The sun sheathed the room in natural light illuminating the red curtains giving almost a sparkling effect that seemed to cause the presentation to hum contentedly, immediately relaxing you as you sat. *Feng Shui to the maximum,* JaDon mused enjoying the plushness of the white arm chair where he sat, Adrian contentedly placed in the corner of the white sofa adjacent to him, maple wood coffee table in front of them.

"Here," Nesby told JaDon nearly thrusting the chilled bottle of water into his hands, jealousy obvious.

JaDon raised an eyebrow but didn't speak. If he weren't here on business, he would have flirted with Adrian just to piss the boy toy off. As it were however, he didn't have time for that luxury, immediately returning his mind to his task.

"Here's your coffee, luv," he sweetly told Adrian handing him the porcelain cup and saucer, his demeanor polar opposite of moments earlier.

"Nesby, Mr. Ivory and I need to discuss some business," Adrian told his lover. "Why don't you run out and get us something nice for lunch," he spoke, more directive than question.

Nesby was visibly agitated but didn't balk.

"Alright luv, I'll be back directly," he spoke instead, pointedly giving JaDon a look.

Sipping his water, he smirked but didn't react. Disappearing up the spiral stairs the spacious apartment held, Nesby left them alone once again.

"I will say that I'm very intrigued that the FBI has shown up on my doorstep," Adrian began, gingerly tasting his steaming coffee and frowning slightly.

"Excuse me a moment," he spoke, rising and heading toward what JaDon knew was the kitchen.

Seconds after he left, Nesby bounded down the stairs, stopping in the sitting room and addressing JaDon.

"Whatever you're up too, you better not harm him," he hissed, uncaring of the man's credentials.

"I'm leaving luv," he called out as Adrian returned to the room.

"Be careful," the man spoke as the two kissed softly and Nesby turned once again leaving through the front door as JaDon continued to fight his devious side and stay focused.

●●●

Life After Death

Showtime, JaDon thought as Adrian again gave him his full attention and waited for further explanation of his presence.

"Mr. Roberts," he began before being interrupted.

"Please, call me Adrian," the man replied, sipping his coffee again.

"OK, um Adrian," JaDon began anew. "I'm a freshman FBI agent, so I'm still going through training classes," he spun the yarn.

"Actually coming to see you is part of one of my assignments," JaDon told Adrian who nodded but didn't speak.

"I was given the Gianni case file, and after researching it a bit noticed that everyone was dead except you," JaDon spoke.

Adrian continued to sit passively and listen.

"I have to do a dissertation, and a video presentation of the case, what could have been done differently, what I agreed or disagreed with, stuff like that," he told him.

"So what is it you need from me," Adrian finally spoke eyes locked on JaDon, and broke his silence.

JaDon swallowed a quick sip of water before answering.

"I wanted to add some pizazz to my presentation, get a better grade I guess, by doing a live interview with the lone survivor of that time," he finished praying he did a plausible job of selling the man on his sincerity and opening up to him.

"And what is it that you think I can tell you Mr. Ivory," Adrian questioned, finished with the coffee, setting the cup and saucer onto the coaster on the table in front of them.

"Well I was hoping to get more of the personal angle from you," JaDon told him, pulling out a small pad and his recorder.

"Do you mind," he questioned as Adrian shrugged.

Turning it on, JaDon began his questions.

"You knew Dezi Gianni aka Devastator, the head of The Clique," he asked.

"Yes, he was a regular customer when I used to wait tables back in the states," Adrian replied calmly.

"But it said in my file you dated his chief bodyguard, um, Monster," JaDon posed, already knowing the answer.

He needed Adrian to open up, to give him more intimate details of the people involved in the Gianni case. His gut told him the man knew more than he was letting on, but JaDon stayed cool not wanting to rattle him or make him shut down.

"Yes, Kevin and I dated for a while," Adrian replied using the man's legal name.

JaDon could see that time didn't dull the pain as the man's eyes immediately filled with tears and he just as rapidly blinked them away.

"But he and I were together, not me and Dezi," Adrian clarified. "I don't know what it is I can tell you except the personal life I shared with Kevin," he went on as JaDon nodded growing slightly frustrated.

"I just am trying to find out about Dezi the man, as opposed to the killer, you know," he questioned switching gears.

Adrian seemed to consider the question for a few moments before touching his chin thoughtfully and speaking.

"Dezi was very nice man, at least he was always pleasant to me," he volunteered.

"He was good to everyone who worked with him, Dirty, Kevin, all the rest," Adrian told JaDon who was scribbling, but not really writing anything.

He just needed to look the part at the moment.

"What about his girlfriend, what was her name, um, Mikayla," JaDon questioned, flipping pages in the notepad feigning search for the information.

Adrian smiled slightly.

"He loved her, without question," he said simply.

"Hmph," JaDon replied. "I have to be honest Adrian, what you're telling me doesn't really jive with anything in the files about this man," he told him. "I mean by all accounts Dezi Gianni was a walking nightmare, so was his partner Dirty," he put into the air trying to gain a reaction.

Adrian simply shrugged.

"People see things differently," he spoke growing quiet again.

"Would you be adverse to me taking a picture of you for the video presentation," JaDon continued the ruse, sensing the talk had come to an end and his trip to London fruitless.

Life After Death

Adrian immediately brightened.

"Not at all," he replied, actually posing on the sofa as JaDon held up his phone and snapped several shots.

"Thank you so much for your time Adrian, I really appreciate it," he spoke standing near the door, Adrian holding it open for him.

"Do you have a card," he questioned. "I may think of something else to help you, never know," Adrian spoke as JaDon smiled and quickly produced it.

"Thank you," he replied taking it from the man's hands.

"Have a safe flight home," Adrian spoke as a final communication, closing the door behind him.

•••

The ringing cell phone disturbed the nap Dezi didn't realize he was taking. Shaking the cobwebs, he sighed softly seeing the name on the I.D., answering as he continued to take in the beautiful ocean rolling softly in front of him. Coming onto the veranda earlier, he made himself comfortable in the hammock and relaxed, intending to simply enjoy a bit of solitude before his business meeting with Arroyo and some new prospects, later this afternoon. Unfortunately the sneakily seductive atmosphere of the ocean breeze, the sea water, and shady oasis encompassing him held other ideas and he unceremoniously drifted off.

"Hello," Dezi greeted amiably.

"Hi Dezi," the soft voice replied. "I hope I'm not disturbing you," they continued as he began to swing again in the hammock, still taking in the ocean.

"Not at all, how are you," he responded, picking up the now watery drink taking a sip.

It was still cool, but not cold, quickly causing him to return it to the table beside the hammock and his attention to his caller.

"I'm fine," they again returned. "How is Kayla, and everyone," they questioned another time.

"Everyone is doing very well," Dezi returned. "I keep telling you that you should come for a visit, spend some time," he added smiling slightly.

Chuckling lightly they spoke again. "I had an interesting visitor earlier today," Adrian spoke, garnering Dezi's full attention.

"Really, and might I ask, who was the visitor," he questioned.

Dezi knew something must be amiss for the man to be calling. Though he found him years ago and reached out to him, they maintained their distance. Not out of any sense of dislike, Adrian told him the memories were still too painfully vivid for him. Respecting his privacy and his feelings, Dezi never intruded on his life, simply giving him the contact information in the event he ever needed him.

"An FBI agent," Adrian replied, bringing a crease to Dezi's brow.

"Really, and what did he want," Dezi replied calmly, fully focused.

"He says he's new, still in training and was working on an assignment," Adrian told him. "He said he came to see me because he wanted to do a human angle to the entire Clique and you as the head of it."

Dezi rolled the information around. There was no reason he could think of that the case would actually be active and after almost twenty-five years, he could see where they might think it a learning tool, except that he received Layton Crowler's assurance the file was triple classified and sealed. The irritation was beginning in the recesses of his calm.

"What did you tell him," Dezi inquired now.

Adrian chuckled replaying the conversation, bringing a smile from Dezi as well. "So basically nothing," he spoke as Adrian again laughed.

"Exactly," he replied. "I have his information," he told Dezi now.

"Hmph, okay, send it to me," he told Adrian.

"I'll email it after I scan it into my computer," Adrian told him another time.

"That's fine," Dezi relayed. "So, when are you coming to see us," he teased dismissing the information for now.

He would address it more seriously later after examining it from all angles, alone in his study.

"No promises, but maaaybe in a few weeks," Adrian replied.

"Sounds good, let me know," Dezi replied. "And if the FBI reaches out again, make sure you call me," he admonished.

Life After Death

"You know I will Dezi," Adrian told him sincerely.

"Have a wonderful evening," Dezi spoke as they ended the call.

He was still thinking about the agent and what the man could have truly been after.

"Maybe he's telling the truth," Dezi murmured rising from the hammock and standing at the banister looking over it.

He didn't want to get ahead of himself and it be nothing, but he didn't want to turn a blind eye and be suddenly overtaken either. His trust factor when it came to the FBI was extremely low. *Perhaps I need to start putting things in order*, Dezi mused. *Just in case.*

"Have a nice nap," Kayla's voice broke his musing as she walked onto the veranda, ice filled drink in hand, handing it to him.

"Why didn't you wake me," Dezi teased, pulling her close and kissing her.

"You looked so peaceful and you needed the rest," Kayla returned, gently stroking his cheek.

"How about a swim," Dezi questioned taking in the sundress blowing effortlessly in the breeze.

"That sounds good," Kayla returned taking his hand as they headed inside, thoughts of FBI agents propelled yet another time to the recesses of his mind.

Life After 14 Death

Aidan continued to observe unnoticed and untouched as his wife perused the rack of dresses in front her. It wasn't her actions at the moment that held his attention; it was the unwavering gaze of the man who continued watching her for the last fifteen minutes, the lust clearly visible in his eyes. Aidan began to follow her into the store, spotting her moments earlier, intending to surprise her. He stopped his progress however noticing the man materialize from an obvious vantage point and follow her as well. Curiosity peaked, he gave them both seven minutes before he slipped into the store and quickly found the current obscure perch he occupied. Still watching, Aidan felt his anger rising, his jealousy keenly focused as the man yet another time slowly scanned his wife's shapely body, licking his lips, before stepping down onto the sales floor and boldly walking over to her. Forcing himself not to move, Aidan continued to watch, wanting to see their interaction. The man said hello as Mariah jumped slightly, startled he knew, since she was still intently searching for the perfect dress. Aidan saw his wife perfunctorily return the man's greeting, her attention immediately returning to the dress rack. *She's not interested, that much is good,* he thought of her reaction and subsequent dismissal of the man.

Still he didn't seem to get the hint, standing and saying something else to Mariah, who once again stopped her progress to regard him. Unfortunately Aidan wasn't close enough to hear the words spoken, but from the look on Mariah's face, they were exactly pleasing. He thought he saw a shadow of fear on her face, leading him to question if the man were menacing to her. *What is this about exactly,* he pondered, still taking in the two in front of him. He saw the man step closer and Mariah take a step back, still trying to maintain the forced friendliness. Aidan knew his wife well. While she wore a pleasant smile, her eyes were cautious and her body language spoke volumes. This was obviously not the first time the man approached her. His blood reached boil when the man touched Mariah, lightly grazing her face with his fingertip. Aidan took several deep breaths pushing the darkness away, blinking rapidly, visions of the man's blood spilling from his body. He saw Mariah quickly move away and say something to the man before turning and striding down another isle toward the front door, shopping forgotten. *You have just made a fatal error,* Aidan thought continuing to watch the man as he sighed deeply and began walking dejectedly in the same direction Mariah just departed.

Life After Death

Aidan waited until they both left before uncloaking himself and following. Stepping into the afternoon sun, his eyes scanned the area for signs of Mariah or the would be suitor. On the one hand Aidan fully understood the man's attraction. His wife was stunning, a prize by any standard. Still he should have known better. The Gianni name was well known on the island, especially by this man, and everyone knew that Mariah was his wife and therefore off limits. *Why do people insist on bringing the worst upon themselves,* Aidan was still thinking as he got into the Bentley and started it. His mind was replaying the scene for him. Mariah didn't say anything to him, but he understood. She probably thought nothing of it, or didn't want him to get angry. Aidan chuckled. He got a bit crazy when he was jealous, he admitted, thinking of a beat down he gave an overzealous admirer when they first settled here years earlier.

"She still should have told me," he murmured passing the car and seeing the man.

Aidan turned to his right, eyes connecting as the man gave him a marginally defiant stare in return. *So we want to play do we,* Aidan thought smirking and speeding away no thought of the man giving chase. Police officer or not, Aidan knew that Stephan Eveson wasn't a fool. He was however about to be a dead man if he didn't keep his eyes and his hands off his wife, Aidan fumed, turning onto the highway that would take him to his estate and he was sure his waiting wife.

•••

"I told you I was sorry Kayla," Chris spoke as she sat in the darkened room, bound by some unseen force, unable to move. "You said you forgave me, but you lied Kayla, you didn't forgive me," he spoke again as she shook her head furiously back and forth that it wasn't true. "What about me Kayla, I loved you," Thomas spoke coming into the room as well. "I told you we could have worked it out, but you didn't want that, you hated me," he accused pointing a dead, rotted, finger at her. Kayla opened her mouth to refute his statement, to tell them both they were wrong, but no sound would come. She tried to scream only to find the room still filled with her silence and their accusations. "Kayla, what did you do baby, what have you done," Black questioned walking into the room joining the previous two. The tears rolled down her cheeks as she tried vainly to rise from the restraints of the chair and over to Black. "They'll find you Kayla, they're never going to stop looking," he spoke again, sympathetically as he walked over to her and kneeled before her, his head in her lap. "He loves you, you know," Black said soothingly. "Who," Kayla spoke shocked herself at the sound of her speech.

"Everyone you love dies," Thomas spoke again, hatefully staring at her. "You're evil and vile inside," Chris chimed in. Black continued to rest his head in her lap, eyes closed.

"Maybe you should die too," he spoke, eyes open now as he stared directly into her eyes. Thomas and Chris began to walk toward her, rage in their dead eyes, figures tall and menacing.

"Baby, baby," Dezi was calling, shaking her hard, eyes searching hers as she finally recognized him.

"Wh-what," Kayla managed.

"You were having a nightmare," Dezi spoke still holding her arms, searching her face concerned.

Kayla shook her head slightly; the images were very vivid and frightening.

"You want to tell me about it," he questioned, finally releasing her, rising to get her a glass of brandy.

"No, it was a fluke," Kayla returned, the bad feeling again in the pit of her stomach.

The dream was somehow an omen she was sure. *But of what,* Kayla pondered taking the glass from Dezi and gingerly sipping the liquor.

"Drink it," he admonished, raising an eyebrow.

Kayla obeyed, coughing once she finished, hearing him chuckle.

"Pansy," he teased as she laughed and pushed him playfully.

"Are you sure you're alright baby," Dezi again questioned sitting on the bed beside her, stroking her hair.

"I'm fine, Dezi, really," she returned, conjuring a genuine smile.

Kayla decided she wouldn't read too much into the dream. If it was indeed an omen she knew more would come. That's how it was with her since Nana died. She would have a succession of dreams, good or bad, when some major life event was headed her way.

"Well if you're sure you're okay, I have to go out for a meeting," Dezi told her rising and walking over to their dresser.

"Yes, I'm fine, too much sun, conch, and that Mai Tai before we laid down," Kayla explained as he chuckled.

"No more Mai Tai's for you," he again teased kissing her lips sweetly before walking out and leaving her with her thoughts.

What in the world could have brought that on, Kayla was thinking recalling the dream.

Life After Death

"Are they really angry with me," she murmured aloud of Thomas and Chris.

Even Black was to a degree upset with her, saying it was her fault they were all dead.

"I'm so confused, what is going on," Kayla again spoke aloud.

Someone was trying to tell her something but she just wasn't getting it. Who was looking? Who loved her? Was Black talking about Dezi? So many questions and no answers to any of them. Kayla's stomach was in knots. Maybe she should have told Dezi, she thought just as easily dismissing it. Dezi would have told her she was being silly. *Dead people can't hurt you,* her mind pressed. Kayla wasn't so sure. Why now? What was triggering the dreams, what in the world was headed for her that would have those three people in the same room? Her cell rang and she heard Jackie's familiar ringtone. Answering the phone Kayla allowed the nightmare to slip into the abyss of lost thought, laughing with her best friend as they chatted pleasantly for the next hour.

●●●

"How was your day," Aidan questioned as Mariah walked into their bedroom from the master bath, having just completed her shower.

Both the children were put to bed and Aidan was preparing to leave to meet his father.

Still he wanted to discuss what he witnessed earlier today before he did.

"It was fine, nothing special," Mariah returned shrugging at the end of the statement.

"Did you find the dress you wanted for the celebration," he questioned leading her into what he truly wanted to know.

Mariah's face shadowed slightly, before she regained her composure.

"No not yet," she told him. "I'm still looking."

Aidan nodded, leaning against the dresser now.

"Mariah," he began, her giving him her full attention. "Are you happy with me, with our marriage," Aidan baited.

Her frown was instant, and severe.

"Of course I'm happy, what in the world Aidan," she asked, genuinely confused and perplexed with the query.

"I know there are a lot of other men out there, and you're a beautiful woman," he began as Mariah walked over to him.

"Aidan where is this coming from, I love you baby, you know that," she pleaded, eyes never leaving his.

Aidan smiled slightly, leaning down and kissing her passionately.

He spoke again when their lips parted. "So I don't have to be worried about Stephan Eveson," he posed waiting for her reaction.

"No," Mariah replied forcefully enough to let Aidan know he hit a nerve.

"But he has feelings for you doesn't he," he questioned now, holding her as he interrogated her.

"Aidan, it's nothing, really," Mariah tried her fear of his reaction evident.

"What has he said, Mariah," he questioned calmly.

Mariah wasn't stupid. She heard the tone, saw the gray eyes go cold and flat. Her husband was furious.

"Nothing Aidan, really," she tried again.

"So he has a habit of touching you," he again fired and Mariah's heart sank.

She immediately knew he saw them in the store this morning. *How, where,* she was thinking as Aidan continued to hold her and look into her face.

"I didn't --, I --," Mariah stammered.

"Has he done something else to you Mariah, something you're not telling me," Aidan asked, growing angrier, his voice rising.

"No, I swear Aidan, nothing," she hurriedly told him hoping to diffuse his anger. "He has a crush on me, but he knows I'm married, and I haven't given him any encouragement, really," Mariah explained.

Aidan believed her, having seen for himself her disinterest in the man.

"Where else has he shown up," he wanted to know.

"The market, sometimes when I'm at the café," Mariah admitted. "Aidan, please, I know that you're angry, but I swear today was the first time he ever touched me," Mariah tried to explain.

"He shouldn't have touched you at all," Aidan flared.

"I know, but I don't have any interest in Stephan, none at all," she told her husband as he smiled at her.

Life After Death

"I know baby, I have no doubt of that," he spoke as they kissed again.

"You're not going to --," Mariah began trailing off without finishing the sentence.

"No worries baby, as long as he doesn't touch you again," Aidan promised, not meaning it, but knowing she needed to hear it.

"Thank you," Mariah spoke softly, garnering another kiss.

"I have to leave now, but when I get home," Aidan spoke, nuzzling her neck, biting it.

Mariah giggled. "I'll be waiting for you," she told him his hand grazing her breast, the moan escaping her lips.

"Aidan stop," Mariah told him lying blatantly as he picked her up, putting her on the dresser, opening the silk robe finding her naked underneath.

"Shhh," he admonished, lips meeting hers again, tongue sliding inside her mouth.

Aidan unzipped his pants, his erection following his lead as he stepped between his wife's caramel thighs, and entered her waiting fortress.

"Mmmmm," Mariah moaned as Aidan took her, his breath warm and stimulating on her neck as he thrust into her.

"Baby, yes," Mariah moaned the orgasm causing her juices to flow fluidly, Aidan's own intensity increasing.

"Aaah Mariah," Aidan growled, thrusting one last time as he too crossed the threshold of release.

Life After 15 Death

Vernon Spoelman, the display showed as Keller held the cell phone in his palm. *About fucking time,* he thought irritably, pushing the green button to connect the call.

"Tell me you found what I need," Keller spoke foregoing a greeting.

"Yes, literally five minutes ago," Vernon returned as Keller took a seat and continued to listen.

"Sifted through nearly thirty hours of surveillance video, all on the low," Vernon told his friend.

"You're sure no one was alerted," Keller questioned.

There were enough players involved and damage control would soon get out of hand if they kept adding members.

"Positive," Vernon replied. "That's what took me so long, hell I could only look here and there when the building was empty and no one was up my ass," he added as Keller mumbled his commiseration.

He was edgy seeing that it took another seven days for him to get this call. Marchant was still on his new assignment and so far causing no problems. They were keeping an eye on the records clerk, Edgar Simons, as well. He was still behaving a bit strangely for Keller, but not enough to warrant them pulling him in. He remained on watch only status for now.

"So what did you find out," Keller asked wanting to get to the crux of the matter. Whoever the culprit, they needed to neutralize them immediately.

"One of our records clerk," Vernon told him, the déjà vu hitting Keller like a stone. "Fresh out of law school, daddy pulls some strings and gets his under qualified ass in the door," Vernon angrily spat.

Keller knew the man was old school having no love for the new recruits or their new methodology.

"What's his name and how the hell did he manage to get the files out of the door without triggering security," Keller now questioned.

Life After Death

He could picture Vernon bristling at the question in his mind. The man prided himself on running a water tight ship, but he just sprang a leak, only exacerbated by the fact it was done by a rookie.

"JaDon Ivory," Vernon replied through clenched teeth. "Been here less than three years," he went on as Keller made mental notes to attach eyes and ears to the man. "He evidently smuggled the file out in a book bag, I'm guessing filled with magazines and newspapers," Vernon told Keller. "I found the security footage of the night he stole the Gianni file, and the checkpoint on duty vaguely glanced the screen, I'm sure seeing just what Ivory wanted them to see, which was nothing," he finished and Keller knew he was breathing fire.

Vernon, like himself, hated to be made a fool of.

"What do you think he's doing with it," Keller questioned now trying to get some sort of handle on why the man would take the file.

He also wanted to have another talk with Edgar Simons. Obviously the man lied and he indeed discussed the file with someone. *He must have opened it, read it, to know it was once held by the FBI,* Keller concluded, his own ire beginning to rise.

"I have no idea, but I would say it's obvious he and your records clerk are in this together," Vernon told him.

Keller kicked the idea around. He may have been right. *But why,* his mind again questioned. *Career jumpers,* his mind answered. Keller was almost positive the two planned nothing more sinister than gaining leverage and catapulting their careers quickly up the internal ladder. *You two idiots picked the wrong case seriously,* Keller ominously considered.

"Well we're already watching Simons, our records clerk," he told Vernon. "I'm going to put eyes and ears on our good friend Mr. Ivory now as well," Keller added.

Vernon didn't balk. There was nothing he could do actually. He was at the CIA's mercy. He couldn't let it get out that not only was a file taken, but it was classified, and the culprit was a file clerk.

"Great, let me know what you need on my end," Vernon told him.

"I'm thinking before it's over these two are going to need to be relocated, permanently," Keller returned hearing Vernon chuckle.

"Oh trust no problem here, I already have a place in mind," came his sinister reply.

"I'm making the call when I hang up," Keller told him. "What's his information," he questioned Vernon concerning the fledgling agent.

Vernon readily supplied the information, asking Keller another time to keep him in the loop, before disconnecting.

●●●

Fuck, what now, Keller groused his other cellphone ringing as soon as he and Vernon disconnected. Taking a deep breath he put his game face back on and answered.

"Good evening Senator," Keller greeted.

"It is if you tell me this Gianni business is put to rest," Layton threw back smartly.

Keller controlled his temper, slowly blowing out the silent breath he took.

"It is under control Senator, as I told you before," he spoke again hearing the man sneer.

"It not under control unless you have the file destroyed, the people responsible fired or disposed of," Layton told him flatly.

"Senator there hasn't been movement from any of the parties involved," Keller responded.

"Really, then tell me why the Gianni file is on the loose somewhere in the general populous," he fired at a stunned Keller.

Fucker has his own moles in place, he thought angrily.

"We have located the person responsible Senator and we're handling that," he told them man beginning to lose the fight with calm and serenity.

Layton Crowler was a pompous ass. Unfortunately he also held Keller and several of his associate's futures in the palm of his hands.

"Hmph, well that much is good I suppose," he relented somewhat. "How long before this thing is completely contained Keller," Layton question yet another time. "I don't have to remind you the dire consequences if anyone, including Gianni, gets wind of this mess, now do I," he spoke, gaining a quick reply from Keller.

"I have agents moving as we speak Senator," he tried to placate once again. "We are going to make sure that there are no leaks, no links back to us, then we're going to seal the case and expose them," Keller finished.

Life After Death

"Fine, but make sure this time Keller," Layton told him. "If Dezi Gianni shows up on my doorstep, trust and fucking believe I'm going to send him to yours next," he added disconnecting without response.

Keller slammed the phone onto the oak desk in his private office; happy he was at home and didn't have to pretend he wasn't furious.

"These two assholes are causing way more fucking trouble than either of them are worth," he growled, pouring himself a triple shot and throwing it back.

He picked up the cell again, dialing his agents.

"Wire the house, I want to know everything this prick is doing, both of them as a matter of fact," Keller yelled. "And do a background on the whore he had a drink with the other night," he added of April, recalling the report on Edgar for that night.

"I want this net so fucking tight, that if they fart, I get the damned aroma," he finished and disconnected, pouring another shot, making another call.

"Hello Michael," Cassandra answered calmly.

"Get Alston to sign search warrants," he told her, again without greeting her.

"For," she returned tiredly, not wanting to subject herself any further to his temper.

"Marchant, his records, personnel file, bank accounts, the damned works," Keller flared yet another time. "I want one for his friend too, Hudson, Gaynelle Hudson," he told Cassandra as she wrote down the name.

"What are we looking for," she ventured to question.

"Any fucking thing that will drum them up out of the police force, in front of a grand jury, or public humiliation," he explained.

Cassandra frowned slightly afraid to ask him anything else, but hating to be left in the dark.

"What is going on," she pushed slightly.

Hearing him sigh deeply, Cassandra's gut clenched. For Keller to be this agitated, things were a code black for real.

"Gianni's FBI file is on the street," he told her and Cassandra swore aloud.

"What the hell, how," she again questioned disbelievingly.

Keller gave her a quick rundown of what was transpiring since she was assigned to North Carolina and Maurice Alston.

"Damn," Cassandra murmured.

"Yeah, so get those warrants signed and executed immediately," Keller fired as she sighed softly.

"Wait Michael," she told him. "I know you're upset, but think about it," Cassandra carefully continued. "Do you really want to tip your hand this soon, what if Marchant has contacted someone else and they know about the files," she tried.

"And this chick Gaynelle, by all accounts she's just a dispatcher who did him a favor," Cassandra explained quickly. "This is too sensitive to go in half assed Michael, Layton Crowler will crucify us, you especially, if this goes wrong," she finished and waited for him to speak.

The silence hung for long, pain filled moments, before Cassandra heard the heavy sigh and the two words.

"You're right," Keller spoke simply and disconnected.

Turning the glass over in his hands, his mind went to the DVD he still held.

"Time for some answers," he spoke, walking into his bedroom opening the small fire safe embedded in the wall behind his headboard.

•••

Layton lay his head back in the huge overstuffed desk chair, feet propped on the equally expansive mahogany desk, mind wandering. *"Don't make me come back and kill you Layton," Dezi growled, eyes flat and cold. "I keep my deals and my promises Dezi," Layton told him. "So do I," the man returned with malice, standing and leaving his home and his life forever.*

"Shit so I thought," Layton murmured aloud.

He wasn't Senator Layton Crowler then. He was Layton Crowler small town mayor with huge ambitions. Meeting Dezi Gianni changed his life, considerably for the better. The chance meeting at one of the city's most exclusive Italian eateries worked out to both their advantages when the waiter slipped Layton the business card bearing Gianni's name and telephone number. Layton wasn't stupid. He knew exactly who the man was and of course what he was capable of. Word was buzzing all over the streets and inside the police department he controlled from his office that Dezi Gianni and his partner Dirty were two of the biggest and best

Life After Death

syndicate connections in the state. Not averse to using dirty money to further his ambitions, Layton called the man an hour after leaving his political dinner.

"Nice of you to stop by Mayor," Dezi greeted as he walked into the expansive office. His partner sat in a leather chair similar to his own, sipping an open bottle of beer. "Drink," Dezi offered as Layton nodded yes. Walking away Layton spoke to Dirty. "How are you tonight," he questioned amiably. "I'm good, you," the man replied cheerily. Dezi returned with the liquor handing Layton the glass. "Let's get to business, Layton," he spoke, Dirty sitting up in his chair as well. Their deal was sealed that night with Layton opening up the city for The Clique and all the illegal dealings they were involved in. Dezi personally saw to his own appetites, no judgment, nor condemnation. *"She's waiting for you at the Miramar," Dezi told Layton the cool autumn night. "Room 1103," he added disconnecting. Layton quickly dressed, grabbing his keys, careful not to wake his wife and slipped out of the house.* The drive was about forty minutes to the hotel strategically located on the outskirts of the city, perfect for rendezvous by those seeking solace from prying eyes. He parked the Cadillac around the back of the hotel, climbing out and going up the stairs, quickly finding the room and knocking.

She opened the door and took Layton's breath away. Juicy, succulent lips touched his own as she invited him inside and loosened his tie. His hands immediately swept over her body caressing the tender supple flesh, firm mounds with pinpoint nipples turning his limp member instantly steel fortified. She undressed him without a word, going to her knees and sucking the head of his throbbing manhood, while he played with the soft dirty blonde hair. "Mmmm," Layton groaned, loving the feel of the lips on his shaft, her tongue sliding up and down coaxing his semen closer and closer to the top. "No, not yet," Layton managed to mumble pushing her away. She smiled as he pulled her to her feet, throwing her onto the full sized bed, pushing her legs apart as he fingered her and felt her opening grow wet with wanton lust. Layton kissed her then, the lips beckoning him with their fullness, his tongue sliding into her mouth as she moaned quietly. Past needy, he ended the kiss pushing her knees into her chest, his shaft sinking deeply inside the glistening pink folds of her love center. "Yessss," she moaned arching her back to take all of him. Layton rode her hard, fast and deep, desperately needing the release her extremely tight crevice would provide. In, god she felt good. Out, damn she was tight. In, he hadn't had sex this great in years. Out, he loved screwing her. In, shit he was about to cum. Out, she cried his name in ecstasy as she came first. In, his semen surged from his tense body, the pinnacle finally attained.

They relaxed after he finished, him lighting a cigarette and handing it to her. "That was incredible," she purred, taking a drag from the lit product, handing it back. Layton enjoyed his smoke as she began to speak another time. "Layton, you said you love me right," she questioned as he absently told her yes. He would tell her that from time to *time when she pouted or made him wait too long to screw her. "We're going to have a baby," she whispered garnering his full attention now. "What, you're pregnant," he replied, mind racing as he blinked rapidly. "OK, that's fine, no problem," he began calming slightly, thinking aloud. "I'll set up the appointment and you can have the abortion," he told her as she flew into a rage. "I'm not killing our baby," she screamed, terrifying him that someone would overhear. "I'm having this baby Layton, you said you loved me," she told him beginning to cry now. He was panicking. This was a nightmare. There was no way he could allow her to have this baby, or their affair to be made public. "I'm sorry baby, okay, calm down," he told her sweetly. "I thought you wanted to have an abortion," he quickly added as she looked at him warily before smiling and walking over to him. "I'm sorry," he added, kissing her now as she kissed him back. Turning she was headed into the bathroom to shower. Without thought Layton picked up the heavy glass ashtray and brought it down on the back of her head.*

She immediately slumped to the floor. Fully engulfed in rage, fear, and self-preservation, Layton hit her again and again, the blood pouring from her caved in skull. He hit her until the adrenaline rush left him and his arm was too weak to lift the murder weapon again. "Fuck," he swore under his breath, common sense returning. "What the fuck have I done, shit," Layton began to cry, blubbering crazily. He needed help. No one could find out about this, but what was he going to do. With no one else to call, Layton dialed Dezi's number. "What happened," the man questioned hearing Layton's hysterical ramblings. "Stay put," the man said simply. The twenty minutes it took Dezi and Dirty to get to the Miramar seemed like twenty years to Layton as he continued to sit in the chair regarding the dead body at his feet. The knock made him jump as he cautiously approached the door. "Open it," he heard Dezi's voice, complying without hesitation. The men's faces were expressionless as they regarded the body. A third man entered moments later, big and muscular, with a large black body bag. He placed the body in it without comment, turning and leaving the room and the three men still inside. "This didn't happen," Dezi said simply as Layton nodded his understanding. "Now, let's talk about your debt," he added and the small town Mayor knew his life now belonged to Dezi Gianni and The Clique. In his mind it was a small price to pay for saving it moments earlier. You didn't have sex with, get pregnant, and then kill, the 14-year old daughter of the city's police chief and live to tell it.

Layton closed his eyes and pulled the ice cube from the glass he still held, rubbing it across his temples to soothe the headache that was raging. He never regretted his merger with the powerful illegal operation, Dezi's financing and connections quickly catapulted him into the position he truly wanted. Even when things fell apart for the organization, Dezi kept his word, keeping him protected and out of the fire. He in turn kept his own promise, using his powerful influence to get the man sent out of the country, the agents removed from the case and both files classified and buried in obscurity. *Damned records clerks of all the fucked up bullshit*, Layton thought hearing his cell ring. Sighing deeply seeing Cassandra's name he picked up.

"Yes Agent Deale," he spoke formerly.

As much as Layton enjoyed banging her, he didn't need any appendages. His wife served her purpose for his political ambitions, no room for scandals, or sprung CIA agents.

"We need to talk Senator," Cassandra told him equally as brusque.

"Alright, what is it," he questioned.

"We have a small problem, but it won't stay that way long," she told him bringing a curious frown to his brow.

"Speak plainly, I'm not in the mood for drama," he told her, growing angry.

"I'm pregnant Senator, you're the father, and I want out of the damned CIA to live my life and raise my child," Cassandra fired, hearing the sound of a crash as the glass fell from Layton's hands.

"Meet me, the same spot, tomorrow night," he spat through clenched teeth breathing hard and disconnecting without another word.

Life After **16** Death

Dezi was listening as Arroyo filled them in on his connections here in London, but his mind was also still examining the information Adrian gave him when he called two weeks ago. The more he thought it over, the more he didn't like it.

"Symon is a good fellow, he will be most helpful to us," Arroyo told Dezi, and Big D.

Aidan stayed behind to make sure the operation continued to stay on point. That was something else Dezi needed to address. Something was bothering his son, but he was yet to speak about it. Dezi made plans to question the young man once they returned to the island.

"How long have you known this guy," Big D questioned, sipping the liquor in his glass.

They were relaxing in the expansive suite Dezi rented for the trip. Each of them had one, in the event they wanted to entertain as Dezi explained to Arroyo. Of course neither he, nor Dezi held any plans of cheating on their women. The man with them however was still single and by all accounts aggressively sexual.

"Symon and I became friends right out of college and have remained close over the years," Arroyo returned, as both men nodded without comment.

"So have you broached the idea of what we want with him already," Dezi now interjected.

"Yes, and he's very excited about your plans," Arroyo again answered honestly.

Big D watched Dezi off and on since they settled and knew something was on his friends mind. Playing his role however, he knew his friend enough to leave it alone, unless or until Dezi asked for his opinion or his help.

"Would he be averse to meeting earlier," Big D asked Arroyo.

The man frowned slightly but shrugged and pulled out his cell. Dezi was looking directly at Big D now, as his friend and partner, returned the gaze. Smiling slightly, he said nothing and finished his drink, the body language between them sharp and on point as per usual, as Arroyo wrapped up the call.

Life After Death

"He can meet us now if you wish," he told Big D and Dezi.

"Excellent idea," Dezi spoke.

He wanted to put everything in place, work through the details, and have the deal on track before going out into the city and meeting with Adrian. He called just before they left the island and Adrian immediately invited him to his home. Rising the men all left the suite and boarded the elevator. Dezi and Big D followed Arroyo's lead as they walked the short distance to the small pub found some three blocks away, walking inside and finding a table. They ordered more drinks, relaxing as they waited for Symon Marion to arrive. They wouldn't be kept in limbo long as the man materialized some ten minutes later, spotting Arroyo and walking over to the table.

"Hello old man," Symon greeted his friend as the two lightly embraced.

"Symon, this is Mr. Gianni and his partner Mr. D.," he told Symon.

"Good afternoon gentlemen," he spoke amiably, taking the seat offered and requesting a beer when the server returned to their table.

"Please call me Dezi," was the directive once they were all seated and served.

"And I'm Big D," came the other correction as Symon smiled and acquiesced to their requests.

"So gentlemen, Arroyo tells me there are a few channels I can help you open that will prove productively lucrative to all of us," Symon spoke as Dezi and Big D took him in.

Tall and lean, hawkish blue eyes, contrasting vastly against the deep ebony skin. Dezi almost smiled thinking how many people he must have unnerved when they first met him.

"Yes Symon, we're looking to expand our import and export companies," Dezi spoke diplomatically. "We are not averse to compensating those who help us, very well I might add, but we have to be sure of their loyalties," he continued, never taking his eyes off the man.

"I fully understand Dezi," Symon returned without hesitation. "I haven't lasted this long in my position without knowing how to play my hand I assure you," he added as Big D smiled slightly, liking the man's directness.

"Trust and believe, I'm interested in filling my coffers and being my own man, the days of my being a yes man to the demands of someone else I would just as soon see in my past," Symon spoke as Dezi again nodded.

"Excellent," Dezi spoke, smiling. "Let's talk routes, contracts, payoffs, and security," he added as the men all began speaking and conversing.

"The head of the port is easily paid without question or regret," Symon told them.

"Good, we have at least three ships that come to that particular port in the month," Big D told him.

"Hmph, you could increase it without suspicion," Symon told him.

"To how many," Dezi questioned, paying rapt attention, liking their new associate very much.

"Have the same three come at least twice a month," he told them, both Dezi and Big D nodding, liking the sound of his plans.

"Good, now let's talk of your compensation Symon," Dezi began anew.

"What did you have in mind Dezi," he questioned.

Arroyo already told him of the man's generosity in percentage, so he was waiting to see what he would be offered before bidding himself too high or too low.

"We're thinking 15% of the monthly hidden manifest, from the ships ported," Big D told him calmly, watching his reaction.

Symon didn't think it was a bad split. From what he observed doing a little research before the meeting, after speaking to Arroyo, that was still almost thirty thousand American dollars a month.

"That's a generous split," he replied as both Dezi and Big D smiled shortly.

"Good, with that settled, let's get back to business," Dezi spoke now.

The men continued to discuss the shipping and port exchanges for the next six months. At the conclusion of the meeting some three hours later, Arroyo announced he and Symon were going to dinner, asking Dezi and Big D to join them.

"I'm game," Big D spoke, rising as well.

"I already have plans," Dezi said simply.

The men graciously accepted his explanation and left him alone in the pub. Paying the tab, Dezi rose, and headed outside, hailing the small yellow taxi passing by and gave him a destination.

•••

Life After Death

Aidan was once again in stealth mode as he watched his wife at the market. Mariah was of course oblivious of her admirer, but Aidan saw him clearly as he watched her examining the fresh vegetables. *This idiot doesn't get it*, he thought inwardly. He missed seeing the man for quite a while, making a few simple inquiries and finding out he was assigned to some training expedition or other. It was apparent he was back however and instantly up to his old tricks. Seeing movement from the corner of his eye, Aidan turned his head back toward Mariah. She was making her way to the fresh seafood, purchasing crabs he was sure. She asked him if he wanted to cook them outside on the deck tonight and he amiably agreed. He loved the sweet spontaneity of her, always coming up with new ideas of things they could do together as a couple as well as a family. *You want that do you*, he questioned seeing the man finally making his move as he began walking toward the seafood area where Mariah was still choosing their catch for the evening. As before, Aidan saw her jump slightly having not seen the man as he approached her from her blind side. He watched as Stephan made himself comfortable leaning against the glass, chattering away as Mariah answered with a word or two, her attention never leaving the squirming crabs behind the glass she stared through.

Aidan plotted than casual observation today. It was time to put a stop to Stephan's attention toward his wife, as well as put Mariah at ease. He didn't want his wife uneasy about going through her normal daily routine, fear of harassment from this man's unsolicited advances. He was halfway inside the market now, eyes never leaving his intended target, as the man continued to regard his wife and try to engage her in conversation.

"Hello Mr. Aidan," the cashier greeted, smiling as he walked by her register.

"Hello," Aidan returned, with a short smile, not wanting to be rude.

Stephan was still deeply engrossed in Mariah and didn't notice his presence as yet. Aidan returned to his task, after the greeting, stopping on the other side of the isle that separated him from the two, wanting to hear what was being said.

"I can help you with those once you're done," Stephan told her.

"Thank you, but I'm fine," Mariah returned amiably.

"Really Mariah, it's no problem," he tried again.

"I haven't seen you for a while, were you on vacation," Mariah inquired as Aidan smiled faintly.

He knew from the tone of the question she was being sarcastic and basically saying she wished he would stay gone.

"No, official business, training," Stephan told her, trying to sound more official.

"How's Vanessa," Mariah questioned now, completing her task, waiting for the crabs to be bagged.

"She's fine," Aidan heard the man return tightly.

Almost chuckling yet another time, he straightened himself and walked around the corner.

"Hello darling," Aidan greeted his wife calmly, kissing her cheek as he walked up to her.

"Hi Aidan," Mariah returned, the fear evident.

She saw his anger plastered on his face.

"Stephan," he spoke evenly, teeth clenched.

"Mr. Gianni," Stephan returned defiantly.

"I was getting our seafood for tonight," Mariah tried, the tension thick between the two men.

"That's fine darling, are you ready to leave," he questioned, eyes never leaving Stephan.

"Yes, I'm ready," Mariah again tried, stepping between them forcing Aidan to look at her.

Her eyes pleaded with him not to do anything crazy.

"Come on then," he told her sweetly, taking the bagged seafood and her arm as they headed toward the checkout.

Stephan's eyes bored into the man's back, breathing hard as they walked away.

"Thank you," Mariah whispered to Aidan as they paid for their purchases and walked outside.

"I'm not going to have you accosted every time you go to the market Mariah," Aidan told her as he put her purchases in the trunk of the Benz.

"I know," she replied. "I haven't seen him in a while, I guess I was hoping the problem worked itself out," she told him as Aidan stroked her cheek.

Life After Death

"I'm going to take care of it," he told her, watching her eyes grow bigger.

"Aidan, no, please," Mariah pleaded as he chuckled aloud.

"Not that kind of take care of it," he teased seeing her visibly relax.

"Oh, okay, then what are you going to do," she questioned.

"Don't worry about it, go home and get everything ready," Aidan replied kissing her again and helping her into the car.

He stood and watched until the car disappeared around the corner, turning his gaze toward the market, eyes meeting the baleful stare of Stephan. Smirking, Aidan turned and headed toward his own vehicle, getting in and heading for his destination.

●●●

Adrian smiled demurely inviting Dezi inside. "Would you like a drink," he questioned.

"Cognac, if you have it," Dezi replied taking a seat on the snow white sofa and surveying the room.

Adrian did have very good taste and Dezi saw that he did very well with all the money Monster left him upon his death.

"Here you are," he spoke again walking back into the room and handing Dezi the glass.

"Thank you," he replied, taking it and sipping the chilled golden liquor contained.

"How have you been Adrian," he questioned now, relaxing.

"I can't complain, like I told you, I'm coping day by day," he spoke again as Dezi nodded slightly.

"So tell me more about your visitor," he began, getting to the crux of his visit.

Adrian sighed lightly, shrugging a bit before speaking.

"It wasn't sinister or anything like that," he began telling Dezi. "I guess it just didn't really seem to jive with what he was trying to sell me, you know," Adrian spoke.

"How so," Dezi inquired.

Adrian shook his head back and forth, as if he were still trying to catalog it himself.

"It was like he was looking for something specific," Adrian put into words.

"A particular person, or was it something else," Dezi again asked.

"A person," Adrian replied looking him in the eye. "He asked a lot of questions about you," he told him as Dezi raised an eyebrow.

The front door opened and the young man walked inside carrying the large take out bag.

"Hello," Nesby said pointedly giving the man sitting with Adrian a look.

Dezi smiled slightly, sipping his drink but not speaking.

"Nesby," Adrian spoke sharply. "This is an old friend of mine and we're discussing some business," he fired off, his irritation plainly on display.

"Put the food in the kitchen, then give us some privacy," he finished as the hurt showed on the young man's face.

"Of course, I'm sorry," he contritely returned before scurrying into the kitchen.

Adrian and Dezi remained quiet until he came back into the room and bounded up the stairs to the bedroom. Hearing the door close and the muted sound of the stereo moments later, Adrian and Dezi resumed their conversation.

"So you think he's fishing for information about me," Dezi spoke.

"Yes, but I don't know the true reason why," Adrian told him. "I mean I guess it could be some class, but honestly, of all the cases they would have since your time on the West Coast, why yours," he finished his rationale of reason.

Dezi wholeheartedly agreed. It was entirely too farfetched now that he got the opportunity to talk to Adrian face to face and get his true take on the visit. That irritation was coming again. Not a good thing for those involved.

"Where is his information," he put to Adrian as his old friend rose from his seat and walked over to a beautifully and intricately decorated black and gold oriental box, opening it and removing the business card.

Walking back to Dezi, Adrian handed it to him. "What do you think he's really after," he questioned knowing Dezi's mind was working.

Life After Death

"Hard to say," Dezi answered. "He may just be a nosey kid looking for a way to climb the ladder," he continued. "He could be someone trying to bring down some of the people in power by digging up old secrets," Dezi told Adrian, who exhaled noisily.

"I just want him to go away and leave us alone," he spoke aloud. "We've been living our lives for years without interruption," he added as Dezi immediately agreed with him.

"Don't give it thought, Adrian," he told him finishing the drink.

"I'm going to reach out to a few people of my own and see just what exactly mister," Dezi stopped for a moment to read the card.

"Mr. JaDon Ivory, FBI, is actually up too," he finished as Adrian chuckled slightly from the sarcasm in Dezi's voice reading the card.

"I hope you're friend isn't too angry when I leave," he teased Adrian who rolled his eyes.

"He's just a diversion for now, so I suggest not," he told Dezi who smiled as well.

"There will never be another Kevin," he spoke wistfully as Dezi sighed deeply in full agreement with him. He still missed both Monster and Dirty to this day, thinking of his friends often, always bringing a smile to his face.

"I'll contact you after I get some more information," Dezi told Adrian, standing at the door. "If you hear from him again, let me know," he added.

"Of course," Adrian replied. "Take care of yourself Dezi," he added, gaining another smile from Dezi who repeated the sentiment to him before walking out of the door and hearing it close behind him.

His mind was already on the call he would make once he made it back to the hotel and his suite.

•••

Stephan walked into the police station, stopping in his tracks seeing Aidan sitting calmly inside Kareek's office.

"Stephan, come here now," he bellowed immediately upon seeing the officer come inside.

Dammit, what now, he groused mentally walking toward the office, storing his temper so that it didn't get the better of him.

"Sit down," Kareek barked as Aidan rose to leave.

"Thank you Chief Anketil," he spoke calmly, not looking at Stephan.

"You're welcome Mr. A. Gianni, I apologize again," Kareek returned solemnly as Aidan nodded and left them alone, walking casually out of the front door.

"Why must you continually make my life hard," Kareek barked at Stephan now that they were alone.

"What are you talking about," Stephan returned, sick of the attitude, especially when he had no concept of why he was being chewed out.

"I'm talking about Mr. A. Gianni coming here and asking me to reign in my officer because he's making his wife uncomfortable," Kareek yelled.

Both Jacob and Joell turned their attention to the chief's office hearing the raised voice, just as quickly disregarding them when Kareek threw a chastising look their way.

"What," Stephan began, flabbergasted. "I have never harassed Ma --, Mrs. Gianni," he protested.

Kareek's eyes narrowed as he regarded the man before him. "You did not approach her this morning at the market," Kareek questioned.

"Yes, but we simply enjoyed a pleasant conversation with me asking if she needed help getting her purchases to her car," Stephan defended; furious Aidan was causing him this grief.

"That's not what her husband says," Kareek returned, emphasizing the word husband.

"He says his wife was visibly upset upon your approaching her," he went on. "I've also gotten reports this isn't the first time you've accosted Mrs. A. Gianni," Kareek told him giving him another look.

Fucking Joell, Stephan thought behind the expression. The man unfortunately saw him at the market and once at a café approach Mariah.

"You cannot abuse your authority as a law officer to intimidate the population you are sworn to protect," Kareek told him angrily.

"You're suspended for three days," he finished as a final point, watching as Stephan's face darkened in anger.

"You're suspending me for having a conversation," he yelled.

Life After Death

"NO," Kareek yelled back. "I'm suspending you for harassing a woman, and intimidating her," he finished, his tone and look daring Stephan to continue the insubordination.

"Fine," Stephan huffed, rising roughly from the chair, stomping from Kareek's office.

Plopping down in the chair at his cubicle, he brought up the computer wanting to log some items before beginning his suspension. His fury continued to boil as he thought about Aidan. *I'm going to make him very sorry,* Stephan fumed.

"Stephan, leave now," Kareek bellowed, seeing him at this desk.

Without another word he rose grabbing his keys and tramped out of the station slamming the door behind him.

Life After 17 Death

Marchant smiled slightly as he stretched getting out of the cruiser. Last night was his final night on special detail. Today he was off, and tomorrow he would return to his beloved day shift. The month he spent helping the undercover narcotics unit seemed like the longest in his life. He was looking forward to getting inside, having a nice cup of coffee and a quick breakfast, showering and sleeping. His neighbor, Mrs. Coleman, unfortunately had other ideas walking across the street, greeting him cheerily.

"Good morning Dwayne," she spoke happily.

Marchant conjured a smile, pasting it on his face as he turned and returned her greeting.

"Morning, Mrs. Coleman," he spoke as she continued to regard him.

"I know you're tired, but I just had to come over and say thanks," she told him.

Marchant held no idea what she was talking about, but decided to simply acknowledge the thanks in the hope it would hasten her departure.

"You're very welcome Mrs. Coleman," Marchant returned deceptively.

She laughed lightly.

"I love when it's your turn for neighborhood watch," she began to chatter again. "Having the officers sitting out here all day and even the evening makes us all feel so much safer," Mrs. Coleman enlightened, immediately peaking Marchant's curiosity.

What is she talking about, he wondered behind the small smile still remaining.

"I see they're gone this morning," she told him as Marchant nodded slightly.

"I hope the car didn't make it too obvious," he fished seeing if he could get her to tell him more.

"Oh no, not at all," Mrs. Coleman answered. "It looked very normal, dark blue, a Ford, I think," she added as Marchant's mind continued to process the information, trying to arrive at a plausible answer.

Life After Death

"I'll let you go now," she told him, reaching over and patting his arm sweetly.

"Thanks again Dwayne, you get some rest now, you look exhausted," she added before turning and scurrying down the sidewalk continuing her morning powerwalk.

What the hell, Marchant was still thinking as his eyes scanned the neighborhood. *Why would an unmarked car be here, what were they looking for, were they watching me,* all the questions barraged him at once, causing him to finally turn and head for his house. The question of why continued to assail him. Was he under investigation for something? Marchant knew one thing, being under surveillance was not a good thing. Mrs. Coleman said they were gone this morning, so maybe they were watching someone else in the neighborhood; Marchant continued to try and consider. In his mind it made more sense for them to be around now that he was home continually. *You were home then, asleep,* his mind recalled, bringing a deep acidic frown.

"Shit," Marchant swore aloud.

He thought about the case he spent the last month working on. Did someone make him? Were these guys posing as cops to get to him?

"Shit," he murmured again.

There was a strong possibility his life was in jeopardy.

Marchant picked up the phone and called Captain Wilmont.

"Hi Dwayne," she greeted amiably once the call connected. "I thought you would be in bed by now," she teased chuckling lightly.

Marchant smiled a bit, before speaking.

"I'm on my way," he told her. "I just wanted to check on something first," Marchant added.

"Do you know of any surveillance assignments in my neighborhood," he questioned the Captain.

Caroline told him to hold on a moment and left him listening to the various wanted bulletins while he held. *This sucks, we need new hold music,* Marchant pondered as the monotone voice of the announcer continued to tell them about one wanted criminal after the other. Captain Wilmont's voice once again filled his ear as Marchant tuned in again and paid attention.

"No, I don't see anything remotely near your house, Dwayne," Caroline told him. "Is something going on," she questioned the concern in her voice.

"I'm not really sure, one of my neighbors happened to mention seeing a car that sounded like an unmarked unit, parked on the street for a few days," Marchant told her as Caroline, acknowledged his statement.

"Do you think it's something," she questioned now.

Marchant thought about it a bit longer before answering.

"Nah, I think maybe just a case of overactive imagination," he told her forcing the chuckle.

Caroline laughed lightly.

"OK, well get some sleep and I'll see you bright and early tomorrow morning," she spoke before disconnecting.

Rising Marchant went into his office, booting up his computer, wanting to check his emails. He was sure there were hundreds by now, not having checked them since before the assignment. *Too tired,* he thought of the long and odd hours the assignment required. The slight bleep of the Windows program loading broke his thought as he glanced at the computer screen seeing it was updating, decided to go and make his coffee. Marchant walked into his kitchen unconsciously glancing out of the window, the information still fresh in his mind about the vehicle Mrs. Coleman saw. Looking up and down the street as far as the window's vision field would allow; he saw nothing. The neighborhood looked perfectly normal. No cars that didn't belong, no strange people walking the streets. Marchant put the scoop of coffee into the coffeemaker and set it to start. Going over to his refrigerator he took out a couple of eggs, pulling the skillet from the cabinet and placing it on the eye of the stove, turning it on. He picked up the loaf of wheat bread, examining it for mold, not sure when it was purchased. Finding none, he plucked two pieces from inside the plastic bag, and placed them into the gleaming stainless steel toaster. Pushing the toast down, Marchant returned his attention to the eggs, heating the skillet and adding a bit of oil, he cracked them dropping them into the sizzling skillet watching them begin to bubble and pop as they cooked. His breakfast complete some five minutes later, Marchant poured his coffee and sat down to enjoy, the fatigue already wearing on him. He decided in the midst of eating that the computer and his email could wait just a little longer.

●●●

Layton Crowler inhaled deeply the fresh sea air, thankful that things seemed to be returning to normal. The drama of the past month wore on him, making him tense and short fused. *Damned Keller,* he thought irritably of the

Life After Death

CIA deputy director. Layton couldn't be too upset however, the man kept his word and effectively neutralized the situation. The records clerks were still under surveillance but so far did done nothing to warrant any further action on their end. As far as he knew, everything in North Carolina was also fine. Thinking about the state brought Cassandra and their last encounter to mind. *"Look Senator, I don't want shit from you except a way out," Cassandra told him angrily after he accused her of trying to trap him with a child he didn't want.* "*And I'm supposed to believe you're going to have this kid, go away, and never come back," Layton fired. "How fucking stupid do you think I am," he continued to rail. "I didn't get this far by leaving loose ends," he told her as Cassandra regarded him evenly. "Look I didn't get pregnant on purpose, trust and believe you are not the man I envisioned fathering my child," she returned hatefully. Layton laughed aloud then. "Yeah, I'm sure, but we both know Michael Keller isn't interested in anything outside of his job," he told her nastily, seeing the tears come and her blink them back. "Anyway, I just want you to pull the strings and get me out of agency without drama," Cassandra told him, not addressing his previous statement. "You don't stand here and make demands of me," Layton yelled. "I can make you fucking disappear and no one would blink or ask a single question," he threatened. "And I can destroy your career with a single phone call," Cassandra threw back. A scandal of this sort would effectively end his senate career and any plans for a presidential bid that may have loomed in his mind.*

"Fine," Layton finally acquiesced. "But you finish this case first, make sure, and I mean damned sure, that this detective does not cause me any more drama, ever," he addressed as Cassandra shrugged. "Deal," she said simply before Layton stepped closer to her, looking into her eyes. "Don't cross me Cassandra, that wouldn't be a good look, or a smart move," he threatened as she sighed softly and turned leaving the suite where they met.

"Hey Pop, mom says to come inside, we're about to eat," his son Layton Jr., spoke breaking his thought.

The smile returning Layton followed his eldest inside the bungalow, heading to the bathroom to wash his hands.

"Please don't let any of this shit come back to bite me," he murmured as he lathered his hands.

Looking at the reflection staring back at him, Layton thought about all the dirt done over the years and asked himself if it were worth it.

"Hell yes," he immediately answered.

The good life was one he never planned to relinquish and nothing, or anyone, would stand in the way of that. *Do you really trust her,* his mind asked another time concerning Cassandra and the child she carried that he fathered.

"Honey would you like wine with your lunch or iced tea," his wife's voice filtered in before he answered himself, dismissing the conversation.

"Wine would be nice honey," he returned amiably, opening the door and stepping out into the hallway, kissing her softly as he smiled at him.

Francine, his wife, was his faithful supporter, partner, lover, friend for over twenty years. True he enjoyed his side trysts, he would never think of leaving her. She gave him two handsome sons, both of whom finished college and were doing very well in their respective fields. Layton was hoping to talk his namesake into following his political footsteps, but so far, the younger Crowler was proving rather unmoved by the political machine.

"This looks wonderful," Layton remarked of lobster salad that graced his plate.

"How are things going at the firm," he asked his younger son, Mark.

"Great dad, got some new cases just this week," he told his father as everyone began to eat and continue to catch up.

Neither of the boys were married yet, but they were in committed relationships. Layton liked Mark's choice far better than Layton Jr.'s, the woman he dated was very cold and superficial. Hopefully he was simply screwing her and not seriously contemplating marrying her. *Might have to intervene before it's over with,* he thought continuing to enjoy his meal. 'Devastator baby, I'm that devastator,' the phone chirped as Mark quickly grabbed it, grinning sheepishly at his mother who gave him a look concerning the rap ringtone. The song itself didn't bother Layton, it was the words that caused him pause. *Devastator,* he thought the involuntary chill running through him. He said another silent prayer thankful that Keller successfully warded off that threat. That was a name, and a man, Layton Crowler prayed never showed up at his front door again.

• • •

Rested and refreshed, Marchant walked inside the local public library. He needed to get out of the house for a while and he knew this place would not only be quiet, but he could catch up on all the latest periodicals and magazines for free. Marchant didn't see the need to subscribe when he could come here, sit in air conditioned comfort, and enjoy them just as well.

Life After Death

Walking over the bank of computers they set up for patron use, Marchant entered his library I.D. and went to his AOL account, logging in. He began scanning the 485 messages the icon told him were present in his in box.

"Trash, trash, trash," he murmured clicking on several messages, marking them for deletion.

He repeated the action several times before narrowing the remaining field to a mere 25 messages.

"Much better," he again spoke aloud, his eyes finding one that intrigued him.

Marchant scrolled down to the message with the subject line, 'Mikayla Bradford', and clicked on it. Taking a deep breath he opened the message and began to read the words from one Stephan Eveson, deputy in Pembroke Parish. *Found you,* Marchant thought excitedly. He quickly sent a reply to the deputy telling him that the woman he described was indeed the one he sought for questioning in a double homicide. Hitting the send button, Marchant smiled broadly. Hopefully the deputy would be willing to help him detain Kayla for questioning. *You want to do more than question her,* the pesky voice in his head spoke up.

Dismissing it, Marchant allowed himself to get excited. Finally she was within his grasp and he would get some answers, real answers, from her. He quickly pulled up the airline websites, searching for ticket prices to the island. Marchant wasn't wasting any time. As soon as deputy Eveson replied to his email, he was going to be pushing for the man to help him and poised to fly over and pick up his prize. *What about the Captain's orders,* his mind again posed. Marchant knew Captain Wilmont would be angry he continued to work the case against her orders, but his bringing back the person responsible would definitely dissolve that anger. *What about the boyfriend,* yet another concern popped up. Marchant was almost positive she was still with the man.

"Maybe Eveson can take care of him," he mumbled, not wanting any negative energy to come into his psyche.

He was too close to looking into the beautiful face of the woman he suspected was a deadly black widow. *Stop lying to yourself Dwayne, tell the truth at least to your heart,* his mind accused as Marchant again adamantly refused to accommodate. His cell vibrated breaking his thought as he glanced at the display not recognizing the number. Signing off quickly, he answered in a hushed whisper, telling the party to hold for a moment as he readily made his way into the outer hallway of the library.

"Dwayne Marchant," he spoke at a normal tone.

"How you doing Dwayne, this is Marty Canfield, from LAPD," the man identified himself.

"Oh hey, how's it going Marty," Marchant returned amiably.

He was curious why the man called, but let the conversation progress without the question being asked.

"Listen, I don't know what's going on fully, but that woman you asked about, Mikayla DeWitt," he told Marchant, his tone hurried and hushed as if he were worried about being overheard.

"Yeah, what about it," Marchant questioned, his own uneasiness descending, picking up on the anxiety in the other man's tone.

"Well it started a damned firestorm here," he told him honestly. "Man, I was called into my Captain's office, busted my chops for over an hour about seeing you and giving you info," Marty told him.

"They don't think I know, but a friend of mine close to the Cap, said the Feds are involved, I don't know how deep, but I just wanted to warn you to watch your back man," he finished and waited on Marchant to speak.

The detective was shaken. *The feds, why, I'm just working on a local case*, he thought inwardly.

"Damn, yeah, that's really crazy," Marchant returned. "Thanks for calling Marty, I'll certainly keep my eyes and ears open," he told him as they disconnected.

Marchant's mind instantly returned to his conversation with Mrs. Coleman.

"Dammit, were they feds," he murmured, reaching into his pants pockets and retrieving his keys.

The magazines and periodicals would have to wait. Marchant needed to get home and study the file and information he procured another time. He was obviously missing something and whatever that something was; some entity of the federal government was definitely not interested in him uncovering it.

Life After Death

Life After 18 Death

JaDon grabbed the file and tossed it into his book bag. Sighing lightly he picked up the prepaid cell phone and texted Gar. The two were the most unlikely of allies these days after being pulled into their respective bosses offices and threatened with suspension over the Gianni affair. JaDon's curiosity was further peaked after the meeting with Vernon. He understood the man's anger over protocol being broken, even the theft of the file folder, but there was so much more Vernon Spoelman wasn't saying and that was the part that titillated JaDon. He talked to April less than an hour after the meeting and returning the file, and she told him about Gar going through basically the same thing. Thankfully JaDon kept presence of mind to make a copy, so they weren't left empty handed. After April brokered a truce of sorts between the two men, they began the tenuous task of actually working together. Whatever the FBI and CIA collectively were trying to hide about this case, JaDon was determined to uncover.

The cell buzzed confirming that Gar was on his way to the meeting spot. JaDon sent another text, this time to April, asking if she found anything else. She was their only set of eyes and ears and unfortunately her clearance didn't allow much, but it was better than nothing. Her reply was swift. 'Nothing new, everyone is quiet,' the message read as JaDon locked his front door and walked to his car getting inside. He began cataloging everything they learned in the last month as he drove. His mind continually returned to Adrian Roberts. *Something isn't quite right there*, JaDon fashioned, turning into the parking lot of the seedy motel. He and Gar took the extraordinary measure of meeting here after their respective lectures. Paranoia was the only thing that kept them on their toes these days. They weren't stupid. The FBI and CIA had very long arms and they didn't put it past either agency to have them under surveillance. JaDon parked and headed into the main lobby retrieving a key. He already made the reservation days earlier. Entering the room he flipped on the light and inspected it. He wasn't sure what he was looking for, but one could never be too careful, JaDon surmised. Satisfied moments later that the room was fine, and taking several peeks from the lone window, JaDon began unpacking the file and all the notes they made together.

The cellphone buzzed again alerting him Gar was pulling up and getting out. JaDon rose and counted slowly to ten, opening the door just as the man walked up, coming speedily inside.

"What's up," JaDon greeted.

"Nothing really," Gar replied, putting his own bag down and unloading a second set of notes.

"So what do we have actually," he questioned as JaDon sighed deeply.

"Hell, nothing from what I can see," he replied honestly.

They were following every lead and hunch from the files archives and each time hitting a veritable dead end.

"Are you sure this guy, Adrian Roberts, are you sure he's telling you everything," Gar questioned looking at JaDon steadily.

"Probably not," JaDon conceded. "But what can I do, he's only going to tell me what he chooses too, and I have no jurisdiction otherwise," he told Gar who nodded, but continued to gaze at the notes thoughtfully.

"OK, what I'm about to say is going to sound farfetched, but hear me out," Gar began as JaDon gave him his undivided attention.

"All the leads we've followed lead us to a big fat nothing," Gar began. "It's almost like someone planted them in here just for that very reason," he continued as JaDon withheld comment. "It started to make me wonder why; why go through all this drama for a case that is supposedly closed and solved," Gar threw out, to which JaDon had no answer; at least not one he wanted to embrace.

"Like I said, this is going to sound crazy, but I think this Gianni guy is alive and well someplace far, far, off the radar," he finished and waited on JaDon to speak.

●●●

"They're at the Comfort Inn, Westside," the agent told Keller who listened intently.

"Who else is there," Keller questioned.

"No one," the agent returned.

"Keep an eye on them, when they leave let me know," he directed.

"You want them trailed," the agent questioned again.

"No, not yet," he returned and disconnected.

Life After Death

These two jackasses are making my life hard, he thought making himself another drink. Keller suspected the two men didn't give up their quest. At the rate they were going, killing them both was becoming more and more a viable option in his mind. Keller didn't forget the reaming he received from Layton Crowler a month ago. *Asshole,* Keller continued to think. He smiled slightly however thinking about the DVD and its contents. When he was ready he would use the information and get Crowler off his back permanently. *Shouldn't drink and talk,* Keller again thought chuckling aloud. His cell rang again and he answered.

"Yes Cassandra," he spoke amiably enough.

"Hello Michael," she returned calmly. "Detective Marchant is off night shift now," she told him, confirming what he already knew.

Keller wasn't taking any chances. He put his own agents in North Carolina, ones he knew were fully loyal to him. Cassandra thought he didn't know about Layton Crowler and them screwing a few months back. He did, and he was still pissed about it.

"Has there been any movement," he questioned, already knowing the answer.

"No, for now he seems to be content to do his job, no other questions about Mikayla or Gianni," she informed.

"How is the good judge," Keller questioned pointedly.

"He's fine and still a team player," she returned dryly.

"Good, see that it stays that way," he told her, his mind formatting a scenario he was thinking of employing. "We may be needing him sooner than I planned," he added hearing her murmur her understanding.

"Keller, listen, I need a favor," Cassandra began anew.

Intrigued, he asked her to continue.

"If anything should happen to me --," she started as he interrupted.

"What's wrong Cassandra," he fired knowing the assignment wasn't dangerous.

"Nothing, it's just that --," she began and hesitated once again.

"OK, if anything should happen to you, what," Keller questioned, not pushing for the reasoning just yet.

"Have a cup of coffee at our spot and think of me," she told him and he instantly understood.

"Of course, I'll think of you very fondly," he told her.

"Thank you Michael," Cassandra returned softly.

Keller frowned slightly. Cassandra Deale was no one's bitch. What in the world, or who in the world, could have her frightened enough to put insurance in place?

"But unless there is something you aren't telling me, that you should, you're going to be just fine Cassandra," Keller returned trying to draw her out.

"I promise when we have this Gianni case under lock and key once again, I will tell you everything," Cassandra returned ending the conversation as she disconnected.

Keller's mind was racing at speed of light. Yet another mystery he needed solved. Keller didn't like being in the dark about anything and this secret with Cassandra was cloaked in midnight.

•••

JaDon was still thinking about their plan. It was dangerous if they were caught, but the curiosity was driving them both over the edge. *That's got to be the real reason,* he thought recalling Gar's words. JaDon immediately told him it didn't sound crazy at all, making perfect sense to him as well. Of course if they were right, that only brought about an entirely new set of questions. Why did they fake this guy's death? Who is Dezi Gianni holding dirt on? Where was he now? Question after question piled into his mind as he continued to drive. They decided that Adrian Roberts was their best lead. They needed to talk to him again, really press him for better answers. Gar was going to London this time. JaDon's bank account still was yet to recover from the first trip. Gar informed him that he already set money aside for a vacation later this year and would simply use that. *Must be nice,* JaDon thought fleetingly, wondering if his reluctant partner would get more out of the man than he did.

Gar was going to use the same ruse, saying he was working with JaDon on the project for class, which wasn't that far of a stretch. He would tell Adrian that JaDon left off some of the more important questions and he wanted to ask them, as well as get the interview recorded live with pictures as well as voice. They talked it over, rehearsing several times so that it sounded plausible. Gar would make the call tomorrow and let him know if Adrian

Life After Death

agreed. *Please let him say yes,* JaDon was growing more and more excited. If Gianni was indeed alive and they could find him, they would rocket up their respective ladders, especially after they exposed all the crooked internal players who set up the scenario. *Money definitely will be hella better,* JaDon thought as he pulled into his driveway. His apartment was okay, it beat the streets, but an apartment on the posh northern side of the city would definitely improve his status.

"For once let this jerk be able to do something right," JaDon murmured getting out of the car and heading for his front door.

Walking inside he put his keys on the foyer table and walked down the short hallway into his living room.

Relaxing on his couch JaDon continued to think about the Gianni file.

"The son," he murmured aloud a revelation hitting him.

The young man was alive and well according to the last update in the file. *Wonder if April can locate him,* JaDon thought. That was a great place to start. Surely the son would know where his father was.

"What if they told him he was dead too," JaDon again murmured aloud.

"Shit," he groused going back and forth still in his mind.

It was worth a try he finally decided, texting April and telling her what he needed. 'Will try, might be a while, things are very tense' she texted back. JaDon typed another reply before rising and heading for his bedroom. Undressing he climbed into the shower letting the hot water cascade over his body. *What are you doing,* his mind began. *If this thing goes sour, your FBI career is over, done, finished,* his conscience continued. *This isn't TV, you don't get a new episode next week, if they fire you, you're done forever,* the thoughts continued. *You'll be lucky to get a job as mall security,* the final thought hit as JaDon frowned severely.

Yes it was risky, but the intrigue and mystery surrounding this man was just too delicious not to have a taste.

"Just have to make sure it goes right," he again murmured finishing his shower and stepping out of the tub.

His Blackberry chimed, the familiar ringtone causing a deep sigh as he answered.

"This is JaDon," he spoke crisply.

Never mind that it was 10PM and he was off work for hours, when Vernon Spoeling called, you answered the phone.

"Be in my office tomorrow morning, 7AM," he fired devoid of greeting.

"Yes sir," JaDon replied hearing the prompt click of the phone disconnecting.

What now, he questioned wearily. *Maybe he's reconsidered and is going to fire you after all,* his fear spoke up. They were getting closer, he needed more time. Whatever he had to do tomorrow, or say, to convince Vernon not to fire him, he would, JaDon vowed. *He's probably mixed up in this bullshit someplace too,* JaDon thought, pleased to believe he may be able to prove the theory and rid himself of the man permanently.

"Come on Gar, pull this off, we need it," he mumbled once again, pulling the covers back on the queen sized bed and climbing in.

Closing his eyes, JaDon was in a deep sleep almost instantly, any further contemplation put aside until a new day.

●●●

Keller was still drinking and brooding. There was too much going on, too many players, too many loose ends. *How the hell can anything be contained within all this chaos,* he thought moodily, sipping the vodka letting it slowly burn its way down his throat. His agent reported the two men left the motel heading it seemed for their respective places of residence. They were up to something, that much Keller was sure of. He called Vernon and told him they needed to take more drastic proactive measures. Both men were being reassigned. He already handled his end with Gar Simon's superior, and Vernon was dealing with JaDon Ivory in the morning. They were being put on babysitting detail for the most part, each shadowing one of the Senator's daughters. It would keep them out of the office, away from FBI and CIA files, and highly visible for Keller's teams. He was done however. If the two men insisted on pursuing the Gianni case, Keller put more sinister plans in place to deal with them. Plans that would guarantee they never caused any more trouble, all without a slight ripple in the agency pools. *Let's hope for their sakes, they don't make me take it that far,* Keller surmised, finishing the drink and rising to head to bed.

He fleetingly thought of Cassandra again as he undressed, deciding on a morning shower, and falling into the king bed. She was a reasonably good lay when they shared sex, but he didn't love her. *That's what she wanted,* his mind told him as Keller sighed lightly.

Life After Death

"Don't they all," he spoke aloud of women in general.

Keller wasn't married and was in no hurry. He enjoyed female companionship, but until he reached the plateau of his career, settling down was simply not on the menu. *She might have been a viable candidate, that is, until she slept with Layton's lecherous ass,* he thought and frowned again, admitting only to himself the slight hurt, anger, and jealousy he felt. *Thought you didn't love her, liar,* his mind instantly taunted.

"Water under the bridge," Keller murmured aloud closing his eyes as sleep quickly found him and the dreams took over.

"I had nothing to do with any of this," Layton Crowler was speaking eloquently as the microphones held took in every word. "Deputy Director Michael Keller was the mastermind and the chief conspirator to allow such a dangerous criminal as Dezi Gianni to leave this country and circumvent prosecution," he continued without pause. "Lying sonofabitch," Keller yelled producing the Luger pistol, firing three shots, each of them hitting their mark. He saw Layton fall slowly, crumpling to the ground, as he heard the screaming and felt the burning. "Gun," the first agent yelled. "Take him down," another barked as they shot Keller again and again. The pain was ebbing as his breathing grew shallow. "Get medics," he vaguely heard. "Is the Senator alive," another asked. "We have a weak pulse," was the answer as Keller struggled to breathe. "What about this one," the agent asked venomously. "Don't let his ass die, too easy," came the acidic reply. "We want the pleasure of disgracing and locking his traitorous ass up." Keller bolted from his sleep, sweat pouring, gasping for air until his surroundings became recognizable again.

"Christ," he murmured the dream replaying as he sat and gathered himself. "Time to finish this shit for real," Keller again murmured, collapsing back into bed, exhaustion finally taking its toll as he again slept, this time devoid of dreams.

Life After 19 Death

Stephan was still smiling as he opened the computer again, heading straight for his email account. *Looks like the tables are about to turn on fucking Aidan and his arrogant ass father,* he thought recalling the reply he received from Detective Dwayne Marchant. He was indeed a legitimate detective and he was indeed looking for the same Mikayla Bradford, aka Gianni, which resided here on the island. The screen came to life and Stephan typed in the URL, waiting to be taken to the page. The computer seemingly took forever, his impatience beginning to overtake him. Finally the login screen appeared and he typed in his user ID and password. Hitting enter, the screen whirled again, bringing up his inbox as Stephan's eyes greedily scanned the unopened messages landing as a final point on the one he was looking for. Hovering the mouse pointer directly over it, he clicked, watching it open, eager to read the contents. 'Thank you for the information you sent Officer Eveson,' it began. 'I believe that your Mikayla Gianni and my Mikayla Bradford are one in the same person,' the message continued as Stephan's smile grew with each word. The detective told him he was interested in questioning the woman, asking if they could work out an agreement for him to travel to the island and do just that.

Stephan thought quickly. He of course wanted the detective to come, but he must be careful. Kareek was unquestioningly loyal to both Gianni's, with Arroyo Trufont now snuggly in their pockets as well. Stephan knew he could use this situation to not only unseat Kareek, but bring down both Gianni's in one fell swoop.

"And have Mariah all to myself," he murmured, his mind recalling the woman again for him.

Stephan smiled slightly still trying to conjure a plan that would accomplish all his goals quickly, quietly, and effectively. Deciding he needed to buy a little more time to think, Stephan instead clicked open his photo file atop his computer's desktop and found a photograph of Kayla. He kept pictures of them all from various events, around town, and daily life. Stephan was plotting for a long time to enjoy the lifestyle of the Gianni's and Trufont's of the world. Now Dwayne Marchant was about to provide that to him on a silver platter. Attaching the photo to the email, Stephan began to type his reply. 'Detective Marchant, before you take the long flight, and it possibly be a wild goose chase, I've attached a photograph of the woman here known as Mikayla Gianni,' Stephan typed. 'If this is the woman you're

Life After Death

seeking, please let me know and we will then make plans for your visit and her detention for questioning,' he finished and hit send.

That would buy him a few more days to plot and make plans, Stephan mused, knowing he would simply ignore the computer for the next few days until he was ready to move forward. Detective Marchant was on his time schedule, and this time, everything would move when he said so. His mind went to Kayla and how he would get her to the station without Dezi's knowledge or intervention. *There needs to be another trip,* Stephan mused thinking of the past deep sea fishing trip. Still there must be a way, he just wasn't seeing it yet. Picking up his keys Stephan headed out of the front door. He was on the last day of his three day suspension. His cell phone chimed almost simultaneously as he sat behind the wheel and started the vehicle.

"Hello Vanessa," he returned actually cheerful.

Stephan's mind was busily enjoying his latest acquisition of information and the perceived power and wealth it would eventually reward him.

"Hi darling," she purred into the phone. "I'm all alone," she told him, intriguing his interest, knowing her father should have been at home as well.

"Why is that, where is your father," he questioned, growing slightly excited that the man might possibly be out of town and one or both Gianni's with him.

"He's at the office silly," Vanessa returned, deflating his hopes and dashing his good mood.

"Oh, okay," he managed to reply without resentment in his voice.

"Why don't you come over for a little while," she again cajoled.

"Only for a little while Vanessa, I have some errands to run," Stephan told her deciding he could use some stress release and not wanting her clinging to him all day.

There were still plans to make.

"That's fine, I'll see you soon," Vanessa returned as Stephan chuckled silently and turned the car around heading toward the Trufont mansion.

●●●

Marchant strangled on his drink scrolling to the bottom of the email and seeing the photo of Kayla.

"God, she's still breathtaking," she murmured, his eyes following every curve presented as she smiled and posed beside the yacht, the sexy, tastefully cut, one piece swimsuit allowing his imagination full reign as he continued to stare at the woman.

Still think she's a black hearted killer, his mind questioned tauntingly. Marchant sighed deeply. Beautiful or not, he was convinced Kayla wasn't as innocent as everyone believed. He felt in his gut she knew far more about Thomas Bradford and Christopher Lynch's dying than she admitted.

"She's going to talk this time," he grumbled, quickly setting the empty liquor glass down and typing out a response to Stephan.

He assured the officer this was indeed the woman he sought, and thanked him for the visual confirmation. Marchant went on to query when he might be able to question the woman, with the officer's full participation of course. He wasn't a fool. Marchant needed to stay on the good side of the authorities there if he wanted any help in extraditing the woman back to the states. *Just how are you going to pull that off considering you're not even supposed to be on this case,* his mind again crashed his fantasy.

Marchant knew Captain Wilmont would have his back once he delivered the confession and the killer, but what about the call from Marty about the FBI? He admitted the thought of the Federal agency's involvement disturbed him. Crossing them would cost him a whole lot more than just his badge. They could feasibly bring him up on criminal charges and lock him up.

"But why, why the hell are they even interested," he continued to muse, speaking aloud.

Marchant was treading seriously dangerous ground and he knew it; but the delectably delicious savor of solving this case and bringing a criminal to justice was too good to let go. *Hahahahahahahahaha,* Marchant heard the loud laughter in his head, frowning slightly. *Why don't you stop Dwayne, admit it, say it, stop lying already,* his conscience again badgered. Marchant frowned severely rising and refilling his glass, taking a large gulp of the vodka and enjoying the tingling in his nose as it went down.

"I'll admit no such thing," he growled aloud, snatching open the kitchen cabinet and grabbing a bag of chips.

Why, are you scared, you too big of a punk to say why you really want to see this woman, the conscience aggravated. *That why you were sitting there with a hard dick looking at her in that swimsuit, thinking about how much you want to fuck her, to bury every*

Life After Death

inch you possess inside her, the screaming in his head continued as the laughter returned.

"Fuck you," Marchant mumbled aloud, stuffing a handful of chips in his mouth.

No, idiot, fuck these lies you're telling yourself, his mind said one final time before his cell rang and released him from the continual torment.

"Yeah, this is Marchant," he spoke, swallowing his mouthful and washing them down with the vodka.

"Yes, tomorrow morning will be fine," he returned before securing a time and disconnecting.

The call was from the local heating and cooling company. Marchant's unit was giving him issue and he placed a service call. The small reprieve ended, his mind instantaneously went back to Kayla and he found himself in front of the computer looking into her beautiful eyes again.

"Please be innocent," he spoke barely audible, his finger now tracing her face, following the path to her body.

"I need to believe you," Marchant whispered once again, finishing off the drink and deliberately turning off the computer unable to endure looking at the woman any longer.

Are you still going to try and bring her back, even if you find out she's innocent, his mind questioned evenly, no accusation this time. Marchant sighed silently, closing his eyes as he tried to answer that question. *"Admit it Dwayne, there's no one here but you, say it aloud, unburden yourself,"* the soft voice of Sonia, his dead wife, whispered as he frowned deeper, but didn't open his eyes. *"I won't be angry, you can say it,"* Sonia again spoke.

"I'm in love with her and I'll do anything to bring her back and have her with me," Marchant mumbled aloud, the relief instant.

"There, now isn't that better," Sonia spoke before he drifted into the soothing release of sleep.

● ● ●

This guy is six kinds of crazy, Keller mused as he listened to Marchant carry on the conversation with himself. He didn't listen to the live feed often, preferring to simply have his team alert him if anything is said he needed to here. Today he was slightly edgy with nothing else to do for a few hours and tuned in. Witnessing the episode today Keller was even more uneasy about the man's intentions.

"He's a loose cannon," he murmured as his mind questioned his next move.

They honestly needed to take Marchant off the street. Even though Cassandra told him there was no movement on the Bradford case, or any questions about Gianni, Keller's gut told him something was afoot. He wasn't going to easily dismiss the thoughts this time. Picking up his phone he dialed Cassandra.

"Hello Keller," she greeted amiably.

"Bad time," he questioned hearing a tone.

"Not at all, the Judge and I are having lunch," she told him as he murmured his understanding.

"That's fine, just listen," he fired, continuing without her acknowledgement. "I want you to turn the heat up on Dwayne Marchant, find me something, anything I can use as leverage and get this guy bounced off the force," he told her.

"Alright, is there a time frame," she questioned carefully.

"Five days," Keller threw back.

"I'll get right on it, sir," she replied sounding official.

Keller was nonplussed knowing it was for Maurice's benefit.

"Good, call me later, when you're alone," he added and disconnected.

Keller was scheming. First they would disgrace Marchant, get him fired. Then he would begin a series of events to discredit him publicly, lastly he would relocate him, permanently.

"Hopefully that will be the end of this bullshit, now that we have those other two idiots under control as well," he murmured thinking of JaDon and Gar.

His cell rang again and Keller pursed his lips watching it for a few moments more, snatching it up at the last minute and answering.

"Yes, Senator, how are you today," he greeted far calmer than he actually felt.

Keller was developing an even deeper loathing for the man on the other end of the phone by the day.

Life After Death

"I'm fine, and I want you to tell me the same thing of this Gianni fiasco," Layton replied icily.

"Senator, all is well, I told you that already," Keller returned, his irritation fighting to push through, and him struggling to contain it.

"Keller, let me tell you something," Layton returned, his voice edgy as if he were about to freak out. "Dezi Gianni is no fucking joke, and I've gotten it on good authority that he's starting to travel again," he told Keller who withheld comment.

"I don't have to tell you what a disaster it would be if he decided to visit the United States again, now do I," he fired and Keller took a deep, sustaining breath.

He closed his eyes and counted to five, before reopening them and speaking to the man on the other end of his line, yet another time.

"Senator, there is absolutely no reason for Dezi Gianni to step foot on U.S. soil," Keller patiently spoke. "Everything and everyone he loves is in Bermuda with him," he added hearing the Senator exhale.

"Keller, be sure, I don't care what it takes at this point, but be sure," Layton returned and Keller finally heard the fear.

He wondered the root of the sudden angst but didn't question it in this conversation. That time would come soon enough and he would get answers to a lot of questions he carried.

"I here you Senator," Keller returned. "And now that I have your full blessings, we'll begin a clean sweep," he finished ominously.

"Good, the quicker the better," Layton returned, knowing full well what Keller meant and having absolutely no issue with any portion of it.

"Whatever you need is at your disposal," Layton again assured.

"Thank you Senator, we'll get started in five days," he told the man, Dwayne Marchant returning to his mind.

"Good, I feel much better," Layton returned and Keller heard the change in his voice.

"Call me when it's finished Keller," he admonished on final time before disconnecting.

Keller smiled slightly when he disconnected. He was already planning to kill them all, Marchant, JaDon, Gar, and Vernon; now he had Crowler's full blessing, and he every word of it was recorded, Keller again smiled, recalling the wiretap he secretly acquired and placed inside Layton Crowler's phone two weeks ago.

Life After Death

Life After 20 Death

Gar rolled his eyes behind the dark shades as the teens continued to giggle, getting on his precisely frayed nerves. He was given the babysitting assignment for Barbara Prather, Senator Dan Prather's oldest daughter, only three days ago. Barbara or Barbie as her friends referred to her, was a spoiled, narcissistic, high school sophomore with a superiority complex second to none. Typical all American type, blonde hair, blue eyes, way too skinny but thought she was fat. She bossed him around from the time of their introduction. Gar didn't dare speak out, or act against her wishes, knowing that not only would he get an earful from the Senator, but Deputy Director Keller would have his head on a platter. He wasn't stupid. This assignment was direct punishment for the entire Gianni file fiasco. So Gar kept his mouth shut and put up with the abuse the brazen miniature bitch dished out.

"Gar, my friends and I are going inside," Barbie barked gaining his attention. "You stay out here, we don't want you crowding us," she told him condescendingly.

Gar nodded slightly, having absolutely no intention of staying outside. His job was to watch her, and he was going to do just that. The only upside so far to his being assigned to little miss Barbie, was the trip her class took to London. Now he would be able to see Adrian courtesy of Uncle Sam.

Gar let the group of girls enter the small tourist shop, giving them a full three minutes before he slipped inside, inconspicuously perched in a corner away from their view, allowing them some measure of privacy to flirt with the teenage Brit's they followed inside. *Already a tramp in the making*, he thought observing Barbie as she allowed the young man to feel her up. Gar previously walked in on her and one of the young boys from her class having oral sex. *Bet Senator Dan doesn't know his precious daughter is a head mistress*, Gar thought again bringing a tight smile to his lips. He continued to watch as the pair disappeared down another isle, away from the shopkeeper's eyes, but still in his line of sight. Gar saw them kissing and touching, before breaking apart and exchanging information. He was almost certain a late night rendezvous would be in order. *Too bad because I have business of my own tonight*, he thought recalling his earlier connection with Adrian Roberts. He called the man a day ago right before they left the states, requesting and being granted, an audience with him. Tonight he would visit and try and get the missing pieces to the puzzle he and JaDon were trying to solve.

Gar sighed lightly seeing the girls begin to ready themselves to leave. He quickly slipped outside of the shop, standing in the same spot once they remerged, Barbara giving him a smug look as they all turned and headed toward the hotel. Gar continued to hold his temper, slowly taking deep breaths and blowing them out as the girls continued to chatter incessantly, pulling out hidden cigarettes and smoking.

"You can have the rest of the evening off," Barbara told Gar with her full authority once they reached the hotel and the girls switched back to their good girl personas.

The rest of the group began arriving from their earlier excursion, chaperones in tow. Barbara's group was allowed to go their own way, mainly due to the CIA presence, but Gar was more than sure it was because of the hundreds of thousands of dollars the Senator pumped into the exclusive private school for both his daughters. Crystal was the younger daughter, an eighth grader who was well on her way to being a carbon copy of her repugnant older sister. JaDon was sentenced to shadow her.

"Thank you," Gar replied crisply as Barbara smugly waved a well-manicured palm his way and headed inside the hotel with the rest of the group.

Dusk was just beginning to fall and Gar felt the need for something stronger than the coke he drank earlier. Turning back the way they came, he headed for the pub he scoped out earlier, ordering a double shot of vodka once he arrived. The meeting with Adrian was in two hours.

●●●

Marchant smiled as the phone connected and he heard the voice.

"How are you Detective Marchant," Stephan questioned amiably.

"I'm fine Officer Eveson," Marchant replied. "But please, call me Dwayne, the other is far too formal."

Stephan acquiesced asking Marchant to do the same.

"So Stephan," Marchant began. "I would like to come and question Mikayla, do you think that can be arranged," he questioned trying to keep the excitement of seeing the woman again out of his voice.

"I've been working on that very thing, Dwayne," Stephan replied. "I think it can be arranged, but it will take me a few days."

Life After Death

Slightly disappointed, Marchant wasn't deterred. It was still a yes, just a postponed yes.

"That will be fine Stephan," he told him, going over plans in his head.

He would need to request vacation time. Going back to the conversation Marchant tried to get a better timeframe from the officer.

"So do you think perhaps this week or next," Marchant questioned.

It was Wednesday and if he could get to her by Friday, even Saturday, arranging the time off wouldn't be an issue. He just needed a boundary to work with.

"No, probably not this week for sure, but next week does look promising," Stephan told him without elaboration.

Again Marchant didn't push. This man was doing him a monumental favor detaining the woman at all.

"Mikayla has agreed to come into the station next Thursday," Stephan lied. "Can you be here then," he questioned as Marchant smiled on his end.

"Thursday is perfect," he answered, already jotting down notes, mentally preparing to book his flight.

"Excellent, let me give you the particulars," Stephan told him giving Marchant the station address as well as the name of several hotels in the area.

"This is wonderful Stephan," Marchant told him. "This will be a huge help in solving this long overdue case," he added hearing the man murmur slightly on the other end.

"Do you really believe Mrs. Bradford guilty of these murders," Stephan probed.

Marchant carefully thought over his response. He wanted the man to help him, but he didn't want to divulge any more than necessary. He still didn't know about the boyfriend fully and the man may have been connected. There was also still the possibility that Stephan Eveson could be setting him up as well.

"I'm not fully sure Stephan," Marchant hedged. "That's one of the main reasons I want to question her, to find out wholly once and for all how much Mikayla does or doesn't know concerning the death of her husband and his best friend," he answered and hoped it would suffice to satiate Stephan's curiosity for now.

"I understand," Stephan returned. "Well I won't keep you Dwayne," he added now. "I will call you again on Wednesday to make sure your plans haven't changed," Stephan finished.

"I'm sure they won't, but yes, Wednesday is fine," Marchant replied amiably as the two men disconnected.

Just as quickly Marchant grabbed his keys and headed out the door, once again journeying to the public library. He supposed he might have been just a bit paranoid, but he didn't trust his home computer anymore. He was entirely too close now and after recalling Mrs. Coleman's account of the men posted in the neighborhood keeping watch, the call from Marty, Marchant felt every justification of the emotion. The drive was short and he quickly found a park, getting out and going inside, signing up for and getting onto one of the public terminals. Marchant began searching for flights to Pembroke Parish for Thursday. He wavered slightly on booking the return trip, unsure just what he may or may not uncover. *I may not be coming back alone,* he thought recalling his purpose for visiting. If he could get Kayla to admit to anything, he would use it to substantiate bringing her back to the states. *What if she doesn't,* his mind questioned.

"She's coming back," he mumbled almost angrily.

There it was, finally. The truth spilled from his lips. Marchant planned to bring the woman back to the states, innocent or guilty. He simply wanted her here, wanted her with him. The case gave him opportunity and motive, but it was his personal attraction that in reality additionally fueled his drive. Finding a reasonable flight, Marchant booked an open ticket since he wasn't sure of his return. On Wednesday night he would touch down in Pembroke Pines. On Thursday morning he was walking into the police station and claiming his prisoner.

•••

Adrian invited Gar in, offering him a seat and something to drink.

"Thank you," Gar responded taking the bottled water from the man as he sat on the expansive white sofa.

"So you're working on the same project as, um, JaDon," Adrian questioned stumbling a moment before recalling the man's name.

"Yes, that's right, Mr. Roberts," Gar returned pleasantly.

"Oh please, call me Adrian," came the smile filled reply.

"Thank you, I will," Gar returned, pulling out his small notebook and flipping it open.

Life After Death

"I would like to ask you some background if I could," Gar began as Adrian nodded and the man started talking.

He asked trivial questions about Adrian's recollections of the West Coast from years ago, his education and training, before finally broaching his true subject.

"So how did you come to know Mr. Gianni," Gar carefully posed.

Adrian paused wistfully, exhaling a deep breath, before answering.

"He was a regular customer at the restaurant where I used to wait tables," Adrian told him truthfully.

"Very nice man," he added as Gar smiled slightly and jotted down a line or two.

"Did you ever socialize with him," he questioned as Adrian chuckled.

"Are you asking if he was gay, or if we dated," he threw back, slightly flustering the young man.

"No, I mean um, I was just --," he tried before Adrian raised a palm and chuckled aloud.

"I'm just giving you a hard time," he told him, picking up his martini and taking a sip.

"Mr. Gianni was my customer," he told the young man as Gar frowned slightly.

"But I thought you dated one of his associates," he spoke aloud, flipping pages in the spiral bound steno pad.

"Kevin Bradley, known on the streets as Monster," he quizzed, looking into Adrian's eyes.

The pain was instant hearing the man mention Monster, bringing all the bad memories flooding back for Adrian. He saw and relived the night Kevin died all over again, saw the agents yelling at him, saw the love of his life crumple before him, his last words leaving with his last breath.

"I'm sorry, I didn't mean to stir bad memories," Gar spoke sensitively seeing the emotion the question evoked.

"No, it's fine, I just need a moment," Adrian replied, rising and heading into the bathroom.

Gar looked around the flat while he was alone, loving the rich opulence of it. *This guy must have come into some serious money, going from waiter to wealthy lay about*, he thought and quickly reigned himself in hearing Adrian returning.

"Yes, Kevin and I dated," he told the man returning to the original question. "But that had nothing to do with Mr. Gianni," Adrian added as Gar nodded and scribbled again.

"Did you know that he died," Gar asked now.

"Who," Adrian questioned.

"Mr. Gianni," Gar returned.

"Oh yes, of course, it was front page news," Adrian again answered.

Gar was finally starting to understand JaDon's frustration. Clearly the man knew more than he was telling, but he was very expertly playing the game of cat and mouse with both of them.

"Adrian, I'm going to be very blunt," Gar began anew, deciding to try a new strategy.

Raising an eyebrow Adrian waited on him to speak.

"I think Dezi Gianni is alive and well, and I think you know exactly where he is," Gar fired wanting to gage a reaction.

Adrian gave him a look, finishing the martini and placing the glass back onto the coaster, before regarding him and speaking yet another time.

"Gar," he began diplomatically. "You're a very brave man," Adrian went on, his tone never changing. "First you come all the way here to London, you and your friend JaDon," he spoke, checking his manicure now. "The two of you have put yourselves in a very precarious position, opening doors best left closed, awakening corpses better left dead," he fired as Gar became more excited.

He hung on Adrian's every word.

"I don't know what the two of your hope to accomplish, what possessed you to even begin this quest," he said finally reclining and crossing his legs in front of him. "But you've both made the biggest mistake of your lives," Adrian added rising and walking to his bar.

"What do you know Adrian, tell me, you don't have to be afraid anymore," Gar boldly spoke, feeling the man a mere seconds from breaking down and spilling all the secrets the CIA and FBI had been collectively trying to keep.

Adrian burst into laughter at his statement, perplexing the young agent.

Life After Death

"Gar, I'm not the one who should be afraid," he said simply as the three men walked into the room from the same hallway Adrian exited to the bathroom earlier.

"He's right," Dezi spoke frostily regarding the young man, gray eyes cold and flat.

"Gianni," Gar breathed, voice a hushed whisper.

"In the flesh," Dezi returned smiling malevolently.

Life After 21 Death

Gar was sweating bullets as the man continued to watch him without comment. Chancing another glance at the other two, he immediately identified the younger man as Aidan, Gianni's son. The third man was a mystery to him.

"You and your friend are causing me a lot of wasted time," Dezi spoke coldly, sipping the liquor in his glass.

They left Adrian's flat almost an hour ago coming to this small hotel room where they now held him captive. Gar fleetingly thought of resisting the men when they first ordered him to his feet and out the door, but thought better of it, his curiosity overruling his fears. Gar hoped he would be able to get useful information from Dezi Gianni and talk the man into letting him leave, the promise of sworn secrecy to his continued existence.

"We didn't want drama, we just wanted answers," Gar tried as Aidan sucked his teeth, giving him a disgusted look.

"Some things just aren't your business Gar," Dezi told him evenly. "Did you and JaDon consider that," he fired, growing angrier.

Gar quickly tried to speak up, recalling the heinous atrocities the file held and not wanting to add his own name to the list.

"I swear Mr. Gianni, we weren't trying to bring you any drama or trouble, we just --," he got out before Dezi slapped him hard.

"Shut up," he growled, almost fully angry.

"So you and this JaDon character, what are you two hoping to get out of this shit," the third man Gar didn't know, spoke up.

"This is my partner, Big D," Dezi diplomatically introduced. "His patience isn't as good as mine, so if I were you, I would speak up," he advised, picking up his liquor glass again.

"We just wanted to get off shit detail, babysitting gigs," Gar told him.

"We wanted to be treated like real agents," he added as Dezi chuckled.

"Ladder climbing," he spoke as Gar nodded, praying continually with each passing second.

He was terrified now that the dream hunch turned into a nightmarish reality.

Life After Death

"Stupid," Big D growled, accepting the drink Aidan handed him now.

"Where's your partner," Aidan questioned, leaning casually against the dresser the room contained.

"He's in the states," Gar answered without hesitation, wishing he could trade places with JaDon right now.

"Gar you're about to answer some questions for me," Dezi began now. "And you're going to tell me the truth, you're going to answer quickly, and without my repeating one question," he spoke, Gar paying rapt attention.

"Do you understand me," Dezi now questioned, voice icy, look deadly.

Gar fought to swallow the rock hard lump in his throat, the dry parched tract of esophagus making the journey rigid and arduous.

"Yes sir," he replied respectfully as Dezi grunted slightly and stood up, looking down at him.

"Who knows you're here," he fired.

"The CIA, I'm on assignment," Gar answered honestly.

"Looking for me," Dezi questioned and he shook his head no.

"I'm guarding one of the Senator's daughters," Gar answered.

"Which Senator," Dezi again fired.

Gar told him all about Senator Prather and his daughter Barbie. Big D chuckled, as did Adrian, when he described the young woman.

"Sounds about right," Dezi returned, his expression unchanged. "Who else," he again put to the agent.

"JaDon, but that's it, I swear," he pleaded, praying the man believed him.

"So there is no official investigation," Dezi wanted to know.

"No, Mr. Gianni, honestly," Gar again answered truthfully.

"Hmph," Dezi replied walking away.

The punch came square to his chest, the air forcefully pushed out as Gar wheezed in shock and surprise.

"I don't think I believe you," Aidan growled, standing in front of Gar now. "You and this JaDon character don't strike me as bright enough to have figured all this out alone," he insulted, but Gar didn't argue.

He was still struggling to breathe and praying to get out alive.

"Who sanctioned this witch hunt," Aidan questioned, right hook to the cheek bursting Gar's lip and loosening two teeth.

"No one, the case is closed, classified," Gar returned, almost screaming. "I swear we were on our own with this one, we've been reassigned because we broke protocol," Gar tried, the tears coming now.

He wasn't about trying to play tough or hard. Gar wanted to survive, live to fight a new day.

"How's Michael Keller these days," Dezi questioned, returning to the bed in front of the chair Gar was bound too.

The man's eyes grew large bringing a smile from Dezi.

"Oh yes Gar, I know Deputy Director Keller very well," he enlightened. "You and your partner probably wanted to know that too hmm," he teased.

"Who is JaDon's boss," Dezi asked looking into Gar's eyes.

"Spoelman," he returned still wheezing a bit.

"Vernon Spoelman," Dezi queried and Gar nodded yes.

"Hmph, interesting," he returned recalling exactly who the man was.

"Give me his cell," Dezi spoke as Big D handed him the instrument.

"You're going to call JaDon and tell him everything went well with your meeting," Dezi instructed, Gar listening without interruption. "You're going to tell him that he'll get filled in when you land, but you have really positive news," he finished and Gar nodded yes, dialing the international call, and waiting on it to connect.

"Are you crazy," JaDon fired in lieu of greeting.

The phone was on speaker as the four men listened to the conversation.

"Look it's paid for, I don't have an international plan," Gar returned, quickly relaying Dezi's message.

"Really," JaDon questioned the excitement in his voice.

"Yes, the two sisters will meet once we touch down, so I wanted to make sure everything was arranged," Gar spoke in code knowing JaDon would get it.

The Prather girls were both their assignments so no one would think any the wiser about them meeting up.

"Done deal," JaDon replied.

"Tomorrow evening," Gar added and again JaDon told him okay, disconnecting.

•••

Keller's phone rang almost instantly. "They made contact," the agent told the Deputy Director.

"What was said," he questioned of Gar and JaDon.

"They're meeting tomorrow," he replied having seen through the coded smokescreen.

"Hmph, okay, make sure you're there," Keller spat as the agent acknowledged his orders and disconnected.

His next call was to Cassandra.

"Hello," she greeted sounding sleepy.

Glancing at the clock Keller noted it was after 2AM.

"Sorry, didn't notice the time," Keller told her semi apologetically.

"It's fine, what do you need," Cassandra responded.

"Do you have what I told you to get on Marchant," he fired, sipping the vodka he poured into the glass as he questioned her.

"Yes, found a blip on his file from about four years ago," Cassandra told him. "Seems he was a bit too aggressive with a perpetrator, ended up breaking the man's arm," she told him bringing a smile to Keller's face.

"What happened," he questioned.

"Perp's family tried to sue, but IA found no cause to indict and they couldn't find an attorney willing to take on the county," she told Keller sounding fully awake finally.

"Hmph, we know where the family is now," he again questioned.

Cassandra enlightened him the family and the victim were all still living in the small town.

"Good, get to them, you know the angle," Keller told her. "Get them to talk, raise a stink," he added as Cassandra assured him she would handle it.

"Time for the judge to earn his keep," Keller began anew. "I want a warrant for Marchant as soon as these people file their complaint," he ordered and Cassandra voiced her understanding.

"I'll get started on it in the morning," she replied.

"Good, that chapter at least should be closed by the weekend," Keller groused talking partially to himself.

"Are we finished here then," Cassandra questioned and Keller picked up something in her voice.

"As long as everything goes smoothly, yes, we're done for all intents and purposes," he returned, wanting to question her further.

"OK that's what I needed to know," Cassandra returned.

"What exactly is going on with you Cassandra," Keller finally put to her point blank.

"Nothing, I'm just ready to leave North Carolina," she returned evenly.

"It can't be that bad," Keller again fished, not for a second believing her answer.

"I'm just ready to be at home in my own bed, and not on the road," Cassandra again tried to pass off.

"Cassandra right now there's a lot of bullshit going on, so I'm going to allow you to slip under my radar with that load you just fed me," Keller returned. "But we'll talk again, soon," he added and disconnected, going back to original task.

His agent would be in place when JaDon and Gar met tomorrow, letting him know what, if anything, the man uncovered. His suspicions told him that Gar would try and contact Adrian Roberts while he was in London. Keller was well aware of the school trip and his being there as well.

"Getting rid of these two cannot come quickly enough," he groused aloud.

Everything was starting to come unglued and Keller didn't like it. *I will not be left holding the bag on this bullshit,* he mused the nightmare of a few weeks ago screaming vividly into his mind. Keller already knew the great Senator Crowler was ready and able to lay this madness at his feet should the truth come out. *Oh but I'm not going down alone,* he continue to muse. Keller had his evidence with no problem using it should the need arise.

"Calm down," he told himself.

Life After Death

This was handled. He was taking care of Marchant before the week was out. Gar and JaDon were already being strategically placed and once they were all permanently silenced, things would go back to what they used to be; peaceful and Gianni free. Satisfied for the moment, Keller drained his glass and headed for his bed. Maybe sleep wouldn't be such an elusive beast this morning.

• • •

Gar's body hurt in places he didn't know he would feel pain. The three men took turns working him over, firing question upon question at him. He prayed they possessed everything they needed now and would mercifully let him go. He gave them JaDon's address, and after the second beating by Big D, told them about April being their inside link to the FBI. Gar was ashamed on the one hand for selling out April, even feeling bad about JaDon, but he held fast to the sliver of hope that Dezi would let him go and leave them all unscathed.

"Gar, I want to thank you for being so helpful this evening," Dezi spoke diplomatically.

Big D and Aidan were picking up their belongings, wiping down the room. Gar's hope began to build, thinking the men were about to leave him secured to the chair until the maid arrived and found him, bound, but alive.

"I appreciate your honesty as well," he continued as Big D smirked, and Aidan smiled faintly. "I regret however, that I'm going to have to kill you now," he told Gar, his face falling.

"B-b-but Mr. Gianni," he stuttered. "I won't say a word, I swear it," Gar tried the sweat popping onto his face, turning it an even deeper crimson.

"I can't take that risk Gar," Dezi told him pretending sorrow.

"Besides, having read my file, you have to know I don't ever leave witnesses," Dezi told him the tone changing.

Gar shuddered. He did recall, vividly.

"Don't kill me, please," he pleaded the tears coming now.

"Really Gar, this is your own fault," Dezi continued as Big D stepped out of the room.

"I know Mr. Gianni, but pl --," he got out stopping as the door opened and Big D returned, pushing the hooded figure into the room, duffle bag on his shoulder.

Gar immediately recognized the form, even with the hood still on.

"Wh-wh- what," he managed as Dezi continued to coldly regard him.

Big D unzipped the bag, Aidan walking over and retrieving a large bottle of vodka, turning and coming back to Gar.

"Let's have a drink," he teased as Dezi and Big D chuckled.

"Mmletmm," came the muffled cries from the hooded visitor.

A well placed punch to the stomach from Big D silenced them, as they fell to their knees. Striding to Gar, Big D grabbed his head, forcing it backward, mouth open. Aidan quickly opened the liquor, shoving the bottle into Gar's throat, the liquor cascading down his esophagus as Gar half swallowed, half choked the entire contents. He immediately felt his head begin to spin, the urge to wretch strong, but unfortunately never manifesting. He just as quickly felt something being tied around his arm and the pinching prick of a needle as something very warm was injected into his bloodstream.

Things began to move at warp speed for Gar. He felt like he was on a rollercoaster, rising and falling, whipping around curves, then the huge stomach clenching drop off the edge. He was conscious, but not particularly cognizant.

"There now, I bet you feel so much better don't you," Dezi calmly regarded, nodding toward Big D who snatched the hood from the quaking girl now standing before them, regarding them fearfully.

Aidan reached out and snatched the duct tape from her mouth as she immediately began to scream at them.

"Do you know who my father is you assholes," Barbie yelled, face beet red with fear and anger.

They snatched her from the corner as she waited on the boy she met earlier, having snuck out of the hotel once Gar left on his errand.

"Do something you fucking idiot," she screamed at Gar.

He burst into laughter, bringing a smirk from Dezi, Aidan and Big D.

"Loosen up you little cunt," Gar returned in his impaired state, farting loudly at the end of his statement.

"Useless bastard," Barbie again screamed before regarding the men.

"Listen my father has money, he'll pay you," she tried, looking from one to the other.

Life After Death

"I think you should take Gar's advice," Dezi told her calmly, as Big D grabbed her, holding her immobile and Aidan repeated his earlier performance pouring another smaller bottle of vodka down her throat, adding two ecstasy pills along with it.

Letting her go, Barbie fell to her knees dry heaving, trying desperately to clear her spinning head.

"Ple--, hell--," she tried, speech failing her.

Dezi walked over to the chair where Gar was still bound, high, watching the girl hatefully.

"Don't you want to punish the little bitch," he spoke quietly near the man's ear as he casually untied him.

"Look at her, not so great and mighty now is she," Dezi continued to goad.

He almost laughed but didn't. Dezi wasn't stupid. He did his homework and knew all about JaDon, Gar, and little miss Barbara Prather before ever talking to the man. He used his own network to check them all out once he received Adrian's call. Gar simply acted as confirmation of the information received.

"Go ahead Gar, take care of your business, show her who's in charge, who's the man here," Dezi went on as Gar's anger grew.

He hated the bossy little bitch at his feet. *Teach her little spoiled ass a lesson,* his fury taunted.

"Gar, Garrrrr, do something," Barbie managed to slur, half screeching, grating everyone's nerves in the room.

Dezi, Big D, and Aidan, however didn't lose focus. Gar, on the other hand, was done. Jumping from the chair he descended on the helpless girl, slapping her face back and forth, screaming at her.

"Shut up little cunt, shut the fuck up," Gar yelled spittle flying.

Dezi glanced at Aidan, smirking, seeing the man's erection grow each time his palm connected with the girls face.

"Freak," Big D murmured as they all chuckled.

Gar didn't hear anything. His rage was full blown, as was his erection, when he forced it into her mouth.

"Suck me bitch, suck me," Gar yelled pumping furiously as Barbie gagged, scratching and hitting him trying to remove him from her.

The three men watched impassively, the madman in front of them as he continue to strangle the girl beneath him with his wildly bucking hips, smashing his groin against her nose, his balls slapping her chin with each movement.

"Mm, yeah, that's it cunt, suck it," Gar mumbled, pulling out without warning, his semen squirting all over the girls face.

Barbie didn't flinch. Her eyes told the story. The girl was dead and Gar's final act of desecration had no effect on her.

"Yeeeeah," Gar breathed, sitting back on his haunches, flaccid penis lying on the girls still chest.

Big D shook his head, Aidan smirked doing the same. Dezi sauntered behind Gar, kneeling, Gar's service revolver in his gloved hand.

"She's dead Gar," Dezi told him as the man's eyes popped open and he regarded the girl beneath him.

His head was still spinning; the vodka and heroin weren't done with him yet.

"You'll get the chair for this, that's if the CIA doesn't have you killed first," Dezi goaded as Gar began to hyperventilate.

"16-year old girl, Senator's daughter, your cum all over her face," he went on as Big D and Aidan casually watched, sipping from their own bottles.

"You'll be disgraced, your family will never live down the shame," Dezi told him as the first tear rolled down Gar's face.

"Can't you see it Gar, your mother, your father, head's hung in shame as they watch you being pushed into the courtroom in shackles," Dezi again spoke.

"No, I can't do that to them," Gar whispered, his back to Dezi unable to see the smile on the man's face.

"End it Gar," Dezi told him, putting the service revolver in his hand. "No more pain, no embarrassment, no drama," he spoke soothingly as Gar continued to regard Barbie and her dead blue eyes accused him, finding him guilty on the spot.

He began to nod his head slowly, as Dezi guided the gun into his mouth. "Take your destiny into your own hands, Gar," he spoke yet another time. "Fuck the CIA, fuck Keller, you are your own man," Dezi whispered, seeing the change in Gar's eyes. "Damned right," Gar mumbled with the gun in his mouth, fury at full throttle once again thinking of all the hell he endured

Life After Death

over the last few months, the demotion, the embarrassment at headquarters and the final insult, being put on babysitting patrol.

Enough!

"Fuck them all," Gar again mumbled pulling the trigger.

The sound reverberated inside the small room as Gar's brain matter exited the back of his head through the hole created by the .9mm slug that passed through it. Dezi smiled again rising from his knee as Gar's body slumped forward landing atop Barbie in a macabre picture of sexual satisfaction. Aidan gathered the empty duffle bag as they wiped the room down one last time to remove any of their DNA. Exiting and leaving the door slightly ajar, they got into the rental and casually left the hotel.

"Who's next," Aidan questioned eyes on the road, driving, as Dezi lit the cigar and relaxed in the backseat.

"I think it's time to visit American soil," he said simply as both Big D and Aidan smiled slightly and asked nothing more.

Life After 22 Death

Something was afoot and Stephan was out of the loop. He glanced around seeing Kareek and Joell talking in his office, tones hushed. He returned to work four days ago being given all the back reports to log and file. Kareek then placed him on bike patrol, taking the squad car away. Stephan was pissed but didn't speak on it. His time was coming. In just a few days Detective Marchant would land and he would finally get his chance to shine. Thinking about the man brought Stephan's mind back to the ruse he would need in order to accomplish his goal of getting Kayla alone. Stephan had absolutely no intention of bringing the detective or the woman to police headquarters. This was his takeover and he wouldn't allow anyone to interfere.

"Hey, you heard," Jacob asked conspiratorially sitting down beside Stephan and pretending to be busy.

"Heard what," Stephan answered casually, playing along with his friend as he continued to look at the report in front of him.

"Arroyo and Kareek are leaving town for the week," he told Stephan who fought to hold the whoop of joy that wanted to burst from his chest.

"Annnnd," Jacob began anew, eyes twinkling.

"I heard the Gianni's and their partner, D, were leaving town as well," he told Stephan, proud of the gossip he procured.

"Really, all of them, same time," he whispered back as Jacob nodded.

Stephan couldn't believe the fates. He would have free reign of the island while all these men were away.

"Is that what those two are scheming on," he questioned nodding slightly toward Kareek and Joell.

Jacob sneered before answering.

"Yes, he's leaving that ass kiss in charge," he told Stephan.

"Figures," Stephan replied irritably.

"No matter, we still get a full week to ourselves to enjoy," Jacob returned, having no more sinister plan than to goof off or take extra-long naps and breaks.

Life After Death

Stephan however sequestered a whole other agenda. With the proverbial cookie jar wide open, he would have free reign to require Kayla's presence for questioning. Joell would definitely need to be watched, but that's where Jacob would come in. *I need to find a way to get Mariah there as well,* he thought deciding that the Imperial Palace, the hotel Detective Marchant would be staying in, would provide the perfect location. *Now, what is the cover story,* Stephan thought as the answer literally fell in his lap. He read over the police report filed by Kayla some three months earlier about a theft as she attended a luncheon at the hotel. *Perfect,* Stephan thought. He would call her, tell her he found the item in question, her diamond bracelet, and ask her to come to the hotel and identify it. *OK but how do you ensure Mariah comes too,* his mind again questioned. He was stumped momentarily but quickly recalled that Thursday's were their spa days. They would be together already.

Stephan decided he would call after 10AM, ensuring they already left the house together, but not yet arrived at the spa. He was watching and learning Mariah's habits long enough that he knew their entire schedule from memory. *Yes, this is coming together very nicely,* he thought and smiled again at the prospect of having Mariah, alone, in a hotel suite. He would sit with her while Marchant questioned Kayla. *We'll talk, I'll get her to relax with me,* he continued to daydream, the thoughts taking on a very erotic overtone. He saw them in his mind's eye kissing and touching each other, her moans of pleasure permeating the suite as his hands touched and massaged her hard clit, the slippery silkiness of her arousal, easily guiding his fingers inside her as she moaned his name in passion.

"Stephan, did you hear me," the raised voice quickly ended the pondering as Stephen catapulted back to reality, looking at Kareek's severely frowned face.

"What is it," he returned barely masking the distaste for his boss.

"I said I will be out of town for the next week and I'm leaving Joell in charge," he repeated evenly, never removing his eyes from the officer.

Stephan shrugged and nodded nonchalantly.

"Sure, fine," he replied without emotion.

"Hmph, see that you do your job and give him no trouble, or there will be hell to pay when I return," he fired looking from Stephen, to Jacob, and the other two officers the small force employed.

"We understand," Jacob replied diplomatically, Stephan defiantly said nothing.

•••

Cassandra was irritated and trying hard to mask it as she once again knocked on the shoddy wooden door, badly in need of paint, and waited for it to open.

"Hello," Cassandra greeted the young man eyeing her suspiciously.

It didn't matter that this was her third visit, they still didn't trust her. *Why should they*, her mind questioned.

"Jace, move and let the woman in," Cassandra heard the woman's voice.

The young man sullenly moved aside allowing Cassandra to once again enter the home. She was entirely familiar with the interior now, making her way down the short hallway into the living room and taking the seat offered on the well-worn, brown and beige sofa. This was the home of Rebecca Myles. She was the mother of Lonnie Myles, aka Loonz, the man whose arm Marchant had broken during his arrest. Cassandra took in the family photos that lined every wall of the room it seemed. The chiffon yellow paint a bit sickening to her palate but blended well with the furniture and potted flowers used to décor the room.

"Would you like something to drink Agent Deale," Rebecca questioned.

Cassandra smiled.

"No, thank you," she responded.

Rebecca Myles so far was a very hospitable host, a small statured woman, she clearly weighed far more than her frame was comfortable hosting.

"Ms. Myles, have you and Lonnie given any more thought to my proposition," Cassandra questioned getting right to business.

Time was short and Keller made sure she knew this when she talked to him this morning.

They wasted a week already tracking the family down and actually gaining an audience with them. It was now Monday of a new week and Keller wanted the ball rolling or them to move on and find something else.

"Hell yeah," Loonz spoke coming into the room. "I want to see his crooked ass locked up," he fired as Rebecca sighed deeply.

Cassandra smiled slightly glad that the young man was finally speaking up. She only saw him the first visit and he curtly told her then it was up to his mother whether they proceeded or not. Obviously, things changed since then.

"Lonnie," his mother began fearfully.

"Ma, look we can't keep being scared," he tried as Cassandra, took note and interjected.

"Ms. Myles, please don't let fear keep your son from getting justice, and you as well," she told her as Rebecca continued to nervously chew on her lip.

"They will harass us again," she told Cassandra.

Frowning slightly, she asked the woman to elaborate. Rebecca told her of the unwarranted traffic stops, the harassing of her son's, her brothers, as they walked the street. Cassandra asked for names which Lonnie gave without hesitation. Scribbling them down, she returned her attention to the woman again.

"I promise you Ms. Myles, these officers will be disciplined," she told her sincerely.

"Now, what do you want to do about the man who overstepped his authority and broke your son's arm," Cassandra questioned looking right into the woman's eyes.

Rebecca looked from the Agent to her son, then back to the agent again before finally answering.

"Where do we need to sign," she questioned as the smile graced Cassandra's face and she pulled the documents from her briefcase.

● ● ●

Kareek was still staring at Stephan waiting for a response.

"I heard you, Joell is in charge," he returned, quickly going back to his reports.

He heard the man mumble something inaudible under his breath before retreating once more to his office.

"Prick," Jacob murmured bringing a titter of laughter from Stephan.

"Don't worry about him, he's leaving in a while and we'll be free," he offered as Jacob snorted and nodded yes, turning around and facing his own computer, booting it up to begin working.

Stephan didn't let Kareek's tirade affect him. He was too busy plotting his takeover. Joell would easily be subdued and he had friends enough to push for Kareek's removal once word leaked that he helped harbor a wanted fugitive, taking bribes, and payoffs. While he worried slightly about Arroyo, he knew enough to know the man wouldn't risk his own future standing up for Kareek. He would cheerfully allow the police chief to be thrown under the bus if it meant saving his own skin. *Then he and I will come to an agreement,* Stephan thought of Arroyo Trufont. His thoughts yet another time turned to beautiful Mariah and them being together.

He knew when Detective Marchant took Kayla back to the states; the elder Gianni would follow in an attempt to free her. Stephan would then take the opportunity to dethrone the son and throw him in jail. He would have more than enough charges once Kareek talked, and he would talk, especially after the beatings Stephan planned to have administered. He would talk just to save his own life when Stephan finally offered him a deal.

"It's time for your patrol," Kareek yelled breaking Stephan's thoughts yet another time.

Huffing, he rose rudely from his chair, intentionally pushing his desk chair violently into the wall.

"Patience Stephan," Jacob told him, hushed.

Gathering a deep breath, he brought the anger down heeding the man's words. They only needed to endure Kareek a few more hours. After he walked out of the door and stepped onto the airplane with Arroyo, the new age of Stephan Eveson, chief of police was about to begin.

"Have a good trip," he told Kareek giving him a fake smile as the man scowled and turned his head, effectively dismissing the officer.

"Arrogant bastard," Stephan mumbled, grabbing his bike helmet and heading out into the scorching summer sun.

Thursday and Detective Marchant arriving could not happen soon enough.

"Mariah, my love, it's almost time," he murmured as he pedaled toward the center of town.

Stephan couldn't wait to hold the woman in his arms, to kiss her beautiful lips, and to make her his once and for all. The thoughts were still dancing vividly in his mind as he arrived at the market, parking the bike under a shaded tree and watching, the smile on his lips, as Mariah got out of the Benz, smoothing her dress and turned heading inside.

Life After Death

"Love of my life," Stephan murmured still smiling as the door closed behind her and she disappeared from his sight.

●●●

Maurice was pleasantly surprised to find Cassandra in his chambers when he entered, having just left the bench for a fraud case he was hearing.

"Well hello," he greeted the beautiful agent with a smile.

"Hello Maurice," Cassandra returned, embracing him as he reached out, pulling her into his arms.

"You look lovely," Maurice complimented, kissing her after his statement, taking in the powder pink t-strap sundress she was wearing.

It flattered her every curve, especially her hips and butt. Cassandra blushed slightly, before thanking him and taking her seat once again.

"What brings you by," Maurice questioned, taking off his robe and hanging it up.

"Well the time has come for that help I told you we would need," Cassandra told him as Maurice nodded, coming and sitting atop the front of his desk, directly in front of her.

"Certainly Cassandra," Maurice amiably replied. "As I told you then, whatever you need," he added smiling, as she smiled back.

"Thank you Maurice, that makes thing so much easier," she told him pulling out the documents and handing them to him.

Maurice looked them over seeing the accusations contained and the charges they wanted brought.

"When do you want the warrants issued," he questioned, turning to get a pen from his holder, on the side of the expansive mahogany desk.

"The sooner the better Maurice," Cassandra told him. "I promised Ms. Myles and Lonnie, swift justice," she offered as Maurice nodded absently, signing the documents that would enable the Agent to arrest Marchant and the other three officers listed in the complaint.

"I think you should go through their Captain however," Maurice told her handing Cassandra the packet back and laying the pen down beside him.

She frowned slightly as he smiled and elaborated.

"This thing is going to blow all the way up once the media gets wind of it," he told her, pulling her to her feet and back into his arms. "It would be better if you took the warrants to Caroline Wilmont and let her handle gathering the officers and locking them up," Maurice finished, his lips on Cassandra's neck now.

"Hmm, I don't see any harm in that," she told him, his hand now caressing her breast.

"I'll go see her after I leave you," she told him, his lips finding hers again, hands sliding under the dress she wore, fingers sliding inside the thong.

"Mmm, your honor, this is hardly the place," Cassandra returned breathlessly.

She couldn't lie and say she wasn't turned on; her moisture would have immediately called her a liar.

"It's the perfect place," Maurice returned, fingers slipping inside her wet opening.

"Maurice, mmm," Cassandra moaned, eyes closed, case momentarily forgotten.

Maurice worked her clit with his thumb, while his fingers slid in and out of her, her hips slowly gyrating in rhythm with his movements.

"Like that," he questioned, kissing her neck again.

"Yessss," she returned, whispering.

Cassandra's hands found the top of his pants, unbuckling them and easily sliding the zipper down, freeing his hard member.

"Maurice, my god," she again whimpered, dangerously close to finishing.

The next stroke of her clit sent her over the edge as she clung to him, her sex spasm, tightly contracting over the fingers still inside her.

"Better," Maurice teased, sliding his fingers from her as he climbed down from the desk and turned Cassandra toward it.

She pliably laid across the desk, dress hiked around her waist, thong pulled to the side as Maurice slid his hardness deep inside her still dripping sex, their skin slapping audibly as he thrust into her again and again.

"Yeeeeesss," Cassandra hissed, yet another orgasm heading her way.

"Cassandra, Caassaannddrraa," Maurice growled from his chest, his thrusts picking up stamina.

Life After Death

Cassandra spread her legs wider wanting him deeper as Maurice readily obliged pumping furiously, his semen inching ever slowly up his shaft.

"I'm cuming Maurice, oh yesss, I'm cummming," Cassandra again moaned, her creamy essence covering his shaft as Maurice moved deeper, holding her hips tighter banging her mercilessly.

"Fuck yeaaaaaah," he moaned some three minutes later, his cum springing forth and filling the writhing woman beneath him, both of them breathing hard.

Gathering themselves, Maurice spoke as he zipped his pants. "Caroline is out of town until Wednesday, but she'll be back first thing that morning," he told Cassandra who again hated the delay but saw no harm.

"Alright," she told him, standing close again. "But I'll be in her face by 9 AM when Wednesday comes," Cassandra told Maurice who chuckled.

"I'm sure you will darling," he told her kissing her again as Cassandra prepared to leave.

"Dinner tonight," Maurice questioned.

"Sounds good," she returned opening the door and smiling as Maurice blew her one last kiss and she closed it behind her.

Patting the briefcase with the signed documents, Cassandra smiled again, relaxing just a bit; they were almost at the finish line.

Life After 23 Death

Mariah was moaning softly as her husband continued his quest to satiate her. Aidan's tongue was greedily circling her clit as her flow ran freely and her chest heaved its chaotic symphony of breath. She was so close, so very, very, close. The next taste from him dropped her over the edge and she cried out his name, holding his face immobile as he obediently drank her finish, growling ever so lightly. Mariah pulled her husband up to her as the sensations from the powerful orgasm began to wane, their lips connecting yet another time, his hardness replacing his tongue, her muscles contracting welcoming him inside her.

"Mmm, baby," Aidan murmured, pushing his full length inside his wife as she vocalized how much she wanted it.

"Yes Aidan, oh god, that feels so good," Mariah moaned passionately, grasping her husband's firm butt and pulling him even deeper.

"You want more baby," he questioned, biting her neck lightly.

"Yes, more Aidan, more," she again groaned.

Aidan quickly took her legs, spreading them widely, putting them over her head as Mariah's gushing sex showed her pleasure.

Aidan was lost in erotic euphoria feeling firm flesh with each thrust, his wife grasping him tightly in her volcanic rapture.

"Shit Mariah, damn," he again growled almost animalistic, his rhythm increasing with each moan from his wife, her sex even more porous and pliable.

"Ohhhhhyeeessss," Mariah cried out cuming hard yet another time.

Aidan felt his body trembling, the orgasm fighting its way to be released.

"Aarrrr," he cried hoarsely unable to contain himself any longer as his seed forced its way from his body inside his wife's welcoming warmth.

Aidan collapsed atop her as Mariah stroked his back softly, kissing his shoulder feather light. After collecting himself a few moments more, he kissed her, moving from atop her, lying down beside her.

"You, Dezi, and D, need to be extremely careful," Mariah admonished as they continued to lie together.

Aidan reached out and caressed his wife's cheek.

Life After Death

"You know we'll be careful baby," he told her sincerely seeing the worry in her eyes.

"We're going to handle business, getting back on the plane, and coming right back here," Aidan again spoke as Mariah sighed and nodded.

"I guess I just thought once we left the states we would never need to go back," she murmured as Aidan pulled her closer and kissed her again.

"Baby, we have to handle this so that our lives remained undisturbed," he explained patiently.

Mariah again nodded. She understood in theory why they had to travel back to the country she was born and raised in, but the wife and mother in her didn't want her husband in any danger.

"No one will ever be the wiser we were there baby," Aidan again reassured.

"Okay, but call me Aidan, let me know how things are going," Mariah replied.

"I will honey," he told her in response.

"Have you seen Stephan lately," he questioned now, changing the conversations course.

Mariah frowned slightly, honestly having given the man no thought until Aidan's mention of him.

"No, thankfully," she replied as her husband chuckled.

"I thought you might miss your best friend," Aidan teased as Mariah playfully rolled her eyes at him.

"If he harasses you baby, let me know and I'll have Kareek take care of it," Aidan told her as he rose and headed for the shower.

"I think he got the message," Mariah told him rising as well.

She threw on her robe and left the bedroom heading down the hallway to check on the children. Preston was sleeping peacefully in his bed, covers tussled, leg hanging off. Smiling Mariah carefully placed his leg back onto the small jungle motif bed and covered him. Walking next door, she pushed the door open revealing her daughter, Livvy, asleep, deeply furrowed under the pink princess comforter that adorned her bed. Closing that door as well Mariah returned to the master bedroom hearing the water still running as she removed the robe preparing to join her husband.

"Please let this go well and bring them all home safely," Mariah prayed quietly before opening the bathroom door and walking inside.

●●●

"So who is this guy that Dezi is going to see," Jackie as while she and Big D relaxed and he smoked a blunt.

"Someone with a long nose that stuck it in the wrong business," he replied, inhaling deeply on the blunt.

"Damn, well his own fault," Jackie returned matter-of-fact. "You make sure you're careful D, and you come back here in one piece, all of you," Jackie admonished as he released the smoke and turned to look into her eyes.

"It's straight baby, in and out job," he replied confidently.

"Yeah, well still, just the same," Jackie replied and Big D could see the angst.

Putting the blunt out, he turned to her again and pulled her into his arms, looking directly into her eyes as he spoke.

"Baby, we're not going to the states to set off any alarms, or bring any attention to ourselves," Big D explained. "We're headed there because these idiots are threatening our way of life, and we can't have that," he told her as Jackie nodded.

"So will that end it," she questioned.

"Yes," Big D replied confidently. "There were three of them working on the case, plus the others Dezi has on his list," he explained to Jackie.

"You're going to kill all of them," she questioned.

Big D smiled slightly. He loved Jackie's forthright manner. Knowing her man killed people didn't rattle her cage, or cause her to look at him strangely. For her it was simply a part of their life and she accepted it as such.

"Right now no, but we'll play it by ear once we're standing in front of them," Big D told her.

He began kissing her neck, turning her on he knew.

"See, don't be trying to change the subject," Jackie murmured as she grew heated.

Big D chuckled.

"I'm not," he told her, lips tracing the tops of her breasts now as he removed the bra.

Life After Death

"I can talk and make love to you at the same time," he told her. "What's wrong, you can't concentrate," Big D teased, licking the nipple now.

"Huh, mm, I --," Jackie got out before he chuckled again taking the nipple into his mouth and sucking forcefully.

"Shhhhit," Jackie groaned loving his lips at the moment.

Big D's fingers slithered between her legs, finding her clit and stroking it, feeling her gates open and the pool begin to fill.

"Mmm D, damn boy," Jackie again murmured.

Big D trailed the kisses down her body until his tongue held her clit firmly between his teeth, lashing it again and again as her hips bucked wildly and Jackie came hard, her creamy offering begging him to take it. Big D immediately moved further down, his tongue invading her opening, scooping her out as she continued to writhe and moan.

"Oooooooohhhh," Jackie's poignant cry resonated through the bedroom as the all-consuming second orgasm descended and took her to a new level of bliss.

Her worries, anxiety, and reservations about their trip momentarily disappeared as Big D entered her, all thoughts directed toward the tumultuous pleasure of the orgasm that was teasingly at the edge of her consciousness.

●●●

Dezi continued to watch Kayla. She remained extremely quiet and pensive most of the day since their earlier conversation and he told her about his trip back to the states.

"Honey, are you all right," he finally questioned, coming to her as she stood on the veranda looking at the night sky, arms around her waist, looking over her shoulder into the ocean before them.

"I just --," Kayla began, faltering.

Dezi turned her toward him, tilting her chin up so he could look into her eyes.

"Just what baby," he questioned sensitively.

"I have a bad feeling Dezi," Kayla returned. "I don't know if I'm just being silly, but I just have a very bad feeling about you leaving, all of you," she told him as he saw the tears gather in her eyes.

"Baby, I promise you I'm going to be careful, and you know Big D and Aidan will as well," Dezi told her calmly. "I have to do this Kayla or we will never get a moments peace," he added and she nodded her understanding.

"Honey if you need anything all you have to do is call Joell," he told her, having been alerted earlier by Kareek of his absence.

"I'll be fine Dezi," Kayla told him trying to push away the still nagging doubt and fear.

"You just come back to me," she admonished as he smiled and kissed her passionately.

"Nothing, and I do mean nothing, could keep me from you Kayla," Dezi sincerely replied.

She smiled at the declaration knowing it was true. Of his love and devotion Kayla was never more assured. That wasn't the source of her angst. There was a nagging in her psyche. Something that just would not leave her alone and it continually blared danger. Deciding she wouldn't put any more undue or unwarranted stress on him, Kayla forced the thoughts away before she spoke.

"Everything will be fine Dezi," she told him stroking his face now. "Handle your business and then come home," Kayla added, gaining yet another kiss from him in response.

"You had a doctor's appointment today," Dezi questioned recalling the reminder from the office earlier.

"Hm, yes," Kayla replied thinking nothing of it.

"And," Dezi questioned, eyebrow raised.

She burst into laughter seeing his expression.

"I'm fine Dezi, it was just a routine checkup," Kayla returned, kissing him again.

"OK, just checking," he replied, kissing her back, turning passionate as they clung to each other.

Dezi felt her trepidation as he held her. He pulled away and looked into her eyes one more time.

"Kayla, listen to me baby," he spoke calmly and soothingly. "I am going to be invisible in the states, I'm going to shut down the drama brewing and threatening our lives, and then I'm coming home to lie in your arms and live our lives together," he finished as she finally smiled fully and relaxed.

Life After Death

Dezi smiled with her, pulling her to him and kissing her again, quickly slipping the silk teddy from her body, and laying her onto the chaise lounge. He loved making love to her on the veranda. The sound of the ocean crashing beneath them helped turn him on as he caressed and aroused her.

"I love you so much baby," Dezi murmured, taking her breast into his mouth.

"Mmm, I love you too Dezi, with my whole heart," Kayla breathlessly replied, his fingers sliding inside her, sexing her deliciously slow, more and more saturated with each motion.

"Yes, baby, yes," she moaned right at her peak.

Dezi sucked the nipple harder, biting it as Kayla's body shuddered, nirvana reached; her flow at torrent. Dezi removed his fingers sensuously licking them as she looked into his eyes, her own hand gently manipulating her stiffening clit. Kayla's glance traveled down his still chiseled frame landing on his rock hard manhood, seductively calling her to it. She kissed the head lightly, flicking her tongue through his opening as Dezi groaned aloud. Smiling a bit knowing he was pleased, Kayla methodically introduced his girth to her mouth's salivating warmth.

"Kaayla," he breathed, loving each nuance as his hips began to move back and forth in time with her motions.

Her hands lovingly caressed his taunt thighs, finding his balls and massaging them gently. She felt his member begin to pulsate, increasing her momentum.

"No, shit, Kayla, baby stop," Dezi pled, trying to free himself.

He managed to extricate himself, pushing her onto her back, leg on his shoulder.

"Bad girl," he teased, sinking his swollen shaft to the hilt of her depth, watching as Kayla's eyes rolled back into her head.

"Dezi, Deeezzzziiiiii," Kayla screamed as she came, his aim at her g-spot dead on.

Unable to hold his own torrent at bay, Dezi came right behind her, his body shaking as her contracting honeycomb milked him for every drop his body excreted.

"Be safe and come back to me Dezi," Kayla whispered in his ear, feeling him kiss her neck.

"Without fail baby, without fail," he murmured before his lips met hers, tongue invading her mouth, starting the heat all over again.

Life After Death

Life After 24 Death

Marchant was once again seated in front of the public library computer, checking his email. He didn't see anyone watching his house since he was alerted, but he wasn't taking any chances. He was far too close now. Kayla was actually within his reach, now was not the time to mess up. Clicking his inbox open, Marchant began looking for the familiar email address when he saw a message about his hotel reservations. Taking a deep breath and praying it wasn't bad news, he opened the email and read with interest the contents. Seemed the hotel was willing to offer him a substantially lower rate with the addition of another weekday. Marchant mulled it over a moment deciding that arriving a day earlier couldn't possibly hurt. *Give Officer Eveson and I a chance to really go over the case file,* he perused quickly clicking on the link to accept the offer. Marchant then went to his flight reservation, amending it as well. He would leave later tonight and arrive on the island by 10AM their time.

"Nice just to relax a moment or two," he murmured aloud going back to his original task, finding an email from Stephan just as he hoped.

Marchant opened it. 'I have spoken to Mrs. Bradford and she has agreed to come to the hotel,' the message read as Marchant began to smile. That would make things so much easier, and put her far more at ease he was sure.

Quicker confession, he thought smirking slightly, having not given up on getting the woman to admit to a crime. Marchant returned to the message seeing that Stephan set up the meeting for 11 AM.

"Perfect," Marchant murmured, typing a reply and sending it back.

He updated the officer on his plans to be on the island tomorrow, and asked if they could get together to go over the file and be fully prepared to question Kayla when they all met on Thursday. Marchant hit send and released the breath he subconsciously held. His pulse began to speed ever so slightly. He seriously gave thought to what he was about to do. It was absolutely illegal and if the woman didn't admit to anything, or he couldn't get her back to the states with some charge or other that would stick, his career was done. Marchant could see Captain Wilmont stripping his badge, turning his case over to Internal Affairs and bouncing him straight off the force. *Don't forget about the Feds, they seem awfully interested in you and this case,* his mind quickly brought to his recollection. Marchant felt the headache begin its dull throbbing, rising and making his way to his car. He drove slowly taking his time eyeing the scenery before him, mind still pondering his impending task. *You haven't gotten on the plane yet,* his mind tried yet another time to reason.

"I have to do this," Marchant murmured, stopping at the small neighborhood park and finding a shady spot.

He didn't leave the car, instead opting to roll down the windows and enjoy the fresh breeze. Marchant watched the mothers with small children as they chatted pleasantly and the children played on the small jungle gym, slides and see saws. He saw the dogs chasing Frisbees or balls that their masters threw indiscriminately, the happy yelps of the beasts resounding in the open area. *You're convinced this woman is guilty, what if she isn't, what if she's just an innocent victim of happenstance,* his mind yet another time tortured.

"Nobody is that innocent," Marchant resolved, speaking his thought aloud.

She must know something. You didn't have all that death going on around you and remain totally clueless. Marchant's gaze fell on the couple sitting together on the park bench, romantically embraced as they looked into each other's eyes. He couldn't hear their conversation, continuing to observe them as the man stroked the woman's face and she smiled. His heart took control and he and Kayla became the couple. Marchant saw himself looking into her gorgeous face, his lips ever so lightly brushing across hers, his tongue flickering over the bottom lip as it quivered in response. The shrill sound of his cell phone broke his thought as Marchant irritably answered.

"Your extra day was approved," Captain Wilmont's secretary told him as Marchant brusquely thanked her and disconnected.

"Tomorrow," Marchant spoke wistfully, starting the car and leaving the park, heading home to pack.

●●●

Today was shaping up to be an excellent day in Stephan's estimation. Kareek and Arroyo were gone. The Gianni's and Big D left earlier this morning, and now Detective Marchant's email confirming his early arrival provided the crescendo. Stephan was more than ready to have his alone time with Mariah and this questioning of her mother would provide him amply. Stephan began to think about when the Detective would undoubtedly want to return Kayla to the states with him. *Mariah will call Aidan and he'll tell his father,* he thought frowning automatically. He couldn't allow that to happen. *How are you going to stop her,* Stephan continued to

Life After Death

ponder. An idea came to mind, but it was drastic and he really didn't want to resort to it. Still, his plans couldn't fail. This was his one chance. The island was ripe for the picking and this time Stephan held every intention of coming out on top. Joell of course clueless he was being plotted against. Stephan was the model officer this morning as not to raise any suspicion. *He's the first thing I need to get rid of,* the man pondered as he continued to leisurely cycle his beat. Stephan made note to go see Vanessa. He would sleep with her today so she would stay off his back and not interrupt his plans. The sex was good, but Vanessa came with far too many attachments.

"Need to be careful," Stephan murmured.

So far they were lucky and she didn't conceive a child. He certainly didn't want that to change. The only babies he wanted were the ones he and Mariah would have together. *She's not going to be hearing anything along those lines for a long time,* his mind shattered the fantasy.

"It will be fine," he groused trying to convince himself.

Stephan hated thinking of Mariah and Aidan together. He hated knowing that the woman did indeed love the man. He hated knowing they made love and she enjoyed being touched by him.

"I'll change her mind," Stephan growled pedaling faster.

His adrenaline was flowing, his anger fueling his speedy ascent up the treacherous hill.

"The reign of Dezi and Aidan Gianni ends this week," he barked arriving at the top and pulling out his cell phone.

He needed to relax.

"Hello lover," Vanessa purred into his ear.

"Hi Vanessa, can I come by," Stephan quickly questioned.

"Of course darling, I'll leave the door unlocked," she replied as the smile found his face.

"I'm on my way, I need to shower," Stephan told her feeling the sweat rolling down his body.

"Mmm, that sounds delicious," Vanessa replied giggling lightly.

Stephan continued to smile, coasting down the other side of the hill he just climbed.

"I'll see you soon," she added and disconnected.

"Mariah Eveson, nice sound to it," Stephan mumbled of the woman who truly held his heart as he turned the bike toward the Trufont mansion and continued to daydream.

Stephan was so caught up in his thoughts of Mariah the mansion almost surprised him jumping into his line of sight. He quickly applied the brakes on the bike, almost throwing himself from it. He climbed down and placed the bike inconspicuously along the side of the mansion, near the garage where he entered the house.

"Vanessa," he called out not wanting to startle her.

"In here lover," he heard the voice, following the melodious sound.

She was waiting for him inside her bathroom, tub drawn, towel in her hand.

"Take off your clothes and get in," Vanessa sweetly voiced, helping him with the first button on his shirt.

Stephan quickly unbuttoned the rest, as well as his pants, and removed them quickly. He took off the underwear, growing erect, as Vanessa stood near him in the sheer peek-a-boo camisole and matching panty.

"Get in," she cajoled seeing his expression and noticing the rise.

Stephan obediently stepped into the water. It was perfect. The temperature was soothingly warm, but not hot. He took his time sitting in the huge garden tub, actually big enough to accommodate his height and laid back, eyes closed as Vanessa squeezed water over him from the large sea sponge she held and casually dunked into the tub.

"You like it," she questioned as Stephan sighed, nodding yes.

He was feeling extremely relaxed, almost to the point of nodding off.

Vanessa however certainly had other plans as he felt her hand slink down his stomach, his semi erect manhood now held firmly in her grasp. Stephan's eyes opened lazily, taking her in as she smirked and removed the camisole, pert breasts standing at attention with the hard nipples pointing the way. Stephan didn't move or react when she removed the panties and stepped gingerly into the tub with him. He loved sex with Vanessa, it was always one adventure after the other. Stephan smiled faintly as she went to her knees, giving him an underwater blow job, no regard for her hair or the water getting in it. *Damn, she can hold her breath pretty good,* Stephan thought as his erection quickly stiffened. Vanessa was able to raise her head from the water, still gobbling his shaft eliciting a few choice curses from Stephan's mouth regaling her skill. Closing his eyes again, his mind rapidly went to Mariah. He stiffened even more, still feeling Vanessa's warm mouth, but

Life After Death

picturing Mariah's dripping sex. He saw himself between her legs, licking her clit, sucking the juicy outer lips of her femininity. Stephan's breathing started growing choppy and short as his orgasm loomed. Vanessa sucked harder, relaxing her throat and allowing his shaft passage, the sensation and visual Stephan was enjoying, pushing him over the edge. Vanessa swallowed without flinching the hot cum rolling from him seemingly endlessly. Stephan was flaccid again within minutes. He hadn't experienced an orgasm like that in ages. Vanessa began bathing him, smiling back as he opened his eyes and looked at her, the lazy smile remaining on his lips.

●●●

Marchant did one last cursory check of the house before walking out of the back door and locking it. He didn't leave from the front knowing that his neighbors would be watching. His paranoia was still full blown as he peeked around the side of the small house, surveying the street both East and West, as well as directly in front of him. He didn't see anything. No unmarked black car, no strange men sipping coffee or eating sandwiches. *Maybe they backed off,* his mind spoke. Marchant did nothing to draw attention to himself since his trip to the west coast. He didn't hear from Marty again, so maybe things were okay and died down. Still, he couldn't be too careful, so he turned and walked through the back gate surrounding his home, small carryon in hand. The little path through the patch of woods made easy to follow by the numerous kids and dogs that used the shortcut to get from one street to another. Emerging from the wooded patch a scant eight minutes later, Marchant walked down the small residential street to the corner, knowing he would find the 24-hour convenience store. That was another quick walk and he was standing outside the brightly lit establishment some nine minutes past. Pulling out his cell Marchant dialed a cab. Giving his location, he turned and went inside the store, quickly purchasing a pack of gum and a fruit juice.

The cab was rapid and within fifteen minutes Marchant was on his way to the airport. His stomach was doing flips as the cabbie drove. The excitement and trepidation all were having a turn inside the cavity. When the entrance came into view, Marchant was downright exuberant. Climbing out of the cab, he jovially paid the cabbie and gave him a nice tip, turning and entering the airport. Marchant made his way to the counter and confirmed his flight, opting to take his bag onboard with him. He was now heading through security, praying he would have no delays. The officer doing the search paused when the metal detector went off.

"I'm a police officer, I do have my service revolver on me," Marchant told him honestly.

"I'm sorry sir, only the Air Marshall's are allowed to be armed," the security informed him. "You can check the gun as luggage and it can accompany you," he added as Marchant shrugged.

"That's fine."

The security officer called another over as they packaged the gun and took care of the necessary paperwork, having Marchant sign it before allowing him through the gates toward his plane. He wasn't bothered however. Marchant was steps away from months and years of painstaking police work. There wasn't much that could bring him down right now.

"Hello sir," the flight attendant greeted.

Marchant returned the smile and the greeting as the man looked at his ticket and directed him toward his seat.

"Thank you," Marchant returned, putting his carryon in the overhead and making himself comfortable.

The plane quickly began to fill and Marchant fretted they would be cramped and uncomfortable, but to his approval and relief, there were still several empty seats when the doors were closed and the pilot came over the intercom and announced they were cleared for takeoff. Marchant sat back, closed his eyes and fully relaxed feeling the plane begin to taxi down the runway. His thoughts took flight right along with the airplane as it left the ground and became airborne. Marchant recalled the night of the benefit when he first saw the beautiful woman married to the local pastor. He could still see every line and detail of the sexy red halter dress the woman's porcelain smooth skin was wrapped in. The perfect circumference her sexy breasts outlined as the dress's bodice kept a bit of the mystery. He would never forget the jolt of electricity that careened down his body when their eyes met. He was smitten, right then, right there. *Now you're trying to make the woman out to be the worst black widow killer in America,* his mind again threw in his face. Marchant shook the unpleasant thought preferring to remember the lightness. His next memory was the day she came to police headquarters after her husband's mistress was killed in their home. He smiled at the memory, able to feel her warmth in his arms as if he were holding her right now. Her perfume was heavenly making his heart sing, even as she cried and poured out her pain. *Why don't you leave the woman alone and let her live her life,* the irksome conscience returned.

Life After Death

"Because she belongs with me," Marchant murmured aloud, eyes opening as he stared in the darkness from the planes window eagerly anticipating their landing.

Life After 25 Death

Dezi threw his bag onto the bed, turning around and heading back into the main area of the suite in search of a drink.

"I ordered a bottle, should be here in a few minutes," Big D told him seeing the look and knowing what his friend wanted.

They arrived only a few minutes ago, but he knew Dezi was well past ready to handle his business. Big D knew Dezi didn't like being in the states and he didn't like being away from Kayla. Aidan walked into the main room just as the knock came to the door.

"Good, perfect timing," Dezi murmured as Big D went to the door.

"Hey how you two doing," he greeted, stepping aside and allowing the party entrance.

"Ahh K.C., Cedric, how are you gentlemen," Dezi greeted smiling now.

"How you doing Mr. Enzo, been a minute," K.C. returned.

"Yes it has," Dezi returned, greeting Cedric now as well.

Another knock came. This time it was room service with the bottles of Cognac, Crown, and Cîroc, they requested.

"This is my son Aidan," Dezi introduced the two men.

K.C. and Cedric greeted Aidan, immediately picking up the resemblance between the two men.

"I didn't expect you two to come, I thought you would send a soldier or two," Dezi told them honestly.

He located the two men, finding them on the West coast through some of his contacts and doing very well. They carved their own niche in the area, moving product effectively and making a nice living at it.

"Nah Mr. E, respect, you know that," K.C. told him as Dezi graciously thanked him for that.

"We got the information for that chick you wanted first, April," Cedric told him as Dezi sipped his drink.

"You have her location," he questioned, ready to get the ball rolling.

Life After Death

He was going to take care of the small players first, then Dezi harbored plans to visit an old friend.

"Yeah, she gets off work in about fifteen minutes," Cedric began. "She'll head to her favorite pub, Lennon's, then she'll head to her apartment," he told Dezi who was impressed with the wealth of information the men gathered in such a short time.

"Good, let's not keep her waiting," Dezi replied as K.C. and Cedric smiled.

Aidan liked the two men instantly; glad they had the help since they were effectively blind, not having been in the states for the past three plus years.

"What about security," Aidan questioned knowing the woman worked for the FBI.

"She's small shit, they don't worry about her," K.C. answered plainly, shrugging at the end of his sentence.

"Just another random chick to get popped, no biggie," Cedric added as the men finished their drinks and rose heading out into the night.

Time to go to work.

●●●

"Damn, glad to be off," April murmured lighting the cigarette and taking a deep pull from it.

She quickly unlocked the VW and climbed inside, just as quickly locking the doors back. Starting it, she backed out of the slot she found upon her arrival this morning and headed out of the parking garage. Reaching the street, April looked to and fro, assuring herself of no oncoming traffic before easing out and turning left, Lennon's on her mind. She needed two or three stiff drinks. Vernon was all over her ass all day today. Everyone was a bit edgy after Gar's suicide and Barbara Pender's murder. *What the fuck was he thinking,* April wondered turning into the bar. Finding a spot reasonably close she got out of the car, again looking around, slightly uneasy for some reason. Locking her car, April hurried inside glad to be in the light and surrounded by people. She found an empty barstool and climbed up on it.

"What can I get you," the bartender questioned coming over and placing a coaster in front of her.

"Kamikaze," April ordered without hesitation.

The bartender nodded slightly and moved away beginning to mix her drink. *Sure hope he makes it as strong as Stan,* April thought of the regular bartender. The guy could mix once seriously strong drink. He was also sexy and attractive. He was older, but that didn't matter to April. She wanted to screw him, but so far he wasn't receptive to any of her flirting.

"Here you go," the bartender interrupted her thought, putting the drink down and collecting her money.

April's mind went once again to Gar and the fiasco of the last week. Every major paper with the headline plastered on the front page. 'CIA Agent brutally rapes and kills Senator's daughter.' April still couldn't believe Gar capable of something like that, but the DNA couldn't lie. His semen was found all over the girls face, as well as skin and hair from his penis inside her mouth and throat. *Jeeesh,* April again thought draining the glass and asking for another. She scarcely spoke to JaDon since they got the news. Vernon almost immediately took him off watching Senator Pender's younger daughter and assigned him to a desk deep in the bowels of the basement's file room. April hoped all the madness would end and everything would go back to normal. The one conversation she managed with JaDon, they agreed to let the Gianni case go and move away. *"I feel like all the pressure pushed him over the edge,"* JaDon spoke sympathetically of Gar. *"Yeah, there was a lot of bullshit going on, especially from higher up,"* April returned as they drank and commiserated with each other. *"Shit, I wish he never mentioned that damned file or that I went and pulled it from the archives,"* JaDon murmured almost to himself. *"It's not your fault JaDon,"* April assured. *"Hell if Gar was that unstable, if not that case, another one that would have driven him over the edge,"* she told him, garnering a slight nod of understanding from him.

"You want another," the bartender questioned seeing the second empty glass.

"No, I better not," April returned, even though she really wanted too.

The last thing she needed was waking up with a raging hangover or worst yet to get stopped for a DWI trying to make it home. Getting down off the stool, April made her way outside and to her car, the liquor only amplifying the paranoia. Her cell rang and she uttered a short scream, jumping from the suddenness of it. A couple entering the bar gave her a peculiar look, but said nothing as they continued their way and went inside, leaving her alone in the parking lot.

"Hello," April answered, unlocking the car and jumping inside, again repeating her ritual of quickly locking it behind her.

Life After Death

"Hey April, just checking on you," JaDon's voice spoke as she started the vehicle preparing to leave.

"I'm okay, how about you," April replied, turning on the highway once again and heading for her apartment.

She heard a heavy breath as he spoke again.

"Sick of looking at fucking files and walls," JaDon returned with an edge to his voice.

"Hopefully it's not for much longer, you know Vernon can be a real dick," she told him hearing a small snort in return.

"Don't I know it," JaDon added.

"I'm going to the memorial service for Gar tomorrow," April told him.

"Yeah I thought about it, but I doubt I go," JaDon told her and she didn't push.

"You home yet," he questioned, hearing her driving.

"Yeah just pulled into my spot," April returned giggling.

"Cool, well see you in the morning," JaDon returned as she disconnected and got out, securing her car and walking to her apartment door, opening the door and coming inside.

Turning on the light, April stopped in her tracks, the scream stuck in her throat as she looked into the face of a dead man.

● ● ●

"Hello April," Dezi greeted calmly as the woman continued to stare, slack jawed.

"I see you're speechless," he added, chuckling at the end of his sentence.

Big D smiled a bit, as did Aidan. Cedric and K.C. remained stoic. She swallowed hard, unsure what to do or say at the moment.

"You and your friends were looking for me I'm told," Dezi began anew, still sitting comfortably in the easy chair, arms resting easily on his lap.

"No, we were --, um --," April stuttered still in a state of disbelief that the man was in her living room, alive, well, and scaring the hell out of her.

"You were just sticking your nose in shit that you should have left alone," Big D growled, irritated with the specimen in front of him.

He was thinking of all the drama they were enduring to come back to the states to handle this nonsense. The time and money wasted. Not that they missed it, but it was principal.

"We didn't mean any harm, we just wanted to know about you," she told Dezi, wringing her hands nervously now.

"Why don't you have a seat April, let's talk," Dezi told her still watching her intently.

April quickly moved to the other armchair her living room contained. Before the serene greens and fluid melons and reds made her feel safe and comfortable, tonight they all screamed pain and chaos as April began to silently pray, saying a rosary she thought she forgot ages ago.

"So here we are," Dezi told her, sitting up now. "I'm here, so what did you want to know about me," he fired and April saw the change reflected in his eyes.

They changed from lively and mesmerizing, to cold and emotionless in one fallen second.

"I --, I -," she stuttered, annoying Big D and Aidan as well.

"Speak up bitch, seriously, you're about to work a nerve," Aidan growled taking a step toward her.

"Please Mr. Gianni, we didn't mean any harm, and no one will know you were here," April pleaded as Dezi smirked.

"Oh they'll know I was here April," he told her as K.C. and Cedric finally showed a bit of emotion in the knowing sneers they wore now.

"Please, I swear I won't tell anyone," she tried again, the tears stinging her eyes.

"Do you have JaDon's number," Aidan questioned.

April nodded yes.

"Call him," Dezi ordered. "Tell him to come see you, now," he added the tone leaving no room for discussion.

April's hands were trembling making it hard for her to hold onto the phone, but she managed to press the numbers and wait for the call to connect.

"Hello," JaDon answered smoothly.

"Hey, I was wondering if you wanted to come over," April spoke, praying like hell he said yes.

Life After Death

"It's kinda late April," JaDon hedged.

"Please JaDon, I don't want to be alone," she told him truthfully.

She heard him sigh and prayed even harder.

"OK, fine, I'll be there in about twenty minutes," JaDon returned.

"Cool, see you then," April returned disconnecting.

"Very good," Dezi told her. "When should we expect him," he questioned now.

"Twenty minutes," April replied as he smiled and her fear tripled.

Dezi got up and walked over to the chair where she sat and looked down at her. "When I talked to Gar, he told me some very interesting reasoning why you all were looking for me, at least why he was looking," Dezi began, never taking his eyes from her. "So now why don't you tell me why you were looking for me," he fired and waited on her to answer.

"I wasn't, not really," she quickly responded. "JaDon and Gar, they were the ones hot and heavy to find out what happened to you, who you were, what you held over the heads of the higher ups," April poured out.

"But yet here you are," Dezi again spoke.

"I um --," she got out before he slapped her hard knocking her from the chair.

"See April, one thing I despise is to be lied to," Dezi told her snatching her from the floor and hitting her again.

"I'm not lying, please," April yelled trying to plead her case.

"You picked the wrong friends April," he growled and her blood ran cold.

"I've worked hard to have my life, to be left alone, and I have no plans of giving any of it up because of bunch of nosey ass punks with too much time on their hands," Dezi finished, punching her in the face, hearing her nose break as she crumpled to the floor.

"Noooo," April screamed as Dezi snatched her up from the floor again shaking her like a rag doll.

"Here I am April, here I fucking am," he told her angrily. "Are you happy to see me, glad you found me," Dezi fired, whipping the razor from his pocket.

Big D smiled marginally watching his friend in action. Dezi was in rare form and sadly for April she was going to bear the brunt of his fury, at least until her friend arrived.

"You should have learned to stay in your damned lane," Dezi told her as he continued cutting her and the blood stain grew.

"I'll --, plee--," April tried as Dezi kicked her hard to the ribs.

"Who else," he railed, grabbing her head and pulling it back painfully.

"You, Gar, JaDon, and who the fuck else knows about this bullshit," Dezi questioned.

"Vernon," April managed struggling to breath.

Dezi gave Big D a look. They both knew the director of the FBI long before that title became his.

"Who else," he growled, still furious.

"Keller," she whispered, barely clinging to consciousness.

Aidan saw his father's eyes narrow and knew the man just made his father's kill list.

"I'm done with you now April, time for us to depart," Dezi spoke as her eyes held his, fear laced, begging, pleading with him not to kill her.

The door chimed, garnering the men's attention for the moment. Dezi gave K.C. a look. He and Cedric headed to the door, Cedric behind it, K.C. opening it as they snatched a shocked and surprised JaDon inside.

"What the hell," he murmured angrily, preparing to defend himself.

"Don't be stupid," K.C. shot back, Cedric holding the .10mm on him.

JaDon allowed himself to be led through the foyer into the living area, his breath leaving him as he saw April, but his heart stopped beating momentarily when he saw the man holding the gleaming straight razor to her throat.

•••

Fuck me, JaDon thought as Dezi Gianni looked back into his eyes.

"Thank you for coming," he spoke calmly, never taking his eyes from the man standing in front of him. "I understand I have you to thank for this little resurrection visit," Dezi told him, April whimpering in pain.

Life After Death

He yanked her head harder, straining her neck more, in response to her protests.

"Gar was the one who brought you up," JaDon quickly defended.

"Yes, but you stole the file, made the copy, went to see Adrian," Dezi slapped back into his face.

JaDon's mind was racing he tried to think fast.

"You and I need to talk, but let me finish this bit of business first," Dezi spoke evenly, the razor blazing a ruby red trail around April's neck as he cut her throat.

JaDon felt the bile rise in his throat pressing his fingertips into his palm as hard as he could to contain the impending escapee. April's eyes grew big as she realized she was dying, hands around her throat trying to delay the inevitable. Apparently patience wasn't on Dezi's menu tonight as JaDon watched him hold out his hand and one of the men who snatched him inside, put a .9mm silencer laden pistol in his hands.

"Loose ends, hate them," Dezi spoke calmly as he put three slugs into April's head, her body jerking with each bullet, spasm one final time and became still.

"Now," Dezi spoke, rising and taking the lit cigar offered. "Let's deal with you," he added and JaDon began blink rapidly.

"You don't have to kill me Mr. Gianni," he quickly threw out.

"Why not," Dezi humored as he continued to smoke.

"Because I can be useful to you," JaDon told him. "I was only looking for you because honestly I envied the hell out of what you did," he went on as all the men regarded him, and Dezi allowed him to talk.

"Why would I believe a word of what you just said," he questioned and JaDon swallowed hard.

"Because it's true," he spoke anew. "April and Gar, they might have believed all that bullshit the FBI and CIA was feeding us, but I'm not stupid," JaDon told Dezi. "I know that power, real power, comes from brains, money, and muscle," he went on. "And you have all three Mr. Gianni, that's why you're still alive and that's why everyone is scared shitless that you might come back," he finished and prayed he was getting through.

Dezi continued to smoke.

"So you want what exactly," Aidan spoke up now.

JaDon regarded the man noting the marked resemblance, not only physically, but the ruthlessness was just as brazen in him as his father. Thinking of it, every man in the room was cold and cunning, quick to kill you just as soon as look at you.

"I want what any normal man would want, success," JaDon replied coolly. "I'm just honest enough to admit I don't give a shit whether I get it legally or illegally," he finished seeing a small hint of a smile on Dezi's lips.

JaDon prayed it was enough to keep him alive.

Dezi rose, finished with the cigar and walked over to where JaDon stood, K.C. and Cedric flanking either side.

"That's a great outlook JaDon," Dezi told him. "See my problem however becomes trust," he went on as JaDon remained quiet. "I mean, sure it all sounds really good, but who's to say once we leave this room you won't run to your boss and tell him about me, have the entire FBI and CIA down my throat," Dezi quizzed.

"Because those five minutes of fame won't line my pockets," JaDon replied.

Dezi nodded thoughtfully, still quietly regarding the man as he stood behind him. JaDon felt his knees buckle before his brain registered the hard punch to his left kidney. Dezi gave K.C. a look and the two men began to beat JaDon mercilessly, faces emotionless as they rained blow after blow after blow on him.

"Let him catch air," Dezi spoke as they stopped and stepped back.

JaDon's face was a grotesque smattering of lumps, bruises, swollen cheeks and blackened eye.

"If what you wanted was to be a part of my business JaDon, you would have never involved your friends, especially knowing they didn't share those aspirations," Dezi told him coldly.

"Do you know why I'm here JaDon," he fired now and the battered subdued man simply shook his head no. "I'm here because I don't plan to leave a living, breathing, witness who can ever, ever, raise the kind of drama that you and your friends have brought to my doorstep once again," Dezi finished the sharp pain searing his spinal column, dropping him to his side.

"Wait, please Mr. Gianni, wait," JaDon managed to yell feeling the sharp pain again and again.

Life After Death

"You should have let me stay dead," Dezi told him. "Then you wouldn't be," he finished driving the ice pick deeply in JaDon's temple.

The same pick he used to stab him over twenty times in his back. Dezi turned the man over, using the ice pick to puncture both eyes.

"See no evil muthafucka," he growled, as they trashed the apartment, took any documents that may have pointed back to Dezi, then calmly opened the front door and left the apartment heading for their vehicles parked across the street.

"Fuck me," they voice came low and awe filled.

Dezi's head whipped to the sound as did the others. K.C. and Cedric held their weapons trained directly on the shadowed figure; Aidan and Big D pulling theirs as well.

"Step into the light," Dezi spoke evenly.

The man did as he asked.

"Son of a bitch," Dezi murmured the smile full blown.

He walked over to the man as they embraced.

"I thought you were dead man," Stan told him still blown away.

"Long story, but come ride with me and I'll tell you all about it," he told Taea's brother, thrilled to lay eyes on him again.

Life After 26 Death

Marchant smiled opening the drapes inside his room as he stretched and took in the brilliant sunrise. The room was magnificent too as he glanced around it. Huge king size bed, with an expansive vividly colored comforter, blues, yellows, greens and oranges harmoniously arranged in varying patterns throughout. The walls were a happy melon green, with tan wicker furnishings complimenting the entirely relaxed atmosphere the hotel was striving to provide. He slept better last night, than in ages. His body and mind were in congruence as the sleep came and lasted. Glancing at the clock on the nightstand the hotel room heralded, he saw it was just a little after 9 AM. He and Stephan were having lunch at noon to go over the file and shore up all the details for tomorrow's meeting with Kayla. Thinking of it, Marchant smiled a bit. He was here. She was here. This time he would get answers, this time he would get her. *You better be super careful*, his mind told him for the hundredth time. Marchant knew, from Stephan's Intel, that the boyfriend wasn't in town. This was the perfect opportunity. He would pressure Kayla into returning to the states with him, arresting her on suspicion of conspiracy if all else failed. *Whatever it takes to get her on that damned plane,* Marchant surmised. He made up his mind that he would deal with his Captain and any censure from the Fed's when he got back. He would have Kayla, the evidence, and an arrest to flaunt in their faces. *Are you really going to let this woman go to prison*, the mind queried.

He didn't want too. Marchant prayed she was innocent, but he wanted her back on American soil to prove that fact. He would be good to her, provide a good life for her, his thoughts raced before reality again screeched into his existence. *What if she's guilty, what if she is the black widow you think she is, do you think she won't have you killed or kill you herself if it means saving her life*, his mind pointedly put onto the table.

"Hmph," Marchant remarked aloud, heading for the bathroom and turning on the shower.

The hotel was really nice and he was glad he arrived early needing the time to relax and wind down. It also meant he wouldn't be tired and edgy when he met with Kayla. Marchant didn't kid himself. If she were doing this for as long as he suspected, he knew she would be very good at feigning her innocence. He needed to be on top of his game if he hoped to break her web of lies and make her admit once and for all her role in the murder of her ex-husband and former lover. *How many other men have you killed or had*

Life After Death

killed Kayla, Marchant posed inwardly, stepping under the tepid spray and beginning to lather his body. Sticking his head under the water now washing out the shampoo he used moments earlier, Marchant shored his resolve. He was going to get what he came for, by any means necessary.

Stepping out and drying himself, Marchant began dressing, checking his reflection and deciding he would forego shaving today. Shorts, t-shirt and sunglasses in place, Marchant picked up the card key and headed toward the elevator. He wanted to do a bit of sightseeing, checking out the various shops and scenery surrounding the hotel. The shoreline was visible from his window, so he was sure it was a short walk as well. Punching the lobby button once he was inside the elevator, Marchant leaned casually against the elevator's interior, enjoying the soft Caribbean beats floating through the sound system. The elevator car stopped on two other floors before reaching the lobby and releasing them all from its grip. Marchant headed toward the double glass doors, pushing them open and stepping outside. The humidity instantly assailed him, the small beads of sweat breaking out along his hairline and the back of his neck.

"Damn, this heat is a beast," he murmured as he walked along, casually enjoying the crafts and displays he passed in his wake.

He felt his cell vibrate and pulled it from his pocket.

"Hello Stephan," Marchant greeted amiably.

"Good Morning Dwayne," the man returned. "Are you settled," he questioned as Marchant chuckled.

"Yes, slept great," he told Stephan. "I'm about to enjoy some breakfast at this street café I'm passing."

Stephan asked the name of it and Marchant read it from the sign in front.

"Yes, they have wonderful food," Stephan enlightened. "Relax and enjoy, I'll see you at noon," he finished up.

"Sounds good," Marchant returned as they disconnected and he found a seat, picking up a menu.

● ● ●

Cassandra, true to her word, was sitting in the foyer area of Captain Caroline Wilmont's office waiting for the woman to come into the office. Glancing at her watch Cassandra took in the time, noting Captain Wilmont was so far ten minutes late. *Shit, come on, we need to get this done,* she thought anxiously. Keller awakened her at six a.m. telling her they needed to move right now.

"What in the hell is going on that he's not telling me," she murmured growing increasingly uncomfortable with the situation.

The idleness allowed Cassandra's mind to go to her own issues. She still wanted out of the CIA, that never changed and Layton Crowler was going to open that door for her. She smirked thinking about the conversation and his promises. *You better hope this case is over before he calls your bluff,* her conscience spoke up. Cassandra wasn't stupid. The moment she found out she was pregnant she knew she established a way out from under Layton's thumb. He didn't need to know she never held any intention of having a child from him and that she aborted the fetus the day after their meeting. The threat, so far, was proving to be more than enough to keep him in check.

The sound of voices and laughter shook her from her pondering and Cassandra focused her mind back on business.

"Captain Wilmont," Cassandra inquired, rising from her seat.

The Captain stopped talking to the detective accompanying her, taking in the suit clad woman, her intuition telling her this meeting wasn't going to be good.

"I'll catch you later Caroline," the detective spoke, giving her a look that said he agreed with her inner speculation.

"OK Mike," Caroline returned using the man's name.

Turning her attention fully back to Cassandra now, she spoke.

"Yes, I'm Captain Wilmont," Caroline acknowledged. "And you are," she questioned, eyebrow raised.

"I'm Agent Cassandra Deale, CIA," the woman spoke and Caroline's mouth went dry.

Now she knew this wasn't a good meeting.

"May I speak with you privately, it's a matter of grave importance," Cassandra vocalized.

Caroline nodded without speaking, stepping over to her office door and unlocking it. She invited Cassandra in, offering her coffee. Cassandra declined, wanting and needing to get immediately to business.

"So how can I help you, Agent Deale," Caroline questioned, taking a seat in the large swivel chair behind her desk.

Life After Death

Cassandra opened her briefcase and extricated a large manila folder, laying it on Caroline's desk.

"I have a warrants for the three officers named on the first page, charges ranging from harassment to abuse of authority," she told Caroline who was staring incredulously at the pages in front of her.

"I also have a warrant for Detective Dwayne Marchant, for aggravated battery, coercion, and violation of civil rights against Lonnie Myles," she finished calmly waiting for the woman sitting opposite her to speak.

Caroline's eyes were scanning the documents in front of her, mind racing. She secretly suspected that at some point the Lonnie Myles fiasco would come back to haunt them, she just had no idea it would happen in such a huge way. The CIA being involved definitely negated any possibility of a work around in the situation.

"Why is the CIA involved and not the FBI," Caroline questioned, buying time, and genuinely curious.

This seemed to be far outside of their scope of interest.

"Because there are entities inside the FBI that are suspected in helping to cover this up in the first place," Cassandra smoothly lied.

Caroline nodded shortly, seeing Maurice Alston's signature at the bottom of each warrant. *Power happy bastard,* Caroline fumed, helpless to change it.

"We would like to give you the respect and courtesy of gathering the officers in question yourself, before the CIA questions and determines if further detention is necessary on our end," Cassandra continued to spin the web.

Picking up her desk phone, Caroline made two calls. The first she requested two of the three officers be sent to her office immediately. The second call she requested the last officer.

"What about Dwayne Marchant," Cassandra questioned, noting that the woman made no inquiries about him.

"I'll have to send a unit to his home," Caroline spoke, her tone cool. "He requested time off beginning today," she completed the explanation.

"I understand," Cassandra returned, making a quick mental note to send her own team over to Marchant's home.

"I'll let you handle your officers," Cassandra graciously offered, rising now. "Please contact me once they've all been processed and I will return with an interrogator to question them," she finished as Caroline continued to regard her, the earlier friendliness vanquished.

"Yes, of course," she returned brusquely.

Cassandra sighed slightly, before offering a tight smile and leaving the Captain's office. As soon as she stepped outside, she pulled out her Blackberry and texted the other two men working with her, sending them to Marchant's home. *Can't be too careful,* she resolved getting into her car and heading back to the hotel suite to await word that Marchant had been detained.

•••

Dang, time flies doesn't it, Marchant inwardly mused chuckling aloud as he saw it was almost noon. He spent the morning enjoying the shops, breakfast, walking along the shoreline and holding various conversations with some of the locals.

"Could definitely get used to this life," he murmured aloud arriving back at the hotel and walking inside.

He wanted to get a quick shower, and change before Stephan's arrival. They were meeting inside the hotel's restaurant. Tomorrow however, Kayla would be brought to his suite. Marchant wanted privacy when he questioned her. No interference from bystanders if things got a bit loud or heated. He slid the card key into the lock and heard it disengage. Stepping inside he quickly stripped his sweat dampened clothing and headed once more for the shower. He finished his task, dressed, and arrived downstairs in time to see the uniformed officer he assumed was Stephan, walk inside. Their eyes met and each gave the other a small smile. Stephan walked over to where Marchant stood, speaking as he offered his hand.

"Detective Marchant, happy to meet you finally," Stephan spoke smiling broadly.

Marchant returned the greeting as they turned and headed inside the restaurant, taking a seat.

Stephan pulled out a small pad when Marchant laid the paper brown folder onto the table in front of them.

"And you're sure the boyfriend won't interfere," Marchant questioned yet again.

He didn't want any last minute complications, his nerves flaring just slightly.

"No, he's out of the country actually," Stephan confidently replied.

Life After Death

"Hmph, well that's good to hear," Marchant replied as their drinks arrived and he opened the folder showing Stephan the information contained.

"It's kind of hard to believe you know," Stephan told him, sitting back casually enjoying his tea. "Kayla is one of the nicest people you would ever meet," he added as Marchant nodded in agreement.

"I've only interacted with her on a limited basis, but I would be tempted to draw that same conclusion," Marchant conceded. "However, you can't deny these are some helluva coincidences."

Stephan acknowledged his statement. He formed his own theory, but didn't enlighten the detective. He observed Marchant since they started talking about the woman and he quickly ascertained there was far more sitting in front of him than a detective trying to close a case. Detective Marchant was on a personal hunt of his own. Stephan fully suspected the man was in love with Kayla, using the case as an excuse to find her, and take her back to the states. He almost smiled, but caught the gesture.

"I understand what you're saying Dwayne, and tomorrow you'll have the opportunity to put your theories into action," Stephan baited.

"Yes, and I have you to thank for that Stephan," Marchant replied.

"Just helping a fellow law enforcement officer," he spoke of the compliment. "As much as I like Kayla, if she is guilty of the things you've shown me, well, I have to put those feelings aside and make sure justice is served," Stephan told him.

Marchant nodded, liking the sound of that. It made his next question far easier to pose.

"Stephan, I may have to take Kayla back to the United States, possibly against her will," he began as the man waved nonchalantly.

"I will help you ready her for transport, by whatever means are necessary," Stephan replied his meaning very clear.

Marchant smiled again and thanked him. The server brought their requested lunch entrée's as they began to eat and continued to talk about tomorrow and what they hoped and expected. Stephan's excitement was growing with each passing moment. There were plans for Joell tomorrow as well. The new regime was only hours from being in place. *Going to be some surprised residents when that plane lands this time,* Stephan chuckled silently, attacking his food with new gusto.

•••

Cassandra felt the instrument vibrate, quickly washing her hands and walking back into the main room of the suite from the bathroom.

"Yes," she answered seeing the agent's name on the caller I.D.

"He's gone," the man said and her heart dropped.

"What do you mean gone," Cassandra questioned already hearing Keller's voice in her ear screaming at her about her incompetence.

"He's left town, we're tossing the house now trying to find a clue where that is," the agent told her making her feel somewhat better.

"Find out, our ass is on the line here," Cassandra fired as the man assured her he would and disconnected.

Call Keller, her mind prompted.

"No, not just yet," she muttered wanting to wait to see what the agents turned up.

"Where the hell are you, Dwayne," Cassandra continued to consider.

This was a complication they could certainly have done without. Cassandra opened her suitcase and pulled out the Android phone she kept personally. She knew that everything they did was recorded at some point or other using company issued equipment. What she needed to handle now was personal. Quickly going to the internet, Cassandra typed in a web address waiting for the page to load.

She studied the information presented once she entered her login, satisfied with the results. *As soon as I find out where Dwayne Marchant is, I'm calling Layton and this bullshit is done,* she perused, shutting down the site and going to another. Again, she entered login information and retrieved what she sought. Cassandra finally dialed the last number on her list and waited for the call to connect.

"What," Layton answered curtly.

"When are you taking care of your end of the bargain," she fired just as dryly.

Cassandra heard him suck his teeth, then his voice.

"When the shit is finished and from what Keller tells me, we still have a loose end in your territory," Layton told her nastily. "Why don't you take care of that and stop bothering me," he added testily.

Life After Death

"That will be handled in about ten minutes," Cassandra confidently told him. "I just want to make sure that everything is ready so I can walk away," she finished and again waited for him to speak.

"I haven't forgotten, trust I don't want to see you or that damned brat you're carrying in your belly," Layton told her, gaining an unseen smirk from Cassandra.

"No love lost on my end either," she told him.

"Call me when it's done, not before, goodbye Agent Deale," Layton angrily retorted and disconnected.

"Bastard," Cassandra mumbled just as the Blackberry vibrated.

She took a deep breath and answered, praying she would get some good news. "Tell me you found him," she questioned the agent.

"Yeah, but you're not going to like the destination one bit," he told her and Cassandra steeled herself.

"Tell me," she said simply.

"Pembroke Parrish, Bahamas," the man enlightened.

"Fuck me," she murmured and he immediately agreed with her sentiment.

Dwayne Marchant just became an expendable liability.

"Thanks, let's get ready to move," she told him knowing Keller would pull them out of the state now.

She disconnected, said a short prayer, and dialed Keller's cell.

"What do you have for me," he answered, sounding calm.

Cassandra took another breath, quickly blew it out and began to speak.

"Marchant has managed to slip out of our net," she told Keller, still bracing.

"What does that mean Cassandra," he questioned and she heard the chill enter his voice.

I will not get caught up in this shit, I've got to get out, Cassandra was thinking knowing it was about to get seriously dangerous.

"He's left the country," she again told Keller, not fully enlightening him.

"And gone where," he once more posed.

Cassandra swallowed hard, pressed her nails into her palms and put it out there.

"Pembroke Parrish," she spoke, the silence culpable on his end.

"Be in my office by 7PM," Keller spoke and disconnected without another word.

"Shit," Cassandra murmured her stomach in knots.

The knock at the door scared her and she jumped, letting out a short scream. *Pull yourself together,* her mind told her as she opened the door to a smiling Maurice on the other side.

Life After Death

Life After 27 Death

Stan was still in a state of euphoric surprise. He played a hunch last night when he followed April home. It was the same hunch he was playing for the previous three weeks after overhearing their conversation one night at Lennon's. Stan managed to land the job bartending there after being turned down by just about everyone else in town. He smiled slightly recalling his conversation with Dezi after they returned to the hotel. *"When did you get out, where have you been,"* Dezi questioned as they smoke and drank, getting reacquainted. *"Man where haven't I been is the better question,"* he replied going on to explain his almost nomadic existence since getting out of prison some ten years ago. *"Kids are all grown, wife decided she wanted a new life,"* he told Dezi who nodded sympathetically. *"So you're not attached to D.C. then,"* Dezi questioned, eyebrow raised. Stan burst into laughter and quickly answered him. *"Hell no, I'm only attached to making money, and I'll go wherever to do that,"* Stan told him honestly. *"I think you should come home with me then,"* Dezi spoke without hesitation. *"Where's home these days,"* Stan questioned. Dezi enlightened him, the man's mouth hanging open at the end of the explanation. *"Well hell makes sense now,"* Stan murmured and Dezi asked him to elaborate. Stan explained the reasoning for him being outside of April's house. *"I heard them talking, heard your name, and they were so sneaky and secretive, made me curious,"* he elaborated. *"Hmph, that's the reason I'm here actually,"* Dezi spoke.

Stan was still reeling from the things Dezi shared, but he wasn't the least bit hesitant or remorseful about agreeing to not only help him, but to travel back to Pembroke Parrish with him. The knock on the door broke his pondering as he saw Big D rise and answer it. Stan liked the man almost instantly; they were going to get along very well. Aidan was definitely his father's son, no doubting that one. Not only did they look considerably alike, the young man shared his father's ruthlessness. There was no hesitation or questioning about what was about to transpire. He even made several suggestions about the debts to be paid. *I get to see Kayla again,* Stan thought and smiled slightly. He missed so much of her life. Hell the baby was a grown woman now, married to Dezi's son, and a mother in her own right. *Taea would have been so proud of her,* he again mused as Big D walked over to him.

"Here we are Mr. Herring," he chuckled handing Stan the new documents.

Dezi immediately arranged for a passport and new identification for him once it was decided he would return to the island with them. Stan chuckled and took the packet from Big D.

"Damn, this is good work," he spoke aloud, as the two still laughed.

Dezi walked into the room, greeting them both.

"Aah, I see the package arrived," he noted, making himself a drink.

"Yeah a few minutes ago," Stan enlightened.

Dezi came over and took the documents, looking each one over.

"We about ready to make a move," Stan questioned.

"Yes, we're waiting for K.C., Cedric, and Aidan to return," Dezi told them. "They were making some last minute adjustments to the earlier plan," he went on. "There's an errand I need to run however," he spoke and Big D frowned.

"Not alone," he said simply as Stan immediately concurred.

"Alright, but we need to head out now," Dezi replied.

"Let's go then," Big D spoke, putting the .9mm in his pocket.

Dezi picked up the card key as they walked toward the suite's door. Stan put his own .9mm in his pocket. He bought it off the streets with his first check from the bar, not wanting to be vulnerable and unprotected. They walked to the elevator, pressing the down button, stepping back and waiting.

"When are we leaving," Stan questioned once they stepped inside the metal box and pressed the ground floor.

"I don't see any reason to stay here after tonight honestly," Dezi spoke. "We'll fly back first thing in the morning," he added as Stan nodded and Big D concurred.

"Once we land and you see Kayla of course, we'll let you rest a bit before we get you into the business and find you a place," Dezi told him, the doors coming open.

"Not too much rest," Big D teased. "I got plenty for you to do," he added as Stan laughed again.

Yes, he and Big D were going to be cool together. Stepping outside of the hotel, Big D hailed them a cab. Getting in Dezi gave the man an address, receiving a strange look from the driver before a quick shrug of his shoulders, turning around and pulling down the meter, away from the curb and toward their destination.

● ● ●

"Let me out, you can't keep me in here, Stephan, do you hear me," Joell screamed again.

He couldn't believe the audacity of the man. They attacked him as he entered the station this morning. Stephan and Jacob, subduing him as they dragged him here to the back of the jail, locking him in the solitary cell designed for criminals awaiting extradition to other jurisdictions. No one would hear him, or let him out. *I've got to get to a phone,* Joell continued to think. He overheard Stephan last night talking to someone. They were making some sort of plans, and whatever they were Mrs. D. Gianni was involved.

"He's crazy," Joell again thought of Stephan.

He knew the man was in love with Mariah, but he never expected him to go off the deep end like he this.

"Are you sure he's going to be undetected," Joell heard the voice.

He recognized Jacob, assuming he was talking to Stephan.

"He'll be fine, you just make sure he stays put," he told this gullible friend.

"Do you really believe Mrs. D Gianni is a killer," Jacob asked as Joell frowned deeply still paying rapt attention to their conversation.

"No, but this detective from the states is going to help me bring down those two arrogant bastards," Stephan growled irritably.

"What about Mariah, she'll be devastated if this man takes her mother away," Jacob spoke yet another time.

Takes her away, what the hell is going on, Joell pondered his stomach clenching.

"I'm going to take care of Mariah," Stephan returned, further distressing Joell.

"She'll call her husband, what then," Jacob questioned.

"No she won't call him, I'll keep her occupied, and I have plans to keep her away from a phone," Stephan again replied.

How long has this loon been planning this foolish venture, Joell's questions continued.

"Well I hope this all goes right Stephan," Jacob told him. "Neither Gianni is a man I want to cross," he added hearing Stephan scoff.

"To hell with them both," he fired arrogantly. "By the time they return, Kayla will be gone, Mariah will be with me, Kareek will be out of power and Arroyo will be kissing my ass to keep his life," Stephan fired confidently.

Joell had heard enough. He had to get out of the cell and call Dezi. He was extremely pleased now the man gave him his number. *How are you going to do that,* his mind questioned again.

"I'm leaving now, so make sure you keep an eye on him, and that Leeks or Salaim don't go back there," Stephan ordered, calling the other two officers by name.

"I got it, just make sure it goes right Stephan," Jacob once again worriedly spoke.

"Relax Jacob, when this is over you will be my chief deputy," Stephan again cockily assured.

Joelle heard the front door to the precinct close seconds later and the familiar sound of Jacob plopping down in his chair and propping his feet on the desk. Joell prayed that today he would be true to form and fall asleep, knowing that Leeks and Salaim would be in shortly.

•••

Marchant was nervous, continually chiding himself for the emotion. *Relax, pull yourself together, you have to be professional,* he tried to boost, arranging the documents on the small coffee table in the room. He had bottled water and juice inside the small mini fridge the suite possessed. Checking his watch Marchant saw that it was almost 10AM. Stephan phoned a little over ten minutes ago letting him know he would be arriving soon. He checked his supplies again, seeing the handcuffs as well as the zip ties. He asked Stephan to bring those for him, praying he didn't have to use them, but wanting to be prepared just in case. *Your hard work is about to pay off, three long years,* his mind spoke eliciting a deep sigh from Marchant.

"Now comes the hard part," he mumbled.

He found her, and arranged a meeting, now it was time to make her admit her involvement in the entire fiasco. The knock came to the door startling him as Marchant took another deep breath, steeled his reserve and walked to the door. Opening it he was slightly disappointed to only see Stephan.

Life After Death

His expression must have conveyed his thoughts as the officer chuckled a bit and walked inside.

"Relax, they will be here in about five minutes," he told Marchant who frowned at the word they.

Stephan again correctly read the man's response. "Her daughter is coming with her," he enlightened, gaining a relieved nod from Marchant.

"That's fine, but I want to question her alone," he told Stephan.

"That's not a problem," he returned. "I'm going to take Mariah for a walk around the hotel while you two talk," Stephan told him.

"That's fine," Marchant replied as Stephan's cell chimed.

"Speak of the devil," he murmured smiling and answering the call. "Yes, I'm on my way down to get you," he told the party. "No problem, just glad I could help," he added and disconnected.

Turning to Marchant he spoke.

"I hope you're ready, here we go," Stephan told him as he retreated from the suite heading downstairs to get the two women waiting for him.

Marchant's heart began to beat rapidly, his pulse starting to race. In a scant few moments of time he would be face to face with the woman who occupied his every thought for the past three years. He would be close enough to touch her, inhale her scent, look deeply into the beautiful brown eyes that held him transfixed all those nights ago. *Focus, you're supposed to be getting the truth out of her,* his mind again recalled, slightly nudging him back toward the true task at hand. His heart however still had a full agenda all its own. Marchant cracked the seal on the bottle of water and drank almost half of it, his mouth suddenly feeling like dried parchment. Thankfully, the burp came before the knock.

Marchant took a huge breath; lungs filled to capacity, counted to ten, and then strode toward the door. He opened it, his eyes meeting hers. Kayla's expression quickly showed her confusion.

"Please, Mrs. Bradford, come in," Marchant spoke as Kayla glanced toward Stephan.

"Please," Marchant spoke again, his voice a bit more forceful.

"You said you found my property Stephan," Kayla told him getting a very bad feeling.

"I'm sorry, but this is official business," he told her, his tone stiff and formal.

"What's going on," Mariah questioned her anger beginning to rise.

"Who are you and what do you want with my mother," she fired at Marchant.

"Mariah, come with me, this is police business," Stephan began.

"What police business, who is this man," she yelled, turning on the officer.

"I'm going to have to insist Kayla," Marchant tried again as she regarded him silently.

"OK, fine," Kayla finally spoke.

"No mommy, it most certainly is not fine," Mariah again railed.

"It's okay honey, I'll be fine," Kayla told her daughter, simply wanting to get whatever this was, over with.

"Come on Mariah, we'll take a walk," Stephan sweetly posed.

Mariah gave him a scathing look.

"No, I'm going to stand right here, better yet, I'm coming inside and listen to what you have to say to my mother," she told them, looking Marchant in the eye.

Deciding he wanted to avoid a scene, he invited them both in.

"Would you object to your mother and I speaking in the other room," he tried genially.

Mariah was again quiet for a while before deciding it would be okay since she was so close.

"Fine," she again fired as Marchant smiled slightly thanking her, walking over to the bedroom and opening the door, picking up the file as he followed Kayla inside and closed the door.

"It's going to be fine Mariah," Stephan told her rising and getting her a bottle of papaya juice.

He opened it for her, pouring it in the cup he picked up on the way over to her, the sedative sliding easily inside and quickly dissolving before he handed it to her and she began to drink.

Life After 28 Death

Cassandra's mind was racing as she sat inside her apartment staring out of her bay window. She loved the view, it was one of the main reasons she bought the condo in the first place. The meeting with Keller was cancelled by him at the last minute saying something came up. Not one for being kept in the dark, Cassandra made a few calls of her own. Unfortunately whatever was going on was being kept securely under the radar. In her mind that wasn't a good thing. *Too much going on*, she thought sighing and sipping the hot tea she held. Strangely enough Cassandra found herself missing Maurice. He sweetly understood when she told him she was reassigned. *"Well you know of course I've enjoyed our time together,"* Maurice said sweetly as he kissed her. *"I've enjoyed it too, probably far more than I should have,"* Cassandra spoke, not totally lying. She smiled slightly thinking of them making love yet another time before he left her with a final goodbye and a promise to at least text or email him on occasion.

Rising Cassandra headed into her bedroom. She opened the small fire safe she kept removing several documents. Dwayne Marchant's disappearance severely complicated things for her. Layton Crowler would definitely not keep his promise now and her time was running out. Cassandra's intuition told her something horrendous was on the horizon. Honestly she didn't believe Keller's damage control was working. Things were beginning to spiral out of control, and the blackout she ran into last night was simply confirming that for her. Dwayne Marchant started the balling rolling, but the two interns and the Gianni file sparked the flame. *I am not going down for this one*, she again pondered knowing that scapegoats would be placed on the sacrificial altar and offered up to Congress when it all fell apart. An idea quickly came to mind and Cassandra knew she needed to move fast. Pulling out the Android, she sent a succession of text messages, getting prompt replies from a couple. The Blackberry rang, interrupting as she put the Android down and picked up her work phone.

"Hello," Cassandra spoke trying to keep her breathing even, her voice neutral.

"Have we got eyes on Marchant yet," Keller questioned.

He ordered three agents to the island yesterday when Cassandra gave him the man's whereabouts.

Cassandra frowned slightly. "No, I haven't gotten a report from any of the agents," she told Keller hearing him suck his teeth.

"Unacceptable, hell there are three of them," he fired and she withheld comment.

"I need to brief you, so be in my office in one hour," Keller told her disconnecting without her confirmation.

Not going to happen, Cassandra made up her mind. She heard the tone in Keller's voice. He was trying to play it cool, but he wasn't. Something was very, very, off kilter. Layton Crowler wasn't the only one she worried about killing her. Michael Keller would eliminate her without thought if he even held an inkling of doubt about her loyalty. Cassandra was on overload. She hovered near burnout for months now and this case put the final straw on the camel's back. Throwing the Blackberry on her nightstand, Cassandra methodically collected clothing, passports, cash she kept in the safe, and a few sentimental mementos, placing them all in the standing suitcase she owned. She left everything that was CIA issue, knowing it was GPS equipped and could track her whereabouts. Finished in twenty minutes, Cassandra walked out of her front door for the last time, getting into the cab she called, leaving her assigned vehicle in the driveway.

"Dulles International," she told the driver, calling the airport by name.

The man smiled faintly, nodding before he pulled away from her curb and merged onto the street heading for their destination.

•••

Marchant gestured to Kayla to have a seat on the bed, which she did, sitting right at the edge, eyes never leaving him. He took refuge in the wicker chair that adorned the bedroom.

"I don't know if you remember me, but my name is Detective Dwayne Marchant," he began.

"Yes, I remember you," Kayla said simply, waiting for him to continue.

Marchant cleared his throat and opened the file folder he still held.

"Well since you and I spoke last, certain things have come to light concerning your ex-husband and ex-boyfriends deaths," he told her, watching her closely for any reaction.

There was none. Kayla sat impassively, silent and waiting.

"I'm here today to ask you about those things, to try and get clarification so we can solve these murders," Marchant told her.

Life After Death

"You do want to solve them don't you," he baited as she sighed impatiently.

"I promise you Kayla if you're forthright with me about this case, I'll be out of your hair very quickly," he again spoke, as she nodded almost unperceptively.

"Let's start with your ex-boyfriend, Christopher Lynch," Marchant told her. "According to what I've been able to uncover, he was shot several times when you two lived on the West Coast, is that correct," he fired, looking into her eyes.

"Yes," Kayla answered simply.

"Did he ever tell you who he suspected of trying to kill him," Marchant again questioned.

Kayla tried to keep her face as neutral as possible. She wasn't a good liar, Dezi teasing her about it coming immediately to mind.

"No, he never said," Kayla told Marchant who was still watching her closely.

She's lying, he immediately thought. He interrogated enough people over the years to quickly spot those being deceptive.

"Hmph," Marchant replied looking through more notes. "You two were still dating at the time," he questioned another time.

"No, we hadn't been seeing each other in over a year," Kayla spoke truthfully.

Marchant nodded, flipping more pages.

"You ex-husband, Thomas Bradford, did he have enemies," Marchant questioned seeing the slight frown before she dismissed it.

"I wouldn't know that detective Marchant," Kayla told him somewhat irritated.

"You said you found new information, but these are the same questions you asked and I answered three years ago," Kayla told him wanting to leave his presence.

She left the life in North Carolina never to look back, yet here this man was still dredging up old news and bad memories.

Marchant sighed dramatically dropping the file onto the floor at his feet, interlocking his fingers, eyes boring into hers as he opened his mouth deciding to play harder.

"The interesting thing about both murders Kayla, and even Chris Lynch's first attack, is that you're always the common denominator," Marchant told her, his inference clear.

Kayla's jaw clenched but she didn't speak.

"It seems that whenever you're tired of a man he ends up dead," he zipped at her wanting her to react.

"So I began to wonder, could it be that the woman playing so very innocent in all these murders actually be the one responsible, the black widow if you will," Marchant added seeing Kayla's breathing begin to increase.

"Detective Marchant, I have never killed anyone in my life," she told him her anger beginning to rise.

He chuckled evenly.

"Oh I'm sure of that part," he told her sarcastically. "That's where the boyfriend comes in isn't it," Marchant threw out, playing a hunch. "You play the helpless victim role and he comes running, takes care of the dirty laundry and you're home free."

Kayla's head was beginning to hurt. She was ready to end this conversation and leave his presence.

"Do you have proof of that, are you going to arrest me," Kayla questioned, pushing back.

"I have enough to detain you as a person of interest, yes," Marchant bluffed. "And that's exactly why I'm here, to return you to North Carolina to answer questions to our satisfaction," he added, seeing her visibly blanch.

"You can't do that," Kayla whispered, terrified.

"Yes, I can Kayla, and tonight we're flying back to do just that," Marchant told her seeing the fear mirrored in her face.

"No, I'm leaving, I'm calling my attorney," she told him, raising her voice as she stood.

"You will be given an opportunity to do all that once we land and get you processed," Marchant told her, pulling out the handcuffs.

"No," Kayla yelled, trying to step around him as he grabbed her and swiftly subdued her, putting the cuffs in place as she began to cry.

●●●

Life After Death

Stephan heard the commotion smirking slightly knowing the detective had told Kayla of his plans to take her back stateside. Mariah never moved. She was still unconscious as he looked down at her stroking her cheek gently. Stephan carefully laid her on the couch, rising and stepping to the still closed bedroom door knocking softly. Marchant came and opened the door, and he peeked over the man's shoulder seeing Kayla lying on the bed, handcuffed still sniffling.

"What time is our flight," Marchant questioned.

"10PM," Stephan replied, having deliberately chosen the late hour to avoid prying eyes and undue questioning.

"What about the daughter," Marchant questioned worriedly.

"She's taken care of, I'm about to leave and get her settled, then I'll be back at 9:15PM to pick you both up," he told Marchant who nodded just as Kayla began to quiet.

"Did you give her the pill," Stephan asked, tone hushed.

Marchant nodded yes and Stephan grunted his approval turning and striding back to the couch, easily lifting the defenseless woman and heading toward the door. Marchant came and opened it for him, watching as he left and headed toward the service elevator.

Stephan smiled as he unlocked the cruiser and placed Mariah on the backseat. He quickly got into the front, starting the vehicle and turning the air condition up to full capacity. He glanced into the rearview seeing her sleeping peacefully and smiled. *Finally the woman I love is going to be with me*, he thought and pulled into traffic. He would get Mariah settled then he would head over to her home and retrieve the children. Stephan thought about the housekeeper knowing he would need to silence her. Nothing was going to thwart his plans. He could see the light on the horizon. In a few hours Dwayne and Kayla would be in the air, Mariah and the children would be moved in, his allies would move to strip Kareek of power and put Stephan in his place. *What about the other woman, Jackie*, his mind questioned. Stephan frowned slightly. He didn't need her to look for Kayla or Mariah and call either of the Gianni's about their disappearance.

"Shit," he murmured knowing he couldn't call Jacob.

He needed him to stay put and handle Joell. Stephan saw his small house come into view, pulling into the driveway, straight into the one car garage and shutting the cruiser off. He got out and unlocked the door, leaving it open so he could bring Mariah inside.

She was still easily pliable as he lifted her again and brought her into her new home. Stephan walked to his spare bedroom and placed her lovingly onto the full size bed contained. He kissed her lips without reaction from her as she still breathed deeply and evenly. Glancing around Stephan double checked the room assuring himself there was nothing inside it she could use to escape or as a weapon against him. The lone window was barred, so there was no escape there. He took the time to install two heavy duty deadbolts to the bedroom door, only accessible from the outside.

"You'll learn to love me," Stephan whispered in her ear, kissing her lips yet another time.

He checked her one final time, reaching inside her pocket and removing the cellphone. He removed her wedding rings as well, angry at the sight of them, reminding him of her attachment to Aidan. Rising finally, Stephan forced himself out of the room, turning and locking both locks. He was going to visit Jackie first, then he would go and retrieve the children, spend some time with his new family, before returning to the hotel and picking up Dwayne and his prisoner.

●●●

Keller was furious. Cassandra was a no show for the meeting and he wasn't able to reach her all afternoon.

"Too much bullshit going on at one time," he murmured parking the car in his reserved space and getting out.

He was finally home and ready to relax just a little. He received word about JaDon and April from Vernon earlier. The police were calling it a home invasion gone wrong but both men knew entirely better. Keller's worst fears were playing in his head. Dezi Gianni was here and he was systematically eliminating everyone who knew about him. *Shit, maybe that's why you can't reach Cassandra,* his mind told him as his breathing increased slightly and he placed his key in the lock, turning the deadbolt and unlocking it. Vernon was rattled, giving Keller yet another point of angst. He didn't need the man to have a meltdown and ruin all their well laid plans. *What about Layton and your own future,* his mind again questioned as he stepped into his foyer. Keller carried no doubt how the events would play out if Vernon blew his cool and started talking. They were all fucked, royally.

Absently, Keller tossed his keys onto the bar of his kitchen, rounding the corner to walk into his living room, the smell causing him pause. Looking up, the thoughts took life. Sitting comfortably in his living room, sipping a drink and enjoying a cigar, was death himself.

Life After Death

"Good evening Deputy Director," Dezi greeted pleasantly, still enjoying his drink and smoke.

Keller glanced around noting the two other men in the room, his survival chances dwindling before him.

"Come in, sit down, make yourself comfortable," Dezi again spoke, eyes cool and aloof.

Keller did as he was told, taking a seat in the other upright Queen Anne leather chair the room held. Dezi finished the drink, placing the glass on the oak and metal contemporary living table in front of him, dropping the half smoked cigar inside as well.

"So, here I am, sitting in your house, highly displeased that I have to be here," Dezi told him, the tone making Keller's blood run cold.

Dezi sighed, rising and walking over to Keller's chair.

"You can't seem to keep a lid on your zoo these days Keller, what's the problem," he questioned, as the other two men accompanying Dezi watched Keller intently.

"They're all dead, but I'm sure you know that," he returned, careful to mind his tone.

Dezi backhanded him, lifting him slightly from the chair, but not dislodging him.

"Give me one good fucking reason I shouldn't end your existence right now," he growled, right up in Keller's face.

Mind moving to warp speed, Keller quickly formulated what he was thinking, verbalizing it just as speedily.

"Because Layton Crowler is weak and he's going to break," he told Dezi.

Big D raised an eyebrow; Stan continued to watch Keller emotionless.

"Explain," Dezi replied evenly, stepping back slightly.

Keller took another quick breath and put his plan into action. He was not about to leave this life tonight if he could help it, no matter who got hurt in the meantime.

"I wanted your files shredded years ago, had them slated for just that, and Layton told me no, made a couple of copies and said he put them in strategic places," Keller told Dezi.

"Is that so," the man replied coldly.

"When the file first was stolen, I wanted to cancel the players then, make it a quick accident, no harm no foul," Keller continued.

"And Layton didn't want that either," Dezi questioned, giving him another look.

"No," Keller spoke plainly.

Dezi glanced at Big D, then at Stan. The two men gave him their agreement without verbalization to let Keller continue to talk.

"So he wanted what, to just let them go on about their quest," Dezi queried.

"He made me put them on other details, kept a closer eye on them, but I warned him, warned him they were nosey and tenacious and wouldn't stop," Keller spun the web.

"Even when I told him about JaDon's visit to Adrian Roberts, he still didn't want to do anything," he told Dezi.

The man didn't speak, still regarding him coldly.

"Listen Devastator," Keller began using the nickname from a lifetime ago. "I'm not interested in holding anything over your head, in my mind the shit is done, I say let's shred these files once and for all and keep it moving," he went on.

"I know the secret you hold over Layton, he's a chitter-chatter drunk and I have it on tape," Keller explained.

"But," Dezi added for him.

"But I don't have proof of what he did, and that's what I need to unseat him," Keller answered.

"Tell me Keller," Dezi began, starting to circle the chair now. "What exactly is it you want from all of this, I mean really," he questioned, stopping and standing behind the man making him extremely uncomfortable.

Life After 29 Death

Joell heard Jacob snoring, continually praying one of the other officers would come in. He had to get out of this cell and alert Mr. Gianni of what was happening. *Stephan has absolutely lost his mind*, he pondered finally hearing footsteps. Joell steeled himself awaiting whoever was on the other side of the door, holding onto the doorknob he watched turn. The door creaked slightly, opening it seemed, in slow motion as Joell continued to watch, wait, and hold his breath. He didn't need Stephan coming in and administering yet another beating. Joell heard another loud snore, deepening his angst, knowing at least that it wasn't Jacob who was entering the dimly lit room outside the solitary cell. Another few inches and the door creaked again, progress immediately stopping. Joell frowned a bit, confused. Enlightenment dawned on him and he realized whoever was coming inside was trying not to awaken Jacob. *Please let it be someone else but Stephan*, Joell prayed not putting it above the man to sneak in and kill him in the cell to permanently keep him quiet. After a measurable pause and another snort from Jacob, the door began its snail pace of opening yet another time.

It was finally open enough for someone to squeeze through and Joell paid rapt attention as the shadow began to fill the space and he instantly recognized it, releasing the pent up breath he held.

"Leeks," Joell hissed, careful not to be too loud and startle the man causing him to cry out and expose both of them.

He saw the man pause and frown slightly as if he were trying to figure out what he heard.

"Leeekss," Joell again hissed the man turning directly toward the cell this time. "Leeks, it's me, Joell," he whispered again as the officer walked toward the cell.

"What are you doing in there," Leeks questioned, careful to keep his voice down as well.

Tall and sinewy, the blue eyes were watching Joell with curiosity.

"Let me out, it is a very long story," Joell returned fearful Jacob would catch them before he could be liberated.

Leeks immediately complied without question, pulling out the ring of keys from his pocket and using the one marked S to release Joelle.

"Listen to me," Joell told him as he stepped out and intro freedom. "We have to get Jacob into this cell," he told Leeks who frowned deeply, his porcelain skin turning a deep crimson.

"Why, what's going on Joell," he questioned now, fully confused and uneasy.

Joell gave Leeks a quick update on the events of the last few hours. "Stephan is mad," Leeks spoke concerning the man's sanity, gaining instant agreement from Joell.

"We must hurry," he told Leeks now. "I still need to contact Mr. Gianni," he added as Leeks nodded. "First we have to subdue Jacob and then I need to find out where Stephan is, and if he has done anything to Mrs. D Gianni," Joell spoke as they both peeked from the open door seeing Jacob still asleep, mouth agape, snoring loudly.

Joell observed his posture. Both arms were hanging limply at his sides, giving him an idea.

"Leeks, see his arms," he told the bigger man.

Leeks nodded in the affirmative, waiting for Joell to elaborate.

"I think he is sleeping deeply enough that you can attach one cuff, then I'll wake him up, he'll jump and you can grab the other arm and subdue him," Joell spoke.

"Fine, let's hurry," Leeks told him. "Stephan is still on the loose and Mrs. Gianni is unaware of his intentions," he told Joell who fully agreed.

The woman was extremely cordial and forthcoming with them. They wanted to make sure Stephan didn't cause her harm. Tiptoeing into the room, they moved quickly. Leeks moved behind Jacob, carefully putting the metal ring around his still hanging wrist and quietly fastening it. Nodding and giving Joell the signal, the man slapped the sleeping officer hard across the face. His reaction as exactly as Joell predicted, allowing Leeks to grab his flailing right arm and clasp the other handcuff around it.

"Put him in the cell," he told Leeks who began dragging a screaming, protesting, Jacob into the solitary holding cell that was just his own private hell moments earlier.

"I'm going to the spa and see if she ever made her appointment," Jacob told Leeks, having gotten Kayla's schedule from Dezi when he asked him to watch over her.

Life After Death

"Keep an eye out and if Stephan comes back, disable him first, ask questions later," he admonished as Leeks assured him he would, watching Joell as he walked out of the front door.

• • •

Jackie heard the knock at the front door, frowning a bit wondering who could be on the other side of it. Kayla and Mariah were at the spa, so she didn't expect to hear from them. They were all meeting for dinner in about an hour, then heading to a show. Looking through her front window she saw the police cruiser. Opening the front door, Jackie found Stephan standing outside smiling pleasantly.

"Hello Ma'am," he greeted amiably.

"Hello Officer Eveson, how are you," Jackie returned, well aware of the man's identity.

"I'm good, Mrs. Wilson," Stephan returned.

Jackie and Big D were married almost a year after they came to the island. He insisted, saying he wanted it official.

"I was wondering if you heard from either Kayla or Mariah today," he baited, expression serious and worried.

Jackie instantly frowned.

"No, what's wrong," she questioned becoming anxious.

"Well I'm not sure anything is wrong actually," Stephan told her, exaggeratedly wiping his forehead.

"Oh, I'm sorry Officer Eveson, please, come inside," Jackie told him catching the gesture.

Stephan smiled and accepted her offer. It put her in exactly the position he needed. Closing the door behind him, Jackie offered him water.

Stephan politely accepted taking the time to quickly case the house as she gathered it in the kitchen. He didn't plan to kill her. There wasn't a need in his book, but he did need her incapacitated. Jackie returned with the ice cold bottled water, handing it to him.

"Thank you," he replied opening it and drinking a small amount.

"As I was saying," he began, spinning the lie anew. "One of the ladies from the spa called the station, slightly alarmed because they never made their appointment," he told Jackie watching the worry come to her face.

"That's not like them at all," she murmured as Stephan nodded agreement. "Let me try and call them," Jackie spoke, turning her back to pick up her cell phone.

He moved swiftly arm around her throat, holding her immobile as she tried to fight back. Stephan knew the hold wasn't lethal but it would render her unconscious in a matter of moments. Jackie was giving him her best, causing Stephan to apply a bit more pressure. She was turning out to be quite the handful. Slowly the adrenaline began to wane and Jackie's movements slowed. Stephan held her tightly until she stopped fighting completely and slumped in his arms.

Picking the incapacitated woman up, Stephan took her into her kitchen and sat her in one of the chairs the dinette set contained. Stephen rambled around the various drawers, heading into the pantry off the kitchen, not finding rope, but a couple of extension cords. Deciding they would do, he returned to the kitchen, securing Jackie's feet to the legs of the chair. He used his handcuffs to place her arms behind her back. Stephen dragged the chair, with her in it, to the small closet he spied while she was in the kitchen getting his water earlier. He took the duct tape he found in his earlier rambling and put two pieces over her mouth. Stepping outside of the closet, Stephan checked her one last time. Jackie was breathing evenly, the tape not hindering her air flow. Satisfied, Stephan closed the closet door, going the extraordinary step of propping a chair behind it before he turned and headed back into the kitchen. Stephan picked up Jackie's purse from the kitchen table, searching it quickly for her keys and any additional cell phones she may have. Finding the keys, he pocketed them, walking back into the dining room where the cell phone still lay peacefully on the table. Stephan put the instrument in his pocket as well and strode toward the front door. Taking one last glance at the closet and satisfied Jackie would stay put, he walked out of the front door and headed for the mansion Aidan and Mariah owned, prepared to eliminate the housekeeper and retrieve his new family.

•••

Mariah awakened with a start sitting up and blinking rapidly as she took in her surroundings.

"Where am I," she murmured as the unfamiliar surroundings continued to take shape.

Life After Death

"Hello," Mariah called out, rising from the bed, stopping momentarily to steady herself as her head spun.

Able finally to regain her balance Mariah tried to recall how she may have ended up in the modest bedroom. It was immaculate, nicely done in olive green, with white accents.

"Mommy," Mariah thought back, becoming alarmed.

The hotel, the man with questions, the juice, she cataloged before realization hit her.

"Stephan drugged me," Mariah murmured knowing she was in trouble.

The man was obsessed with her and she was his prisoner now. Mariah quickly went to the door seeing the two deadbolts, as she frowned angrily.

"I've got to get out of here," she mumbled again glancing at the window and seeing the bars and the sinking sun.

Not giving up, Mariah continued to look around the room searching for a way to get out. She looked at the door, glancing all around it her eyes focused solely on the hinges. She watched enough home improvement shows to know she could pry them up with the right tool.

She began to slowly walk around the room, opening various drawers on the nightstand and dressers. She struck pay dirt in the last drawer finding the rusted flathead screwdriver.

"Yes," Mariah murmured walking over to the door and putting her ear to it.

She had to make sure Stephan wasn't around or anyone was in the house. She would need to pound on the screwdriver to dislodge the hinges, especially given the age they seemed to have from her closer inspection. Glancing around the room once more she saw a midsize paperweight. Mariah decided she would use that as a hammer and help push the hinge pins up and out. She held her breath, hearing nothing. The house was deathly silent. Mariah prayed that meant she was alone. Shoring her resolve, she placed the screwdriver to the bottom hinge, using the paperweight to strike it. The hinge pin didn't move. Taking another deep breath and waiting, Mariah listened to see if her effort brought anyone to the bedroom door. Hearing nothing for another solid five minutes, she tried again, striking the pin harder this time. It creaked a bit, raising almost imperceptibly, but enough to bolster Mariah's hopes she could dislodge it. *I've got to get out of here and get to mommy, it's getting dark,* she thought striking the pin yet another time. This time it raised noticeably and she smiled, striking it again and again until it finally fell harmlessly to the bedroom floor.

●●●

Stephan wasn't happy. The housekeeper was out with the children and he didn't know where.

"Damn," he groused not wanting or needing the loose end.

Right now however there was nothing he could do until he got to the house and questioned Mariah. He would make her call the housekeeper and have the children delivered to them. *She's awake and angry by now,* his mind told him. Stephan knew it would be an uphill battle with the woman, but he was determined. He thought about swinging by the station, but decided against it. Jacob didn't call, so that meant everything was fine in his mind.

"How hard could it be," he murmured of keeping Joell locked in the solitary cell.

Glancing at his watch, Stephan noted the time. It was a little after seven. He needed to get home, get the children delivered, Mariah situated, and back over to the hotel to pick up Dwayne and Kayla in a little over two hours. Sighing, Stephan picked up the cars speed heading for his house. His mind took him back over the events of the day. He accomplished quite the coup in a scant few hours.

"How do you like that shit Kareek," he murmured arrogantly thinking of the soon to be deposed Chief of Police.

His cell rang and Stephan answered amiably seeing Marchant's name on the caller I.D.

"Hello Dwayne, is everything alright," he questioned, hoping there weren't any unforeseen issues.

"Yes, fine, Kayla is still out," Marchant replied as the relief washed over the officer. "I was simply calling to make sure everything was still on schedule and that the flight was booked," Marchant told him.

"Everything is on schedule Dwayne," Stephan told him truthfully.

"Relax, in a few hours you'll have Kayla back on American soil and in your capable custody," he added flattering the man's ego.

"Yes, you're right," Dwayne answered. "I'll see you in a couple hours," he added and disconnected.

Life After Death

Stephan saw the house in the distance, readying himself for the battle he knew was awaiting from the beautiful woman he now called his own. He was still smiling mere moments later when he pulled into the driveway, opening the garage and pulling in. Stephan turned the car off, reaching in his pocket and retrieving the keys and cellphone he liberated from Jackie Wilson earlier. He reached over and put them in the glove box. Task complete, Stephan opened the car door and walked inside his kitchen, darkened now that the sun was down. He glanced down the hallway, eyes finding the door now laying on its side hanging into the walk space.

"What the --," Stephen got out before everything went dark as Mariah hit him hard over the head with the cast iron stew pot she found seconds before he walked inside.

Life After 30 Death

Keller chanced a glance at the man sitting to his immediate left. The expression remained unchanged. Dezi Gianni had blood on his mind and when they landed there was no doubt he would get his wish. Keller thought back on how they got to this place. How he ended up on a chartered private jet on his way to Pembroke Parish, in league with the most dangerous man he knew on this side of death. *"What do you want out of this Michael, I mean really,"* Dezi posed, just as his cell chimed. *"Pardon me, you can think a little longer,"* he told Keller calmly, answering the call. Keller watched the man's expression darken, his eyes go cold and flat, and knew whatever he was hearing wasn't good. He recalled praying that it wasn't information that would seal his death warrant. *"I don't have time for you, so I need to kill you, kill Vernon and Layton and leave this wretched country,"* Dezi growled after disconnecting. *"What's up man,"* Big D fired at his friend. Stan was watching him questionably as well. Keller listened intently as Dezi told his comrades about the rogue police officer. He didn't interject until he heard the name Dwayne Marchant.

"He's a detective from North Carolina," Keller spoke as Dezi returned his attention to him. *"Tell me everything,"* he told him, his tone and expression daring Keller to lie or refuse. *"He's been digging into your wife for a while, trying to tie her to the murders, the husband and ex-boyfriend,"* he told Dezi who nodded without speech. *"He connected with this detective in LA, but we diffused that situation, at least we thought we did,"* Keller freely admitted. *"We issued a warrant issued for him a couple of days ago because he became a liability, but --,"* he got out before Stan spoke up. *"But he managed to slip through your CIA bullshit,"* he growled just as angry as his friend. Keller swallowed hard and quickly nodded. *"I can get you to her, quicker than a commercial jet, and I already have three agents on the ground over there,"* he offered up as Dezi continued to watch him and withhold comment. *"You never answered my question Michael,"* Dezi coolly posed. *"What do you want?"* Keller again took a deep breath, verbalizing his thoughts. *"I want to be CIA director, have basically unlimited power,"* he told the man. *"Layton Crowler however poses a threat to that,"* Keller added waiting for a response.

When none came he continued. *"I can destroy him with the confession, put him in prison, and I have enough Senate power to get me confirmed, especially after the Prather fiasco,"* Keller told Dezi yet another time. *"And you need corroboration,"* Dezi questioned as Keller nodded yes. *"Get me to Pembroke Parrish and once I kill Dwayne Marchant and Stephen Eveson, we'll handle your problem,"* he replied. *"Done,"* Keller instantly replied. He wasn't stupid, that was as good a deal as he would get. He also knew well enough to know if Dezi Gianni needed to get to Bermuda he had enough money to make that happen with or without his help.

Life After Death

"Did you make the call," Aidan questioned giving Keller a hard look.

"Yes, before we took off," he told the younger Gianni.

He almost wanted to feel sorry for the detective, but the man's blatant stupidity brought his fate knocking. The pilots voice came over the speaker alerting them to fasten their seatbelts as they were about to descend for landing. Keller again saw Dezi Gianni's face, almost gleeful at the prospect of actually seeing the man in action first hand. He was also inwardly celebrating his new position at the CIA, knowing his new allegiance carried the clout to see it come to fruition. Keller felt the wheels of the plane touch the runway and his adrenaline began to flow. He loved the thrill of the chase.

•••

Kayla carefully opened her eyes. She was awake for a while now but continued to feign unconsciousness. She heard Marchant moving around behind her. She quickly took in the objects in her view. Kayla was plotting. She wasn't going to be victimized anymore. Dezi taught her a bit about protecting herself and tonight she was going to put it to good use. If Marchant took her back to the United States, she held no doubt her future would include a uniform and bars. Even though she wasn't guilty, she did know who killed the men. Kayla would never tell; and because of that they would place the blame on her and lock her up for the rest of her life. There was really nothing in the room that could be construed as a weapon. Her eyes swept it again, coming to rest on the telephone sitting on the nightstand. It was one of the older ones with the push buttons. She knew they were reasonably heavy and if she could hit Marchant just right, she could at least knock him down long enough to escape through the suite's front door. *How are you going to get your hands free,* her mind questioned. The handcuffs were still securely in place, her arms becoming numb.

"Hello," Kayla called out softly, seeing as she expected, Marchant materialize moments later.

"You're awake," he said sweetly, actually smiling at her.

"Yes," Kayla replied careful to keep her voice neutral. "I need to go to the bathroom," she told him laying the trap.

"Alright, I'll help you up," Marchant told her, reaching onto the bed and sitting her up.

Kayla allowed him to help her to her feet, looking into his eyes now.

"Kayla, I didn't mean to frighten you earlier," Marchant told her sincerely.

Kayla saw it now. The man was emotionally involved. *Has he been carrying this torch for three years,* she wondered of the obvious attraction.

"Are you still taking me back," she questioned.

"Yes, but all you have to do is answer questions, provide evidence and you're free to go," Marchant deceptively replied.

"Hmph," Kayla responded. "I can't use the bathroom with my hands behind my back," she told him still looking into his eyes.

Marchant watched her wordlessly, trying to decide whether to trust her or not. He recalled her history and that she was never prone to any violence the he was aware of. The woman was by all accounts very docile.

"OK, I'll take the cuffs off if you promise no more stunts like earlier," Marchant told her.

"I won't," Kayla told him trying her best to sound sincere.

Marchant smiled slightly, uncuffing her.

"Thank you," Kayla returned softly, turning and heading for the restroom.

She closed the door, actually using the facility as her mind raced. She needed to get to the other side of the bed, and then get him in front of her. *What if it's bolted to the nightstand,* Kayla's mind pushed. Truthfully she was scared as hell, but not scared enough not to fight for her freedom. Finishing, she flushed, washed her hands and exited the room finding Marchant sitting on the corner of the bed waiting.

"Are you hungry," he questioned.

Kayla nodded, thankful when he went to the phone and picked up the handset. She saw the base slide out of place alerting her that it wasn't bolted. *Thank you,* she inwardly mused, listening as he ordered them both a grilled chicken salad before disconnecting.

"It should be here in about thirty minutes they said," Marchant told her as Kayla smiled slightly and nodded.

He walked back to where she stood now, close enough to touch her.

"I know you're scared Kayla," Marchant began. "I promise I won't let anything happen to you," he added, reaching out and stroking her cheek.

"Thank you for that," Kayla replied, stepping around him, walking back to the bed where she lain earlier.

Life After Death

"This isn't about hurting you Kayla," Marchant tried as she turned to face him, hands behind her back as she carefully began lifting the phone. He was walking toward her now.

•••

Joell met them as soon as they walked down the three steps of the small plane. "Mr. Gianni," he greeted as Dezi began questioning him. "I haven't been able to find him, and Mrs. A. Gianni is missing as well," he spoke garnering Aidan's full attention.

"What about my wife," Big D questioned, concerning Jackie.

"I have an officer going to your house now to see if she's there," he told him while they walked toward the Suburban.

Opening Dezi's door, Joell waited for him to get inside before repeating the gesture for Aidan, Big D, and Stan. Keller opened his own door and got inside, pulling out his cell.

"What have you found," he fired to the first agent that answered. "Hmph, yeah, keep it on the ground, by any means," Keller instructed and disconnected.

"They found a flight plan for United States, North Carolina," he told Dezi, who nodded.

"We need Stephan, Joell," he growled coldly, sending a shiver up the man's spine.

"I'm trying Mr. Gianni, I thought we would go to his home," he told them as Dezi grunted his approval.

He was content for the moment knowing that Marchant wouldn't be able to leave the island. Still his gut gnawed at him. The man found a way to slip out of the country once; he may be able to do it again.

"Who --," Joell mumbled as they saw the disheveled figure run into the woods.

"Stop," Aidan spoke, the figure familiar.

Getting out of the truck, he headed into the woods, Stan and Big D on his heels. Dezi, Joell and Keller remained in the truck. Aidan heard the branches breaking, following the sound, careful not to call out just yet.

"Let's flank them," he whispered to the two men accompanying him.

Nodding their understanding, Big D went left, Stan right, as Aidan continued his path. Stealthily the men made their way through the dense brush. He heard the branches still breaking, the thud of a body falling, then scrambling as they rose and continued to run forward. Aidan caught a glimpse again, opening his mouth to call out when he heard Stan's voice.

"Hey, stop, hey," he yelled as Aidan heard him begin to run.

All of them were running now, following the sound of Stan's voice as they pursued the elusive figure. They came to a clearing and Aidan saw them, still running, heading straight from the one hundred foot drop he knew as at the end of the cliff in front of them. Recognition kicked in and he yelled loudly.

"Mariah, baby, stop running, it's me," Aidan screamed as she turned around and lost her footing.

Aidan saw her hit the ground, tumbling straight for the edge of the cliff, her screams piercing the night air.

"Maaaarriiiaaahhh," Aidan screamed, racing top speed to catch his wife before she went over the side and left him forever.

"Aiiidaannn," Mariah screamed as she reached the edge and began going over, disappearing from his sight.

Aidan's heart stopped. Dirt dispersed into the air, rocks flew at crazy angles, the air swirled with activity, even the insects buzzed angrily at the disruption of their ordered night.

"Gotcha," Stan yelled, diving to the edge of the cliff, holding her by one arm as she dangled precariously over the edge.

Aidan and Big D arrived simultaneously pulling them both back from the edge to the safety of solid ground. Aidan hugged his wife tightly as she sobbed hysterically terrified he was sure. His own heart was racing in his chest realizing just how very close he came to losing her.

"Shh, baby, it's okay, you're safe," he tried to soothe, still holding her tightly. "Shh, come on," he told her as they stood and he picked her up, carrying her back to the truck.

Aidan placed her inside, still crying, sliding quickly in bedside her.

"Shh, baby, where is Stephan," he questioned sensitively.

He knew from the direction she came and the fact she was walking, she at some point met up with the man.

Life After Death

"At his house, I think I killed him Aidan," she whispered, eyes big, horrified by the thought.

"It's okay Mariah," he told her as he and his father exchanged glances.

"Honey, where is Kayla," he questioned knowing Dezi was about to burst.

"The Princess hotel, with that awful detective," she answered angrily.

Dezi didn't need to utter a word as Joell made a U-turn and Keller made another call for an agent to come and retrieve Stephan.

Life After 31 Death

Stephan slowly came around, head pounding. He opened his eyes, blinking as he tried to focus. The room was starting to retard its spinning and he was able to see one image instead of three. He looked around finding his vision limited by the handcuffs restraining him to the hard metal chair he was seated in. Glancing down Stephan saw the chair secured to a large concrete pillar in the middle of the room, his ankles also shackled to the legs of the chair. *What the hell*, he wondered looking up and seeing the two men inside the room with him. They were unfamiliar, but he knew they weren't his saviors. The men were dressed in black suits, the bulges obvious where their weapons rested in their holsters. *FBI*, Stephan wondered as he continued to regard them and they ignored him. He pulled against the cuffs knowing they were secured, but hoping just the same. The metal cuffs clinked harmlessly against the exertion he placed on them and one of the men glanced his way with a satisfied smirk. Stephan ignored him; instead he began trying to recall the earlier events of the evening. He drove home, parked his car, walked in his house, then it went dark for him.

Mariah, shit, his mind instantly recalled his heart beginning to pound. She was out. He remembered now. The door lying in the hallway. He didn't know how she did it, but Mariah somehow escaped him. Where was she now? Did she get to her husband? *They're out of the country,* his mind reasoned, yet the question loomed, who were these men holding him and who were they holding him for?

"Hey," Stephan called out.

The men continued to play cards without disruption.

"Hey," he called, louder this time as one of them turned to him, clearly irritated.

"Where am I, who are you guys," he threw out.

The man watched him a while longer and Stephan thought he wasn't going to reply.

"You're in a warehouse, and we're the CIA," he said and returned to his card game without further explanation.

Stephan was stunned. *The CIA, what in the hell is going on*, he thought becoming very uneasy. He was still deeply mired in midnight. Stephan didn't think his attempted takeover was CIA worthy, so what were they doing here with him as their prisoner. His mind again traveled to Mariah and finding her. He couldn't do anything right now though, except sit and wait. One of the men's cell phone rang and he answered giving short one and two word answers to whoever was on the other end. He rose and walked over to Stephan putting the phone to his ear.

"Say hello," the agent barked as Stephan jumped slightly.

Swallowing the sudden dryness in his throat he opened his mouth.

"H-h-hello," he stuttered.

The line remained silent, causing him to wonder if the other party disconnected.

"In one hour I'm coming to that warehouse and pick you up," the voice spoke. "And then I'm going to kill you," Aidan finished and disconnected as Stephan began to quake, and pray.

●●●

Kayla was trying to remain calm as Marchant continued to walk toward her.

"I know everything is probably very chaotic in your mind right now," he spoke disarmingly.

"Why Detective Marchant," Kayla questioned as he stopped walking and regarded her curiously. "Why did you go through all this trouble to find me, just to take me back for questions," she clarified.

"Because two men are dead Kayla, and their families deserve to know what happened to them," he told her. "Because there is a murderer roaming free who needs to pay for their crimes," Marchant finished as Kayla's grip on the phone tightening.

"Is that the only reason," she again questioned never taking her eyes from.

He didn't have to answer. Kayla saw it earlier when she arrived; she heard it in his voice when he spoke. Detective Dwayne Marchant was in love with her and she was more than convinced that was the entire reasoning for his coming to Pembroke Parrish and trying to take her back to North Carolina. *What the hell is he thinking, that we'll live happily ever after,* Kayla pondered as he took another step toward her, close enough for her plan.

"It's not the entire reason, no," Marchant answered honestly, lifting his arm readying himself to touch her.

Now, hit him now, her subconscious screamed. Kayla snatched the phone up, base first, swinging it at the Detective. The force was enough to topple the nightstand as the cord came disconnected from the wall, the crash loud and furious. Marchant was quick enough to avoid the entire brunt of the phones force, but Kayla managed to clip him right below the temple, knocking off his balance and equilibrium. She didn't waste time. Kayla pushed him hard helping his fast descent to the floor, scrambling hastily over his twisted frame, racing for the front door. She tripped over the ottoman she didn't see as she ran, breathing ragged and uneven, pulse raging in her ears as she heard him calling her and coming toward her. Kayla made it to the suite's door, grabbing the lock bar and flinging it backward, hands on the deadbolt and doorknob simultaneously.

"No, Kayla, dammit," Marchant yelled, close enough for Kayla to feel his breath on his neck.

Reacting, she threw a wild elbow backward, luckily hitting him in the stomach and knocking the wind from him. She turned the lock now, hearing the thud as it unlocked; grabbed the bottom knob and turned it as well.

"Nooooo," Marchant managed, lunging as his flailing hand connected with her ankle.

Kayla kicked at him, shaking the foot vigorously before he could get a solid grip on it, slipping out of her shoe, turning and opening the door, blindly running into the hallway, eyes filled with tears.

The arms encompassed her and Kayla began to struggle in earnest, to out of breath to scream, not wanting to waste the energy.

"Kayla, baby, it's me, calm down honey, I'm here, I'm here baby," Dezi told her still holding her tightly.

Hearing his voice, her nervous system shut down and she collapsed into his arms, consciousness almost lost.

"Put her in the truck, stay with her," he told Stan who nodded and gingerly took Kayla from him, his own nerves on end.

He was excited about seeing her, but not like this. Dezi waited until Stan stepped onto the elevator before turning back toward his destination. The man stumbled out of the room right into their line of sight, still shaking his head back and forth trying to clear his vision. Dezi's eyes narrowed as he strode directly in front of him causing Marchant to stop in his tracks and take in the man before him. His head was pounding but he recognized this face. This was the boyfriend and he was in a world of trouble. Marchant's body obediently dropped to its knees as the blow was delivered with power and precision to his solar plexus. Dezi hit him again with two overhand rights, his knee now on the man's throat.

"Not yet Dezi," Big D told his friend, intervening.

He knew the man wanted to kill the specimen in front him, but there was a plan and they needed to stick to it.

Keller's cell went off as Big D and Aidan dragged Marchant to his feet, pulling him toward the service elevator and truck waiting downstairs.

"Yeah," Keller barked. "Is she all right," he questioned and all movement ceased.

The three men regarded him silently waiting for him to finish his call.

"OK, yeah, take her over to the Gianni mansion, the main house," he spoke and disconnected.

"Found your wife in a closet, bound and gagged, but otherwise unharmed," he told Big D who nodded slightly, the relief evident.

Returning to their task they arrived at the elevator and boarded. Dezi watched Marchant with icy hatred the entire ride. The man was barely conscious, but Dezi fully planned to rectify that before he killed him. He was absolutely furious with the idiot detective who came to his home and tried to take away his heart. *No one touches my Kayla, absolutely no one,* Dezi continued to murderously think. The ding of the elevator finally broke the trance and Dezi turned away from the man. Big D and Aidan dragged him the SUV, opening the back and throwing him into it, binding his hands and feet, stuffing a gag into his mouth. They got into the truck and started it heading for the warehouse where Stephan was being held. Dezi traded seats with Stan, holding Kayla as she lay obediently in his lap, having fully awakened moments earlier. They were talking when he got into the truck, so Dezi knew they at least covered the basics of reacquainting themselves with each other.

"Did you kill him," she asked softly looking into his face.

Dezi looked into her eyes, furious again thinking of the man hurting her.

"Not yet," he answered truthfully.

"Do you want me to spare him," Dezi questioned, knowing Marchant could hear.

Kayla put her head right over his heart listening to the melodic beat of it as his strong arms comforted her and his body heat warmed every sensor in her body.

"No," she said simply, eyes closed as she relaxed.

Dezi smiled.

Marchant allowed the tears to come and roll down his face as he heard her answer.

•••

Joelle walked into the police station to loud screaming as Jacob continued to yell aloud.

"What is going on," he questioned Leeks.

The man sighed before giving him a look. "He's been going on like that for the past two hours," he returned.

"What does he want," Joell questioned.

He was tired, exhausted actually. The Gianni's thanked him for his service and dismissed him some thirty minutes ago. He didn't know exactly what was going to be done, but Joell knew not to expect to see Stephan or the American detective ever again in this life.

"He's screaming for you," Leeks said simply, rising and walking by Joell.

"I'm going home," he said merely leaving the room before Joell could object.

Taking a deep breath, he took his time walking back into the small room where Jacob was being held.

"Why are you causing all of this racket," Joell questioned testily.

His head was beginning to pound and his patience was extremely short.

"Joell, let me out of here, please, right now," Jacob pled.

Joell gave him a look, turning to walk out of the room.

"No, wait, please listen," he tried again as the man gave pause and turned around.

"Make it quick, I'm tired," he fired irritably.

"Is Stephan dead," Jacob questioned fearfully.

"Not yet," Joell answered plainly.

Life After Death

Jacob swallowed hard and nodded. He remained quiet for a few moments longer, chewing on his bottom lip.

"Joell, please, let me leave this place," he began anew. "I'll go and never come back, please, don't let them kill me," Jacob continued starting to blubber as he cried.

"What makes you think they would kill you," Joell humored knowing very well Jacob was definitely on the Gianni's death list.

He cried harder, wailing now.

"Because I helped Stephan, because I'm stupid," he continued to lament, getting more and more on Joell's nerves.

"So you want me to let you go and put my own name on a death list," he returned, feeling little sympathy for the pathetic man before him.

"No, I have it figured out," Jacob told him as Joell sat down in the plastic chair outside of the cell.

"See, you will tell them that you came into the cell to bring me dinner and then I attacked you, knocking you out and escaping," Jacob told him, eyes shining with hope.

"It's a good story Joell, they'll believe it," he continued to cajole.

"I don't know Jacob, the Gianni's are very shrewd," he humored.

"Yes, yes, I know, but Joell this is a good plan, its foolproof," he told the man as Joell assumed a thoughtful look.

"Hmm, maybe," he murmured as Jacob pounced.

"Yes, it is Joell, it will work I tell you," he again attempted to persuade the reluctant participant.

"Where will you go Jacob, all you know is here," Joell questioned rising and stepping closer to the cell.

"I have a cousin in Haiti, I will go there," Jacob responded. "It's a long way from here and they will never see me again, I swear it Joell," he spoke.

Joell continued to remain quiet a few moments longer.

"I'm not pleased about you having to hit me," he told Jacob.

"No, I don't," he replied. "You don't tell them until the morning, you will have been unconscious for a few hours the lump will have gone down that would have been left," Jacob explained.

"Hmm, you really have thought this out haven't you," Joelle questioned.

"Yes," Jacob returned. "I've had plenty of time to ponder the complete idiot I've been trusting Stephan."

Joell nodded agreement, stepping closer to the cell door, keys in hand.

"Thank you Joell, thank you so much," Jacob rapidly fired as the key slid into the lock and the cell door opened.

"I swear Joell, you will not regret this, I swear," Jacob told him wiping his tears with the back of his hand.

"Go out of the back door," Joell spoke as Jacob nodded and turned his back, reaching for the doorknob.

The bullet pierced his heart, instantly stopping it. Jacob's eyes grew big as the shock registered for the scant few seconds of life left.

"You really are stupid," Joell said simply as the man fell against the door sliding callously onto the floor beneath it.

Joell looked at the dead man without emotion. He didn't forget the beating both he and Stephan administered.

"Now we're even," he murmured, picking up the phone and calling Leeks, telling him how he killed Jacob as he tried to escape.

Life After 32 Death

Aidan stroked Mariah's face as she continued to sleep. The doctor gave her a powerful sedative in the wee hours of the morning when he paid the house call. They were all here in the main house. Dezi wanted the women in one place so they could be well guarded until they were sure of no more traitorous interlopers. As far as he knew, both Kayla and Jackie were also still heavily sedated. Rising, Aidan stepped out of the second massive master suite and turned left heading down the hallway. He carefully opened the second door he arrived in front of, sticking his head inside. Both Livvy and Preston were still fast asleep. Their housekeeper, Abigail, was in the room next door and would see to the children once they awakened. Aidan was extremely grateful for the woman's intuition yesterday. Abigail told them she saw the police officer as he came toward the house, and quickly exited the rear door, going down the path to the beach below where she called a cab and took the children into town. She simply said; he didn't look peaceful. She didn't return until Aidan called her, seeing the missed calls on Mariah's cell once her purse was retrieved from Stephan's house.

The anger was instant and searing when he thought of the man. Stephan Eveson earned his number one ranking on Aidan's death list. *Crazy bastard*, he thought of the man's obsession with his wife. Aidan asked the doctor to examine Mariah once she slipped into the deep sleep. He wanted to know if the man violated her, even though Mariah assured him nothing happened. The doctor confirmed his wife's assertion, setting his mind at ease. Still Aidan planned to permanently remove Stephan from all their lives in just a scant few hours. Leaving the children sleeping Aidan headed to his father's study. He was almost positive he would find the man there. His father's fury was virtually at overflow. Aidan understood; he felt the same way. He knew Big D did as well, noting the venomous looks he gave Stephan when they picked him up from the warehouse last night. The two men were being held while things were being finalized. Keller was playing his role very well, and Dezi told Aidan they would need to make one last trip to the United States, if he wanted to go. He of course instantly agreed having a bit of unfinished business of his own there.

Aidan turned the knob and walked inside the room, the aroma of the finely crafted cigars his father smoked greeting him.

"How long have you been in here," Aidan ventured.

Dezi was staring intently out of the window, watching the surf below. His eyes were cold and flat, the jaw clenched, the vein in his temple pulsing.

"All night for intents and purposes," Dezi replied, sipping the liquor in the glass.

"Is Kayla still sleeping," Aidan now questioned, making himself a drink.

"Yes," Dezi replied. "I asked the doctor to sedate her heavily, I don't want her awakening until we're finished and back at home," he told Aidan finishing the drink and putting the glass down.

Big D and Stan walked into the room right after Aidan added the ice to his glass.

"You two want a drink," he questioned the men.

"Yeah, cool," Big D replied.

"Sure, vodka though," Stan replied seeing the brown liquor.

Aidan nodded and proceeded to make the requests.

"I'm ready to end these muthafuckers," Big D growled.

"Just waiting for a call, then we're heading out," Dezi replied, casting a look at Aidan now.

"Which bastard is first," Stan questioned taking the drink from Aidan.

"Thanks," he told the young man as he smiled slightly and nodded.

Big D took his, saying thanks as well, before drinking half of it in one gulp.

"Simultaneously separate," Dezi replied and Big D chuckled.

Aidan was still unsure how it would turn out, and Stan was simply lost. Choosing not to speak on it, they continued to drink finishing just as Dezi's cell rang and everyone's anxiety level went to overload.

• • •

How the hell did all of this go so terribly wrong, Marchant pondered in the darkness. He didn't know where he was, but he was uncomfortable as hell. That much he could certainly attest to. He was blindfolded with soundproof headphones on. It was creepily eerie, the silent darkness that held him. He smelled wood, and dust, thinking he was inside a factory of some sort perhaps. He couldn't tell if it was day or night; if he were alone or under guard. Marchant was hanging by his arms, thick heavy metal chains suspending him from the floor. The aching stopped hours ago. Now he was simply numb, disoriented and scared. His journey the last three years was continually playing on a loop reel in his head. He saw every file he looked at, every question he asked. Marchant regretted with everything in him that he didn't heed that inner voice that continually begged him to stop, to let Mikayla Bradford be a distant memory. No, he followed his heart and now it was about to be stopped by the man she controlled. *Well you got the answer to your question didn't you,* his mind interrogated another time.

Marchant recalled the inquiry the man asked and the answer she gave. She was indeed the cold, black-hearted spider, he suspected but didn't want to admit. Marchant wanted to kick himself again and again. He also felt bad dragging Stephan into the sordid mess this trip became. *He had his own agenda, you didn't force him,* his conscience tried to relieve. Marchant didn't feel vindicated at all. He knew if he never sent the email, the officer wouldn't be in whatever mess he was now. *Is he being held too, did the boyfriend kill him,* the questions seemed to continue to come. Marchant couldn't even offer the man any assistance, hell he couldn't help himself. They were both presumably about to die in this mirage of an oasis. *I should have arrested her three years ago,* he continued to cogitate concerning Kayla, the hurt mixing with the anger. Marchant finally admitted even knowing she was guilty, he still loved her. He still wanted to touch her, to hold her, to know the pleasure of making love to her and hearing her call out his name. *How fucking stupid am I,* he mused feeling a slight breeze. Marchant prayed for a miracle; prayed that someway, somehow, Kayla would change her mind and tell her boyfriend to spare his life. He was on the first thing with wings or a boat motor heading for the U.S.

He felt the sting, the burning, before his head started to spin. *Drugged,* his groggy mind managed before he felt the chains being loosened and felt his body drop to the floor, cold, concrete, and unyielding as his head banged it setting off a cacophony of multi-colored stars. The pain shocked his numbed nervous system and he involuntarily cried out. The fall knocked the headphones askew and he could hear a tiny bit. There were voices, lots of them, speaking languages he didn't understand, rapid fire and angry. *Where are they taking me,* Marchant tried, fighting to hold onto the tiny bit of consciousness. He was losing the fight, the darkness quickly taking him over and the fear gripping him with an iron fist. Marchant heard the one voice now, familiar, still deadly enough to bring chills to his spine.

"Put him inside the room, under," Dezi's voice spoke.

Marchant felt his stomach begin to lurch unable to stop the assent of the hot rancid combination that came spewing forth as he vomited and the man carrying him cursed, dropping him rudely onto the ground another time.

"Bastard," he screeched, kicking Marchant hard to the back as yet another frontal assault came and he hurled again.

"Get him inside, it's just puke," Dezi growled as Marchant heard the man apologize profusely picking him up and moving again.

The last thing he remembered hearing was the loud, screeching cry, then silence.

•••

Stephen watched them load the incapacitated man, dumping him almost at his feet, blindfolded, bound, headphones in place to block sound.

"Brought you some company," one of the men threw out as the other one laughed and they turned leaving them inside the room, locking the door behind them.

Stephan recognized the detective even with the severe bruising to his face. *The elder Gianni no doubt,* he thought of the man's obvious beating before looking away and back out of the small window. This was certainly not where and how Stephan saw himself after the takeover. Hearing voices, he returned his attention to the door, seeing it open and Kareek walk inside, accompanied by Joelle. The Chief looked his former officer over, the disdain obvious in his acrid frown.

"Look at you," Kareek barked angrily, walking closer to him.

Stephan posed no threat. He was suspended from the ceiling by his arms, feet secured to the metal pole dead center of the room. He was gagged, so even speech failed him presently.

"You're a disgrace," Kareek spoke again, slapping him hard at the end of the declaration.

Stephan's eyes narrowed his anger apparent.

"What were you thinking, hmm," Kareek questioned again, this time a closed fist to the midsection knocking air from him, making his breathing through the gag very laborious.

"Jacob is dead," Kareek told him calmly seeing the shock, surprise, and eventual pain of the revelation.

Stephan cast a glance at Joell, his eyes meeting the man's cold and indifferent smirk. *Bastard probably killed him,* he thought as Kareek again spoke.

Life After Death

"You've brought this on yourself," he fired, hitting Stephan again. "Maybe you should have spent all this energy trying to take over into learning how to play the game and you wouldn't be about to meet hell through the front door," Kareek told him coldly, stepping away and out of the door, leaving Joell alone with him.

"I killed Jacob," the man told him evenly, never moving from the spot he stood. "I enjoyed it immensely too I must confess," he added chuckling ever so slightly.

Stephan was seeing red. Jacob was a good man, slightly misguided and definitely gullible, but he didn't deserve to die for that.

"Oh don't give me that look," Joell scoffed. "You are the reason Jacob is dead, remember that," he fired and the guilt took Stephan's breath away for a second time.

"You and your stupidity, thinking you could overthrow the entire power structure that has kept this parish operational, put food on tables, able bodied men and women to work, and why, so you could feel like cock of the walk," Joell's fury bubble over.

"Oh, but you're about to get your reward Stephan," he said anew, laughing once again. "Yes, that you are," Joell concluded turning and stepping to the door and opening it. "Enjoy the scenery Stephan," the man again taunted. "This is the last time you'll see it," he concluded walking out and locking the door once again, Stephan's hopes dashed, thoughts of making his final peace permeating his mind.

Life After 33 Death

The hatred still coursed through his veins like liquid iron as Stephan stared defiantly into Aidan's face, the man standing right in front of him. The lackey's came and removed he and detective Marchant over an hour ago, bringing them to yet another holding place, binding them in place in the hot sun until the deadly men before him now, decided to arrive. The salt air assailed his nostrils but Stephan couldn't appreciate the familiar and normally comforting scent. The seas where choppy today causing the boat to toss more than usual, Marchant becoming sick as he continued to vomit from his own precarious perch. *Drowning is the worst death,* Stephan thought taking in the water that surrounded them. He didn't know how far out they were, but there wasn't a speck of land visible. There was however another boat and that made Stephan slightly hopeful. Maybe they were taking them out and losing them to wander and drift aimlessly in the sea. *I certainly pray so,* he thought as Aidan continued to regard him coldly, expression without explanation. He couldn't tell what the man was actually considering behind the bland façade.

Stephan's attention was momentarily averted when Big D walked over to him. The man's presence was ominous yes, but the object in his hand made Stephan swallow hard. Big D's gaze never left him as he hefted the tire and draped it over the man's head, encasing his neck and lifting his arms slightly, trapping his shoulders inside the rubber collar.

"How's that, comfy," Big D questioned coldly, a small smirk on his face.

Stephan didn't speak. Not caring for the defiant look, Big D pulled out his switchblade, cutting him across the face, deep angry cuts that bled profusely. Stephan cried out in pain.

"Bastard," he yelled as Big D smiled, backhanded him, drawing blood, and stepped away.

"You really are an idiot," Aidan began, his eyes smoldering.

"I told you to stay the fuck away from my wife didn't I," he growled as Big D and Stan came back, bearing buckets.

The smell instantly terrified Stephan.

"Wh-what are you doing," he stammered, watching the men go about their task without interruption.

Life After Death

"Kidnapping her, setting up this dumbass stunt with jackass there," Aidan continued, ignoring the question, throwing a quick nod toward Marchant who was watching the scene with interest and dread.

"Mariah is too good for you," Stephan returned, the gag removed from his mouth some semblance of bravery returning.

Aidan burst into laughter, moving close to his ear.

"Trust me when she's screaming my name as I slide in and out of her wet dripping honeycomb, I am more than good enough for her," he spoke cruelly as Stephan frowned deeply.

The visual of the two of them making love hurt him far more than he ever imagined or wanted to admit.

"How are you going to explain killing me, even you aren't above the law," he tried lamely, needing to stop seeing the image in his mind's eye.

Aidan glanced over his shoulder at the men leisurely viewing the scene unfolding.

"Kareek, are you going to arrest me for killing Stephan," he questioned eyes level with the officer in question.

"I don't know anything about Stephan being dead," Kareek returned calmly puffing on the cigar he smoked. "Stephan left the country after unsuccessfully trying to overthrow the law by way of political coup," he finished as Aidan smirked at Stephan and shrugged.

"There you have it," he told him as the cloths simultaneously were placed inside the tire.

The pungent aroma quickly assailed Stephan's nose, his eyes instantly watering, the cuts burning and still seeping slowly on his face.

"Why don't you be a man and let her choose, you're killing me because you're weak," Stephan tried to bluff.

Aidan punched him hard to midsection.

"Ass, get it through your head, Mariah loves me," he told the man as more rags were stuffed into the tire. "She loathes you, fears your presence because she thinks you're unstable," Aidan burst Stephan's bubble.

"That's not true," he fired defensively.

"Of course it is Stephan," Aidan again taunted. "But you're done harassing my wife, my father, our business, Kareek, Arroyo," he fired naming the people standing on the boat.

Stephan jerked and pulled against restraints to no avail. He was securely held in place and the tire was now full of the saturated cloths.

"Last words," Aidan questioned as Stan lifted the container.

"Fuck you, fuck all of you, you're all going to die, watch and see," Stephan screamed helplessly as Aidan nodded and Stan emptied the contents of the container over him the discomfort maddening as it made contact with the open cuts.

"Maybe we will one day Stephan," Aidan told him, pulling out the cigar and biting the tip. "But not today," he went on placing it in his mouth and pulling out the wooden match. "Today you're going to die and we're going to watch," Aidan told him as he struck the match, casually lit the cigar, and flicked it directly onto the tire.

The gasoline that Stephan was doused with spontaneously sparked and he was fully engulfed in flames. The men all watched devoid emotion as Stephan screamed, painful wails of pain and terror. The smoke was thick and acrid as it rose, black and menacing from the effigy that zenith before them. The mingling of charred flesh and melting rubber proved once again too much for Marchant who began to wretch yet another time. The cries began to quell as the fire grew in intensity, the tire melted, melding with bone, marrow, and charred flesh to morph an absurdly fashioned human statue.

"Nice," Dezi murmured of his son's choice of demise.

"No loss," Kareek remarked, the men agreeing with his sentiment.

●●●

Layton's nerves were on end. He was trying to reach Keller for almost two days without success. There was a firestorm brewing, with Senator Don Prather leading the charge. Of course he was still distraught over his daughter's murder, pulling together a group of his cronies to begin an in-depth investigation into the agent assigned and the hiring practices of the CIA, as well as their liaisons, which of course Layton was a central part of. Adding insult to injury the man picked up the scent of the two dead agents found together in the same two days he continued looking for Keller. The police quickly surmised it a home invasion gone wrong with JaDon Ivory walking blindly into it and losing his life. Layton wasn't so sure. Something about the entire set-up bothered him. It was familiar, too familiar. Picking

Life After Death

up his cell he dialed Vernon Spoelman again. The man was avoiding him, giving him the brush off the two times he actually spoke to him.

"Yes Senator," Vernon answered calmly.

"Where the fuck is Keller, and don't give me that bullshit that you don't know," he fired. "I know about your affiliation, so remember who you're talking too," Layton added angrily.

He heard the man sigh slightly before his voice filled the stratosphere again.

"I honestly have no idea where Keller is," Vernon told him yet another time. "He hasn't returned my calls either."

Layton sucked his teeth, frustrated and anxious.

"Well if he calls you, call me immediately," he ordered and disconnected.

I've got to find him, we need to pull together a strategy, Layton continued to fume, sipping the gin and tonic in his glass.

His mind went to Cassandra. That was another loose end, another missing loose end. No one saw or heard from the agent. She didn't show up for debriefing, to teach her CPR class, not even the neighbors, grocers or local Zumba instructor laid eyes on her. *What the hell is she up too, I don't need all this fucking drama,* Layton continued to drink and consider. There was still the very real threat of the child she carried. He wasn't in the mood for scandal, having secret plans to remove the woman permanently from his life. Her or the child surfacing later, neutralized. Now everything was pandemonium. Everyone was blowing in the wind; there were three dead agents to contend with, a senator on the rampage looking for his head on a platter. *Any excuse,* Layton thought of Senator Prather.

The two weren't friends, barely co-existing, and Layton knew the man was always envious of his power and prestigious position on the various committees and the game-changers who favored him. *I've got to get this nonsense handled,* Layton thought his mind cataloging the remaining rank of the CIA. If Keller thought he was irreplaceable, he was most assuredly wrong, Layton angrily formatted. It was time to shift into self-preservation mode. Deciding he would give Keller until morning to contact him, Layton headed into the master bedroom to shower. He was expected at a press conference in forty minutes to try and downplay the death and mayhem of the past few weeks. He was the consummate performer if nothing else, Layton thought as the water cascaded over his head. He weathered worse and came out on top; this time would be no different. *Don Prather will never be me, he'll never have my power,* Layton believed arrogantly, drying himself and stepping into the massive walk-in closet choosing a deep navy blue single breast suit, white shirt and navy tie; conservative and believable. Satisfied after he dressed, Layton regarded his reflection in the mirror. *Go show that loser Prather why you're top dog,* his mind bolstered as Layton smiled at his own reflection, turning and striding toward his front door, secret service waiting outside as he stepped up to the curb and the sleek Lincoln Town car pulled up, driver getting out and opening his door.

●●●

Marchant kept glancing involuntarily at the charred mess that used to be Officer Stephan Eveson. The stench still permeated the boat even in the openness of the sea; the wind only seemed to intensify the nauseating excrement. *These people are sick as hell,* he thought before movement caught his attention and he turned to see the boyfriend approaching him. They tied him to the middle mast of the ship, arms by his side, secured. His waist, thighs, and ankles were secured as well. Marchant swallowed hard as the man stood directly in front of him, not speaking, simply staring. *How long has this guy been killing for her,* he wondered seeing the man's icy demeanor. The gray eyes were like individual cubes of ice floating inside the sockets. Marchant tore his eyes away from the man, glancing around the boat taking in the others, his gaze found one of them staring more intently than the others. Marchant didn't know who he was, but there was something very familiar about his demeanor and mannerisms. *Damn, how wrong could I have been about her,* he began to think all over again as Dezi once again garnered his attention, taking the cigar from his mouth, dropping it onto the deck and regarding Marchant yet another time.

They removed the gag so he was free to speak. Marchant decided if he were going to die he wanted answers. He felt he deserved that much at least.

"How did you end up killing for her," he fired.

Dezi gave him a curious glance, raising an eyebrow.

"You think what exactly Detective Marchant," he questioned calmly, allowing the man to speak his mind.

"I think you're being tricked by a beautiful woman to do her dirty work," Marchant replied.

"So you believe Kayla to be what, a cold, demented mistress of death," Dezi again put to the man, the amusement apparent in his voice.

Marchant swallowed again, dismayed how deeply deluded the man was about the woman's true essence.

Life After Death

"She's a manipulator," Marchant answered. "She's beguiled you with her beauty, a little affection, to do all the evil things she doesn't want to dirty her hands doing," he finished up as the men burst into laughter.

Dezi only smiled however. Keller remained stoic, continuing to watch. Marchant was confused by their reaction. Did she have all of them brainwashed like the man in front of him.

"Detective Marchant," Dezi began anew. "Do you even know who I am?"

Marchant was honest and shook his head no.

Dezi calmly crossed his arms before him and enlightened him.

"My name is Dezi Gianni, and killing people is as natural to me as breathing," he told the detective, watching the shock register on his face.

"That's not possible," Marchant breathed.

He recalled the things he learned from Detective Canfield.

"Certainly it's possible detective," Dezi told him. "Especially when you have friends in high places like CIA Director Keller here," he added, nodding toward the man Marchant earlier noticed.

His mouth dropped. Keller's expression remained unchanged; his eyes blank as if he were watching a boring movie. Dezi continued with Marchant's attention refocused.

"Kayla doesn't have an evil bone in her body," he told the man.

"Yeah," Marchant scoffed. "Is that why she told you to kill me," he fired angry and hurt.

Dezi did laugh this time, gathering himself moments later.

"Detective what you heard was a woman who finally, finally, has learned to put herself and her existence first," Dezi spoke evenly. "Kayla has been fucked over by the best in the name of love, law, and justice," he growled, growing irate Marchant could tell.

"But I saved her from that," Dezi told him calming himself.

Marchant's look begged him to continue as Dezi took another breath and blew it out. "I came to North Carolina, took care of her issues with the dear Reverend Thomas Bradford," Dezi told him. "Christopher Lynch, well he was an old debtor who managed a new debt," he told the man, glancing over at Big D.

"I vaguely remembered you, but now you've placed yourself squarely in my radar," he told the detective back on task. "Kayla is happy, she's loved and provided for here," Dezi patiently explained. "Her family is here, everything she could ever desire is here," he went on. "Now here you come with bullshit trying to drag her back to the hell she escaped, from the life she readily shed, and take her away from everyone and everything she holds dear, and for what, to prove you're some super crime solver," Dezi threw out.

"Or perhaps detective you held a far deeper, greatly more personal reason for trying to take her back, hmm," he accused as Marchant's gaze shifted guiltily.

"Aaah, I see," Dezi told him, stepping just a bit closer.

"Just so we're clear detective," he started in again. "No one, absolutely no fucking one, touches my Kayla," Dezi told him punching him hard to the face, shattering his nose. Marchant's mouth instantly flew open to catch air, the blood streaming from the injured appendage dripping onto his still heaving chest.

"You won't get away with this, I'm an American citizen," Marchant tried; sound very much like Stephan moments earlier.

The laughter came again, the men completely enjoying the show before them. Keller finally broke his silence, addressing the detective, looking him in the eye. "Detective Dwayne Marchant fled the country after an internal investigation found him in league with several known corrupt officers, who were part of a huge extortion and drug ring," he spoke evenly.

Marchant's expression was disbelieving.

"Detective Marchant came under scrutiny after a victim of his brutality filed a federal suit against him for violation of his civil rights," Keller continued on. "Rather than face prosecution and subsequent incarceration, he chose to flee, his whereabouts at present are unknown," he finished, returning to his previous posture.

"What! You can't be serious, no one will believe that," Marchant yelled, veins rising in his neck.

Keller shrugged and Marchant wilted. He knew the man was right. People were like sheep, they believed anything you told them if you found or fabricated enough evidence to make it look plausible.

"Today my beautiful Kayla, my family, my partners, are going to once again be at peace," Dezi told him, as the gleam caught Marchant's eye.

Life After Death

The knife was quick, slitting his throat in one fluid motion. He instinctively put his head down, hoping to staunch the flow of blood and his imminent death. Big D and Stan were instantly at Dezi's side, pulling the man's head back to an upright position, the blood coursing out with each pump of his heart. Marchant's eyes never left Dezi's as he saw the man's hand move upward.

Keller flinched; even Kareek and Arroyo frowned as they watched Dezi reach through the hole in Marchant's throat. The detective was going into shock, gagging and trying to cough away the invader coming up his esophagus. Finding what he sought, Dezi wrapped his hand around the man's tongue ripping it backward, down and out of the same hole he stuck his hand and opened via the knife.

"Jeeesus," Arroyo murmured a new respect for Dezi's depravity.

Big D and Stan were emotionless as they all watched Marchant's last breath heave, his bodily functions give way and death descend on him. Keller pulled out his phone using it to take the necessary photos of Marchant, putting it harmlessly back into his pocket. Using the same knife, Dezi opened the man's chest cavity to his abdomen, stepping away as the intestines tumbled forward.

"Let's go," he said simply as they all turned and left the two dead men, stepping onto the yacht that floated alongside them.

"Finish it," Dezi told the two men they hired.

The men nodded after Stan, the last man of the group, stepped off the smaller vessel. The tugboat tied itself to the dead floater and began pulling it further out to sea, where it would be scuttled and allowed to sink, bodies gone, threat ended.

"Now, let's talk about Washington and a certain senator," Dezi spoke as they all enjoyed cigars and drinks inside the cool innards of the luxury yacht, heading back to the shore and the Gianni compound.

Life After 34 Death

Layton breathed a huge sigh of relief seeing Keller's name appear on the caller I.D. His nerves were brittle and frazzled. He was fielding call after call this morning from his committee friends and other Senators he formed liaisons with over the years. They were all concerned about the unwanted attention Dan Prather was bringing to their various pet projects.

"Where the hell have you been," Layton questioned angrily as he answered the call.

"Handling the situation," Keller returned calmly.

"What's wrong," he questioned, already fully apprised of the current state of affairs.

"Dan Prather, that's what's wrong," Layton returned disgusted.

"I need you to handle the damage control from these three agent's deaths," he went on, pausing only to take a gulp of the gin and grapefruit he mixed while talking to Keller.

"Those deaths were already handled by the police, and we've covered our tracks with Edgar Simons," Keller again spoke, no hint of distress in his voice.

"Well obviously it's not enough," Layton almost yelled.

"Dan Prather is on a personal fucking witch hunt," he fired. "Trust me Keller, like I told you, I will not go down alone, do you hear what the hell I'm saying," he ranted, about to lose control.

Calming himself slightly, Layton began anew.

"We need to meet, right now, I want to know what you plan to do about this damned drama," he told the Deputy Director.

"Fine, my schedule is free, let's meet at your bungalow," Keller spoke.

"Yes, that's fine, thirty minutes," Layton again directed and disconnected.

"This bullshit needs to be over like yesterday," he murmured aloud.

Finishing the drink, Layton headed toward his study. Arriving he sat down in the huge leather chair, the scent of the cowhide wild and gamey. Layton let his eyes roam the room taking in the huge built-in mahogany

Life After Death

bookshelves, lined with every imaginable book on law, politics, and policy. The desk he was seated behind was also a huge mahogany wonder, polished to a mirror finish, sturdy and befitting a man of his political stature. Sighing deeply he closed his eyes rubbing is temples. Dan Prather was a huge thorn in his ass right now, Layton mused. The man wasn't hearing reason when he tried to apologize and offer up every peace offering and incentive known to political man. He wasn't biting. Dan Prather had one objective it seemed, and that was the utter annihilation of Layton Crowler's career.

"That certainly will not be happening, no matter what," he growled, eyes glazed over as he began searching for his original purpose of coming to the room.

Even with the sturdy oak wood door closed and locked, Layton's eyes kept glancing up toward it as he carefully turned the tumblers on the floor safe right beneath the desk. It was casually covered with the heavy area rug, no hint of its presence visible. Hearing the final tumbler click into place, Layton pulled back the small handle and the steel door opened to reveal its hidden manna. He removed the thick manila folder, laying it on his desk. This was the file he kept on Keller. Layton was no one's fool and he didn't get this far by being sloppy or stupid. Throwing it into his briefcase and closing the lid, Layton closed the safe, locking it once more and rose leaving the office. He paused for a moment pondering whether to leave a note for his wife, deciding he would text her instead and picked up his keys. He passed through the foyer, glancing at his reflection in the mirror stationed on the wall above it. Deciding this case put too much stress on him causing a deepening of the worry lines he saw etched around his eyes and jawline, Layton made note to call his travel agent and book a vacation. Sun, sand, and surf, was definitely in order he continued to ponder, getting into his car and heading for the villa.

●●●

Vernon parked the Lexus and got out, locking the vehicle and engaging the alarm. Subconsciously straightening his tie, he headed toward familiar destination, mind whirling as he walked. He received a call from Michael Keller some twenty minutes earlier basically demanding his presence. *This is his and Layton's mess*, Vernon concluded irritably. Granted he lost two agents, the police did a very plausible and believable investigation into the deaths. It didn't matter what he believed or who he believed truly killed April and JaDon, the case was settled and that was all that mattered.

"Always some damned drama," Vernon murmured, almost at the door now.

He wasn't going to let the two of them push him around this time. Layton Crowler seemed to think the Bureau was his own personal arsenal and playground; that the agents there were simply set in place to serve his every whim and desire. Vernon's jaw clenched, the years of resentment beginning to simmer beneath the calm demeanor he was struggling to maintain as he arrived at the front door and prepared himself to ring the bell.

Vernon did another quick tie check, taking a deep breath and blowing it out slowly. Closing his eyes and repeating it again, counting to twenty this time. Vernon repeated the exercise for the next ten minutes, still standing on the doorstep, until he calmed enough to get through the meeting with the pompous politician and the emotionless CIA Deputy Director. Using his index finger, Vernon finally rang the doorbell, the chime light and melodious. He heard movement behind the door, readying himself unsure which of the two would answer the door.

"Hello Vernon," Keller greeted kindly, stepping back and allowing the man entry. "Thank you for coming so promptly," he added as they began walking down the long hallway.

"It's not like I had a choice," Vernon replied testily.

He didn't see any point in either of them thinking the visit was friendly or that they were anything other than three people whose survival depended on the other.

"We're meeting in the den," Keller responded not reacting to the FBI Directors snarky comment or attitude.

The men continued to walk wordlessly, arriving less than three minutes later at their destination.

"After you," Keller told him, as Vernon pushed the slightly ajar door open and stepped inside.

●●●

"Please, have a seat," Dezi said calmly taking in the shock registered on Vernon's face.

Swallowing hard the FBI Director did as he was told. Layton Crowler was already seated, pale, and terrified.

"Gentlemen, it would seem we have some unfinished business," he continued, sipping the cognac in his glass.

Vernon looked to Keller, relaxing in the leather rolling chair and instantly knew only himself and Layton were on the losing side.

Life After Death

"Layton," Dezi began, regarding the terrified Senator. "I made you a promise years ago didn't I," he questioned.

"Dezi, listen, I --," Layton began before Dezi raised a hand, silencing him.

Vernon ventured to turn his attention from Dezi momentarily to take in the other men present. Seeing the resemblance as well as the photograph in the files, he recognized Aidan. He also recalled the mug shot of Demetrius Wilson aka Big D, knowing who the other man was as well. The last man with them however was a mystery to him, though he supposed now it really didn't matter as he turned his attention back to the master of ceremony and paid rapt attention.

Layton looked ready to cry as he watched the man before him intently.

"I told you as long as you didn't have anyone in my face, I would keep your secrets and do your dirt," Dezi told him eerily calm.

"But you couldn't do that simple thing could you Layton," he questioned again.

"I did Dezi, I kept my word, it was Keller, he was the one, him and Vernon, they couldn't control their damned people," he railed, quickly laying blame at the feet of the other two men present.

"So it was Vernon who sent JaDon Ivory to see Adrian," Dezi queried, turning his attention to Vernon now.

"Hell no, Layton's a fucking liar," he expeditiously answered. "I was working with Keller," he went on without prompting. "We were ready to ship them out, someplace cold and distant, but this asshole told us not to make a move," Vernon explained.

"Liar," Layton roared.

Dezi smirked, clearly amused by the two men.

"Keller's no fucking angel either Dezi, don't trust him," Layton tried. "He killed one of his own damned agents," he fired and Dezi saw Keller blanch.

Intrigued, he questioned the man a bit further.

"Who," he spoke and Layton quickly answered.

"Donovan Black," he told Dezi who raised an eyebrow.

Keller's expression darkened.

"Why would he do that," Dezi again questioned, simply curious.

He hated Black; the man's death meant nothing to him.

"Because he started digging again, finding some notes his ex-partner inadvertently left in a file," he told him.

Dezi shrugged, perplexing the Senator.

"Then I would say Keller did his job, the exact opposite of you two," he again spoke crossly.

"Do you remember what I told you Layton, all those years ago," he questioned now. "That if I ever showed up on your doorstep again, what would happen," Dezi questioned rising from his seat as Layton visibly quaked before him.

"Dezi, please, listen, it's over, the files are safely where they should be," he tried to explain.

Dezi backhanded him, knocking him from the chair to the floor where he continued to grovel, the lone tear rolling down his cheek.

"The files are gone, shredded, and destroyed, like they should have been years ago," he fired, nostrils flaring angrily. "Since you and your cohort Vernon here were so fucking incompetent, I found a new source of help," he told him, glancing over at Keller.

"Should have known, you damned snake," Vernon spitefully spat.

Keller chuckled, shooting him a bird.

"Shut up," Dezi roared causing both men to jump.

Big D smiled slightly, Stan and Aidan were slightly alarmed but on full alert. Aidan never witnessed his father at this level.

"Weak and fucking useless, the two of you together can't make one brain," Dezi insulted. "I don't like having my friends harassed, my family threatened, you of all people should know this Layton," he fired as the man nodded profusely that he understood.

"Today the shit is finished however," Dezi began, calming slightly, but not much. "I came here with every intention of killing you Layton," he told the man, gray eyes burning into him.

"But Director Keller here, has made me a much better offer," he told him.

Vernon's eyes narrowed hearing the title Dezi designated. He was angry, angry and jealous, knowing if he received the chance first he would have done the exact same thing.

Life After Death

"You're finished Layton," Dezi told him coldly, putting on the brass knuckles. "I'm not coming back to this country for any foolishness, not now, not in the future," he spoke, snatching the senator from the floor.

Big D and Stan stepped up, holding the man immobile as Dezi worked him over, careful not to hit him in the face. Dezi punched him again and again to the torso, the ribs, the stomach, the fury and force enough to bring the man's dinner flowing up and out of his mouth onto the floor beneath them. Dezi hit him again in the ribs, hearing them crack. Layton was breathing rapidly, legs buckling. Nodding slightly, Big D and Stan released him, his body thudding heavily as it connected with the floor, his face rudely landing in the same vomit and bile that moments earlier left his body.

"I gave Keller everything he needs to ruin you, and he had a nice little conversation with Senator Prather," Dezi told him as Layton groaned pitifully.

"Seems he wasn't too happy that you knowingly sent a predator to guard his precious daughter," Dezi taunted.

Layton tried to shake his head, only succeeding in smearing more of the vile bodily excrement onto his face.

Kicking him hard to the midsection, Dezi turned his attention to the FBI Director regarding him warily.

"Vernon Spoelman, FBI," Dezi spoke contemptuously.

"I'm not a threat to you, I want this over just as much as you do," the man quickly spoke.

"It should have never begun," Dezi fired coldly.

"I told you, it was Layton, he was the roadblock," Vernon again tried to explain.

"Keller, do you think we should let the Director live," he questioned, never removing his eyes from Vernon.

"I think a new administration should start with a clean slate," he returned flippantly.

"You smug sonofabitch," Vernon yelled, almost rising from the chair to attack Keller, catching himself at the last instant, recalling Dezi standing in front of him.

"My, my, doesn't sound like you two are friends at all," Dezi again spoke sarcastically.

"He's no one's friend and he'll fuck over you too Dezi, the first chance the snake gets," Vernon said aloud.

"Hmph, is that true Keller, are you planning to fuck me over," Dezi questioned.

"No, unlike these two, I'm neither weak nor stupid," Keller truthfully answered.

He witnessed enough of Dezi Gianni to know far better than to ever cross him.

"Hmph, I think I believe him Vernon, which is bad news for you," he told him, as Vernon noticed his son walking toward them.

"This is Aidan, my son," Dezi diplomatically introduced. "He wasn't very happy about your fuck up," he explained.

Vernon watched, mesmerized it seemed, as the young man withdrew the silencer laced gun from his pocket. *Ruger*, Vernon recognized, as the first bullet penetrated his chest. Air left him, shock set in, his neurological system began to shut down. He still saw however, the hand that now was elevating. *What is he --,* the thought began as the second hollow point entered his skull, the disruption expansive. Sight left, sound began to fade, pain was a distant memory, breath was non-existent; then there was nothing.

Life After Death

Aftermath

Caroline Wilmont stared at the badge her mind racing well past warp speed. How did they here? Dwayne Marchant was one of the best officers she ever had the pleasure of working with. The charges and accusations leveled against him she still couldn't bring herself to believe. Caroline knew it looked bad, especially with his disappearance. They still were not able to find the man, his trail ending with his flight to Brazil. *Why Dwayne, dammit,* she thought as the hurt descended. Caroline prided herself on being a great judge of character. Marchant was a lot of things; stubborn, willful, hardheaded, defiant, but dishonest was never among the traits she felt he possessed. For months she fought hard to clear his name, to tell the FBI they made a mistake, but even she couldn't refute the evidence that was continually coming to light every day. The other three officers involved cut deals naming Marchant as the ringleader, drawing shorter prison sentences, some no time at all. Of course they were immediately fired upon their indictment, but there were rumblings that the police union was gearing up to fight for reinstatement for those who received no jail time and entered no guilty plea.

Sighing, Caroline continued to toy with the badge. It was taken from the wall where they placed replicas of all the officer's badges for public display. Dwayne Marchant's name was met with scorn and ridicule these days and she was only happy that his wife had already passed on. *This would have destroyed her,* Caroline thought of the woman enduring the shame and embarrassment. Still in Captain Caroline Wilmont's mind there was the looming question of why. Detective Marchant by all accounts still lived a middle class existence. They FBI showed her several bank statements showing offshore accounts where Marchant supposedly hid his ill-gotten monies. She scoffed at the memory, the amounts miniscule in her estimation, only averaging a total of ten thousand dollars. *Why would he risk his entire career for peanuts,* she continued to muse. It wasn't adding up for her and no matter what the FBI said, there were things that weren't being said. Still she couldn't argue anymore. The case was done as far as they were concerned and they moved on to the next big bust. They only people caring or mourning Marchant's loss were the friends he still kept in the department and her.

Deciding she wasn't helping sitting in the chair brooding, Caroline rose and grabbed her coat. Winter descended on the city, lending fuel to her already melancholy mood as she stepped outside greeted by a brusque wind and a light snow that covered the ground. Getting into the unmarked car, she headed to Marchant's house. The Feds were done tearing it apart and granted permission for the detectives personal effects to be packed and disposed of. Caroline volunteered to personally handle the task. Arriving at the small home moments later, she parked in the driveway, Marchant's car still sitting undisturbed. She opened the driver's door and climbed out; using the key given by the FBI, and went inside. Instantly appreciating being out of the elements, Caroline flipped on a light switch, pleased that the electricity wasn't disconnected. She found the thermostat and turned on the heat, looking around the house trying to decide where to start. Going into the bedroom, armed with several large trash bags, Caroline began emptying dresser drawers. She filled three by the time she made it to the nightstand, pulling the drawer completely out, and dumping the contents into the large plastic sack. Without thought, Caroline threw the drawer violently to the floor, the sobs coming heavy and deep. She felt the spirit pass through her almost as if Marchant were standing in the room and she knew in that instant they would never find him. Dwayne Marchant was dead. She didn't have a body, and she didn't have proof, but in her heart Caroline Wilmont knew she would never get an explanation or see her friend again on this side of the Jordan River. Pulling herself together, she finally decided she was okay with that and continued packing. Some things she supposed were better left unexplained.

•••

"Slow down mister," Cassandra playfully fumed as she ran to keep up. Shaking her head she continued to chuckle as she watched him bouncing, falling, getting up and running again.

"Slow down," she called out again, just as promptly ignored.

Curious as ever, the flowers, dandelions, grass and dirt made perfect play companions for his exploration as he promptly examined each, evening tasting a couple of the flowers, the dandelions escaping a similar fate by blowing in the wind before they could be devoured. Cassandra burst into laughter seeing the perplexed look on his face as the particles floated away and out of his reach.

"That's what you get," she spoke finally catching up and scooping him into her arms, squirming to get down again.

"No, it's time to eat," she spoke turning and beginning to walk back the way they came.

"Woof," assailed her ears as Cassandra chuckled again, kissing him, as they got closer to the house.

Life After Death

She glanced around at the majestic tree lined view they held, the rolling meadowland before them and how peaceful it all was. Walking away from the CIA two and a half years ago was the best thing she ever did. Of course she spent the first year looking over her shoulder, but finally able to relax, Cassandra began enjoying her new life.

Montana was beautiful country and they fit right in. The community they lived in was small but friendly, everyone watching out for their neighbors and lending a helping hand if need be. She used the money from her offshore accounts, having removed it weeks before leaving the agency that day. Cassandra didn't spend a decade with the CIA to be stupid or sloppy. She knew they would look for her; well Keller would look for her. Thinking of him made her sigh. She knew all about his new position as well as Layton Crowler's demise. *Serves his bastard ass right,* she thought as the sound invaded her ear again.

"Woof," it came loud and piercing.

She giggled again, holding him tighter.

"No more animal planet for you," she laughed putting him down and allowing him to run again, the rear of the house in view.

Cassandra swallowed the lump that formed in her throat as she watched him. He was absolutely perfect and she thanked God every day for him. Alston Michael Deale was a spunky, healthy, happy, well-adjusted little boy who gave Cassandra a reason to get out of bed in the morning. She discovered her pregnancy two months after leaving the CIA. Maurice was his father, but she'd never told him. They still emailed occasionally with him asking her if they could meet and her deflecting him each time. *You're not being fair to Alston,* her mind chastised yet again

Cassandra didn't want to deal with the drama. She didn't want Maurice to feel obligated and she didn't want anything from him. Their son was the most precious gift he could have ever given her and she would always be eternally grateful to him for that, but Alston would be spared the hurt or shame of knowing he was the product of an illicit affair for his father and an assignment for his mother. Shaking the thoughts, Cassandra caught up with her son pretending to race him the rest of the way home, intentionally letting him win as she feigned exhaustion.

"Win mommy," he told her smiling his brilliant smile, eyes twinkling, melting her heart all over again.

Alston was exquisite blend of both she and Maurice, his personality however was all his own.

"Yep you sure did," Cassandra told him taking his small hand as he allowed her to lead him inside the house.

"Can you go and wash your hands, and face, and I'll make you some lunch," she questioned the two year old.

"Yes mommy, sketti-o's," he told her making his choice known as she chuckled and told him okay.

Cassandra opened the can and poured the contents into the bowl, popping it into the microwave and pushing the start button. The knock at the door distracted her as she frowned lightly, wiping her hands on the kitchen towel and heading toward the sound.

•••

Keller caught the smile and laugh that wanted to escape as he watched the expression changes on Cassandra's face.

"May I come in," he questioned as she continued to stand in the door.

Nodding mutely she stepped aside and allowed him entrance. Keller took in the house. It was very quaint, calm and serene, very warm and relaxing. He turned to the sound of her voice as she spoke and broke his thought.

"Would you like something to drink," she questioned calmly, but Keller saw the nervousness.

"Lemonade sounds good," he replied after she gave him a few choices.

Smiling slightly Cassandra left and headed toward the kitchen. Keller took a seat in the oversized leather recliner, still taking in the house. The colors were neutral, lots of browns, beiges, and blacks here in the living room. He was pretty sure the rest of the house wasn't quite as conservative recalling Cassandra's love of vibrant color. He heard her moving around slightly disturbing his thoughts yet another time. It took him quite a while to find her. He gave her credit; the woman hid herself very well. *With good reason don't you think,* his mind questioned as he thought about the child.

Keller knew everything about her; about her life after she left the agency, the house here, the little boy she conceived with Maurice Alston, and the man's ignorance of the fact. Even during all the turmoil with Layton being disposed of and his rise to CIA Director, he never forgot her or his determination to find her.

Life After Death

"Here you are," Cassandra spoke coming back into the room and handing him the glass.

Alston bounded into the room moments later, stopping as he eyed the stranger sitting in their living room.

"Hi," the tiny voice piped up, walking over, fearless, and standing directly in front of Keller.

He smiled slightly returning the child's greeting. He caught Cassandra's anxiety from his peripheral vision.

"Who are you," Alston again inquired.

"Honey, that's not nice," Cassandra carefully chastised.

"It's fine, a legitimate question," Keller told her looking into her eyes now.

She swallowed hard, averting her gaze.

"My name is Michael," Keller told the little boy.

"Really," Alston giggled. "My name is Michael too," he proudly made known.

Keller was taken aback. This was one fact he didn't know. He looked to Cassandra who was examining her hardwood floors at the moment and refused to meet his gaze.

"It's my middle name," Alston diplomatically explained, the d's sounding like b's in his baby speech, as Keller chuckled.

"Oh, I see," he replied as the little boy turned to his mother, basically dismissing Keller's presence.

"I'm hungry," he informed bringing another small smile to Keller's face.

He said nothing as Cassandra excused herself and took the little boy into the kitchen, setting his lunch before him. She gave him his spoon, told him she would be back in a few minutes admonishing him to eat all his food and not make a mess. Keller regarded her as she came back and took a seat, her eyes finally making contact again.

"Why are you here Michael," she asked quietly, the fear causing her voice to quake slightly.

"Cassandra, you left me without explanation, without regard for your oath, just walked away," Keller returned, intentionally not answering her question. "I asked myself, what would make my best operative do that," he went on as Cassandra fidgeted, casting a glance into the kitchen occasionally as Alston ate, signing along with the cartoon playing as he watched the small TV attached to the countertop.

"I could only conclude that you wanted to get away, but I think what disturbed me most was the fact you didn't tell me," Keller told her gaining her total attention again.

"Michael I --," Cassandra faltered.

"I suppose you know about my appointment, and Layton's fate," he questioned and she nodded yes.

"Hmph," he replied, sitting up on the edge of the recliner, face inches from hers. "Did you also know that I am in love with you and it broke my heart when you left me," Keller questioned.

Cassandra gasped, frowning at the revelation.

"You must have known Cassandra, suspected as least," Keller pressed.

He was positive she didn't know. He was a master at hiding his emotion. True he was furious with her for sleeping with Layton, but he found out the truth of why as well as her being pregnant from the Senator, having the abortion, and blackmailing him to help her leave. Cassandra was perfect for him and he knew it. Keller vowed once he got his life situated and found her, he would pursue her until she relented and became a lasting part of his life. Finding out about Alston didn't dampen his plan, and now after learning the child's full name, he knew his feelings weren't unrequited.

"Michael I never knew you even thought about love," she told him honestly. "Sex yes, but love didn't seem have a place in your life," Cassandra added with a twinge of bitterness.

Keller reached out and took her hands, holding them between his.

"I've loved you for a long time Cassandra," he admitted freely. "I was livid finding out you slept with Layton, were pregnant with his child," Keller told her watching the tear roll down her cheek. "But I didn't understand fully then, I was just hurt and jealous acting off impulse," he explained as another tear joined the first.

"Cassandra, is it too late for us," he questioned praying she said no.

"I have a child Michael," she answered skirting a direct response.

"OK, so what," Keller replied. "He already has my name, so what's the difference," he went on. "No one will question that you and I engaged in an affair, you became pregnant, we worked it out," he told her, lifting her chin.

Keller leaned in and kissed her, hungrily, pulling her in his embrace. Cassandra broke the kiss, pulling away guiltily looking toward the kitchen. Alston was oblivious to the two adults, still singing and dropping sketti-o's on the floor.

"Are you sure this is what the Director of the CIA wants for his life," she questioned, her heart screaming at her to say yes and accept this man into her existence.

Keller smiled fully.

"Have you ever known me not to know what I want Cassandra," he questioned as she chuckled.

"No, I don't suppose I have," she returned quietly.

"Let's be a family Cassandra," Keller pleaded. "I know it's a lot and its sudden," he began again. "So let's date, I'll come and see you, you and Alston come spend some weekends with me in DC, get reacquainted with each other," Keller proposed.

"That might work," she acquiesced as Keller pulled her close and kissed her again, his breathing erratic.

He was aroused and so was she. Rising she went and headed back into the kitchen. Alston was nodding slightly, but trying valiantly to fight the sleep that tried to descend. Keller chuckled, helping her clean the sleepy toddler up, picking him up when she was done and following her to his bedroom. True to his earlier thought, the room was alive and vibrant with color. Cassandra took Alston from him, placing him on the small bed shaped like a car, the child never waking. As they stepped outside of the room, Keller again embraced her kissing her deeply.

"Can I see your room now," he questioned huskily, his erection pressing against her stomach alerting her fully of his intentions.

"OK, but only for a minute," she teased taking his hand and leading him down the short hallway.

Keller appreciated the colors in hers as well, the five minutes he took it in before turning and stripping the clothes from her, enjoying their reconnection as she moaned his name in ecstasy and he finished inside her hoping for a girl this time.

Horizons and Sunsets

Stan smiled as Kayla walked back onto the deck. Existence was great here on the island and he never regretted for a moment his decision to leave the shambles of a life he lived in the United States. His pockets stayed filled with money, he bought a beautiful home, quickly learning the business with Dezi, Aidan, and Big D.

"Here we are," Kayla told him sweetly, handing him the ice cold mango and pineapple juice.

He acquired quite the liking for it.

"Thanks," he told her as she sat.

"Are you really okay Stan," Kayla questioned, looking at him closely.

He smiled slightly, sipping his juice before answering.

"Just get a little melancholy sometimes, you know," he replied honestly.

Kayla nodded. She absolutely understood, especially times like this when she looked out onto the ocean and wished with everything in her that Taea was there by her side.

"I miss her too Stan, so much," Kayla spoke aloud the subliminal thought rolling through both their minds.

He smiled again, taking her hand this time.

"I know you do," he replied and they both sipped their drink and continued to gaze into the ocean lost in private thoughts.

His cell broke the mood as he scrambled to answer it and quiet the shrill ringtone.

"Hi," he greeted. "Yes, soon," Stan added, ending the conversation quickly as Kayla gave him a look and chuckled.

"Vanessa," she teased as Stan laughed and told her yes.

"I'm happy you found her Stan," Kayla told him again of the woman.

The two were instantly smitten when they met over two years ago at the huge launch party Dezi threw on the island to celebrate yet another overseas trade route they established and won clientele for. They quickly grew closer with Vanessa becoming pregnant and giving birth to their daughter Zoië.

Life After Death

"Yeah so am I and Zoië is definitely the brightest spot in my reality," he added and Kayla again heard the sadness.

"Have you tried reaching out, letting them know where you are," she questioned referring to his other children, all grown now.

Stan sighed lightly.

"No, I think it's best to let that life go, you know," he told her calmly.

"I still love them, and I'm still their father, but I wasn't there for their entire life," Stan acquiesced referring to his incarceration.

"I understand," Kayla told him.

"So are you and Vanessa going to have another baby," she questioned as Stan scoffed.

"Not anytime soon, shoot, Zoië is barely two," Stan protested.

Kayla laughed aloud. "Don't wait too long."

"Whatever," he sulkily replied as they finished their juice.

"I'm going to head out now, Kayla," he told her rising.

"Tell Vanessa hello for me," she replied as they embraced, hugging each other tightly.

"I think she would have liked it here," he murmured as the tear rolled down Kayla's cheek.

"I know she would have," she replied.

"Happy Birthday sis," Stan spoke again as they once more gazed at the ocean.

"Happy Birthday Taea," Kayla added as she felt Stan's hand slip from her own and heard him leave her standing on the deck listening as she heard Taea's laughter escaping from the waves before her and knew that everything was all right in both their worlds.

●●●

"Daddy, daaaadddyyy," Livvy impatiently screeched garnering finally, her father's full attention.

"Watch this," she told him as she swung higher and without warning, jumped from the moving swing.

"Livvy," Mariah yelled, terrified her daughter would hurt herself.

Preston, their precocious three year old, was a captive audience and clapped, squealing loudly in delight at his sister's death defying feat. Aidan chortled lightly, before speaking.

"Hey that was pretty good," he told Livvy who promptly grinned and climbed into the swing again.

"No you don't young lady, get down," Mariah told her, her heart finally starting to slow its rampant pace.

"Aww mommy," Livvy pouted.

"Let her swing honey," Aidan tried. "I mean okay yeah it was a little dangerous, but she's a kid," he patiently tried to plead.

Mariah looked into her daughter's disappointed face and relented.

"OK, but if she breaks something YOU are going to the hospital with her," she told Aidan, who kissed her cheek and promised he would.

"Go for it space girl," he told Livvy who cheerfully returned the swing, pumping her small legs to gain more and more altitude.

Preston watched amazed, his eyes glittering.

"Now this one will be trying it," Mariah mumbled still slightly miffed that she was hoodwinked by her husband and daughter.

"Someone's a little cranky hmm," Aidan teased, kissing her neck.

Mariah smiled a bit before pushing him away. Abigail materialized almost instantly, walking over to them as they sat inside the gazebo watching Livvy ready herself for another launch.

"I'm about to head into town," she told the couple. "Would you like me to take the children with me," Abigail questioned.

"Yes, please," Aidan replied very dirty thoughts on his mind.

Abigail smiled as she took Preston's hand and called for Livvy to stop swinging. Defiant as ever, Livvy continued to push herself higher.

"Livvy, now," Aidan told her, voice heavily bass laden.

Knowing her father wasn't kidding, Livvy swung once more jumping from the swing again, landing on her feet as usual, beaming with pride at her accomplishment as she looked to her father for approval.

"Flying squirrel," he teased grinning at her as she grinned back.

Life After Death

Abigail took them both as she headed around the house to the garage. Aidan saw the car leave seven minutes later and turned to his wife.

"Come on, let's see what we can do about your crankiness," he teased, grabbing her breast.

Mariah swatted his hand, jumping from her chair and running inside.

Aidan caught her as she turned the corner of the hallway that led to their bedroom.

"Mmhmm, gotcha now," he teased, biting her neck, arms wrapped tightly around her waist.

"Stop, Aidan," Mariah giggled as he pulled her down the hallway kicking open the bedroom door when they arrived.

"No, quit it," Mariah continued to laugh.

Aidan was smiling as well, expertly popping buttons on her dress, removing it speedily, as well as the silky powder pink bra beneath.

"Mine now," he murmured, lips locking onto the hard nipple.

Mariah moaned loudly, her temperature soaring. She removed Aidan's shirt, caressing her husband's bare chest. She licked his nipple as his fingers slid between her legs caressing the slick wetness found there.

"Aaaaidan," Mariah moaned as he connected with her engorged clit.

She sucked his neck, her hands wrapped around his hard thickness as it jumped slightly in her hand. She stroked him slowly, rubbing her thumb through the slick moisture at the tip, oozing slowly from him as his pleasure increased. Aidan ventured inside her dripping opening with two fingers, gliding them in and out of her, feeling her breath on his neck, raspy and uneven. Mariah felt it building in the deepest regions of her womb, spreading quickly to her pelvis, her pubic bone, her opening, and finally her clit as the scream left her mouth, the magnitude of the orgasm jolting her entire body.

She heard Aidan groan in her ear, her strokes as she held him growing faster and more fluid. His manhood began to pulse in her hand. Her husband was close.

"Shit Mariah, mmmm," Aidan grumbled, grabbing her hand and stopping her.

His lips found hers as they began to kiss and he pulled her onto his lap. Mariah threw her head back hissing loudly feeling her husband's thickness invade her fortress.

"Baby," she heard him whisper, holding her hips tightly and going for release.

Mariah rode him with steady, measured strokes, teasing him as she held him prisoner in her securely structured walls.

"Ohh gooodd, arrrgghh," Aidan again moaned feeling the continual contracting of her insides.

"Good honey," Mariah teased, rising almost off his erection.

"Mmmph," Aidan managed, lids closed, eyes rolled back in his head.

Grabbing her hips he roughly pulled her back down onto his throbbing erection, aiming for her g-spot. Mariah tried to hang on and tease him more, but Aidan took control, hitting her spot and her clit in rapid succession, she lost the battle screaming aloud again as he held her breasts in his hands, hips pumping furiously.

"Aidan, oh yesssss, right there, I'm cummmmming," Mariah voiced hoarsely, feeling his body shudder right before the encompassing warmth of his finish settled inside her.

Mariah drifted off quickly as Aidan held her. He caressed her face as he watched her sleep. Even though Stephan was dead two years now, Aidan never forgot. Every time he thought of the ordeal, he wanted to kill him all over again. *Shark bait now, stupid bastard,* Aidan mused, smiling slightly. Things were good in their lives again. The business expanded by leaps and bounds. Stan was a great addition to their family and he learned a lot more about his father, Kayla, and their lives before they all settled here together. Aidan thought about the letter he received last week. While they were in the states looking for the agents to squash the nonsense arisen, he reached out to the prison system looking for his brother. He was clueless where DeSean was transferred after he left the country. Years passed since they spoke. It took forever it seemed, but the letter arrived and gave him the information he sought. Now Aidan needed to decide if he would really reach out. He loved his brother, but that time and that life seemed so far removed from him. Would it disturb the balance if they reconnected? There were so many questions too, Aidan still pondered. He had a niece or nephew out there somewhere that he held no knowledge of. So many questions, so many loose ends; pushing it aside, Aidan pulled his wife closer surmising DeSean wasn't going anywhere and he would make a decision in due time.

Life After Death

●●●

How the hell did this happen, Layton Crowler mused for the thousandth time. He was promptly impeached and thrown out of office, criminal charges brought for misconduct, extortion, intimidation, and finally an almost thirty year old murder. *"Life, without possibility of parole,"* the stern judge spoke after a jury took less than four hours to find him guilty. For two years Layton survived at the maximum security prison. He did things inside this place he never thought possible; endured degradation and shame all in the name of survival. Mark and Layton Jr., visited faithfully the first year. Now they came sparsely, if at all, most times opting to send him letters, cards, and money for his commissary. Francine was broken. The loss, the revelations, the entire ordeal was too much for her. She suffered an emotional breakdown and was admitted to a sanitarium. Released some six months ago, she filed for divorce. Layton still felt the hurt as he recalled the smirk from the guard who delivered their mail.

Today was a new beginning. Layton felt good. He felt confident for the first time since this all began. He thought of Keller and how craftily the man unseated, shamed, and destroyed him. *Always was a sneaky bastard,* he mused of the man and his ambitions. *He's in bed with the devil now and it'll destroy him soon enough,* Layton told himself to ease the seething anger that still held him firmly in its vice. That was one thing he regretted. Not being able to exact revenge on Keller or Dezi Gianni right then and there. *Arrogant bastard,* he thought of the man who casually sauntered into his home, beat the hell out of him, and snatched away everything he worked so hard to build. *I wonder if she had that damned baby,* Layton groused of Cassandra Deale. He heard, over eight months ago, through the very scant sources that still talked to him, that the woman left the agency and disappeared from sight. *Bet his haughty ass didn't see that coming,* Layton cheerily thought, regarding Keller. *That's why I fucked her to start with, she was beautiful yes, but she loved him and I knew he cared about her, even if he never admitted it,* Layton patted himself on the back. He was going to pay them all back now though. He planned it all. He laughed aloud at the thought.

"Hey princess," the male prisoner crudely spoke as he walked by Layton's cell giving him a crude gesture.

"I'll see you later tonight," he added before laughing with the other three inmates accompanying him.

Layton didn't allow the boorish behavior to dampen his spirits. Today was a good day. Walking over to his bunk, Layton carefully lifted the ramshackle mattress and removed the manila envelope. He meticulously opened it and removed the contents.

"Let's see you dig yourself out of this," he spoke of the classified documents inside.

Engrossed in the documents, Layton never saw the man slip inside his cell and walk up behind him.

"What's up bitch," he heard menacingly in his ear as the huge arms encompassed him.

Layton opened his mouth to cry out when the dirty rags were instantly stuffed inside.

"Come on man, hurry up," one of the others told him as Layton's pants were stripped and he was placed spread eagle on the bunk, face in the makeshift pillow as he felt the man rip into him, thrusting hard and deep.

"Mmm shit, this is some good ass," he mumbled, humping with all his might.

Layton closed his eyes, the searing pain mingling with the repulsion, bringing tears to his eyes. He was assaulted like this before, but lately took to paying and bartering his way out of the sexual interludes.

"Shhhhhiiittt," he man groaned as he finished.

"Dezi Gianni sends his regards," Layton heard, eyes growing big as he felt the homemade toothbrush shank sinking deeply into his temple.

Death was mercifully quick and Layton felt nothing else as the men collected every scrap of paper from the cell and slunk out undetected.

●●●

Dezi enjoyed the full bodied flavor of the cognac, sipping it and savoring the taste before allowing it slide effortlessly down his throat. He leaned back in the massive black Italian leather desk chair, eyes closed, relaxed. It wasn't something he allowed himself to do often, but when he did, he enjoyed it fully. Here at home he found solitude. Kayla was still his heart and just knowing she was near was enough to still the raging beast inside that continually wanted to raise its head. Business was great. Stan never lost a step and they moved right long as if twenty plus years never happened. *Him and Vanessa Trufont, never would have seen that coming,* Dezi chuckled as he pondered the affiliation. He only thought that because of Vanessa's penchant for coming across as arrogantly snotty. Stan quickly brought her to reality however. *Before fucking her silly,* Dezi again mused laughing aloud at

Life After Death

his thought. He also knew her secret. Arroyo had no idea his daughter was screwing Stephan Eveson. He more than likely would have disowned her. Dezi however knew. He had her fully investigated when Stan started seeing her, especially when she became pregnant. He wasn't going to let her pull a fast one on his friend.

Things were going well now however with everyone involved. He smiled again thinking of Jackie and Big D. *Told him*, he thought smiling again as he refilled his glass. Seemed Jackie wasn't as safe as she thought finding out she was three months pregnant. They were of course monitoring her given the fact she was in her forties, but the doctors assured them that so far everything was fine. To say they were shocked would be an understatement. *"Damn, well um, should we worry about that," Kayla asked Dezi as they discussed it one evening. He laughed. "Baby, we're fine," he reassured. "Oh, okay, you had the procedure," she questioned. Dezi nodded slightly. He had the vasectomy almost seven years before he found her deciding he didn't want any children if he couldn't have them from her. There was also the small matter of the pregnancy scare with one of the woman during a quick affair here in the parish.* Dezi hoped the child came healthy and whole. Big D was playing it cool with Jackie and everyone else, but he and Dezi spoke and he admitted how excited he was at the prospect of having a child on this earth. *It'll work out*, Dezi thought and sipped the drink again.

His thought finally came to rest on Keller, now director of the CIA. Dezi kept his end of the bargain, even secretly attending the congressional hearings. Things went smoother than silk and no one was bold enough to publicly challenge Dan Prather's recommendation of Keller's appointment. *"I do have one question," Dezi spoke as the two men met for the last time inside Dezi's suite. "Yes," Keller returned waiting for the man to pose it. "Why did you kill Agent Black," he questioned. He saw the man sigh deeply, frowning slightly before he replied. "It wasn't a pleasant task," he explained first. Dezi patiently listened. "Black was always extremely meticulous, to a fault," Keller explained with a bitter laugh. "He picked up your file again, saying something didn't sit right with his gut," Keller explained as Dezi nodded. "He began questioning things, requesting certain documents, basically causing ripples in already calm waters," the CIA Director told him. "Layton Crowler made it clear that you were never to resurface again, at any cost," he went as Dezi saw the picture emerging. "I sent him on the assignment, then had one of my trusted operatives slip the prisoner a gun with instructions to kill Black, in exchange for his freedom," Keller told Dezi. "I somehow doubt you kept your bargain with the convict though hmm," Dezi questioned as Keller again laughed the short, bitter, laugh. "No," he said simply. Dezi left the conversation alone, satisfied with answer and not really caring, having no love for the dead man. His question was curiosity, nothing more.*

"Honey, are you alright," Kayla asked softly as she cracked the door.

She was knocking for the past five minutes without response.

"Hmm, oh I'm sorry baby," Dezi replied dismissing the thoughts forever.

Keller was in place now and the man proved himself to be trustworthy. They were even in the process of working on a new deal together. As long as the Director stayed in his lane and played his role, Michael Keller would be rich beyond his wildest dreams until the day he died. Dezi of course put insurance in place however, if Keller ever decided he wanted to renegotiate.

"I'm fine, just relaxing and I think I may have nodded off," Dezi admitted as she giggled and came to him.

Dezi reached up, pulling her into his lap.

"I love you so much, do you know that," he questioned, kissing her at the end of the statement.

"Yes Dezi," Kayla returned looking into his loving gray eyes. "I know without a shadow of a doubt that you love me, and you've been more than good to me," she told him as he smiled at her.

"For you Kayla, I would stop the world from spinning," Dezi earnestly spoke.

"I know baby, I know," she replied as they began to kiss passionately.

As he made love to her Dezi, wondered yet another time how differently things might have been if she became pregnant with his child all those years ago. It was the one and only regret he ever felt when it came to her.

"Mmmmm Dezi, yessssss," Kayla breathed severing the thought as he felt her body's pleasure and held her tighter going deeper.

I have her and that's more than enough, Dezi thought as a point of end, his own orgasm descending as their satiated cries filled his study and they clung to each other, bond stronger than ever.

Life After Death

Also, check out these other offerings from the Author KR Bankston available www.krbankstononline.com and other online retailers: Amazon.com (https://www.amazon.com/author/krbankston), BN.com, and more.

THE GIANNI LEGACY:
A Deadly Encounter
Sins of the Father
Smoke & Mirrors
Life After Death
Aftermath
Sinister Alliance
Requiem

THIN ICE – THE SERIAL:
Thin Ice
Thin Ice 2 - Hide & Seek
Thin Ice 3 – Armageddon
Thin Ice 4 - Resurrections
Thin Ice 5 – Checkmate
Thin Ice 6 – Hangman & Socrates
Thin Ice 7 – Echoes of Reckoning
Thin Ice 8 – Separazione Finale
Thin Ice 9 – Epiphany
Thin Ice 10 – Ambition
Thin Ice 11 – Homecoming
Thin Ice 12 – Siren Song

NOIR FROST SERIES:
Shattered
Evolutions
Darker Shades of Light
Crosshairs
Reawakening

THIN ICE GENERATIONS:
Blood Legacies
Dark Confessions
Malevolence
The Wedding
Eldest Son
Friends & Liars

OTHER BOOKS:
X-Mafia: The Rise of Pirate & Creeper
Unholy Empire (pt1 & 2)
Christian
Atomic
Shattered Peace
Interception
Three The Hard Way
Now You're A Star
The Agency
The Master Orchestrator
King of the Game
One of the Boys
No Take Backs
Gold Plated Dreams
The Destroyer
Unwell

Life After Death

About the Author:

K.R. Bankston is an established Romantic Suspense author with some 40 published works to her credit, including the highly successful Thin Ice and Gianni Legacy series. KR is the CEO of Kirabaco Media Group, LLC which houses her works. In addition to being an author KR is a Publishing Consultant, and Public Speaker. KR also writes Contemporary Romance under the pen name Kay Raneé within the Cayenne Drama label.

KR's "BookOpera" series Thin Ice was voted Serial Novel of the Year and Urban Fiction of the year. Her other series The Gianni Legacy has been touted as The Godfather of modern day. Her novel, Christian was voted #75 of Top 100 Books of the year. Her novel X-Mafia was voted Urban Fiction of the Year. KR invites you to step outside the box of assumption and pop open a title and allow the stories to enrapture you.

You can find the Author on the following networks:
https://twitter.com/KRBankston
https://www.facebook.com/KRBankstonAuthor
https://www.patreon.com/KRBankston
https://youtube.com/@KRBTheAuthor
https://www.amazon.com/author/krbankston
https://www.instagram.com/bookoperalegacy
https://www.clubhouse.com/bookoperalegacy

www.ingramcontent.com/pod-product-compliance
Lightning Source LLC
LaVergne TN
LVHW091533060526
838200LV00036B/597